J. E Chamberlain

Cotton Stealing

A Novel

J. E Chamberlain

Cotton Stealing
A Novel

ISBN/EAN: 9783337082192

Printed in Europe, USA, Canada, Australia, Japan

Cover: Foto ©Andreas Hilbeck / pixelio.de

More available books at **www.hansebooks.com**

A Novel.

—"WHO RICHES GAINS BY WRONG,
IS BUT A THIEF."

CHICAGO:

JOHN R. WALSH & CO.

1866.

CHICAGO:

J. W. TIDMARSH,

PRINTER.

CHICAGO TYPE FOUNDRY,

J. CONAHAN,

STEREOTYPER

PREFACE.

Every phase of the Cotton Trade, within the army lines during the war, was so conducted that it obtained the name of "COTTON STEALING ;" and the parties engaged were called "COTTON THIEVES." The mere fact that a man was concerned in cotton speculating, was *prima facie* evidence of corruption, putting the speculator before Treasury Agent, Army Official, and Detective, as saying—

"I AM IN THE MARKET—LEVY BLACK-MAIL ON ME."

Early in the trade, *small* thieves could steal small lots of cotton, and enjoy the proceeds. After Army, Treasury, and Navy sharks fell on their track, not only their profits, but the cotton and capital invested was lost, while their precious bodies were overshadowed by a military prison, and their mouths gagged by a bayonet. Then the business fell into the hands of *great* thieves, who shall be nameless.

"Truth is stranger than fiction." Although every incident set forward is believed to be true, still, as fiction, the work must either stand or fall. No one man, no single State, nor any particular year is designed. When names are mentioned, the acts are removed as far as possible, to prevent identification;

because, although founded on fact, and built of materials furnished by actual experience of the cotton trade, the novel is a witness rather than judge—written by no believer in the doctrine of human perfection, nor the possible power of any individual to remodel the age, nor the probability of a single work reaching the moral heart of the nation. It has been written by a Western man as a cotemporaneous novel, to stand the test of to-day—by a Western man whose whole nature revolts against the attempts to deify the participants of the war, by magnifying virtues and extenuating faults, in some cases ignoring them entirely. There is one tribunal among a free people which no wrong-doer can escape—enlightened public opinion. At its bar let friends and neighbors try every officer or soldier who comes home rich beyond his monthly pay. Wealth greater than this must be explained to the home tribunal, which alone can inflict the punishment of public condemnation. Will they do it? Keeping this in mind whenever the "I" appears, and any shall ask—Who is this "I"? this is the answer:—I am a Western man with a story to tell. Will any one read—will any one hear it?

Cotton Stealing.

CHAPTER I.

" Detail for picket—Fall in, fall in ! " " Count off." " One, two—one, two." " Shoulder arms." " By the right flank—file left—March ! " " Right shoulder shift arms—Forward ! "

Last evening, the brigade commander sent orders to a regiment of Missouri Volunteers, at Helena, Arkansas, to detail a lieutenant, sergeant, corporal, and fifteen men for picket duty.

This morning, rub-a-dub-dub, rub-a-dub-dub, one, two, three, four taps, called the attention of the men to orderlies' call. On their return from the colonel's headquarters, each reported to his captain the order for picket, and the quota allotted to their company.

" Company I. One corporal and five privates ; " whereupon, going to the company quarters, the orderly sergeant calls :

" Corporal Jones."

" I am sick," he answers, crawling out of his tent,

after a dozen voices have called " Corporal Jones," and one man opened the tent to hunt him up.

" Sick be d—d! You are always sick when your turn comes for picket."

" I am sick, orderly. I have a bad cold and cough, and the Arkansas quickstep, so I can hardly move. I reported at sick-call this morning, and got some pills."

" Yes, I remember. I saw you going to the bone-yard."

" Who is next?—Williams ? "

" He is on guard to day," said one of the boys. " There is Henry."

" My turn comes to-morrow. Don't put me on. Put on Manet."

" I don't want to put him on. He is almost sick. He never refuses, sick or well, and I would rather favor him than any one of you."

At this moment the captain came to see how the detail was progressing. Henry was a favorite; the weather was cold and inclement from rain ; and he took sides.

" Put on Manet."

" As you say, Captain," said the orderly, " but it is rather hard on a good man." He was unwilling to oppose the captain, for promotion depended on keeping the right side of his officers ; moreover the captain did not like Manet, and the orderly knew, as did the captain, that no other corporal could get men to go with him on picket more readily than that same Manet.

" Corporal Manet."

" Here ! " A young man, not more than twenty-five, came out of a tent in answer to the call—a firm, quiet man—not six feet, nor below five-feet-six, whose answer, " *here* " was characteristic.

" You will report to the adjutant at headquarters for picket duty, immediately, with a detail of five men from this company."

" Yes, sir."

The detail obtained in the usual manner, reported. They were inspected by the adjutant and found correct. Then the officer in charge was called away, and the men placed themselves at ease, growling after the manner of soldiers, who, when ready to march, are compelled to wait for some dilatory superior. At length the lieutenant came and gave the orders which begin this chapter.

The picket-guard were in plowing dress—army blue—which had furrowed the long land from St. Louis, through the battle of Pea Ridge, and the rocky mountains, barren hills, and desolate swamps of northern Arkansas. A blanket rolled into a cord, was knotted by a string under the left armpit ; below this bounced a haversack, unbleached muslin when new, un-acquainted with a wash-tub since hard tack and cooked rations were introduced long months ago. Some men wore boots, others the common army shoe. Clothes and shoes stained with mud ; only one thing bright, their guns, set off by the inseparable belt and ballot box, which contains forty votes for the Union. They marched through the hamlet—soldiers moving are always marching; but little does that word *march* convey the motion of a company of soldiers through Helena at that time. The soft soil of the Mississippi bottom, wet up by rain, was churned by the thousand teams of mules, and by wagon wheels, to neither butter-milk nor butter. In some places the bottom had "fell out." The side-walk alone was navigable, in some places hardly that; crossings were made on stepping-stones. The traveling was abominable.

To call the insignificant collection of houses and stores, the two hotels and three small, diminutive churches—the collection of various buildings composing the Southern town of Helena, a *hamlet*, may seem arrogant to the wild *bar* of Arkansas, whose idea of a big city had only been formed from Napoleon and Little Rock, while any one of those fourteen thousand soldiers who, under General Curtiss, won the battle of Pea Ridge, and cursed the miserable roads, rugged mountains, and thirsty bottoms they sweated and toiled through, in their long, tedious march to the Mississippi, could have named villages by scores, which, without a millionaire planter, or a negro slave, were more beautiful, more populous, and possessed more of the true essentials of a city. Yet the town of Helena was the outlet of all the cotton and tobacco of a large and rich extent of territory, monopolized by a few, whose interest excluded free labor and smothered the life of a town which, under Northern auspices, would have made a broad mark on the history of the nation. Whatever of insignificance belonged to Helena has past ; the large force which occupied and fortified its hills—the battle there fought—its important relation to the cotton trade, have become history.

Those who accompanied that march will remember how beautiful, how inviting the sight, how superb the emotion as the first glimpse of the Mississippi fell on their weary columns, toiling over the hills ; how home-like the quiet town, dotted by a few mansions of wealthy planters, set in gardens of green; they will remember how soon wheels of army trains cut the wet streets into ruts. until "no bottom" could, with the same truth, be said as of the Mississippi, leaving between fence and fence a sea of mud ; how the flock of carrion birds (camp pirates,) bastard offspring of sutler shops—lit on the gardens and front yards, building booths of cracker-boxes and fence-boards, in which pickles, ginger-bread, old eggs, and spoiling dainties not of army rations, tempted thirteen dollars per month out of privates' pockets ; how soon after, followed the trade store, by special license of the commander-in-chief.

The streets and side-walks were full ; mules and wagons were in knee-deep possession of the straits of mud. Officers in shoulder-straps and pistols, cavalry in yellow trimming, sabres and pistols, artillery-men in pistols and red, and infantry in U. S. brass and bayonets, were jostling each other on the side-walk in the freedom of American volunteers passed out for the day.

Cake shops, cider barrels, cabbages, onions, pota-

toes and apples, were great centers of attraction.
Whisky, at a dollar a pint, and brandy at seven and
eight dollars per gallon, were contraband, and sought
with all the avidity of contraband goods. Here and
there some boy-soldier was reminding himself of
home and Fourth-of-July by a dime's worth of candy.

All the blue men were cheerful and happy. They
had won the victory of Pea Ridge; New Orleans
was in our hands—Donaldson, Fort Henry, Island
10, Nashville, Fort Pillow and Memphis, were ours;
and they themselves were in comfortable quarters,
with plenty to eat, for a long rest, after their tedious,
toilsome campaign. In marked contrast, were individuals clad in tatters, or well-worn homespun, dyed
by oak or butternut bark, soured into the hue of
dead leaves by ignorance of civilization. They were
secessionists who had been conquered—good Union
men while the army of the North was in possession,
looking with greedy eyes on the clothing, boots, and
shoes, pins and needles of the Jews, articles of which
they had known the value since the war commenced.
There were women, too. not well dressed· as New
York or Paris would have called half-decent ; common calico reduced to first principles, breadths scanty
as before slave labor had made clothing cheap. All
made way for the guard which came ploughing along,
elbowing to clear themselves of the Scylla and
Charybdis of mud, dangerous, with no song of the
Syren.

While the guard was passing one group of men
and women, a young person of prepossessing features,

elegant form and manner, despite her poor bonnet
and dress, with the insolence of beauty, and knowledge of man's natural politeness, with the dare of a
proud, unconquered will, maintained her dry footing
while her companions shrank shinglewise by the
fence. A few gave her the road unjostled, others
following encroached, until the line of guides naturally came where she was standing. The rebel female
courted insult, conscious of ability to cut more
keenly. The sergeant in front of Corporal Manet,
who was acting as sergeant, resented the position by
a muttered " She-devil," and gave her the place ; the
corporal caught the word, looked, and their eyes met.

The eye has no expression. Taken alone, it is
simply an eye. Cut off the forehead, hide the face
below the under lid, and every expression is the same.
Mirth, anger, sparkle of passion, flash of excitement,
convey no meaning—nothing but an eye looking
straight forward. Character is written in the facial
lines. The gentle eye has a gentle heart writing
night and day on pliant cheeks. The timid eye has
a heart susceptible to the slightest wind of danger,
putting fear on the lid and in the blood to blanch
when it breezes. The blue eye, the black eye, the
gray eye, the hazel eye, have power only as the features write or have been written distinctly over with
the inside life of the soul. The soft eye, hollow eye,
firm eye, have meaning; as brow, nose, cheek, lips
and chin, have held constant intercourse with the
emotions of each day. But the eye has its tongue,
its daguerrean power, can communicate, can receive

electric sympathies, electric antagonisms, recognize weakness, discover strength: alone, it is nothing; combined with the face and soul, it is a fighting member that reaches beyond fists, declares hostilities. and informs the combatants of the duration of the contest, the difficulty of victory or the impossibility of peace. Some eyes say, "Never, never, *never!* I can die—never, never will I yield; you may vanquish, but I conquer when I am dead." These eyes thus meeting said these words, recognized this will. Before any contest between a soldier and a woman was possible, a man of the woman's party put a strong hand on her shoulder and drew her from the way.

"Le-ette!" said the man. She started at his voice; she yielded to his hand. Was it more the hand or more the voice power? This woman yielded that will which would have died in the soldier's path, to the voice, the hand of this other man, who had an eye—a black eye—with its firm "never" as firm as her own.

When the guard reached the outskirts of the town, the lieutenant divided his command into three squads, stationing them at different points which were within his instructions. One of these squads of men, much smaller than the others, was assigned to James Manet, acting sergeant, who had been stationed here before.

"Lieutenant," said he, "you are making the guard too small. When we were stationed here, this road was considered most important, and was most carefully guarded."

"Who asked your advice?"

" I only offer you my opinion."

" Opinion be hanged."

" I only do my duty."

" Your duty is to obey. If you do not keep a cool tongue I will put you under arrest. Fall in guard—March !"

In silence the men proceeded to occupy the post assigned them. They reached the top of a hill, where they paused a moment for breath. Some had been here, and knew the place as selected by their commander for the picket-post—a place admirably adapted to watch all the surrounding country, and particularly the road they were guarding. Of course they, as volunteers will, began to break ranks.

" Who in Lucifer told you to stop ? Take your place in the ranks. Forward ! until I order you to halt."

" Lieutenant, this is the only safe picket-post on this road for a mile. I have been over the ground, and know."

" Corporal, speak when you are spoken to. This is the second time you have meddled. Be careful not to do it again."

The Lieutenant led his men down the hill, looking for a post, passed over a bottom, then up and down a short swell, and stationed his guard under a walnut —a huge, hoary giant with Briarean hands, each finger-end a leaf; an agreeable spot, but unprotected on either flank, dangerous in front, and susceptible of being cut off in the rear.

The men saw their danger, but would not remonstrate with their officer, who had no extraordinary surplusage of brain, and was " putting on style " for effect.

During the day he remained with them, attending to his duty as officer of the picket, examining passes and permits, and searching for articles contraband of war. Toward evening, he put the guard into the corporal's hands while he went away.

Soon after, so soon as almost to seem that he left to avoid responsibility, wheels were heard approaching. The guard prepared to fire, but the drivers seemed intent to stop, and the miserable place was good excuse for apparent violation, or full intention to pass beyond army lines. A number of women were riding in each wagon and no one could fire on them. There were also several male and female riders on horseback, in the rear, who at the same time halted at the headquarters of the picket.

Here was abundance of trouble. Nightfall, wagons loaded, a large company, whose passes must be examined and " plunder " searched. All were impatient to proceed. The responsible officer on duty was absent, and a corporal, with this small guard, compelled to do it alone. It looked like treachery—it looked like *Cotton*.

The corporal knew his duty. Stationing a man at each flank approach, he ordered the guard to form a line around the men and women, while he and two men proceeded up the hill and examined the wagons.

Immediately the butternuts began to show the

passes, their permits, and deprecate delay, to occupy
his time by clamorous calls for im̄ediate attention,
protesting against detention, as night was near,
pleading to go on, reiterating in loud tones their
faithful Unionism. Their earnestness was suspicious ;
they were too officious. He asked them if the teams
belonged to them ; they answered "Yes."

"Then you will wait here until I see them all
right. If I find anything wrong, you shall go to
Helena together."

As he reached the foremost wagon, one of the
women asked permission to speak to the officer in
charge. She had chosen her man skilfully, and enforced her request by a *smile*, in the soldier's dialect
—a bottle of whisky. She walked her horse to the
opposite side of the wagon from the corporal, then,
suddenly starting, the animal flew up the hill.

"Halt, or I fire."

The woman did not even give him a glance, but
rode more swiftly. As he spoke the corporal sprang
to the road-side. His gun dropped to ·a sight ; the
report, the zip, zip, zip, of the minie-ball, and the
dropping of her horse in the road followed.

"Back ! back !—stand back, I tell you," said the
guard to the prisoners, who would have rushed to see
were she dead or alive. The woman rose from the
ground and then fell on the neck of her horse. The
corporal loaded his Springfield rifle on the run, and
she confronted the same eyes that had met her's now
full of tears, when he said,

"You are my prisoner."

Instinctively the woman put her hand to her pocket. The movement was such that the corporal said, putting his bayonet at a charge before her breast :

" Hand me your pistol."

In his eye she read a will, firm as her own. She changed her determination, drew out her pass, and as she gave it to him, the spirit of resistance asked :

" Why did you kill my horse ?"

" Your pass is correct. Why did you attempt to run the guard ?"

She made no reply, her attention being called to the horse struggling to get up.

" I thought I creased him," said the corporal. But when he put out his hand to take the bridle, the animal, which had recovered, jumped away. At a word from his mistress the horse came, and the woman put her arms about the animal's neck, again shedding tears, and saying, " Janie—dear Janie."

The corporal noticed that her hand was twisted in the mane, and not knowing but she might again try to escape, advanced and took the rein.

Le-ette looked at him, drawing her upper lip like an iron ligature around her front teeth, which glistened with a deadly white, while impatiently gnawing her lower lip. With a mighty effort restraining the volcano within, she said,

" You might have shot me."

He answered proudly, "I should not have killed a woman. You had no reason to run guard, unless, " A guilty conscience needs no accuser." Stand one side I shall have to search you. Perhaps you are a spy."

Then he continued to himself, "Where can that lieutenant be?"

"I wish he was here," said she.

"Bad! Bad—business. There are too many—something is wrong! What can I do?"

Then, he ordered a man to take her to the others, and "watch her closely."

He went to the wagons, took the papers offered, and found them official and correct. If he was only sure the articles were none but those permitted, they might pass. That was the rub; that was why he was here stationed. Every parcel ought to be examined. Then it flashed over him that they belonged to the party of the female who had attempted to escape, and all ought to be detained.

Le-ette spoke to a man of the company, when she came back, and the corporal found them posted when he asked, "does this person belong to you?" The man answered, "No!" though there was a half "yes;" and one who had not received the hint was checked by the emphatic injunction, prefaced by an imprecation on his soul—"Dry up."

A faithful picket is suspicious. He has no right to take anything for granted. Eyes, ears, the whole consciousness ask questions, receiving the plainest answers with a doubt. Tens of thousands of minds are consolidated in him. The life of the army is in his keeping. The responsibility admits of no temporizing, gives no discretion, and calls for absorbing attention. Where was the lieutenant, officer of the

2

picket? Gone—bought off. In an instant James had decided.

"Turn back every one of those teams ; take out the horses and corral them under the trees. The rest take positions and keep the whole company under guard until the lieutenant comes. I shall report him for leaving his post."

The women and men were not in tears. Sterner emotions dry up such moisture in contact with war. Actual starvation, absolute destitution of comforts and luxuries, had compelled them to seek the Federal lines, to take an oath they hated, to humiliate themselves before a clerk of the Treasury Department, to beg like a slave for the addition of one pair of shoes, one more pound of coffee, of sugar, of tea, one more pattern of calico, one more box of pills ; .when this was over, a similar battle had to be fought with a clerk of the provost-marshal; and even then, the chief, with a pen-stroke, dashed out the choicest hopes. Afterward the commanding general, in some unaccountable way, had interfered, and now, necessity, not the lighter task-master, regarded inexorable in peace, but the inflexible, stern, heartless necessity of war arrested them on the lines, within sight of the promised land of secessia, where they would be safe. They were almost escaped, almost home, almost free —one move more ! In such a moment the soul poises, as a sailor who has mounted the shrouds, passed man-ropes and foot-ropes, clear above royal-stays, until he has climbed the naked spar, and stands on the main-royal-mast truck—poises on the brink of a great

hope.   They were almost home.   That order dashed
their hopes to the bottom.   Arrested!—Prisoners!—
oaths all nothing, goods seized—confiscated.   The
future was bottomless as the ocean.   They crowded
around the private, who by the fortune of the hour
held their destiny in his hands, to try if they could
persuade him to let them go.   They besought, en-
treated, threatened, promised.

   At this moment one of the guard fired.   With the
report came the sound of horses' feet.   The sight of
his men scattering into the bush, the volley, and the
answering pistol shots, together with the charge of
the guerrillas, was instantaneous.   Dropping Le-ette's
bridle, which he had retained, the corporal leveled
his musket, whereon came a flash, with its report.
One guerilla in advance threw up his arms, and dropped from his horse.   A foot remaining in the stirrup,
his head was dragged against the rough road, until
the saddle turned, and the affrighted animal, maddened with terror, disposed of both seat and rider.
A howl of rage fell from the gang.   Two avengers
spurred up, one with sword, the other with leveled
pistol.   One horseman's arm was broken by a blow
from a musket.   The same blow changed to the
guard-against-cavalry, receiving a deep dent from the
sword it warded off.   The riders were carried past
by their impetus, one with the addition of a bayonet-
thrust also, to take along.   The next rider drove his
horse over the corporal, taking his sword from his
head as the horse's chest struck his right side; this
impetuous rush felled the Union soldier prostrate,

and, as if that were not enough, a stone-cut opened his left temple.

When the corporal awoke to consciousness he was jolting through dark woods, his body promiscuously doubled over the articles in one of the wagons ; rain was falling in his face; he was wounded, and a prisoner. He tried to move, intense pain admonished him of the uselessness of any attempt to escape. He felt, and found three ribs broken; then he thought of home, of mother—and wished to die.

CHAPTER II.

The party came to a halt about daylight, opposite Friars' Point. Here a man, not captain, neither officer nor member of the band, took charge of affairs. A mysterious power belonged to him. Savage specimens of humanity, regardless of their superiors, treated him with deference—a deference he acknowleged with that quiet dignity which accompanies men conscious of authority. The tie which bound them was not the war-link of officer and soldier. Said he:

" We will now divide the plunder."

As soon as he had spoken, a shaggy ruffian exclaimed—

" I'll be dyed ef yuh do !"

" Then, you will be dyed."

It gives pain to think of the grevious, shocking profanity which is the usual dialect of passion. The war was impregnated with oaths as with an atmosphere. All must breathe air : with each breath of such air comes a certain pollution. Still, no true history can be written which fails to notice this characteristic iniquity ; nor can an accurate representation of the men who act in these pages be made without an indication of the hot words steaming, fetid,

from their tainted souls. The language of heaven
cannot come from the heart of a demon. To avoid
this as much as possible, the changes, present, past,
and future, of the word "damn," are rung upon the
word "*dead*"—since the dead only can receive that
punishment of awful fire and brimstone which is com-
passed in the eternal penalty "damned." Men whose
hearts are a sewer, have a mouth from whose funnel
vapors pour (as cones in a volcanic crater send forth
noxious gasses), foul mouths, always in eruption,
belching oaths, as Ætna or Vesuvius throw out rocks.
This guerilla was such an one, and speaks, first invoking the Almighty:

"We need them 'ar, a heap mor'n them uns, 'nd
ef we'd'nt come in, whar'd they be? They 'longs
t'us; our boys paid for 'um—what's berrying yonder."

A ferocious gleam passed through his eyes. The
calm demeanor and conscious strength, the acquiescence of others who gathered around, and another
something, of which the guerilla knew, held bound his
hand, ready to shoot with the deadly revolver. Slavery produces material for cold-blooded assassins.
They existed before the war; they have multiplied
like August-flies since, and the nearer the destruction [it is not yet destroyed,] of their pet institution
—that sum of all villainies—approaches, do many
more threaten to become guerillas, cut-throats, ban-
dits, and assassins, if their way is not given them.

As if recognizing the inevitability of those words,
the uselessness of contending against the band, that

point was abandoned; but only to open a valve for suppressed fury, which found expression upon the prisoners.

There were four unwounded ; two others beside the corporal wounded. These last had been moved from the wagons, and were lying beside a tree. All were under guard, but the wounded were not so closely watched ; there was no danger of their running away. This blood-hound [Can the Chinese doctrine of transmigration of souls be true?] in human shape, when unable to bite his superior, drawing his pistol on one under guard, was on the point of firing, when the sentinel checked him, saying :

" Oh, Hugo ! Jim, what's the use ? Let 'em starve at Belle Isle."

" By ——, that's so !" adding, " I must kill somebody. I'm dyed wolfish this morning."

" Then give it to that one," was the reply; the guard pointing to a poor soldier in Union blue, whose leg was broken by a ball above the knee.

The prisoner heard the remark, and attempted to avoid death. So strong is hope of life—so strong the hope of living through all this torture, to meet a wife and child at home he raised himself on his hands to crawl away on the unshattered knee, drawing his useless leg after him in its bloody garment.

The guerilla, profanely ejaculating His name who died for sinners, added, " See the hog escape !" then placed his gun-barrel [he had put up his pistol,] at the man's ear, and fired the charge through his head.

The wad and ten buck-shot enter, making a hole

the size of a door-knob—but leave none of the other
side. Shot, skull, brains, blood, and soul, went out
together; and then the guerilla kicked the lifeless
form. Another came up to see the "sport," cursed
him in hell-dialect for a "——fool, to waste a shot
on a Yankee skunk who couldn't git up an' git."

Others also gathered to see the doings; among
them an officer. To him one said: "Jim has finished
one dyed son of a Yankee log of wood; and, by the
way, his foot is planted on that ar one's belly. I
reckon his biler'l bust."

The prisoner subjected to this indignity, scarcely
twenty-one, was almost girlish in appearance. A
heart too large for his body volunteered to endure
the hardships of war. The poor frame, after the pri-
vations, almost starvation, of the march, had been
drained of its life by the fearful camp dysentery;
yet the heart, the will, never refused duty; went on
picket, stood faithful at his post, was wounded by a
pistol-shot in the abdomen, and was dying before that
cruel foot crushed its weight down. Then the officer
spoke, invoking the Almighty—

"——rot your soul, Jim. What are you doing?"

" He was trying to escape."

" The sarpint! he was! Don't you see death in
his face?"

" I kinder reckon he won't run much furder; didn't
calkerlate he shood. That ar 'un I'll fix him 'fore
I'm dun."

The corporal sat against a tree, bolstered thus by
one who had a remnant of soul. It was the easiest

position he could lay in; and from it he could witness
the horrid scene, and anticipate the future which
awaited him. His thoughts were like those of the
drowning. The solid memory of the past and this
experience were present—a picture in which every
thought had the identity of a leaf, limb, tree—a
brain-forest, whose foliage, distinct as reality, was
imperishable as eternity.

He saw his mother in her mourning widowhood,
and in the mind-laden duties of to-day, happy in ignorance of him threatened with death—felt the suspense, when the lagging report of his company, attacked on picket, reached her; endured the throbs of
dread, passing in combat with wishes of hope, that
the missing might prove alive. Dreary, so dreary,
to live betwixt and between death and life, sustained
by the possibility contained in the word "missing."
Home, native state, sisters, loved one, country, the
future of the war, his foster-brother's death and
lonely burial; this attack; comrades dead—happy
to be shot dead. This torture from a human form!
Oh, there must be a hell! If there is no hell, let
all decent people call that part guerillas frequent in
heaven by the name HELL! and keep away from it.
His mind was illuminated, as a forest in a midnight
storm is lit up by an unearthly flash of lightning, re-
vealing an infinity of impression during the short instant, between the words of the men, as they left the
gasping boy and came to him.

No word of expostulation, no appeal for mercy
fell from the corporal's lips. He would no more ex-

pect or ask this of that creature than of a carniverous
animal, whose eye shone implacable over a hungry
open jaw, whose glittering fangs contrasted savagely
with a long red tongue, dripping with anticipation.
He looked not him, but death, in the eye—an eye
alike in man or beast—seen before with a will which
kept every muscle firm—kept his eye unmoved.

A groan, the last expiring labor of the young life,
attracted a new observer to the scene—Leette, riding
by with the captain.   They were in season to see a
blow—a cowardly assassin's answer to a steady look,
which knocked the corporal prostrate, whence slowly,
with great agony, he was only able to lift his head,
put it on the hand of his unwounded arm, and turn
his face to them.   His eye met Leette's, and she recognized—not entreaty, nor defiance—but endurance, waiting without fear or hope.

" Hell-cat ! " she exclaimed.   That poor white, of
no account, not even a nigger, ornary, trash, was an
object of loathing.   All of nobleness in her nature
revolted against a blow upon a wounded man—one
who was too chivalrous to shoot a woman when he
had the right.   The man looked to his captain, and
said :

" He killed two of we 'uns, 'nd I thout I'd spare
the trouble of toting his carcass to t'other side."

" That's so," said the captain.   " We cannot be
bothered with wounded."

" I fixed them 'uns," said the brute, pointing to
the two dead men, with the assured look of one confident of approval.

By this time the whole band were gathered about the prisoner, and among them the citizen who had been dividing the spoil. He asked:

" Who will take care of him ? "

" Leave him in the bush," said some one, " to starve and become food for hogs and turkey-buzzards."

" Let me kill him," said another.

" Throw him into the river," was the voice of a third; while a fourth used the English classic which we have changed to " dead," and exclaimed, in contempt :

" What a dyed fuss about a dyed Yankee! "

" Will any one be responsible for him ? " asked the captain.

No one replied. The band, with a roving commission, had no fixed quarters; no surgeon, no hospital. Their own men were abandoned to the chance of care which the poor white's hovel or the slave's cabin afforded.

" I reckon I mout 's well send him tu hell, 'long with t'others. I don't often ax yah, Captain; I'd take it mighty kind on you to guv this yer."

Before the captain could reply, the citizen above alluded to asked :

" Did your mother ever keep boarders, in New Haven ? "

The young man was, from pain, unable to speak, but nodded " yes."

" I thought so. I boarded at her house. Leette, that chap made my fire, and blacked my boots, when I was in college. Can't you do for him ? "

" Yes; give him to me. I will take care of him."
Leette perceived a frown of disapproval, which
was not confined to privates. Their indignation was
braved by this defiant excuse:

" He spared my horse; I would spare him for that.
Janie has done more than you all together; I would
not exchange her for a dozen Yankees."

" You hear what the lady says?" The captain
addressed the corporal. " Give your parole of honor
not to attempt to escape."

" No!" was his reply—hardly heard, it was so low
—unmistakable from the emphatic negative of the
head.

Put the word " dog " after three strong, profane
intensives, and you have what the guerilla captain
said; follow them by " Bully for you! He has good
pluck; I like him the better. I will take the responsibility; he cannot run at present:" and you have
what Leette said—the words that decided the question, and saved his life.

There were, however, murmurs of discontent among
the men; one face, in particular, was black as a
thunder-cloud. The storm was not to be. The citizen leader had reasons for keeping peace. He addressed them :

" Boys, you can afford to give Miss Leette her
own way, when you know how she has outwitted the
Yankees. The barrels of salt she brought from Helena have powder and caps for you all; the barrel
of sugar is sugar only on the outside—the inside is
made up of quinine and morphine. I cannot tell you

everything she has brought through the lines ; but
you can judge of its value to our army when I assure
you its cost was twenty thousand dollars in greenbacks. Nor is this all. She has brought for you a
supply of army-shoes. There are a few dozen woolen
shirts, and a choice collection of other valuable articles. These are all for you. Now you can understand our anxiety to get these wagons safely through
the Federal lines. You know why I insisted on the
attack, and forbade your burning the " cotton " you
brought in. It is true, we have lost some of our
brave boys, but their lives are well spent for their
country—they have bought medicines, ammunition—
articles priceless, as we were destitute.

Some of you were unwilling to give a share of the
" plunder " to those women who brought it out ; they
did not know that it was only through them Miss
Leette got the permits which concealed these articles.
Now, when you know that your own share, the proportion of the government, is not diminished by the
small lot they receive, I am sure you will have no
objections to their return home with all I have given
them."

" No, no, no !" responded the band, astonished at
the magnitude of the operation in which they had,
unwittingly, been engaged. Leette, too, was astonished. No one but the cotton speculator, and his
agents in Memphis, knew of the secret importance of
those rusty barrels of salt, and flour, and sugar—the
contents of those harmless boxes of ladies' wearing
apparel. Nor can any one, who has not made the

experiment, form an idea of the amount of valuable war material which can be compressed into a very small space. The cotton speculator was not yet done. He noted the change among the guerillas, determined it should be complete, and continued—

"When Miss Leette was coming out she saw the teams had been stopped, and knew all was lost if any examination was made. By agreement, the officer in charge of the picket was away—but his subaltern was too honest. He had ordered the whole party under arrest. On this, Leette, at the peril of her life, dashed by the guard to come to you and obtain aid. This man fired—the shot which gave us the alarm—and brought us so opportunely on the ground. Had he chosen, he might have killed Leette; as it was, he did not even wound her horse. Here is the bonnie mare to-day, ready for another brush ; or, and I may as well tell you this, now, ready to take Miss Leette to Yazoo City with some most important news which she has obtained, of a new expedition against Vicksburg—Gen. Grant's design to attack in the rear, while McClernand and Sherman go down the river and attack in front. She will make the trip in thirty hours—impossible without the bonnie bay mare Janie !"

"Hurrah for Miss Leette, and the bonnie bay mare!" said the guerilla captain. And three hearty cheers were given with a will.

"Now," resumed this man, "I vouch for Miss Leette's having no share in a single article she has so successfully brought out, and ask, shall she not have the man who spared her mare?—I may say her own life; especially when the prisoner, as soon as he gets well enough to march, will be sent to prison at Richmond, where he will be exchanged for a better man, now in a Yankee prison; or where he may have the pleasure of catching the small-pox, or starving to death in the glorious old Libby, or on the sands of Belle Isle?"

"Let her have the dyed Yankee." "Bully for Miss Leette." "She's a brick." "Let her take him." "Let him go, if she says the word."

These, and other words of approbation were falling from the men, as, with pleased smiles, they left the corporal (sorry, now, he had not killed Janie,) to go to the precious spoils which the bribery of cotton had successfully passed through the Federal lines.

The goods were unloaded on the ground. A team (Miss Leette's) sent back to a swamp, where a large flat-bottomed scow was carefully concealed. This was raised bodily on to the wheels and drawn to the river. When launched, it made a long, narrow batteau, capable of carrying ten bales of cotton, one hundred men, or quite a squad of cavalry.

On this ferry Leette and her horse were set over, also the contraband of war, which was speedily concealed among the houses at Friars' Point.

James was laid on the bottom of the wagon, and driven to Leette's plantation, where he was put in the care of Leette's old "mammy"—where we leave him.

CHAPTER III.

Friars' Point is a little hamlet, on the Mississippi river, some one hundred and five miles south from Memphis, and about fifteen or twenty miles below Helena. A few miles above was once the small town of Delta. At an unfortunate moment, guerillas fired upon boats passing with troops. Speedy punishment followed, in shot, shell, and fire. Delta is now chimneys.

What a sad series of emotions the sight of lone chimneys suggests to the traveler on the Mississippi! When cotton was in its glory, before slavery demanded the neck of freedom for its foot-stool, the picturesque villages of negro quarters, whitewashed and glistening, had a peculiar, quaint look—from the location of every chimney outside, on the end of the house. The chimney of the planter's more pretentious mansion was not an exception. Then the eye, watching the changing scenery, caught sight of chimneys with houses between; chimneys with smoke issuing out; chimneys, with troops of children playing below, martins and swallows playing above; chimneys alive, happy. Now, as then, the eye catches

chimneys—but no houses, no smoke, no children.
All are gone, except the monumental spire of brick—
tombstone of southern rights, standing on the grave
of the unpaid life-service of the negro.

Above Friars' Point, toward Helena, the river
spreads over a wide bottom; at high water making a
broad lake, at low water drawing the current into a
Gulf stream on Sandy Tortugas, making the channel
difficult and treacherous, bringing the deck-hand to
the port and starboard-lead, singing the song echoed
by the officer of the deck to the pilot perched in his
wheel-house—a martin-box on lofty Texas.

That funny refrain—"And a quarter twain—
nine and a-half, making men laugh. Eight feet
large, then seven and a-half, and you're drawing
seven; now, six feet scant—the last, the last, you
stop with a jerk—your boat is fast." Dingle, dingle,
ding, ring the stopping-bells; jingle, jing, jing, nerv-
ously twang the backing-bells. Then follows a jar-
gon of tingling brass, Greek to every nation, dialect,
and people, save that semi-barbarous, semi-enlight-
ened, semi-civilized, whole-hog, half-alligator specimen of humanity, a Mississippi-river-steamboat-man.
Everything has stopped, while the center of gravity
has gone on, almost knocking overboard the chimneys,
wrenching every timber and brace, and turning crockery and chandeliers into a harp of a thousand strings.
The boat is on a sand-bar; the river is falling; this is
the notorious rendezvous of guerillas; what will be
the fate of boat, passengers, and crew?

The writer was at Friars' Point, on a cotton boat,

3

at night, tied to a stake, steam up, hot water hose in position, and a determined man, who fought with Sigel at Wilson's Creek, in charge of the pipe: engineers were at their station, pilot at his wheel, and everything ready for backing out. Some sixty men, a whole company of guerillas, filled the cabin, drinking at the bar, swearing at us, and cursing every " dyed son of a Yankee hog."

One man came quietly to the office, whose garments could not· hide, to the experienced eye, his eagle mind and lion will. He said:

" You have come to buy our cotton. We will sell, but you must understand this, we must have supplies. Your money is worthless to us, as ours is to you, save as it furnishes us with articles of prime necessity. Our government does not permit the sale of any cotton. I have a commission to burn, and have burnt thousands of bales. I never fired a bale without regret. If Jeff. Davis had taken my advice, not a pound would have been destroyed. I would have fought, I would have conquered with cotton. I would have sold the whole crop, taken your greenbacks, and bought gold. With that gold our Confederate scrip should have been redeemed, and kept at par. Your green-backs would have depreciated to what our paper now is—a bushel not worth a damn. You understand me. I would have shipped our cotton to England, using you Northern men as our commission merchants, paying you handsomely for your trouble. Cotton will bring something in gold. This we would have received. We have burnt our cotton, destroyed our wealth, and our currency is poor as hell. Our rulers are beginning to see their mistake, are about ready to adopt my policy. I will take the responsibility; we must have supplies. If you will bring us them, we will sell you cotton. For the sake of supplies we will take a portion in green-backs. We must have supplies. Now you are in the cotton business, get us supplies; we will not hurt you. When we have *our bellies full*, then look out—we will give you good warning."

Without deciding the accuracy of his reasoning, the correctness of his theory, or its harmony with principles of political economy, the honesty of the man was self-evident: one of those men enthusiastic in defence of slavery, with the idea of a Southern Empire big in their imaginations. This man may be taken as a type of those who saw a future for themselves in destruction; men who owe their genius to American institutions, yet would overthrow the system which gave them oppportunity to rise; who would build up in the New World a monarchial government on a European model, in which they were to be lords and nobility.

In 1853, this man, whose name I call Kendal La-Scheme, was a senior in Yale college, rooming with a Northern class-mate whose name was Sandison. Both were poor and proud, but not equally dependent on their own exertions. Kendal dishonored the North by boarding with an uncle who had been South to conduct the mechanical part of his father's boot and shoe business. That father had married a North-

ern school teacher, a shoemaker's sister. When their
property, invested in business, had been lost in a
commercial crisis, which cost the son his father, the
uncle returned North.' Kendal, however, was bred
among slaves, whereby a natural love of power was
constantly cultivated amid the degrading consciousness of pecuniary want.

His mother, proud of her son's blood, which she
flattered herself descended directly from the lofty
mountains of ancient aristocracy, brought from England in old colonial times, taught him a corn-cob lesson of poverty clad in scanty silks, and, at her de-
cease, had perfected him in the art of deception. He
despised the relations whose riches reminded him of
destitution, and resolved to carve out his own fortune. Too shrewd to make enemies, he secured every
possible advantage from them before he came north
to his uncle; then, entering his uncle's family, went
to school with his cousins, and other children, whom
he despised because they were "mud-sills," arrogating
the pretensions of Southern aristocracy and wealth.
His will, cultivated by slavery, tamed by necessity,
was stubborn and implacable, ever accomplishing that
which he undertook, hesitating never, calculating all
chances, and yielding not to successive failures.

Sandison, his room-mate and class-mate, resembled
him in poverty, and approached him in tenacity of
purpose. Both were friends, because neither could
afford to be college enemies. Sandison would do
smaller actions. This, perhaps, may be an error;
Kendal, being more astute, could make him seem to

do them—for neither would hesitate to do wrong if advantage could thereby be attained; in proof of which, one instance only need be cited:

Boarding with the mother of the corporal, after the death of her husband had thrown her on the world almost alone, Kendal La Scheme, already in debt, forgot to pay his year's bill—a sort of forgetfulness termed swindling, save among honorable men such as La Scheme, who called it "sharp." The loss brought Mrs. Manet behind in her store account. Once behind, the profits of boarding were not large enough to put her out of debt. Then a strong sense of honor led the widow to sell her house, land, and furniture, and move to the West, where the pour of misfortune's shower continued, in the removal, by death, of the brother who invited her to his home. Then, as a choice of evils, she found a home for herself and child by marrying a noble man, whose motherless family of large and small children appealed most strongly to her fond, loving heart.

To unfold more clearly the quality of La Scheme's character, it is necessary to tell how the money to pay this bill had been provided by Kendal's uncle, but, being on a student's extravaganza in the neighborhood of the seminary where Leette was a school-girl, he (not being allowed admittance within the walls,) outwitted the teachers, and, in "doing it up brown," spent the money, and left nothing but a promise, which ruined the poor widow.

Thus much for her; for Kendal's uncle this: the money which should have paid the college debts was obtained by note aud mortgage of this uncle's premises. The same lack of principle refused to pay again—and thus, uncle and benefactor was sacrificed, and that, too, without excuse, as more than the amount was squandered by Kendal in political campaigns.

In their room together, during senior year, these two men, talking, asked each other what they would be—

"I am going to be a politician, Sandison."

"So am I, La Scheme."

"I shall go South."

"I shall go West."

"Very well. You will be a Senator, and so will I. Then, hurrah for the spoils! My principles are to get all you can, and keep all you can get."

"Those are mine."

"We will remember this."

"Yes."

"Whenever you have opportunity, play into my hands; I will do the same for you. Is it a bargain?"

"Yes."

Such was Kendal La Scheme: a crafty man of the world, despiser of Christianity, hating freedom and free institutions, because they give the opportunity of competing with himself, looking on power supreme as deity—mind and matter simply slaves—disciple, yet not a desciple, of Voltaire, because believing in spiritualism. There was a divinity he adored, on whose altar love, country, earth, and heaven, were imolated: that god was *Self*.

During the years preceding the war, he lent his utmost endeavor to promote the hostility growing between the sections, calling upon all his powers, upon a wonderful memory and clear reasoning mind to widen the breach beyond the possibility of union. He staked everything upon the result, and planned for war long before war was conceivable.

After the war had progressed far enough to cloud with doubt the expected easy success of the Confederacy : while others were looking only on the hopeful side, Kendal, alive in every sense, a great deal alive, gazed steadily at the possibility of failure, and became satisfied that mere success in military affairs was insufficient, and that those arts with which politicians managing a campaign are so familiar, ought to be put in motion, to weaken the strength of the National Government at home. He knew there were mercenary men, who would gladly form an Opposition. Like most Southern politicians, he believed Northern office-holders would take a bribe and sink below, rather than be poor and go to heaven. Money was therefore a necessity ; men were a necessity ; women, too, were a necessity—for women tempt men, taunt men. Had not the women of the Southern Confederacy been so fierce, the common sense of the fighting masses would have abandoned the struggle, while terms were possible. Kendal was too far-sighted to overlook any assistant, however mean, to despise any gift, however small—retaining, by a powerful memory, a clear appreciation of every person he met, and their value, as instruments, in accomplishing his plans—when he arrived at a certain point he sought Leette.

Mariette Ledone, called by her slaves "Miss Leette," is a woman of peculiar fascination and power: a rebel, unadulterated: a woman of honor, but such an honor ! a woman who ought to have been a man, and yet no man can do what she accomplished. What a soul that woman had ! When a child, she possessed every element of beauty; the cheek, the forehead, the dark eyebrow, the penciled lash, the small chin, the regular, elegant teeth, small mouth, and rosy lips, superb neck and rounded shoulders, graceful in gesture, graceful in motion. As a child, Leette was the admiration of her circle—as a woman, more than the child promised.

Leette was early left an orphan, under the care of an uncle whose home was her father's plantation, where, by the tyranny of a will, the uncle was supreme and the mistress subject. Little love was wasted in the large plantation houses. Money bought what money buys; affection did not seal the bargain. Slaves, obedient as will, brooking no look of opposition could demand, waited on master and mistress. Leette was a caged sprite, fluttering within the bars, and fighting the jailor; hating the ties of blood, setting guardians, law, and propriety, at defiance. To free themselves from constant battle, the antagonist was sent to school. Here she met the firm, strong hand of discipline, under which her proud spirit chafed, yielding, because a choice of evils, revenging by a secret hate, which never would forgive the Yankee teacher for making her "mind."

The ingenuity displayed by Leette in violating the school regulations, and escaping school penalties: the tact and energy with which her flirtations were managed—her coquetry enticing the brains from love-sick students, until they were half-crazy at her inconstancy, drew the attention of La Scheme as something worthy of him.

Women were, to him, subjects of psychology. Leette became a victim of psychological investigation. With similar coolness the tyro in medicine uses the knife. Studying to know why woman has power over man, he won the love of dozens for the mere sake of testing his own relative strength; deserting them as soon as satisfied, or permitting the trusting heart to love on until he got tired. Here was metal worthy of his steel. He sought an introduction, and stormed her thought-castle. Pain and suffering were not regarded by the cold-blooded animalcule who investigated his own mental states with scientific interest: as a savant may inoculate his body with small-pox, or other disease, simply to know, by experience, the peculiar sensations connected therewith, and the influence of different drugs on the system during the successive stages of disease, between attack and recovery.

Coquette Leette had found her match. To merit his attention she studied; he was an honor man: loved music; she practiced lessons, as never before; to win him—changed from a careless romp to a careful, studious woman.

To him Leette was a plaything, and he threw her

by when he left college, as a boy a top or marble,
when top or marble-time is done.   But when, in the
onward progress of events, he studied the situation,
laid down his position, and shaped his course for future aggrandizement, such a woman became a necessity.   Then he sought Leette, and a ready welcome
greeted his arrival.   There are, in every contest,
blows to take as well as give.   Leette had her plans,
and saw Kendal out of her own window.   On his
part, he sought to convert a good impression into
abiding love, which he knew to be possible to woman's
heart; to this end made entrance behind the family
curtain, won every confidence, and stood everyone's
friend; to Leette offered a deferential homage, which
compounded admiration with delicate worship—a flattery subtle as those fumes which story attributes to
the rose-scented poisons of ancient alchemy.   He was
playing for the stake of her love.   Where woman
worships she will die.   Kendal was alive to fasten
her heart on his life-altar intending to sacrifice it
for his benefit.

In the midst of war, alone, with none to love, what
wonder she yielded!   He wooed delicately, wooed
and won the fiery Southern passion, wherein mind,
soul, body, are perfect, because free slaves.   Oh!
slavery is but an idea, a word, a name—service without a will.   When the slave-holder Leette loved, she
became   servant, La Scheme master.   It was not
slavery, only love—loving service.

Kendal La Scheme infused a willing heart with an
idea of devotion, absolute, because designing to make

a tool : and perfect mastery could not be obtained
with an imperfect confidence, with a blemish of suspicion. A serpent magnetizes a bird. His grasp on
her hand was the soft slime the serpent embrocates
to swallow his victim. He twined serpent-coils
when fondling her head, when patting her cheek, his
finger-fall prickling. Had sensation been fruit, the
apple would have had honey flavor, tinctured with
a citric or tartaric acid, deliriously delicious. La
Scheme did love her, after a fashion. That which
fooled Leette was passion's flame, which in Byronic
natures burns for a thousand, to each new object
sends out a fiery language, ever new and ever thrill-
ing. From a Byron, from a La Scheme, enough to
deceive any woman of mere passion—of more passion than principle. Yet, even when assured of a
victor's impunity, his cold-blooded calculation, his
deadly hatred of the Yankees, was manifested.

" Your will is mine. You are under my control."

" I am not," she answered.

" We will see," was his reply. He made a motion
for her to take a child's place upon his knee. She
had often been girdled by his arm, her head had lain
on his shoulder, but never this. He fixed his eye
steadily, and looked. She rose to go away ; he put
out his hand and stopped her ; she remained. For
minutes the struggle continued. At length, tired of
resistance, she compromised, saying :

" I will not. I never will :" but sat at his feet.
He put his hand on her head ; she took it off, and retained it. Holding her's, he gently drew it toward

him, and she followed the hand. Holding her tightly, he said, "I do love you, Leette."

In all of their conversation there had been no waste of words, in soft, mawkish sentiment. La Scheme knew better. Eyes spoke love; actions spoke affection; but the tongue had words of war, of death against the Yankees, hate against the race of Northerners. They were one in the strongest antipathies of the heart, and, by implication, ought to be united in the gentler and holier emotions. Said he—

"You have yielded to my will-power. I never found a woman before who cost effort equal to that I have expended on you. Experience has now taught the existance of this magnetical influence, and I design to inform how it may be of valuable service in accomplishing our designs against the enemy. No one can ever conquer your will without your consent. Men are educated to yield, and, particularly, soldiers are taught to obey. Possibly you may meet another person who can master your will. I do not believe it. I say this to you now, because our mutual wish is to do all we can against the dyed villains who are attempting to keep us in the Union against our will. I have demonstrated will-power by making you obey. I tell you that you have power, and in this way have unfolded your greatest strength. You have, naturally, beauty; are fascinating, are accomplished. Music, education, cultivated taste, are yours; besides, you know the world. Add to this, money, opportunity, and will. Everything is yours, but opportunity and money; these I will supply. You must come in contact with the Federals, and turn the heads and hearts of their soft young officers. Break them if you can. Seduce them from their fidelity to home and family, and damn them in their self-respect. Oh! it will be glorious! I think I can see you trample on their hearts. I wish I had their united souls under my heel; I would grind out the last drop of blood! You need never flinch, nor hesitate; while you have implicit self-confidence, and exert your strength of will, you cannot fail to overwhelm the foe who controls your destiny. Will acts most powerfully in silence. This is why I have taught you this lesson in will-power."

Leette was disappointed. Hungry for love, when she had made, had acted, a complete gift of herself, she received husks—a "lesson in will-power."

CHAPTER IV.

The mansion and quarters of Miss Leette were behind the levee, at such a distance from the river that they could not easily be seen. The stranger passing on a steamboat can only discover the deep foliage of those beautiful evergreen trees, which are a pride and glory to the south; which seem so much more beautiful than the firs and pines of the North, because their contrast with common vegetation is so distinctly marked; because when leaves have fallen in the Fall, they are so deeply green, so magnificently in harmony with the sad sombre hue of the bare grey of twigs, limbs, and tree-tops.

Mr. Ledone had little taste for gardening. Leette's taste was wild and extravagant. Impulsively seizing an idea, she carried it to an extreme, afterwards abandoning it as a child tired of a toy. Her uncle was practical, caring more for a sweet-potatoe patch than a garden; but he was also systematic in potatoe patch and garden; consequently the walks were always neat, and the borders trimmed. Leette's roses, after her first fancy passed, ran wild in untrimmed luxuriance, and her shrubbery was untamed as her own character. The neatness of the practicalist, and the abandon of nature contrasted in harmony. God's work is always glorious; and in the surroundings there was a quaint fantasy which made Leette proud of her home, which overwhelmed a stranger with crude sensations of ecstasy, too glorious to explain.

After her return from Yazoo, the exultant spirit fell, since Kendal, whom she awaited, expected, did not come. Though he arrived soon after, her spirit had not entirely recovered its tone, and he felt pressed to discover the reason, fearing lest he might be losing his influence. "Leette!" said he. Her reply was a child's action. In love to him, her woman's heart was a child's heart, and nestled in its faith in him. He rested his cheek on her's, and asked,

"Darling, what is the matter?"

"They told me Generals Van Dorn and Price were to attack Rosecrans, at Corinth, to-day. I believed we would wipe them out, but my heart does not feel victory—and you were not here."

"Leette, I am not sanguine of immediate success in this struggle. We shall conquer in the end. You will see times darker, by a thousand, than this. Have you ever been snagged on the river? Do you remember the death-stroke that hit your heart-center when the big cotton-wood tore up the guards, shivered timbers, and smashed the upper-works—the crash which fell from the broken chimneys and the nervous throbbings of every fibre of the fast boat? Can you hear the shrieks of the ladies; the agonizing cries of children: and the tone of fear, which, coming in the voice of a strong man, is terribly awful? I remember, and you cannot forget. What a great look I took into the heart of my Leette! How brave you were! I have never forgotten, shall never forget. Oh, Leette, you are a woman! What a precious one you are!—Were you only a man—But a woman like you can do more than twenty common men. You did not die; you were spared, spared to me, spared to our country, now trodden by the mercenary feet of Yankee hirelings. Our country has not yet seen its darkest, but it will not die; it will live like my own Leette, to be more beautiful than ever. It shall yet be free from any contamination with the fanatics of New England; a nation of our own, the richest, most powerful on the earth.

"But, Leette, we have not struck all the snags, in our progress toward victory. You cannot but remember how hard the boatmen worked to save the boat. How, standing in water up to their necks, they struggled, after the captain had abandoned hope. Do you remember how we were saved?"

"Yes; you suggested the plan."

"Do not despair of our country, even when our great and noble President gives up hope; for, in that hour, it shall be given to some one, perhaps now unknown, to suggest the plan that saves us all.

"Oh! are we in such danger!"

"I fear it. I hope not."

"We cannot fail. Kendal, dear Kendal, oh, we cannot fail!"

"I will die first, Leette."

"So will I. When you die, I will not live."

"My own Leette."

A woman is a child in the arms of a man. When both are fiery hot with passion, the hearts burn into each other. When love and hate mingle—love to each other, hate inspiring vengeance toward a common enemy ; the antagonism of hate makes the pressure and word of love-passion more eloquent than tongue can tell.

"Leette, I am not satisfied with the present manner of carrying on the war. We are only fighting. We ought to have war in the North. Where there is a division of sentiment, a *casus belli* exists. Men at the North, party-men, cordially hate each other as we hate the Yankees. We, our government, ought to foster that hatred, by fanning to a flame political differences. This can be done by a judicious expenditure of money—and cotton will bring this money. We can buy agents and influence on both sides, then array them against each other ; involve honest, unsuspicious men, and throw obstacles in the way of government, which will undermine the power of the administration, and weaken the hands of its friends. We can buy those very friends—for every Yankee has his price. The Yankee minister works for money. His church-member violates his covenant-obligation for money ; and if wife, pastor, or child, are benefited thereby, all will excuse him for the sin against his government, against his country, against his own soul. A man may be a hundred-thousand-dollar

4

rascal, and the whole parish, a whole community, will
sustain him, will raise the loudest clamor when their
friend is exposed.   Eyes and conscience are blinded
by the almighty dollar.   Newspapers control public
sentiment at the North.   Every editor has his price.
We can divide the whole country by a proper application of money, to the right men, in the right
place."

"Kendal, papers do not make public opinion."

"Not make it, Leette, but direct it.   Independent
as the American people are in thought, they are the
veriest slaves in the world to a few leading thinkers,
who block out tracks on which they load cars of people, who believe themselves running the train—while
they are passengers, dead-heads, drawn by another's
steam.   Money makes the wheels turn ; let us sell our
cotton, get money, and buy up the papers of the
North.

"The London *Times* controls the sentiment of
England.   Our principles are identical; and money
controls the *Times*.   Sell our cotton, and we can have
English intervention.   France is an empire ; French-
men are the slaves of Napoleon ; we sympathize ; they
love show.   Money will control the French people.
Sell our cotton, and we can have French recognition.
English intervention, and French recognition, will
make Southern independence.

"Do I tire you, Leette ?   My own darling ?"

"No.   Go on ; show me what I can do."

"I have conceived a plan, which I shall attempt to
carry out, which will, if successful, accomplish my ob-

ject, in which you can take a prominent place, and act a most important part. But your life will always be in peril, and you may die in doing your duty. Are you afraid?"

" Try me, and see."

" I wish to lay down, on golden rails, an underground track, which shall bring into the Confederacy, from the North, arms, munitions, clothing—all the articles contraband of war. Have you courage to undertake, and are you willing to sacrifice all that is necessary to aid me, to aid our country ?"

" I am."

" Even yourself?"

" Yes."

" Even me ?"

" What !"

" If necessary, to marry a Yankee, if thereby you could make your country free ?"

" Oh !—Oh !"

There was an accent of sharpest pain in the aspirated vowel twice repeated. There was more agony in the convulsive clutches, the burrowing of herself into his bosom (as do some insects hide to avoid danger). But La Scheme felt no compunction as he put the knife into her soul. She was to him what other females had been. It was no new experience to absorb the heart-life of a woman. He could as coolly break her heart as he had others.

" Leette, I design to form a plan, by which, every force antagonistic to Abe Lincoln's administration shall be consolidated. It demands secrecy. A thousand different strings must be touched, conflicting influences and motives be trained, until, all uniting, shall sweep the republican form of government out of existence. The plan must be so deeply laid, that men and women shall work blindly against their own property, their own interests, and only open their eyes when they see they have accomplished their own destruction. To do this, money must be obtained. To do this, we must sell our cotton.

"You can help; you must sacrifice. Are you strong enough, are you patriotic enough? I have put before your mind the strongest power capable of holding you back—myself. If I am ready to die for my country, shall I withhold my honor, or my love?"

"It is wrong. Dear Kendal, it is wrong. I cannot do wrong, La Scheme!"

Then, in order to remove every scruple, he enunciated a part of his creed:

"Every person has a standard within, called conscience. None can suffer beyond their capacity; conscience is a measure of capacity. If I never violate my conscience, I shall never suffer any punishment; neither will you, nor any other one. Hell is a fiction. There is no fire and brimstone. Mind is the center of enjoyment, the source and center of pain. When I violate my principles, I shall suffer therefor. Is it right to kill a Yankee? Yes: I shall go to heaven after killing a million. I hate a Yankee. I deceive him: do I lie? No; I shall go to happiness after I have told him a million. When I kill him, when I

make him believe a lie, I do right. I act in harmony
with my conscience; I do right. When a Yankee de-
ceives you, the act on his part is but the same. You
make a mistake, receive an injury; but there is no
wrong. If I make a Yankee violate his own principles of rectitude, of holy honor; if I violate the
sanctity of the heart of a Yankee woman, and tempt
her to fall, and she does fall, conscious of her guilt,
then punishment comes on her, self-inflicted: I enjoy. If you can make a Yankee violate his own integrity, you send him to hell; he punishes himself.
Tempt him, make him fall from his conscience of
rectitude, and he will suffer while you enjoy. That
which is your highest happiness will be his consummate misery. Now, if to accomplish this, a sacrifice
becomes necessary, is the act wrong? No; it is
glorious. The fiction of the Gospel sends God's son
to die for men : Can you not sacrifice your honor?
Leette, you are mine; dear one, you are mine forever. In heart-life, in soul-life, we are one—two
spirits blend; spirits can be united though bodies are
dissevered; and when life shall have passed away,
melting into one grand essence, eternity shall possess
no single joy they do not share together

> "Here on earth we part,
>   There we shall be one;
> Two bodies have one heart—
>   Heaven-hearts have bodies none."

"Do not sob, Leette! It may be unnecessary.
We are very happy now. Our country does not call
for this surrender now. When the time comes, my

all belongs to my country ; I cannot be with you.
My own dear Leette, my heaven-wife, cheer up. Let
us pray that this sacrifice may never be demanded.
We are happy now ; let us enjoy the present.

"Souls united now in one, shall be as one forever.
You are brave, and you are true. You love your
country. I know I can trust you. I know you
possess sublime courage. It is because I know, because I love, because I trust you, that I have confided to a woman, the greatest of her kind, plans
which are to be realized—now only plans.

"I am going to leave you for a time. Money can
come from sugar. I have plans to be carried out for
the sugar of Louisiana ; they will soon be accomplished ; then I will return to you. The same
friends who aid in sugar, at New York, will help
us there in cotton."

A moment's pause followed ; for Leette could not
reply. He asked :

"Where is your prisoner ? "

"I do not know. I have never seen him. He is
in old aunty's care."

"Send for her."

When aunty came, La Scheme asked :

"How is the Yankee ? "

"'Pears as do he can't die. Neber seed such a
sight in your life. Dar's no white spot all ober ;
bruse, an' bruse, an' blud. 'Pears as do he dun
gon' an' wont die. Laws a'mity, if dat's war, ole
aunty don't want tur seed no more on't."

"What does he say ? "

" Nuffin."

" What does he ask for ? "

" Nuflin. Laws a'mity, he just lays dar so quiet. It's cur'us."

" Does he suffer ? "

" 'Spec' he can't help dat ar'. Yer seed, his head's mashed on de top, and's split on de side, and on de tudder side it's black; and dere's his arm shot right tru ; and his side's gone in, and de poo' man's bruse all ober."

" What have you done for him ? "

" Rubbed um wid possum fat, and cubbered um wid leaves. Put de water on to cool de pistol bullet, and de wet rag on his head."

" Is the bullet in ? "

" 'Spec' not, massa. De hol's clar tru."

" His ribs are broken. Aren't they ? "

" 'Spec' da be, massa. De ole man straighten em' out."

" How's that ? "

" He lif' um up and roll um ober."

" Didn't he yell ? "

" Nebber say word. He make no noise. Shut um eye, hammer um lips togedder—dat's all."

" He is a brave man. I saw it when you stood in his way, Leette."

" Is that the man ? Did you know him then ? "

" Yes. I knew I had seen his eye before, though I did not recognize his face. He will make a good aid. He came near spoiling my plans. We ought to have bought him, as we did the lieutenant and the provost-marshal. He is a good subject, and while I am gone I will leave him to you. Try and win his respect and love; make him a traitor; then trample on his affection, and degrade him by your contempt. Besides, you can use him to find out who are the officers of the Federal army best adapted to become our tools. You are a dear girl, Leette; but you have not sufficient control. You need something to fill your mind. Try and play good Union, and deceive this Yankee. It is a good time to begin."

CHAPTER V.

"The next morning, before La Scheme took his leave, he said to Leette :

"Come, let us visit your prisoner. I wish to see if my impression is correct ; to know whether time will be wasted on him. Some Yankees have royal blood running in their veins. On such you do well to exert power. Conquer such and the victory is glory. You do not hesitate to take the path I point out ?"

"No. I am only a woman, but I have a soul burning to aid my country in this struggle. I have a personal hate toward the enemy. I know something of them from my school lessons. They are mean and despicable. I long to do something. Tell me what to do. Show me how I can serve and I will never avoid labor, or danger. I do not understand how you, whom I know to be so very brave, can keep away from the army. You might be a General."

"All kinds of talent are in demand in this war, Leette. The republican idea is destroyed if we succeed, and the men of the North must be made to

compass their own destruction. Nothing in existence can destroy the American Union but the animosity of its individual members directed against
themselves. While united against a common foe,
they are invincible.

"A republic is either the strongest or the weakest
of all governments: composed of independent individuals who give their single, absolute, entire support—labor—life to their country, conquest is impossible: it is synonymous with extermination. This is
why we are so strong—but when severed by interest,
fear, or any other motive, no government can be
more weak; water falling in drops from a precipice,
—so shall we be, when ever our common bond of
union fails our confederacy. This is the reason I
favor a monarchy or aristocracy. This will make
our future government a consolidated monarchy,
with constitutional rights and privileges, whose leading men and women, the governing wealthy classes,
may agree or disagree, while those seggregated
atoms of people at home are mere tools at the beck
of the master-mind, king, who ever he be. I feel
that my part is not to expose my life on the battle-
field. I must preserve it. I have dedicated, devoted
it to discover, protect, foster, forward every element
of disunion at the North. That element union, gone,
war must follow. War at the North will call troops
from our territory. We will side where we please,
being the gainers in the success of either party. The
moment war does come at the North, and it must
come, it shall come. Don't you say so?"

"God grant it!" fervently, said Leette.

"Money will make it. Money comes from *cotton* —that money we can have—you can help me get it. Napoleon said, "God favors the strongest battalions. Money makes strong battalions; let God alone, Leette, and get money, then we will soon conquer these mercenary wretches. We will make a war where state shall fight state; city attack city; town and county have hostile armies among their own citizens; every man fighting for himself; strength and weakness; globules of melted iron, against drops of water. It will come. It must come. Shall it come, Leette?"

"Yes."

"Then help me sell our cotton."

"What can I do, La Scheme? Tell me; show me; I will follow where you lead; trust me; I will not falter."

"Find from this Yankee, who are politicians among his army corps officers. Learn of him the character of every captain and colonel, and mark when he speaks of a wicked one. Particularly note those who have been party men. Politicians know the value of money, and are unscrupulous. We can make tools of them while they imagine themselves masters of the situation. When diamond cuts diamond the sharpest, hardest wins. You can play the coquette with him. If he has a Yankee wife make him unfaithful; if he has a love, make him untrue to her; make him believe you love him; lead him on; play him off—and it may be he will be smart enough,

valuable enough, to use as an agent. We may tempt
him, and make him a traitor. Hereafter you may
find a place in New York to work, and then this fellow may be of service. My mind is full of plans,
projects and hopes. In every one I have hate and
vengeance against our enemy. It may be necessary
to marry some one to aid on our cause. I hope not.
Then, I mistake if you are not ready. When the
war is done, it will be strange if there is no grave for
a Yankee wife, or a Yankee husband. Do you understand Leette? Our country first, and afterward,
peace, home and love. Here we are. Wouldn't it
be a joke if this was your first visit to your husband?"

"I could choke him."

"You may choke by and by, when we are done
with him. I tell you, I enjoy the simplicity of these
green, unsophisticated Yankee farmer sons. They
let out information as freely as laundress Dinah
soapy water—it is all pure gold to me. Let us see
you come the Union woman over him."

The corporal lay on several bundles of corn-fodder
which the old slave had spread open, covering them
with a tattered blanket. She had kindly washed not
only his bruised body, but his clothes, which were
now quite decent. Had they not been covered with
mud, he would have had neither pants nor coat, for
the guerillas took his shoes and stockings. His coat
was spared—too clotted with blood to be an object of
desire. Motionless, on his back he was attended by
a slave girl moistening the cloths on head and face,
arm and side.

They came and looked at him. His eye met theirs. —Waiting.

. " Are you hungry ?" He shook his head.

" Laws-a-mighty, massa, he don't want nuffin. He don't say nuflln. He jest lies dar—jest so. Look at dem yer feet. Dey's quality feet, dem ar. I reckon his mammy'd let on ef she seed him so kinder gone like."

" How do you feel ?"

" Very well."

" Can I do anything for you ?"

The impulsive womanhood of Leette entered her voice. Manet had no interest in La Scheme, had no ill-will toward the man whose word helped save his life. But Leette was a woman, and he saw in her the angel which might be. God gave woman to man as a heaven-token. She is pure and holy, and to the sterner part of humanity is an angel. How sad that angels can ever fall! Manet thought she was an angel. He knew not she had fallen. He answered—

" I thank you."

Leette turned to her companion, " I like him. I will take care of him and have him well when you come back."

" Do not fall in love with a Yankee—I shall be jealous."

"Never fear, I know my duty."

" Corporal, what is your name ? Mine is Leette. You must call me Leette. No, you are a Yankee. My slaves call me Miss Leette, you may call me so too."

"James Manet."

"Mr. James." She caught a notion of respect, from the calm dignity of the wounded prisoner, which informed her of strength and character. "I must go and say good-bye to my friend. As soon as he is gone, and I can safely move you, I have a pleasanter room for you in the house. Get well as fast as you can."

And now, while the man La Scheme throws the whole of his great life, the whole of his great mind, the whole of his great energy into the work before him; while he hastens into the national army lines, forswears himself, and passes North; studies the situation, consults with those friends of rebellion, those politicians like himself who go in for spoils, get all they can, and keep all they can get; those men who made such pledges, such forgone forfeitures of themselves, their patriotism and their country, that Jeff. Davis, Floyd & Co. were confident no war could by any possibility ensue—while he forms organizations, metes out promises, and creates depositories for rebel gold; while he takes advantage through his assistants of the Yankee speculations in rebel lines; while he puts, as far as his great genius can, every friend or foe under obligations, and subsidizes them for the cause—always laying by a safe sum for emergencies—and while Leette assists in every way open to her as a woman, this story runs back to the beginning of the war and narrates some plain and true incidents, which are not fancy, which belong to the history of James Manet, which also belong to the history

of the country, for they are matters of fact. Matters
of fact which Leette learns, one by one; questioning
by kind look, kind word, kind deed; worming her
snake-path into his life; not a snake, nor yet a viper,
a human possibility for curse or blessing, as evil or
good obtain ultimate supremacy over her soul.

CHAPTER VI.

On the first day of January, in the year 1861, when Abraham Lincoln had been elected, but not yet inaugurated, that individual of whom Shakespeare wrote "God made him, and therefore let him pass for a man," still being seated in the presidential chair, I was invited to a quiet dinner party.

The day, if I remember right, was rugged—a mixture of sunshine and more shade; the shade constructed of gray clouds—not built up from earth, but built down from above, until they seemed the gloomy granite of a big prison, whose ceiling constantly threatened yet never tumbled down. I remember how I watched the lake—one of those great seas whose water is not deep enough to be blue—which, reflecting the leaden sky, presented a horrible, cold, relentless color as the waves rolled over and over in mad windrows toward the shore. A shore of white sand in summer; whiter now in the spotless snow, as if a white wave-crest had forgotten to roll back.

There was no fear, though the waves dashed terribly against the breakwater and hurled their icy spray high over the lighthouse on the pier, that they would reach the town, which was safe on a high bluff—a beautiful face looking down at its feet, where our gentle river wound its snow-clad prairie over marshes in which autumn taught the wild rice to ripen, and the untamed duck to gather strength for long flight to the land of summer.

On the far side of the river, the aged oaks, whose babyhood whistled sapling-songs in the ears of Manitou's departed, lifted a thousand thousand moss-grown limbs in defiance of the rude old warrior, whose annual attacks they had ever braved, seeming to shake their sturdy fagots at and in the sky : and this they did ; for squalls drove through the air from the lake, on to the pier, over the beach, over the sand-hills, over the saw-mill, on to the bluff, then through the houses and steeples and over the river into the woods—flurries of snow, without a pendulum and untimed by any clock. How savage every flake! An independent warrior envenomed to kill; but without the ability, though the wind was implacable as a fury, and sharp as the glance of a piercing eye.

Into this I must dive before the warm hearthstone and genial cheer which awaited the invited guests could be reached. The hour hastened, the short day was saying night when the gray opened.

You can always see heaven when the gate is open. How quickly it shut! Then a cloud from the horizon came driving with impetuous speed toward the shore. As it drew nearer it separated from the sky—a cloud-storm on its own hook—an island of storm—a whirl-wind of gray filled with flakes—a distinct wrath an

5

hundred feet high, driving before it acres on acres of white-caps. Just here the sun scowled and illumina-ted the savage flakes, which, between the scowl of the sky, and the scowl of the wave, and the scowl of the sun, became a vivid russet color, a volcano half cooled, which attacked the town—shaking the houses, rattling windows, shutters, doors; whistling in every nail-hole, and filling every crevice with its sifting army of snow.

It threatened in distance like a mountain of thunder;
  It burst on the lake like a torrent of woe;
It was gone in an instant—a twinkling of wonder—
  And left, as a monument, nothing but snow.

That evening the sun set in beauty. This we saw, looking from the table. When, heavier duties being performed, the hale old gentlemen, George Washington Wirtman, father-in-law to James Manet, asked his guests their opinion of the events foreshadowed by such a fitful New-Year's day. I remember, for it seems many years ago,—seems like a dream of childhood, a dream of an old man whose skinny fingers smooth a grandchild's hair,—how, one by one, we wedged our minds a little into the dark future, trying to find a gleam of light.

Manet's mother—holy word!—thinking no evil, could not conceive of any war. A woman whose heart was big enough for her head to swim in; a head made not like a pin's, by a hammer, but thought-ful, educated to teach the youthful and mature mind, and control by the instincts of common sense; a

mother causing a dead name to be held in reverence
in the family of a second husband, and the children
whom she had adopted in the new relation to love her
more for the just affection she lavished on them who
had lost their mother. Her house was home ; not of
riches, for daily toil brought daily bread ; but home,
where love seasoned every feast. This of to-day
was given her son, James, a fine young man, aged
twenty-two, who had a clerkship at twenty-five dollars per month in a country store.

Daily duty confined him from early light until
nine in the evening, when he put up the shutters and
went to bed. Slept in the store : which means a
space separated from the spare catch-everything,
without carpet, stove, wash-stand, or clothes-press ;
gloomy in winter and stifling in summer. He could
not go home save twice a day ; a tin pail being table-
cloth, knife, fork, and dinner company. That tin
pail! Who prepared it every morning? Mother.
And the sweet stories of remembrance it sang; the
little acts of self-sacrifice that every now and then
unexpectedly peered out; the kindness of the bread
and butter to the son loved by a mother who studied
his tastes and anticipated his wants,—oh, tin pail!
many and many a weary, hungry picket night hast
thou stood out in the dark thicket, bedecked with the
jewels of memory, and many a long wish has gone
far back into the past for your return ; and then the
heart has opened its great love and drawn the holy
thought within and folded mother to the dearest spot
of a noble patriot soul. Good bye : you are a jewel.

Ah, when we get to heaven, many a coarse, rough earthen vessel will be found there; while dazling diadems are dross forever! For three long years, barrels, gallons, dimes, dollars, yards, bushels, codfish, fire in the morning, shutters at night, and tin pail had turned like the wheels of an old family wagon, driven to church by a staid New England deacon.

James had done nothing for himself. His wages were willingly given to his mother. God bless that mother! Her boy's heart was of her heart a part,— a big heart, with room to spare,—and James would have died for her. Now he was a man, she had said:

"James, come home this New Year's day. You have few holidays. You must have one good dinner to remember beside Sunday's. I have your employer's consent. You shall invite whom you please, and the party shall be yours. You deserve one happy day, and I offer this as an omen of a happy New Year."

Can you see her quiet, earnest face?—happy— running over—making welcome felt? Her eye is pouring out gifts beyond rubies; shining as the stars shine, beaming as the stars beam. Her voice sweet with kindness; the tone diffusive, common property, enough for all; to be appropriated by whoever choose, with that attribute of possessory right which means me, mine.

In summer, morning brings light and sunshine: Mother is the morning of this summer; gentle sisters—only two—the flowers of this home. Bright-eyed Jennie; Lilly Sue, a drop of life set in gossa-

mer tissue. Alina Sandison (daughter of the Chairman of the County Committee ; the same Sandison
who had been a room-mate of Kendal La Scheme,
and owner of the store where James was clerk) is
here as an exotic, loaned and borrowed—the village
beauty ; but of her more hereafter. James Manet
threw his love away on her? Wait. Love is a
study. Study this love. Alina Sandison to-day is
a mirror. The distinction between mind-mirrors lies
in memory. Eyes reflect, faces shine. To-morrow
will tell whether the soul is mere sand, fused, rolled
and backed with amalgum, or not : to-morrow, when
the soul wakes,—and that to-morrow may not be for
years,—will it remember ?

From early childhood, God's sweet gifts had been
peace to all these daughters. The wind had blown
roughly at long intervals ; brought troubles and trials
which seemed mountains—such mountains as the deni-
zen of the West finds in the rolling prairie, never
having climbed the Alleghanies or Blue Ridge. How
could they imagine what a few short months would
bring ! That the hurricanes of sorrow would beat
on their wounded souls traveling with weary steps to
the summit ; where these elevations of grief are but
rolling prairie to the Andes, the Chimborazos, the
Himalayas of anguish that loom in awful grandeur—
impending in terrible proximity over all the future.
The future to them was a garden—its probable events
beautiful flowers.

There was another member of this circle, son
Henry's wife—daughter Mary—serving in the kit-

chen ; a service of joy : like the Saviour's lowly act
of hospitality to his disciples, which makes the doer
chief in the heart of those whose feet are washed—
standing in the door with her babe in her arms.
Black hair ; dark eyes, now pleasant with joy, but
possessing the deep, distant look of capacity for suffering.   She was of those who are sensitive to
distant danger.   In this case there were no nettles in
the air.   One by one, pleasant joys and glories of
the present set a gleam of sunshine over the spirits
of all.   Even Mr. Wirtman, anxious for the future,
did not believe the acts of secession by the Southern
states more than ebullitions of a defeated party, who
would yield, as they ever had done, to the principle
of republics acquiesing in the will of the majority.

I have seen a little play-mate destroy the pleasure
of a whole bevy of bright eyes and pleasant faces by
a pout, a cross word, or a selfish "I will," or "I
wont."   A destroyer threw this group into deep
thought by saying :

"I believe there will be a terrible war—a war of
eight years' duration."

"Impossible !"   "What do you mean !"   "You
must be crazy !"   "Why !"   "Horrible !"

Surprise was on every side.   From out the kitchen
four eyes—the babe was like its mother—looked over
the table, as if the southern west held a corpse.   The
untrained lips could not say "Father."

"Since the idea strikes so unfavorably, I will re-
duce the time to three years—not a moment less."

"I believe," said Mr. Wirtman, "our Southern

brethren design to show us by their votes of secession how firmly they are determined to maintain their
opinion of their rights; but I do not believe they
will ever attempt to wage war against the national
government. I hardly hope to see them join in the
inauguration of President Lincoln. They will become reconciled, however, and the future will be as
pleasant as the past."

Again came the disturbing voice:

"You do not know the people of the South. Nor
do I, save those met at college and in the law school
at Cambridge. I found them—whom I regard as
types of the whole—large-hearted, open-handed,
quick to resent an injury, and unwilling to forgive;
the best of friends and the worst of foes; the soul
of chivalry and the incarnation of self-will. Their
mother filled her duty by giving them birth; a negro, at the penalty of a kick, or a cuff, or a scar,
trained the child in the way it should go. Their
will, never broken, has ruled the Union; and now,
seeing their scepter passing away, they prefer to die
than yield. They will not yield. They secede.
They wait not for the North, but enunciate their own
proposition: 'Grant us all we ask, and we stay;
refuse, and we never will return. You dare not
fight; if you do, one Southern man can whip five
Northern men at any time. Our forbearance is stigmatized as cowardice. There remains nothing but
war.' "

"Hurrah for war and glory! I am in. There is
a chance for you and me, James. I will be captain, ·

and you shall go cook. I do hope we shall have a little. In six months we shall whip them out and be better friends than ever.

The words of Charles Hardone. Mark him. A handsome, lively, dashing, good boy, fellow-clerk to James. When not at the stove, telling stories, he is at the show-case, among ribbons ;—codfish, mackerel, salt pork, butter, cheese, lard, etc., for James. A trump among the boys, and a lion among the young girls ; a good runner and jumper ; handy at ball or any other game ; not bad at a story ; prompt with a repartee ; the first to laugh and give a joke, and no fool at a song. He, too, loved Alina Sandison, as did all the young men. Who would not love a handsome, wilful girl—the prize of the county—one to be looked up at—one who knew her advantages? Was his love thrown away ? Wait. What is love?

Alina Sandison looked on this burst of enthusiasm with dangerous homage. Women love brave men. Debarred from opportunity to manifest the strength of their own character and will by hard blows, they adore courage, nobleness and daring. With the womanly feeling, composed partly of a quiver, partly of a thrill, she asked, ' Wouldn't you be afraid to be a soldier ? "

He replied by singing to the tune of " Janet and Janot " :

"Oh, I want to be a soldier and go into the war;
For I hear the call of glory, and worship honor's star.
I will gladly leave my home and enter in the strife,
And, rather than be conquered, I will offer up my life.
Oh, if only I'd been there, when Bunker Hill was young,
I'd wrote my name in fire and stamped it on each tongue.
But the days of war are past and the days of peace have come,
With every chance of glory lost, poor I must stay at home,
With every chance of glory lost, poor I must stay at home."

"You seem to believe war impossible, Hardone. I hope it may not come. But let me assure you that the pride of the South will not permit them to retrace their steps, were destruction seen by their own eyes before their own feet. With the chances of success now tempting, they will not, cannot recede. Their honor is involved, their reputation at stake, their self-respect indicted, and they now would experience a thousand deaths rather than face to the rear. Their *pride* is a mountain, which will yield only to death; and when that pride stands against the Union, against the permanence of the institutions entrusted to us by our patriot fathers, that pride must not only yield but be demolished; and if, in such destruction, extermination becomes a necessity, then they must *die*. Fear not, you will have a chance to win fame, honor and glory."

"Mother," asks James, "would you be willing for me to be a soldier?"

"James," is her reply, "Your grandfather's father was at the battle of Bunker Hill. He fought in 1812. When your country calls, go. Your friend takes an unfortunate view of human nature. The time he anticipates will never come."

Problem in 1860. The future. Given, the North and the South and slavery. What will the end be?

Immediate, uncompensated liberty for the negro slave, say the abolitionists.

Non-intervention, says Douglas and the democrats of the North.

Intervention means freedom, non-intervention, means freedom—see Kansas,—say the leaders of the South. Intervention we demand, legalizing, nationalizing, protecting slavery everywhere.

Intervention, says the Republican party, to limit, hedge in, bound and forever block the farther extension of the slave institution.

Non-intervention, means freedom. You are all abolitionists, and we secede from the Union, say the South.

The world does not comprehend the crisis, not even does the country. But the far-seeing statesmen of the South recognize the hand-writing on the wall and forestall the battle of human progress. They strike the first blow because the contest is inevitable. They comprehend the coming struggle in its height, its depth, its far length, its wide breadth. If you yield, grant all, whatsoever we ask, whensoever we call, wheresoever we be, howsoever it may be necessary to be done, make us kings, conquerors, masters, be our subjects, servants, slaves, we will be your friends, your kind masters. If not, if you refuse, if you attempt to maintain the old Union, you must *exterminate* us for we will never go back.

Do not mistake. The mass of southern people comprehend no more than the masses of the North. No better than did Manet's mother: they are not governed by logic, but by hope; the great managing minds, sitting on the lofty summits of thought and will and pride, they alone, gazing from their high elevation were masters of the situation.

In reply to James' mother—for the tone of her remark was kind pity—the disturber said, "I am sorry I cannot see as you do. Since I have given you a new thought, storming the placid quiet of your mind, I will fire a closing volley. I have said there would be war. Of course this is mere speculation. Let me add, war will not end, until battles four or five, perhaps more, will be fought, in which the number of killed and wounded on both sides will amount to forty or fifty and possibly a hundred thousand."

Unprepared for the thought of war, this assertion would have seemed too reckless, too improbable to be worthy of contempt; but that called manner, the something more than words which coming from, goes to the soul, startled an emotion of astonishment, which found vent in the sign language of lungs and heart; tongue and ear were suspended, the organs of insensible perspiration became respiratory, breathed and filled the room with suspense.

Then that mother was first conscious of an infant dread, a babe of death born in her heart. Oh, God! what misery there is in a word! What horror in an indirect conception of the possible!

The old gentleman whose experience was weighty, who was already the watcher in sleepless nights of thought, absorbed in contemplating the *may be* of his country, calmly turned from the speaker to his other guests, with the remark :

" I do not believe such a calamity can be permitted by the good God. Whatever may be in store for us, safety is in his hands. I confess I discover no peaceful solution of this problem, nevertheless, confidence in our glorious destiny does not forsake me an instant. Like my wife I can only be sorry our friend sees no good in the future."

" Far from it," said he, in reply. " I see every good in the future. The impending conflict, permitted by our Heavenly Father, is beyond present conception. We cannot attain to its termination. Schiller says : ' Great evils take great remedies to redress them, and tempests fittest scatter pestilence." If, as I believe, such the evil to be redressed, the moral convulsion will be equal to a tornado on the tropical islands. There will be a new heaven and earth, but the glorious sun will look through purified atmosphere on prostrate palm and evergreen forest; on ruin, wreck and death ; solemn witnesses of the cost of purity. Excuse me for casting a damper on our pleasant gathering. I was only honest to myself in speaking these cruel anticipations. May they prove incorrect. To show my sincerity, I propose with the consent of my hostess to invite the guests here present next New Years' day to dine in this room. We will then be able to

see that I am wrong, and I pledge myself to make
a valuable monument by which to remember my bad
prophecy.

There is a good time coming, if not very nigh—
When "the stars" shall shine in a cloudless sky,
When the flag of the free, and the hope of the brave,
Shall no more droop o'er the home of the slave.
     Let it come! Let it come!

The good day is coming, when love alone,
Shall rule every heart and fill every home,
When the lust of wealth and the pride of power
Shall vanish like smoke and be known no more.
     Let it come! Let it come!

That good day IS COMING. The heart shall stand
And greet every freeman on freedom's land,
The stars and stripes shall spotlessly wave
O'er the land of the free and the home of the brave.
     Let it come! Let it come!

The good day is coming, God speed it on,
Like Spring's rosy morning when winter is gone;
When the South shall bloom like a fruitful tree
With labor's white home, the home of the free.
     Let it come! Let it come!

CHAPTER VII

Looking back, I remember the Republican convention at Chicago. The great wigwam, the young men's Lincoln club, the assembling of delegates and their alternates, the deep subtle schemes and plans of those men who shaped their course by the probable turn of events, so as to seem directors of the public mind, while merely sharpers snatching the floating drift on "*that tide in the affairs of men which taken at its flood leads on to fortune.*" I remember, for it was my fortune to stand in the space reserved for the honorary members of the convention, the mighty enthusiasm which attended the nomination of Abraham Lincoln ; the peculiar broken-downness of those whose hopes were built on Wm. H. Seward. Most particularly, I never can forget the scene which transpired in the office of one of the distinguished lawyers of Chicago, then an important officer in the United States Supreme Court. I remember an alternate delegate, who wrote *Hon.* before his name, and half a million after it was enquiring of the legal gentleman, having had long acquaintance with Old Abe as a lawyer :   "Was he a smart man ?"

And the answer was :

"No; only a first-rate, clever fellow."

"What kind of a lawyer?" continued the questioner.

"Tolerable. We class him as third-rate."

And then was asked this wonderful question:

"Can he tell a good, smutty story?"

"Can't be beat at that."

Which answer was followed by this cutting comment on the qualifications essential in this man's experience of Washington society:

"Well, then, perhaps he will do."

Afterwards the gentleman, entering into general conversation, (for the small knot gathered in the office represented New York, Massachusetts, Michigan, Illinois, Wisconsin and Nebraska,—each giving utterance to the thoughts of the hour; and the successful friends of the nominee were replying to every deprecatory remark by quoting his known character for honesty,) said: "Honest Old Abe may do well enough in Illinois; but when he gets to Washington he will find himself in hell!" I remember my inward comment on the few tears which that old, tough business politician wrung from his eyes, humiliated by defeat into indifference to manly shame. "Pennsylvania sold us. But we would have raised two hundred and fifty thousand dollars in the city of New York alone, to have carried the state of Pennsylvania, and, if more had been necessary, we would have made it up to a million."

Why do I remember these incidents of the past? What, if anything, to do with cotton? Because the

iniquities connected with cotton are the direct offspring of the abuse of free institutions, and the common practice of purchase and sale of personal influence among party men. The morality of a nation
that tolerates the schemes of wire-workers, reward-
ing the most astute and successful by the highest
posts of honor and trust, that nation must suffer the
penalty, defeat in war through incompetent leadership;
the useless sacrifice of valuable life at the shrine of
the god cotton; the wholesale traffic of senators and
representatives bought and sold by a per centage on
all, each and every gallon of whisky drank in the United States. This is the thought of the present moment; the best of present judgment. Throughout this
work the _I_ claims no peculiar infallibility, having too
often been taught that to err is human; having, by
force of circumstances, changed opinion. Change
of opinion is not necessarily degrading. Water without motion stagnates; human thought cannot be perfect. God alone possesses exhaustive knowledge
which is capable of unerring certainty. Consequently that mind, that political creed, that party
which never errs must be divine or else a dead pool,
with neither progress or life. The assumption of
infallibility by a being less than supreme, is itself an
indication of weakness, yet every independent mind
has a certain self-confidence, a kin to infallibility,
without which life and actions are worthless. This
is right, for so far as our knowledge exhausts the
subject, so far our reason and judgment are correct.
To this extent humanity can be infallible. Yet new

ideas should be enunciated humbly, lest crossing the settled notions of the past, they excite prejudice, than which nothing is more difficult to overcome. Whereon it follows, that the most useful, if not skillful arguers are those who state the proposition simply, distinctly, so that every mind clearly comprehends the issue, sees the point. Beyond this, nothing can be done, words, argument, are useless. Conviction is the eating of truth into the mind, and truth needs no assistance, except to be perceived. Could men of education only find terms of expression, definite, decisive, precluding possibility of mistake, the real difference of opinion in the world would be immeasurably reduced and misunderstanding impossible.

I think of this as I remember the convention of the Democratic party at Baltimore. Where the ablest men of the South had gathered, poising for an instant on the beam of destruction, giving the alternative to their old associates and tools, and to themselves saying: "Although we may at your request defer another term, yet dissolution and secession is inevitable, and we will accept your submission that we may be better prepared when the struggle comes."

Honor to Stephen A. Douglas! All honor to the firm, stern patriots he represented! He saw the future, and recognizing its import, refused to be a second Franklin Pearce! It was impossible for him to be a James Buchanan! His party standing behind kept to his support with unwavering fidelity, which was the hand-writing on the wall. They were

6

not abolitionists, they believed in the vested rights of the constitution. They did not even believe in intervention to keep slavery out of the territories, north of the compromise line. They did not care a copper for the nigger, but they were for the Union, and they followed their leaders blindly. To the genuine secessionist, Douglas was more dangerous than an abolitionist. When far down the Mississippi, when with Gen. Sherman, after the first battle at Chickasaw Bluffs, after we had gone up White River, and taken Arkansas Post—we went up to the Cut-off before we entered the Arkansas River, our troops landed at Napoleon, and some stores were broken open and burnt; then a man excusing himself, told me, how in the days before the first hostilities, after the firing on Sumpter, when the last boat was going up the river, the men of Napoleon had come on board with a halter, calling for the d——d Yankee—the God d——d abolitionist, to take out and hang him— and said he, "a Douglas man in Texas, where I came from was stigmatized as a d——d abolitionist." Then he added, "See what I got for being a Douglas man," and he stripped, exhibiting a huge ugly scar half torn through the thick muscle of his arm, while a stab by his collar bone and another glancing over a rib by his heart, were witnesses to his truth. "I had just got well of those, and I said nothing, and now I would sink every rebel in hell. I would burn every house, rob every home, and turn the whole devil-brood into the ashes." Being asked to explain, he replied: "I was a Douglas man, talking poli-

tics, when a Breckenridgeite called me a d——d
abolition son ———. I told him that Douglas was
the only true Union man, that Breckenridge was the
biggest abolitionist, that the man who voted for him
did more to destroy the Union than one who voted
for Abe Lincoln, or any other abolition devil, and
that the quickest way to abolish slavery was to vote
for Breckenridge. Then the cursed son of hell—I
have fixed him since—took me unawares and
stabbed me. Do you blame me for hating the rebels?"

Looking back, I remember, during the campaign,
how the public mind was waiting; how every mind
filled with anxiety for the future, seemed to go out
after what might be. I remember the nightly group
in the store. The wide-awake lamps, and the enthusiasm generated by the fairy dancing of swinging
lanterns and torches.

Chas. Hardone was Lieut. of a company in which
James was private, but while Chas. was always absent from from the store, James could only get out
between hours as on him fell the work of both. Mr.
Sandison as leader in the county committee, was constantly busy and absent, Charles was his useful assistant, but James steady and reliable, what could
the store do without him?

So it happened that Lina went to the store on the
nights of illuminations, that she called the steady
one to keep her company; that he sometimes came,
and when that was prevented, watched lest any insult
should be offered, for such was the excitement in the
little town that every one was in the street, even

little children, and times were when whisky made the
rough men from the woods forget the words proper
-and the actions chaste. Lina's mother had given
James a general charge, feeling safe when he promised to take care, and safer whenever Lina said "I
will ask James to take care of me."

As children they had gone to the same school;
had not spoken often, were not often playmates,
had seldom met at children's parties. As village children know, they knew each other. James
was slow, a vice worked by a lever and screw, gathering together and keeping knowledge. Persons
brought up with such children do not give them credit
for their rich storehouses, but estimate the rapidity of
acquisition without credit for tenacity. Yet the
quince tree bears quinces by and by—and oranges
are no worse because the tree must grow ten years
before it arrives at fruit. Steady James, reliable
James, who knew every part of his duty and did it;
who had no bad habits and was no lion, was regarded
as a safer companion than many who desired Lina's
smiles.

One evening, long before New Year's, when news
was coming from every state assuring the election of
Abraham Lincoln as president, one grand, triumphal
procession was inaugurated, in which a company of
ladies represented the states of the Union. Alina
was one. During the afternoon the celebration was
in carriages and on horseback. In the evening some
enthusiastic persons insisted upon the ladies joining
the procession of the Wide-awakes on foot. Charles

Hardone was very urgent; for Alina would be an
officer. With the judgment usual on such occasions,
they led the procession in the middle of the street—
up, down, forward this way, back that—until the
beautiful girls of the morning were fainting from fa-
tigue, and soiled and torn from the unusual and
improper places through which they were led. The
cause, and the time, and the occasion were the excuse. Pride at carrying through what once had been
commenced alone kept them there, save the necessity
of mutual support. And, as a grand finale, the procession went to the public square, where a mixed
crowd of all sorts were laughing, gibing, and enjoying the license of such a time. Here James found
Alina, and firmly taking her away from her companions, from Charles Hardone himself, obeyed her
mother's instructions and led her into the store.
Nearly exhausted, sustained by nerve power, Alina
was hesitating between weariness and anger; for
pride rejected the right to dispose of her thus.
Nothing in the way or manner of James gave offence
—at least she could not torture such a meaning into
it ; yet she would not have yielded had not he taken
her hand. She did not heed him in the least until
he held her, and then drew her to the support of his
arm. She yielded, too tired to stand alone. The
multitude would not separate from respect, nor cull
their language, nor perfume their breath. She clung
closer, and he took her away.

Excitement! The politicians had wrought upon
the popular mind until a river of excitement—what?

—ran through the land. Every heart was charged, and a telegram was sufficient to discharge enthusiasm all over the country; man, woman and child—those having any claim to humanity—felt its power. Why cannot this mystery of existence be solved? Is this identical with the power which James Manet perceived as Alina Sandison leaned on him! Did he wish forever? Not at the moment did James understand the mysterious emotion; memory and study taught the deep meaning. From that time he knew himself controlled by an instinct—a passion, which read the different changes of the word "Alina."

A regular octave of pet names; Leena the second in the scale, what the school girls called her. Aleen, the long call with the rising inflection, when mother sent word through pantry, bedroom, parlor and shed, for my daughter. Een, the abbreviation, which little baby sister made musical. Ina, the wilful appelation of a fiery mate, who would not do as did the others. Ena, the same softened as her sister spirit, so the school girls called themselves, was always saying in her ear, arms twined together as sister-spirits do to enhance their bliss by the magic of the touch. One more, the chord of the seventh, Allie, which James called her that night. Alina Sandison.

Her father was reputed wealthy. So he is; now worth no one can tell how much. Cotton. Of that by and by. He was the most sagacious politician in that part of the state; invaluable to his party for profound skill in defeating a majority. Her mother —it is wonderful how some unimposing men win elegant wives!—unrested at dawn, worked wearily until night, sinking to rest like a wet bow-string when nerve tension was removed.

Alina Sandison. Lina and Allie. Charles Hardone loved Lina. James Manet loved Allie. We call her now Lina; for the one is. She may be worthy of the name "Allie" by and by—worthy the love which James Manet threw away; for that which he loved and called "Allie" was possible, but had not yet dawned upon the life of Lina Sandison.

Lina's young face was full of possibilities. The forehead white, high; so nearly square in front, as to demand scrutiny to see the curve; so nearly curved, as to obliterate the idea of any angle; the eye-brow arched, delicate as the penciling of nature upon a flower. Her eye full, with plenty of room; straight forward in purpose; arch on occasion; gentle, except when aroused; but when quiet, presenting the slightest shade of hungriness. The cheek was dainty, like a golden apple stained with crimson; not a long care, or hard trouble, had deepened a line or toughened a feature. The nose was delicate and full, which, with a small mouth and chin, completed an oval of beauty which belonged to Lina Sandison —which James Manet worshiped, which Charles Hardone believed the handsomest in the world.

Thus far, Lina's life has been simply a negative. How long will this continue? The heart, once awake, soon finds its polarity. Toward which will it point, James Manet or Charles Hardone?

Between these individuals existed a peculiar affec-

tion.   Charles liked James more, perhaps, because
James loved him.   Few young men are found who
possess the versatility, the humor, the geniality of
Charles.   Certainly, none in that town, dignified in
our West by the name of city, with its mayor and
common council.   The long evenings were short
when he was present; and James would do his work
and give him evenings that might have been private
property; would engage to do double duty to release
his mate from the store, that he might be the soul of
many a gathering, of many a sociable, of many a
committee met to plan, decorate, or prepare for village tableaus, parties and church festivals.   Charles .
was the favorite; could talk, while James could only
work and was dumb.   The dumb can think.   Such
kindness begets a return; all the return possible—
often far short of the spirit of the doer; still the
giver—it may be well—accepts the return as pure
gold, and treasures dross in a heart where sordid rust
gleams with glory.

James, in the stillness of his thought, watching as
one whose heart-life is at stake, had been slowly,
painfully deciding himself away from the heart of
Lina.   She was kind to him, teased him, seemed to
appreciate his attention; yet the something that
would have filled him with happiness never came.
There were times when a thrill would startle; but
sober thought and careful observation satisfied him
of her greater interest in Charles.   Why shouldn't a
young girl, educated at school, singing in the choir,
prefer the smart, talented young man who sang the

leading part by her side? A man almost a poet:
certainly an apt rhymster; the life of every gathering. Why should she not prefer him to the hard-
working man who sat speechless in a corner? Yet,
do what he would, reason as he might, James loved
her. Though he never would tell her a word, never
would permit her to imagine his affection, he could
not help loving, and was not sorry. Every true and
pure affection elevates the heart; nor need the hum-
blest be ashamed of the spontaneous out-goings
toward any one whose beautiful qualities of feature,
mind and heart excite admiration and love.

Of all this Lina Sandison knew no more than the
pleasant realization of attention which flattered her
self-love. The girls teazed her; but no more than a
dozen others. And, when she was invited to the
New Year party, she was only gratified by an attention others did not receive; she was very happy because she was the only one invited by James, and
because Charles Hardone was there.

CHAPTER VIII.

The soldier of the Union, on his bed of corn-leaves, was not conscious of the motive which led the fair-faced woman to smile on him; to bestow care where, perchance, care was useless. Not so; James Manet had tenacity of life. Some men lay down—cases are often seen in hospital. I once saw five strong Irishmen die in a row; before the surgeon or nurse anticipated danger they were dead. Others came in pruned like a tree; cut down, hacked, mutilated; sick with fever and dysentery; at death's door, with finger on the latch, and yet lived on, recovered; aye, went out and fought again: not only once, but more. They seem made of malleable iron, and needed pounding to show their metal.

In such a case, treatment as was Leette's was invigorating; she moved the corporal to her mansion. Resolved to please her lover by winning the Yankee's love and trampling on his affection, she put him in a pleasant room. There were no luxuries of a sick chamber, no tempting delicacies, no store medicine, but kindness, attention, and the semblance of love.

A woman who loves carries the object in her heart. When some work, act, or path has been designated for her by him, strength of affection is manifested by the enthusiasm with which it is followed.

Unconsciously, Leette threw into her kind acts the love-thought she was wasting on La Scheme, or Kendal, as the heart-tongue called over and over to the heart-ear a thousand times a day. The outward act deceived, because the perfect representation of an inward thought which bore the name of Kendal. This was more than a prisoner had a right to expect; and, as he had no suspicion of evil design, as he saw the image and superscription—the eagle, stars, stamp and figure of Liberty—he did not imagine the coin counterfeit. As true and pure a feeling of gratitude was returned as man can offer to any kind, beautiful woman.

For a time their intercourse was confined, on her part, to a "Good morning"; a "How do you do to-day?" "Can I do anything for you to-day?" On his, a smile; "Better"; "Nothing"; "I thank you." Simple words, "I thank you." They had never sounded thus before to Leette.

When very young his mother had taught him: "James, always thank every one who is kind to you. Never fail to recognize the slightest act of good-will. It costs nothing, and every one likes to be appreciated; to know you appreciate them. Even when kindness is mistaken, and is really of no service, recognize the good spirit, and thank the heart for its good-will." James loved his mother, and, from that mother's love, a holy radiance shone upon his "Thank you" which entered the heart of Leette,

without her suspecting what for a neighbor Kendal
had there.

She did not love the Yankee corporal. Love begets love; neither loved the other. Leette, seeking
to win love, won gratitude, from which she missed
that something La Scheme had won from her—which
she imagined had been won from him. The true and
false were defining themselves, taught by this task,
whereby she was soon to discover how cheap she had
sold herself; to know, yet refuse to understand; to
see, yet refuse to believe; to be taught by progressing events how unworthy was Kendal, and yet to
cling on his memory still; to discover how the
prisoner, who, although grateful, would not love—
had, without effort, taken captive that pure respect,
which, without passion, is the only basis of abiding
love. The task gradually changed to a pastime, and
Leette carelessly asked:

"Where are you from?"

"The West."

"I am glad. You Western men are our friends.
We are not fighting you. We hate the Eastern abolitionists. The West and South will be friends, and
our country be the same; but we will never unite
again with New England. No wonder you are brave.
I can take care of you more willingly, now I know
you are of our own people."

She asks no more questions. He speaks no more,
conscious that the Eastern blood is yet warm in his
own veins, and that no boundless West can change
the heart with its instinct for freedom, which, born in

the blood is bred in the bone, and will live, either among the rocks of the hills of the nutmeg state or the alluvium of the American bottom.

At another time, Leette, piqued at his quiet silence, asks :

"What are you thinking about?"

James answers, "My mother."

Quickly Leette asks, as if her care and kindness were called in question, "Are you not at home? What more can I do?"

His reply, following a long breath, is, "Nothing. I am a prisoner getting well. I have not heard from home since my brother's death."

He becomes silent. She waits for him to tell more; but nothing follows, and Leette, believing the cause of his grief something beyond the loss of a brother, —believing the time for confidence ripe, says:

"James,—I must call you James,—I think you mean more than mother."

"Yes" is his answer. "My brother's wife and child."

She waits again for him to speak, knowing that attention and sympathy ask questions more to the point than ignorant words. He continues:

"What will become of them?"

This she cannot answer, and holds her tongue again. What does she care? Nothing. Nor does he for what she may think. His thought is inward, as his next words show:

"I fear lest mother, thinking I am dead, may give up hope. It may be, Lilly Sue will wish to go. She loved us."

Then came a triumphant thought, flashing imagined success through Leette's brain, "Here is the
key to this Yankee heart. Lilly Sue. Who is Lilly
Sue?" and she asked him.

She is disappointed to hear him answer: "My
sister, dear Lilly."

Again, seeking the heart, to which as yet she has
no clue. She inquires.

"For whom do you sigh? I am jealous of sighs.
They do not come. for sisters as deep as that one.
There is another one."

"No." James *no* is a lesson in spelling which so
poorly represents the lesson of deceit, that Leette
places him at the foot of the class, by the instantaneous exclamation :

"You were disappointed in love; you know you
were, and enlisted to fight us, because you could not
conquer yourself!"

"No—lady—I am a prisoner, and not at liberty
to discuss these questions. I buried love when my
country was in danger. I volunteered for the nation,
the whole Union. Could you see as I do, you also
would agree with me. I thank you for all your kindness. I wish these cruel differences were adjusted;
we ought to be at peace—but, much as I think of
you, while we are at war we are enemies."

Changing her plan on the instant, she said, "Is
that all? Now James, I am going to bury the
hatchet for the present. I am a rebel."

"And I a good Union man."

"I like you the better, honest Yank. We will

agree to be foes by and by. Now, and until you are able to fight, we must be friends. Give me your hand."

" So be it then," and James gave his hand.

Both were pleased. She in finding a foe worthy of her care, he in freeing his mind and standing in her presence a friendly foe. This was that anomaly, an armistice, which neither war nor peace mingled in friendly grasp hands prepared to slaughter the other. In such proximity love can, has often burst its barriers and mingled antagonisms in harmony.

" Now, says Leette, holding up her small beautiful fore-finger and throwing a world of playful, coqueting menace into its prohibitory action, " Remember, you must not tell me again, you are a prisoner. I set you free. You cannot escape till you are well. Do not try. I give you permission to leave me. Go, crawl through the briar patches; hobble into the cane-brake, to starve and feed bears, hogs and turkey-buzzards. I shall not seek to find you. Be contented until you are well, then I promise to withdraw my parole and make you a prisoner again."

The corporal would not give his parole, not to escape. Leette put it upon him, as no gentleman could refuse, by confidence in a foe whose life she was preserving. James acknowledged her courtesy by a simple, " I thank you," emphasized by the strongest exclamation point of a great soul—a man's tear. Leette impulsively exclaimed.

" I like you. I wish you were not a Yank. As you are, you must be—but I will never forgive, if at any time you refuse to speak true thoughts, true words and true feelings. Tell me what you think about the war. I wish to know about the Northern people that I may be enlightened as to real differences between us. You must be frank, so will I, and if you get angry it will not be my fault; if I get angry the blame shall not be yours. Is it a bargain?"

"Yes." Then with his answer came a sudden impulse. She had been by his side, a bee over a flower ; the bee has a sting, its destiny is honey, but it can poison. Leette did not sting yet. Her hot Southern blood fastened a live kiss on his face. Her lips had no sooner made and taken that sensation, than the heart telegraphed modesty, which blushed at his look, and then she bounded away.

In two minutes Leette did not care. This mixture of recklessness, flashing anger, flashing pride, flashing love, flashing folly, flashing calmness, disarmed suspicion but had a subtle instinct, as the watching cat perceives the approaching victim, before eyes, ears or smellers detect its presence.

And the corporal was not long surprised, for he had seen since the war began, such incongruities of character—actions so contradictory of all his experience of the possible, that nothing of any nature or character so ever could surprise or astonish him. He was thrown off his guard, thus giving Leette an opportunity to gain a clue to the incidents of the next chapters.

CHAPTER IX.

Some hearts have an instinct of disappointment. The sun may be shining, others radiant, yet faint expectations of calamity impregnate their being.

I am analyzing James as he seemed to me; for he had not studied his nature sufficient to take a joy, leaf by leaf, and, from a beautiful rose, make a general ruin of calix, pistil, stamen and corolla; nor was it possible for him to explain the iron stubbornness that garroted his throat, burned in his eyes and congested his heart, when, day after day, evening mail and nightly discussion excited intensely his brain. One fort after another was seized by the rebels. War is coming. Then the hope entertained by every one, particularly by his father—yet, somehow, he observed that Mr. Sandison never spoke when the others were confident—that President Lincoln would have wisdom to enable him to escape that which seemed so inevitable; that hope would throw doubt on his mind. Yet, after restless thought during the long night, morning would find him with a tired head, an unrested eye, a heavy load all over, and then, when

7

Lina Sandison came tripping into the store and lengthened minutes into an hour talking happily with Charlie, while he waited on all the customers, and only received a kind "Good morning," the shadows of thought sank heavier, and he said to himself, "There will be war. Let it come. I shall go."

Charlie Hardone had penetration to discover the thoughts of James. Perhaps I ought not to use either *penetration* or *discover: imagine* may be correct; still imagination, if true, might be called penetration. Charlie wanted the time, and the thought, and the smile, and love to himself, of not Lina alone, but of every one of his lady friends. His ambition was gratified, he was perfectly happy when the center of their observation. As Lina was the first in social position, she became first in his catalogue. Without any serious thoughts he strove to win her, and parted with so much of himself as was necessary to the object. Here he encountered an obstacle in the wishes of Lina's mother, who chose James to care for Lina. Why? Because she knew too much? No. James himself knew nothing. Had he any jealousy? No; but he would watch. If Lina had a fancy for James it would be strange or he would find a way to put a stopper on that. But did Lina's mother have any design in the distinction? This became a study which at length received answer in the negative. She evidently had no suspicion of him; but trusted James as the oldest, best known and safest. While engaged in this investigation the incident of celebration night occurred. In a moment—for James, by gentle but quiet determination, took Lina from him—there had been an exhibition of strength of purpose, of power, which surprised, and angered, and aroused the evil passion, "I will pay you for this." Knowing himself, to attribute love to James was the first impulse; to suspect Lina, the second; to vow to put an end to the same, and ingratiate himself, and labor to that end, the next. Charles Hardone was a natural schemer; a Yankee school teacher from the East, who came to the West to make his fortune; equally ready to teach music or day school, or take the charge of a prayer meeting. It demands no little skill to manage, with general approbation, the idiosyncrasies of evening meeting, and the whims of .a district where the teacher boards around, and the sensitiveness of a singing school, with a concert at the end. Before he was twenty Charlie had done all this, and graduated in a political campaign, where he beat Mr. Sandison in a minor election. The sharp old war-horse, taking the measure of his antagonist, drove him off the track by hiring him when out of employment. Mr. Sandison justly estimated his clerks, and to him more than his wife was James indebted for the preference. Mrs. Sandison had confidence in her husband's judgment of men. At one time she asked :

"Shall I ask Charles or James to look after her?"

"James," was the decided answer.

"But Charles is a church member."

"I know," said he, "Charles has experienced religion like a steam-engine; dashed through the long

bridge and come out safe on the other side. He is
a Hard-one. James has made no professions; but he
has an iron will, which has accepted a Saviour from
a consciousness of personal need, and I would trust
him with my soul sooner than any minister I ever
saw.''

Time went on. Charles did his utmost to attract
Lina. Gradually he assumed as a right, the privilege granted James, who retired because Charlie was
always before him, and, some how, Lina seemed
pleased. James inherited from his father a sensitiv-
ness which his mother refined—a retiring demeanor,
never put self forward unless in the path of duty.
His love was timid—magnifying its object, and un-
derrating himself. He determined to make one trial
to present to Lina the opportunity of choice, and, in
case of failure, abandon the hope of her love. He
knew when Charlie would go to ask her company to
an evening gathering. He would meet him there
and invite her himself. Should she choose Charlie,
he would accept her decision as final.

These thoughts had worked in James' face; such
always do. His mother alone observed them, and
that evening she asked his confidence by a look that
was answered thus:

"I am going to call on Allie to-night. Charlie
will be there, and I will know which she likes best."

Mother recognized the secret, the confession, the
hope, the fear, and foresaw the end. She could not
speak. To the sad shadow of dread another fear
was added.

Charlie was already there. Cordial greetings were given, while he retained his position at the piano where he had been singing several songs. James took a seat by Lina, at her invitation, and this gave him a hope of joy, observed by the watchful pianist, who now felt sure of wounding and paying for the unforgotten. He believed he had power, will power, and was determined to use it against his friend, although he little thought of the extent of the injury. What did he care? Without seeming to watch, he permitted no movement to escape, and while singing, comprehended every word spoken. James waited until he was through, and then said:

"Miss Allie, I came to invite you to attend the meeting this evening; but, Charlie, perhaps you have her engaged already?"

"No," was his reply, and then he said, "Oh, Lina, I have never sung you my new song. Come, I composed it for you."

> "When the sun brings with the spring
>   Flowers bright, flowers gay,
> Gentle birds on blithsome wing
>   Welcome each new day.
> Every bush and every tree,
>   Every leaf and flower,
> Has a voice of melody
>   Full of wondrous power:
> Singing music of its own—
>   Love's sweet tone, love alone—
> Proving that, though time roll by,
>   Love can never die.

When the last rays of the sun,
　　Fairy soft, fairy bright,
Kisses darkness with its own
　　Twinkling, twittering light,
Every breeze and every star,
　　Every murmuring rill,
Purling through the evening air,
　　Has an angel trill:
Singing music of its own—
　　Love's sweet tone, love alone—
Proving that, though time roll by,
　　Love can never die

Youth's bright sun brings with life's morn
　　Love's bright flowers, love's bright flowers,
And my star of hope is born,
　　Shining for thy bowers;
Every thought and every dream,
　　Of my life a part,
Flows in one pure crystal stream
　　Toward thy gentle heart:
Singing music of its own—
　　Love's sweet tone, love alone—
Proving that, though time roll by,
　　Love can never die."

He threw a whole storm of passion into his voice
and the fervor of love into his words, while from his
eyes as fixed on her a sparkling will danced out, con-
quering by magnetic power. Then without waiting
for an answer to James, speaking as if the question
had not been asked, he said:

"I came for you to go with me, and you will go,
wont you?"

She looked at James an instant and answered,
"Yes." The next moment she would have recalled

the word, for a look came on James' face which cannot be forgotten. Charlie marked it and was glad. "I have hit you now," was his secret thought. James stood for a moment. She tried to redeem and asked,

" You will go with us ?"

" No."

There was something intense in his quiet. No word could reply and no conversation supply the vacuum—triumph for Charles, but regret on Lina's part, destiny for James. He held his ground gently, firmly, while she put on her things and went with them out. To her invitation call again, replied, " I thank you," so that she knew it was a kind " No "— like the everlasting hills. And he said as they parted, " Good bye, Allie."

Charlie strove to divert Lina's mind, to overcome the strong regret that James had been only second, that he should feel so badly. She was not to blame. But there remained the memory, the vacuum, not improved by the painful expression returned her in a smile by James' mother. Did it mean that she knew ? This and more came up for thought. Charlie found his companion absent although striving to be polite.

Lina had the first blow that taught she was no longer a girl. That night came long thoughts. She studied the meaning of James' unusual conduct, his look, and his mother's sad smile. She imagined the possibility of its true meaning. Then compared the two—was not sure she preferred either, certainly loved neither—asked herself if she was ready to love any one. Answered, no. Felt glad she had not made Charlie unhappy, was sorry the thing ever occurred. Blamed fate for the misfortune, and at last slept and dreamed that she was married to Charles Hardone and that at the wedding was kissed by James, who threw his arms around her neck. Then somehow, she seemed to see him with a gaping wound in his breast lying on the ground and her white bridal robes were clotted with gore.

James Manet possessed a heroic purpose and will, only one among ten times ten thousand. Thousands of patriots went into eternity on the battle-field and thousands died in the hospital who will never have a historian or a monument. I could weep tears of blood would they avail as I recall these unknown soldiers without friends, without home, without love, for whom no single tear was shed, who so loved freedom and their free country that they spilt their every drop of blood for it. I see now the long rows of hospital cots in the long cabin of a Mississippi river palace, wounded men after the battle of Shiloh, unwashed, uncared for, untended during seven long days, hungry and thirsty, waiting for their time to have their wounds dressed or their limbs taken off, without a word of complaint, and enduring their agony without a groan or a contorted muscle. James Manet did not blame Lina. Such was the low estimate he placed on himself as compared with Charlie, that he wondered how he could for a moment be such a fool. He was ignorant of the mighty infinity called soul, which God had given him. How many soldiers in this war have manifested heroism, nobility for which no father, mother or friend gave them credit! which would have remained unknown, undreamt of, had not this opportunity been presented for development. Their souls are wide awake and immensely active in the boundless realms of paradise. There is a blessing in a curse, when by it we are taught to prize the quiet spirit near us, which holds the germ of honor, renown and immortality. James was ignorant, uneducated, and knew not the power hurrying him on.

That night in place of going to the church, he joined a knot of young men, who were talking over the possibilities of war on the corner opposite the hotel and by the store. A large number of dry goods boxes were piled up, on which they found seats. Among the number was a tall, sandy-haired, light-complexioned young man, with fiery eye, born in old Connecticut, having the descended blood of a fighting race, brought over from the cavaliers of Cromwell. A proud, haughty soul, a noble, generous spirit, hidden under the apron, tough fists and sinewy arms of a wheelwright. To-night he was clad in broadcloth; straight as an arrow, strong as an oak, proud as a knight, he seemed invincible. War was not new to him. A boy he belonged to the Governor's guards. Hampered by the control of an iron uncle guardian, he ran away and enlisted in the regular army, where he saw service, and when Buford's men attempted to drive the 'free settlers from Kansas, without being an abolitionist, he shouldered his Sharps' Rifle and joined Jim Lane for the fun of the thing.

"I tell you boys what I will do. If war come, and I know it will, I will get up a company and join the first regiment that goes. Those Southern men cannot whip us. I have fought them. They say one Southern man can whip five Northern men. It is a lie! I remember the first fight Jim Lane had. There were only a few of us Northerners, mostly men from Massachusetts, and nearly a hundred of them. We were in a bad fix, between two high banks in a kind of gulch. Perhaps we might have got away, it was a chance, but we had come to fight and could no more than die. They were all mounted and rode down on us, yelling. We kneeled down in the first rank and stood in the second; as soon as they were in good distance we let them have it—and then loaded and fired as fast as we could, expecting to be rode down every moment. They did not come. When we ceased firing and the smoke cleared up, there wasn't a Border Ruffian to be seen, and only a cloud of dust to show where they had gone. I tell you we can whip them in every fair fight. But they wont fight fair. Now I have forty names pledged to go with me from the country where I live, and I think I can easily get enough for a full company. It only takes ninety-six. Don't you think I could, James?"

"Yes," was the answer, "I will go for one."

Then, when Lina and Charlie were enjoying their own thoughts, this group was preparing for war. An instinct seems to control humanity anticipating the events of the future, and the *may be* and *will be* never find the world totally unprepared.

Events continued to hurry on. Arsenal and fort were seized. Every mail brought some new account of hostility until South Carolina became the center of the United States, and one little band of heroes the embodiment of nationality. Hour by hour the nation quivered in its million million heart-strings, while hostile cannon frowned on starving patriots calmly waiting for fate. Moment on moment of suspense, increased to almost agony, until the news came of the first gun on Fort Sumpter. Then excitment became will, the land sprang to arms, and patriotism reigned supreme.

CHAPTER X.

" Why are you a mere private, James ? "

Leete's prisoner has been improving in strength, though not yet strong. He talks more than he did ; still she is the questioner, seeking a little to-day, and to-morrow following up the clue. He answers the question thus :

" My first captain was killed by the time-serving of a political governor. I had an offer of office ; but would not demean myself by doing any act which politicians would reward by a commission ; not even to be in debt for its gift. A debt of gratitude to be paid in kind, I regard as an antecedent sale of soul, of which I never would be guilty. I have one life to give to my country. I knew nothing of war, and refused to assume responsibility as an officer over the lives of others when I was ignorant of the duties of a private."

" How was your captain killed ? "

Leette wanted to ask a dozen questions, but this was the prominent thought to keep before his mind. The ideas she obtained from his answer were : he had a first captain, who was killed by a governor ;

therefore, he has been injured, and this is the opening to make a traitor. James answered:

"He was not killed, only drowned; but the act
was the direct result of the governor's perfidy. Had
Captain Esmons never been compelled to visit the
capital to watch the progress of events, and to try
to make the governor fulfil his promise, he never
would have been on board the steamboat from which
he fell and was lost. I do not like to talk of these
things. It covers a sad past, on which I do not often
look."

For that very reason Leette would make him gaze
longer,—as long as her motive was concealed, and
she could torture without suspicion. She continued
by replying to his first question:

"What a poor opinion you have of yourself!
Hundreds of officers are not so well qualified, nor
ever will be. In the Confederacy talent like yours
would ever secure preferment, and be recognized and
acknowledged by our government."

"I love my country too well to permit my patriotism to be diminished one atom by the evil acts of my
fellow citizens. This rebellion has called me to
jeopardize my life for the Union. How much rather
should I endure the unnecessary indignity and positive wrong-doing of those who profess to be my
friends at home!"

To explain more fully than Leette could possibly
draw from the soldier, watchful even of the reputation of his native state, we go again to the first call
for seventy-five thousand six-month's men. In our

city no one asked "Who will go?" Men came spontaneously and enroled on Captain Esmons' muster-roll. It was drafted by Mr. Sandison, with a copy of the State Militia Laws before him. It was signed by the captain, and James placed his name next.

In that day of uncertainty great doubt hung over leading politicians. All patriotic men determined to sustain the President. But some of the democratic leaders in our city hesitated, influenced by party spirit to antagonism, manifested by a questioning, carping, uncertain, disbelieving, doubting manner. Their patriotism drove them to loosen all party lines and distinctions, and fight for the Union, one and inseparable, but they were not sure of the best interests of the party. There had been no concerted plan or action. The first gun fired at Sumpter shot the Northern heart unprepared. Patriotism, pure and unadulterated, ruled the moment. Politicians were not. The great, true heart of the people responded. Before twenty-four hours Capt. Esmons' company was full. He had been East, passed through the capital on his return, and brought word that the governor ordered individuals who recruited companies to take them into barracks until they could be assigned to regiments; that he would grant commissions as soon as muster-rolls were presented at the State Adjutant General's office.

Immediately the people, with one consent, brought contributions. Every man's heart was full, every hand open; without discussion, taxation, or solicitation, the volunteers were fed. An old warehouse was filled with the stout, stalwart, sons of the country and forest. The drums beat. Men, who had been free as the wilderness of the West, surrendered to the idea of a soldier, and willingly confined themselves to the second and third story, where, hour after hour of day and evening, the tramp of squads, drilling without musket or bayonet, answered to " Front face," " About face," " Eyes right," " One, two; one, two," " Into two ranks form company," etc., etc.

One housewife loaned her unused cooking-stove; another, her great coffee-pot. The hotel sent down its spare spoons and knives; a dozen families contributed crockery; private teams left their work and went to the distant farms to bring straw for the soldiers' beds, while a patriotic committee of ladies gathered spreads, blankets and quilts to provide the men for the night. As soon as the barracks were once opened, every man left his home and joined the company, yielding implicit obedience to every requirement of the new relation, returning no more at morning or evening. Even mother and sister were refused entrance to the dearest of all the earth,— that brother who loved country better than life. Son and mother acquiesced because there was at stake the life of the nation, to which individual life —a hecatomb of lives—are less than the thousandth part of a drop to the whole great chain of lakes, only one of which, with its sunset-horizon of water, expanded north, west, and south of them farther than the clearest sight can reach.

Captain Esmons was the last of his name and race. A small patrimony in ready money was at his disposal, and this he laid on the altar of the cause. Was printing to be done, he paid; was any individual of the class alluded to, unwilling to give the article which some of the boys had procured at his store, he paid. He bore his own expenses to the state capital, met the adjutant general, was welcomed by the governor, and assigned to the second regiment. Quick as had been our movements, others had been equally patriotic, and now not only was one regiment full, but it was certain that the state would answer the call for men. It could be relied on to do its whole duty. The governor said:

"Captain, go back and drill your men. Tell your people, tell Mr. Sandison to keep your company in barracks, and before a week we will assign them to the headquarters of their regiment."

At that time there existed a fear lest the people would not come up to the crisis—feel the responsibility, and assume the burden of the hour. Before the world never had a similar problem appeared. The United States, through a period of unexampled prosperity, had cultivated the arts of peace,—its discordant and inharmonious elements had cohered; but now that a large minority refused to accept the will of the majority,—particularly when that minority had a strong *prima facie* right to be independent, more particularly when a great portion of the population of the non-seceding states sympathized with the South, admitted the right which had been exercised, or were in doubt of the coercive right, or, if right, the ability to coerce, or, if right and able, the advisability, the expediency of its exercise,—the leaders of all parties were so astounded that they stood still; waited to see whither events turned,— the nation took control, and was equal to the hour.

Looking back on that time, I believe in the remark of a steamboat captain,—a strong, plain man, who neither minced his meat or his words,—" Why don't the president call for three hundred thousand volunteers at once, and crush the rebels? We can raise half a million as easily as seventy-five thousand men." Yet this was not to be. The president was not in advance of the people of the United States; all were learners, and to-day are teaching the world a lesson in which themselves are taught, being scholars at the expense of the dearest the heart loves, the most precious blood the heart contains, at the expense of life. Let me write with humility: at the expense to many—alas! how many!—of eternal life itself. Until that lesson is learned there will be no sure, no lasting, valuable peace. When God strikes, man is a fool to anticipate freedom from pain. Nature, offended, never forgives, and if, in the course of the Creator's government, war and calamity fall on a people, permanent, abiding peace will not return until his plans and purposes are accomplished.

Had James Buchanan hung Jefferson Davis, Floyd, Beauregard, Wise, Mason, Yancy, and a score of others as traitors, the curse of slavery would be as

8

deep to-day on a preserved country as ever: the question of slavery extinction deferred indefinitely, and only one step gained, if indeed anything had been accomplished at all, and that merely the building of an imaginary wall to hinder its advance into new territory.

But laying slavery for the moment entirely on one side, a most important lesson to be taught, to be learned is the imperative necessity of purity among those who govern the nation. A mere politician influenced by no higher principles than party, is corrupt as the father of evil, dishonest as that father, and as worthy a place in the lake of fire and brimstone. Note, that there may be exceptions; turpitude is graded by distinctive lines, and while one man for his share of punishment should be condemned to sit forever on a lukewarm flat-iron, there are those who deserve to be confined time without end in a blast furnace of melted sulphurate of iron.

No sooner than the call came for volunteers, no sooner than the companies came pouring in to answer that call than opportunities for fortune presented themselves:—the common profits of ordinary business on the amount of clothing, camp equipage, &c., required to outfit a regiment being equal to the life savings of an ordinary man. The State patronage was in the custody of the Governor and the Adjutant General's office. Immediately the old warhorses smelt the contracts afar off and advanced their claims, based on past personal services, or on pledges of future support; bargains by which present favors are granted in consideration of a future possible contingency. This is partially illustrated in the fortune of James Manet while connected with Capt. Esmon's company.

The Captain returned in great spirits, told his men he had orders to stay in barracks for a week, then they were to go to Shawnee town to camp with the Second Regiment which had already eight companies and the promise of two more. The people heard with joy, made new contributions, sent wheat to the mill, where the miller exchanged it for flour: this was taken by the baker who every morning supplied the company with bread. The ladies gave pies and puddings, the butcher contributed meat, and hams came from every store and every smoke house in the vicinity.

But a week dragged into two, and no orders for marching came. Then Capt. Esmons went again to the capital.

The Adjutant General informed him that the Second Regiment was full and his company had been transferred to the Fourth which would rendezvous at another city in a different part of the state in two weeks. He was sorry for his disappointment but it was the Governor's orders. All the Captain could do was to return, tell the people to support the company in barracks at their own expense for two weeks longer.

The patriotic enthusiasm of the people of the state was so great that companies sufficient to fill twenty regiments had been offered, the state quota did not amount the half. As soon as this became under-

stood, politicians, small men of town caucuses, peti-
fogers of justices' courts ambitious for a title, began
to wire-work the Governor, learned that Capt.
Esmon was entitled to no political courtesy, and
insisted on the transfer of his company which they
accomplished, for he had no friends to notify him of
danger, and even Mr. Sandison had only written a
common letter of recommendation.

Remember, that this was at the outbreak of the
rebellion, before there had been any Bull Run, or
"all quiet on the Potomac," when motives untried
were mere patriotic impulses or instincts, the germ
of then future, of present massive gigantic principles.

Capt. Esmon returned home disappointed and told
his story. Immediately intense indignation filled the
people furnishing an opportunity too good to be
thrown away by the opposition. The friends of the
Governor were becoming his bitter foes. The volunteers felt that the supreme authority of the state had
trifled with them. They asked only their rights.
Why had subsequent organizations in other parts of
the state been preferred when they had the printed
orders of the Adjutant General's office assigning
them to their position ?

Capt. Esmon would not permit the bad faith of a
political Governor to influence his patriotism, but
resolved to move his company to another town whose
sons were his soldiers, which had not yet had the
privilege of feeling personally identified in the good
cause, as a Turk who eats salt with a stranger. He

believed himself safe for the future because he had paid men at headquarters to advise him of any proposed changes, so as to enable him to get on the ground in advance, and plead his own cause. He had also been assured by the Adjutant General himself that no other changes would be permitted.

Lina Sandison had not spoken to James since Sumpter, events had followed in too quick succession. When she went to the store, he had gone,—nothing was powerful to detain men in that hour. My country calls, store, farm, contract must wait. "Let the dead bury their dead." She asked Charlie to go to the barracks with her, but now work demonstrated what James had done. Disposition was ready. It made him mad. Selfish men when angry because forced to sacrifice self or neglect duty, vent the passion on some innocent object. 'James had no business to enlist and leave him the work. James was a fool, and Lina what did she want of a fool.' He promised to go with her at evening, choosing the hour of drill. At that time Lina was again at the store waiting, and this quiet waiting vexed Charles, but he was too wise to manifest the annoyance. The truly noble woman which lay hidden in Alina Sandison's character, the possible which the lofty undeveloped soul of James had seen indistinctly in her beautiful face, which he loved as god-like manliness alone can worship, that new born life struggling with the babyhood of girl thoughts, recognized the value of the old playmate, who never unkind, had been neglected for a late acquaintance. She had wounded the feelings of one who now was giving his life for his country. The next time of her visit James was cooking, too busy for conversation. Once she had an opportunity, fancy seemed to tell her that James was anxious to speak also, she found no words and Charlie came—immediately James hurried away. Once more she tried, going to his mother's, joining Jennie and Sue, but some new order had been issued and James sent word, that he would be glad to meet mother, but thought his obedience to the order would be more valuable to the men. Mother acquiesced; Jennie was indignant; Lilly Sue shed tears, and all went away with a swollen throat. Then, for every man, woman and child in town thought of our boys, talked of them, worked for them, then Lina took from the store, silk red, white and blue, and with some others fashioned a flag to be given to the company.

On Sunday our ministers preached a sermon in the churches for our men, and in the evening all the congregations gathered in one house to bid them a parting God speed. To give them the dear old flag. Poor ignorant people! ignorant soldier boys, not informed concerning war enough to know but every company carried its flag. How different has the reality been to the expectation! What lessons have you not learned since that beginning!

Every inch of room was occupied. The singers seats filled with the choirs of all denominations. Then, rub-a-dub, dub—came the war sound and the company broke into single file and entered by either aisle to the seats reserved. The air was dense with emotion. Hearts were full before a word was spoken. Already more than one mother was intimate with the death alarm, ticking, ticking.

Poor fellows, they are sleeping in the dust of Missouri, in the sun-baked soil of Kentucky, of Tennessee and Mississippi; Louisiana and Alabama hold some; some are invalids for life; a few, how few! have come safely home!

Tears were there and hearts too full to cry. A free people resolved to vindicate their honor and transmit unsullied to posterity what patriot sires had bought for them. The altar was country, and here was the sacrifice.

" We give you this flag, emblem of liberty, hope of the free. Let no act of cowardice dishonor it! Yield it not in defeat, bring it back when you come home. crowned with victory; we promise to hide its soiled and worn fragments in the holiest memory of our hearts. You are blood of our blood, bone of our bone, strength of our strength. In your life we live, in your death we die. But living or dying let that flag wave forever.''

It was given to our captain, who taking it, said:

" I take this flag, still yours, not ours, in the name of our country; no North, no South, no East, no West, one and inseparable, the Union indivisible forever. I thank you for your kindness; we have lived on your bounty and we love you for your care. This flag I take in behalf of my men, and for my part, I am ready to swear never to return to you again unless we come in honor and victory. My men will you thus swear?''

" We will."

" Then swear."

And they rose together a solemn unit in that full audience.   The captain then said:

" We swear not to return again, unless we come in honor and victory."

James Manet now held the flag.

" Raise your right hands;" they were lifted.   " By the flag we swear."

And with those hands raised to the high heavens, in God's holy house, before their fathers, mothers, sisters, brothers, loved ones and friends, they together said,

" We swear."

The next morning they had gone.   Man proposes, God disposes.   But sometimes it seems as if God had left the universe and permitted the devil to rule alone.

CHAPTER XI

"How great a matter a little fire kindleth!" Charlie Hardone felt himself losing ground, when James Manet enlisted; Lina Sandison thought so much of the volunteers. There was but one way to gain position—by also enlisting. He was, however, unwilling to be a private. Already he had partly prepared his work by discouraging men from joining the first company, where he saw no chance for office. His mind ha l started briskly into the future, marching rapidly up the steps of promotion, anticipating that ignificant abreviation "Gen." before his name. This hope, the wish to be a commissioned officer, made him secretly talk against Captain Esmons' company, telling persons under his influence to "Hold on; we are going to get up a better company by-and-by. Don't be in a hurry; wait until these fellows get off." And now they were off, and now James had gone, a fair, unobstructed field, in love and war, was left for him. The field was unobstructed but full of labor; for as yet he had neither company nor commission—without which he could not hope to make a move in the game whose victory was Lina.

He looked at his chances, and then went to a young lawyer, a politician, who had acted in concert during the last election, saying:

" Solenter, why don't you get up a company? I will enlist the men. Army pay for a captain is one hundred and ten dollars per month, *   :ons, which will make twenty dollars more;   .des you have a chance for promotion, and if you only are fortunate, Sandison will use his influence with Senator Wilderfort, through whom you can become a Brigadier General. That pays well, four thousand dollars besides perquisites. Make me second lieutenant. Barker Wentlau will take the first, and we will have a company in no time. It is the best thing to be done. Law won't pay until the war is over, and after it is done, the only successful public men will be soldiers; so you might as well pitch in."

An avalanche may begin in a snow-ball. Solenter was smart, and went to Sandison, Chairman of the County Committee:

" Sandison I want your opinion honestly. I can make it for your advantage. If you will do the fair thing by me I will aid you by my influence among my friends. What is your candid opinion about the war ? "

Sandison said, " I have just received a letter from headquarters asking the state of public opinion here. Government will go in strong, if the sentiment of the North will sustain and back it up. Now what do you think? Have we got back-bone ? "

" Not a doubt of it ! Man, woman and child would die to vindicate the honor of the flag."

"I don't know," slowly said Sandison. "It is an awful risk to take. The Republican party may get knocked to pieces if it goes too fast. We must keep cool, not let our feelings get ahead of our judgment."

"I care for any party. I am ready for the first thing that turns up, if I stand a chance of coming on top. Will the war last longer than six months?"

"God bless your soul, yes. This is only the beginning, although it will not do to talk too loud. But we must be cautious. The party wont sustain too great pressure, President Lincoln is all right and understands the crisis. He will not go one step faster than he is compelled. There are great constitutional questions undecided, and the democrats will take advantage of every mistake; now we are in power we must manage to keep the track."

"Then the war will continue. That is all I want to know. I am going in, and you must help me. I must get in among the first regiments as captain; I have the arrangements all made. From captain I can get to colonel, and the road to brigadier is not difficult. I will make it pay you. Now, how shall we manage?"

Solenter—Captain Solenter—for when Sandison consented to help, his commission was safe as if signed and delivered—had placed the county chairman under obligations by a *kind word* to a rich relative. I make this distinct, and prominent, because to-day, and until the war debt is paid, the people of the United States are, and will be paying the penalty of countenancing such bargains. Because the moral sentiment of party sustains the traffic of soul. Solenter had written of Sandison:

" He is a good fellow, pretty hard up, but he will pay you one of these days. He is chairman of our party, in our county, and may do me a good turn by and-by. I will regard it as a personal favor if you let him have the sum he wants."

The time for payment had come. How is the debt to be canceled? Let us examine the situation. The quota is more than full. The enthusiasm of the hour, from the remote corners, sends company after company to the governor. As they come, each brings the strongest individuality, the most patriotic fervor. They say:

" Do not refuse *me*. It is not fair to make invidious distinctions. Why should we be left out of this struggle because we are not on the line of a rail road? Here you, in the state center, are to have all the honor and glory, and we, poor country people, are of no account."

Captain Solenter without a man has determined to raise a company, and get admitted to the next regiment. Sandison says he will help him: Solenter is successful, and that when forty full companies, whose captains have already what seems to them guaranties of position in the *first* regiment, are therefore keeping up their organization, and in many instances are supporting their men at their own expense.

The path to success is certain, under the principles which govern party men and party measures. The man of greatest ability or patriotism, without party friends or party influence, must be sacrificed at the call of one who has sufficient weight with the leaders. And this was one of the corner-stones of the Southern imagination of success.

Their leading minds pointing at the ease which directed, controlled, governed and moulded political parties, declared that the democratic idea was a fallacy, and the experiment of a popular government fairly tried and exploded. Man, led by the nose, was incapable of self-government. Had they not led the North, until the sight of politicians crawling before them was sickening; characterized by a name derived from an animal which sucks venom from the soil, bloats its loathsome, yellow belly with ugly bugs, and is food for serpents—a toad, toady! The North had toadied until the South were sick and tired of the Union, and they were going to leave it. Ah, there was another side! If,—there was a chance, that power might leave; the Southern star might— it was on the wane; then the crawling, sycophantic politician—the degraded animal they despised— would spit on them. Southern honor could not endure such degradation; the pot got angry because the kettle called him black.

I doubt not that many an honest Southern man, sound to the core,—a patriot of '76 in the idea of a free government of common people,—would return, heart and soul, to the old allegiance, to the old flag of childhood—of his father's—with absolute assurance of a pure ballot-box, an unbought executive, and an immaculate legislature and judiciary.

The danger lies in the smarter, more able, cunning, astuter villain, who supplants the Judas in power before him. The means are equally corrupt; the weapons equally satanic. I give that you may give, is powerful. If you do not give I will expose, has more power. But the superlative of an unprincipled bargain is, when the strong nerve of a relentless will unites " I will give if you will do," together with " I will expose, will ruin, if you do not."

When Mr. Sandison met the governor,—I do not call that man a fool. I forgive him the injury he did those hundred men. Still, can he be relieved from all responsibility for what followed? At that time, so hot were men's passions, they could have killed instantly the head of the state; but since then they have seen acts of greater despotism, before which this falls into insignificance. Thank God! there is a tribunal before which accountability is tried to the remote· consequence, and each man suffers the penalty for his own sin and folly, and no more. For all that, there is true cause of astonishment at the honest patriotism of the common, everyday citizen of this free land, who endured unflinchingly the cuffs and indignities of the little, brief authority placed over him; submitted to red tape airs, obeyed the command of one really his inferior, for the sake of the land of freedom. When Mr. Sandison met the governor; for he had received a letter declining in courteous terms to appoint Solenter to the next regiment, while he consented to grant a commission as soon as a company was raised; at this time the governor said to him:

"Sandison, I would do anything in the world to oblige you; but this I cannot do. I have had trouble enough already. There are forty companies ahead of Solenter's, and I should play hob with the party in other parts of the state by giving him preference. More than that, I cannot do everything. The adjutant general has charge of the appointments. Besides, Sandison, your own people are growling, and I transferred the company before to quiet Senator Wilkins of Deerkill. This much I will say, if you can get the general's consent, and fix anything in good shape, I will do everything man can honorably do in the premises."

When Sandison met Captain Solenter, and gave him the governor's reply, Solenter's choler burst out in the following language:

"Sandison, you and I must get that commission. You must hatch up some dodge. Between us it must be done; or, I will foreclose that thousand dollar mortgage. It can be done. It must be done. I must have my company in the next regiment. Let us go to the adjutant general's office and talk with him."

That evening a letter came to the Captain from Charlie, reporting progress and saying their muster-roll had twenty names. Here was another bad how do you do. No commission could be granted until the muster-roll was filed in the adjutant general's office. Solenter instantly wrote Charlie, "You must fill up a muster-roll before Saturday; send it to me with sixty-six names by that mail; it must be filed in the adjutant general's office on Monday. Everything goes well. Work hard and drive business."

The first step in the game of chess is to learn the board and the value of each chess-man, the moves follow, and then the game according to the skill of the players. Solenter was not a chess player, but is worthy of the name *trump:* he held in his hands rich, influential friends, also acquaintances, at the capital. Sandison was the right hand; the governor, the adjutant general, and his friends were heavy pieces. Where were the pawns? Captain Esmons was one, sacrificed; so, also, were others. But first let me develope the plan, or the sequence, which accomplished Solenter's will, and placed him captain of Co. B (Co. A is No. 1, Captain Solenter of Co. B is No. 2. in the line of promotion. Once out of the line, then on the staff. Step two is lieutenant colonel, and a colonel can easily become a general by the judicious use of proper influences at Washington together with newspaper patronage) in the next regiment.

The acquaintance of the adjutant general had been cultivated amid the luxury of a prime Havana, (five hundred dollars a thousand)—a stock was kept for this purpose. In the vanishing smoke of the fragrant and delicately-flavored cigar, Solenter managed to impregnate the official mind with the valuable quality of good-fellowship: "Smokes a splendid cigar. I like him. Sorry for you. Regiments all full. You should have come sooner. Never mind, a thousand chances yet. The governor is your friend? Shows his good sense. Will do the best I can for you. Sandison spoke to me of you. Smart man, Sandison. We could not manage your part of the State without him. Too late. Nothing to be done until the new call. Will be out soon. Then every one will have a chance. Not the next regiment: have two full already; put you for the next one. An order from the governor; that might do. Hard to work; might be. I will see. Can't look after you alone. Told Sandison so. There is Jones, from Morgan. Why not put your heads together?"

Politician Jones comes in. Sandison says this is useless; for that section of the state having identical hope, expectation and claim, are in antagonism. Can these claims be recognized and reconciled? It seems impossible. Solenter yields not a hair; holds all he can get, and waits for more. Time passes. Monday morning brings a letter from Charlie, with a muster-roll, as per order. He also writes: "Lina Sandison says her father wrote home, that you were having rough work in getting accepted, and twenty companies were ahead of you for the next regiments. Why can't you get up a Western regiment from our part of the state? Our county-seat ought to have a share of the patronage, and a regiment leaves a pile of money."

This is the key to the problem. With this in hand, Sandison and Solenter go to Jones. Jones will

9

help make the new brigadier, if you can use him
right. But Jones is as firm as the hills : " I consent
to a Western regiment from your county; but my
Eastern regiment must be ahead of yours. You say
the governor is your friend. Then, why don't you
and Sandison make him transfer that company from
your town, and give you the place ? "

" Thank you, Mr. Jones.   This is idea number
two.   It will not do to use Captain Esmons thus, lest
the indignation of the community fall on the new
company, on the honorable chairman, or the governor
himself; but you have started a new idea, grafted a
thought on the sectional one. Here is the plan as developed.   Three companies from our section of the
state shall be transferred to a new regiment ; belonging to an old regiment they are entitled to preference.
Jones' company shall take our vacant place ; better
than he had expected. Mr. Sagacious from the
North shall have another, and Senator Hardhead
from the center shall take the last vacancy.   To reconcile the town of Stick-to-it their company is entered on the new prefered list. Three other companies are also taken from the regiment, already
organized, which is number one under the next call,
an influential politician, designated as colonel, and
in caucus the four regiments are so manipulated that
thirty strong, influential party-men, with their res-
pective interests, are engaged to force and consummate the plan.   Each one of these men had the ear
of the governor—had the private entrance to the adjutant general, who, as a party man, must answer

to the calls of party. Thank God, some governors were men enough to rise superior, equal to the emergency! Each of these men and the host of friends they represented pressed on the governor as per agreement.

Captain Esmons too soon learned the new effort, initiated, and left his company to visit the governor personally, to remind him of his word of honor, and, in case any removal had been designed, prevent it, or have the order, if such there was, revoked. On his way to the capital, he met one of his brother captains who had been sacrificed, he said, "You are too late; I have been with the governor all day, so have four of the best men in our town; if they can do nothing, you will be sure to fail."

"My case," was Esmons' reply, "is unlike any other. I have once been transferred. I have the word of the governor, and the pledge of the adjutant general, and more, I have a general order of assignment. I have also a special order to me, as captain, and to Mr. Sandison and the people of our city. You cannot make me believe the governor will ever violate his pledges."

I must hasten over the midnight ride, the unsatisfactory meeting with the adjutant general, the order shown to disband his company and send the men home and wait further orders.

"Send my men home! Wait until further orders!" Then the adjutant general put on style, ceased to use the manners of a gentleman, but tried to bluff a bolder man than himself by the assumption of mili-

tary authority.   He had mistaken his man, met a
Rowland for his Oliver, and again laid all the blame
on the governor.

"I could not help you; I had to obey orders.   It
is no use now; all you can do is to go home and obey.
It will be better for you."

What an amount of petty meanness those words
contain!   "It will be better for you."   That is, I possess the power, and if I ever have the opportunity I
will revenge myself for thus daring to dispute my
acts or question my motives.   Stomach my insults,
eat your own words, be humble, or I will teach you
what you never can forget.

That man came very near the feelings of a slave-
holder.

Captain Esmons was no slave.   He followed the
governor to his own home; met him face to face, man
to man—who said to him:

"Your section of the state demanded a sectional
regiment.   I did all I could for you, but I found it
impossible to satisfy the pressure unless I granted
their request and I was unable to reconcile conflicting interests, unless I transferred your company to
another regiment.   I have done as well as possible
by you, for although not included in the call, you
will be first in the next, which I am assured from
Washington will be very soon.   I advise you as a
friend to accept what cannot be averted; send your
men home, and tell them to stand ready to go into
camp as soon as I call, and by a month or six weeks,
I think you will be needed."

"But, governor, I came to you before you had even a full regiment, and you personally told me you were pleased to see me. You advised me to get up a company; you promised to accept it, and said I should go into the first regiment. I took you at your word; I raised my company; you accepted it, and assigned me to the second regiment. I found no fault; all I desired, all my men desired, was to go. I thought I knew my business better than some, but as both regiments were in the call, it was a small matter whether we were one or two; then without consulting us, (volunteers not sworn in have some rights, although regular soldiers have none, which an officer is bound to respect) we were transferred to the fourth. My men felt the indignity; but as there was still hope of service, no objections were made, and now you disband us, and order us home. Many of my men, like myself, are from the East. They have no home; they have given up their situations, are without work. Where shall they go? More than this, they enlisted for our country, for the war, longer or shorter, and we have sworn not to go home until it is over. You have done us a great injustice, and I ask in the name of my company to have it undone. For myself, I care little, for them everything. I would rather die than go back and tell them the governor of our state is untrue. Can this order be reversed? Must we be disbanded?"

"I see no other way. You have only the one course. I have just returned from the capital, am very weary, and this whole subject is disagreeable.

I have done the best I could. You must make it as easy as you can for the men. Good evening."

Solenter and Sandison had been successful. When they joined the band of scheming men assembled at the state capital, their interests merged and blended with those of the party, and the conflicting claims were arranged as judiciously as possible. Captain Esmons' company, and the others were made to suffer, that a few office-seekers might obtain posts of honor and emolument for themselves or the friends to whom they were in debt, or whose future services would amply repay this investment.

That night Captain Esmons hastened back to his command. Poor patriot ready to do, dare and die, but hindered. Invincible, determined man, quick to conceive and accomplish, he would not be depressed, neither allow his comrades even to feel the force of this blow.

On the steamer he fell in conversation with a gentleman—said he:

"I love this state—my only sister lives here; the last of our family. I wanted to hail from here. I love our neighbors, truer and better people never breathed. But I cannot in honor go back to them. The honor, the word of the governor may be nothing, but mine is everything to me. If I cannot get into service here, there are the border states, Kansas and Missouri. They want men, and all I need do is to write to Jim Lane, he knows me. I can go as a private. I do not know what my men will say, but I think every one will go wherever I lead. If they are ready I will take them to Missouri or Kansas and pay their expenses myself. Besides all this we have sworn."

And then he told this friend and the circle who stood listening to his story of wrongs, the vow recorded over the flag and quoting the words,

"Send them home! Wait further orders!" exclaimed, "I would die first!"

Made a step back, when his foot slipped, and he fell over the steamboat's unprotected guard into the river.

He was a strong swimmer, but every effort in the swift current was unavailing, treading water, he took some valuable papers from his pocket, put them in his hat and then threw them towards the boat, and then went down.

Three days were spent in searching for the body, and at last it was found. It was taken to that sister's, where it was laid out in the unstained silk of the battle flag dishonored by the state executive, and therefore taken from its staff, wrapped around his breast and buried in his coffin.

CHAPTER XII.

The soul is a thread. Time holds the end, called beginning. The other end—where? The same experience of similar events, developes or fails to develope different souls. If ever the mind, questioning, asks why? To what useful purpose are these varied, tremendous emotions I experience—I am called to endure! What beneficial influence do they exert on my character? How do they nourish? for emotions are the food of the soul. Then each question turns back like the deluge dove, without finding a leaf, tree, or flower above the waters, whereon to rest. All these teachings must be good, although the end is hidden, like Jehovah's throne, in darkness. Perhaps they are studies to be appreciated at maturity. If so, what a tremendous maturity there must be somewhere in the future for persons educated by war, as was James Manet!

Look at him—a school-boy, an orphan, leaving home to work for a mother's support. Estimate the amount of mental discipline obtained from a few winters in a graded school. Before even that is

complete, transfer him to the daily routine of a
variety store, where the questions of government
and constitutional law, occupying the public mind,
are discussed by the politicians and lawyers drawn
together at headquarters. This is all of education
he can boast. These are his best advantages. Nature made him a man, and circumstances—I say
God's Providence—makes the United States his
school-house; the American people his school-mates;
and sends him into the army to learn the new lesson,
—to complete his education and graduate. The
head swells with fullness of brain; the heart can with
difficulty retain the bursting emotions which follow
in such quick profusion.

As lightning shot word after word over the electric
wires, dispatch after dispatch was read at the store,
and the busy, silent man held within a load of energy,
determination and will, which none but the All-seeing
knew. When great eternity shall exhibit souls in
place of faces, minds for capacious stomachs, purity
of life-principle in place of color, James Manet will
stand among those of Bramin caste, Caucasian complexion,—a pure white man.

Lina Sandison taught him to love. Something
went out. In time James learned it was love.
Why? How? What for? A thousand questions,
useless as Robinson Crusoe's gold, remain soluble
only in "I know it is so." Inheriting sensitiveness
from a gone-father, he learned how to be unloved by
the dearest one in the whole world.

Then he found solace in his country, and, when

the call for volunteers came, the warm blood became tinctured with excited life; burned in his forehead, scorched in his eye, tingled in his fingers, throbbed in his feet, electrified his limbs, held a grand carnival in his heart and chest; and, on call of an eloquent look, or a patriotic word or act, a heroic self-denial or manly example rippled and thrilled with an intensity akin to faintness, an exhaustion never weary of labor. Self remembered, Lina remembered, mother, —not one of the sorrows of parting forgotten; all remembered; but nothing, less than nothing, compared to the love of country—to the pure patriotism of an American citizen.

When he took the flag—Lina's flag—from the hand of Captain Esmons, the room was dim, his brain whirled, and the staff leaning on the floor was a support. In the bottom of invincible purpose he repeated the words "We swear." The import of the oath, in God's house, was deeply impressed on a mind imbued with religious principle, which had decided not to unite with the church, lest, in the new, untried camp life, he should bring dishonor on the Christian name; a man who could act Christ when those who professed,—may they be forgiven!

Words are feeble to express the soul-torture brought on James, when, after three days' search, he found the body of his dead, drowned captain—the pale, bleached face; those proud limbs, stiffened as water and death stiffen; the wet, sodden garments, the pulpy documents, the sandy hair filled with the siftings of the river. Dead before his time; dead

for nothing; dead without cause; dead, and not a
blow struck for honor, for glory, for country; dead
because a political governor had not integrity, firm-
ness, to keep his word; dead, and the flag he had
sworn never to bring back, except in honor, had been
sent back dishonored in the house of his friends.
He had to take the corpse home and prepare it for
the grave because that oath was a mountain none
others of the company would climb, except to escort
as mourners the body to its forever. Deeply griev-
ing, almost shame-faced, that band of men came
back. Were they to blame? What should James
do with the flag? The governor had refused to fulfil
his word; he might fail again. Without honor once,
twice, three times, what security remained of future
dependence on his guarantee? None. With stern
anguish they consented, and James Manet removed
the flag and gave it to Captain Esmons for a shroud.
He carried the bare, useless staff in the procession,
attracting the attention of the crowd of depressed
patriot friends; pointing to the coffin for explanation, where more than one sacred tear started as they
recalled the moment, when that now useless clay
grasped the banner with joyous life, and, strong in
hope and noble purpose, called on his men to die to
preserve it from dishonor.

When the funeral was over, James refused to go
home. Keenly sensitive, a disgrace, undeserved,
seemed to cling to him. He felt it in the atmosphere; shook it in the hands of old friends; most
of all, in the unusual kindness of Lina Sandison,
which produced that pleasure akin to pain.

"What are you going to do?" She asked the
question when those two beautiful sisters, forgetting
that he was anything but a loved one, put their arms
around him, girl-fashion; coveting the kind support
of his arm, and leaning against his breast, as if
thereby to get their hearts inside of his—Jennie and
Sue, feeling as if the brother was an idol belonging
to them, now recovered after being lost, and they had
determined to part with it no more. "What was he
going to do?" He had asked himself that question
which Lina now put, and it made him glad that all
would hear his answer given to her. At this moment Charlie Hardone, searching for Lina, came.

The grave-yard was on the lake shore. Beautiful
pines, prepared to catch songs and murmurs from
every wind-whisper, stood on the bluff,—what a magnificent requiem they make when the hard, cold north
wind rages!—near whose brink ran the road from
the village. Next was an orchard; then the bury-
ing-ground; new, like the West; rolling; set with
a second growth, save where the sickle of the reaper
had cut them down; long grass dead, long grass
green, creeping vines, and wild-grape tendrils clung
on to the knolls, making the hollows of graves without monuments lost. Wild flowers were in blossom,
and prickly vines tore the delicate garments pressed
by the throng into places not in demand by the ordinary gatherings of funerals. What will he do?

Standing in the shade of a few trees,—one a sugar-
maple, with its beautiful leaves; another an oak sap-
ling, promising by its sturdy young growth to form

a timber for a ship of the line; a tough hickory, and a young sasafras,—they were joined by Mary Wirtman, her husband, and his child. Happy Mary! The world holds everything you love save mother. Soon Heaven will take a clasp on your morning, noonday, and midnight thoughts, and only one wish bind earth to life—this darling who now stretches out the plump child-arms to kind James. He releases sisters and takes the little one; who puts her tiny hands on his face, gives a kiss, and then with shame-faced beauty clasps his neck, hugs tight, and cuddles her face behind his. shoulder, whence she playfully peeps out to see why they are all laughing, assured by the gentle, loving hold that she is welcome, very welcome.

Just now, Charlie hoping to exert a peculiar influ-ence, to appear generous, to wipe out the impression generally prevalent of complication with the enemies of Capt. Esmons, with improper. haste addressed James.

" Captain Solenter wishes me to offer you the posi-tion of orderly sergeant in his company."

He said nothing of a condition; James must secure twenty recruits. This same offer had been made to two others besides the acting orderly. As soon as news of the governor's new order reached town more than half of those whose names were on that muster roll ordered them off. They would not serve with Capt. Solenter. Others said they never put down their names only to fill the requisite number and with the assurance that they should not be called

into service. Of this and other things Charles said
nothing. He came with the most important, labori-
ous useful office in the company, one on the door-step
of promotion and unasked offered it to James.

James forgave all he had unintentionally cherished
against his friend. His mother thanked Charlie
from her whole heart. Jeannie and Sue thought
Charlie was the next best in the world. Lina felt a
warm glow for this unexpected act. Meanwhile the
question, What will you do? was unanswered.

Mary's husband spoke. " James, if I were you,
I would never enter the service of this state; you
have been abused; your honor and your patriotism
made a derision. Not only this; but every one of us
has been insulted by this uncalled for act of oppres-
sion. Will you go with me to St. Louis, Mo., and
join the army? If no other opportunity presents,
we will become regulars."

James replied, " I have no blame to cast on my
state, although the act of its governor has occasioned
such misery. I will go with you. Our company
have voted unanimously to serve as an organization
under no captain but the one dead. And as soon as
these last honors are over, we are going for the war.
We shall keep our vow, although disappointed in our.
hopes to honor Lina's flag as a company. We shall
separate, but none of us I hope will forget or feel
absolved from our oath. In one way or another we
will serve our country until the end."

When Mary's husband said, " Will you go with
me?" when James said, "I will go," a yawning

future opened in Mary's heart. Unconsciously she took her child from James and pressed it to her bosom, to hold husband at home. The sisters, Jeannie and Sue, left James for Henry, Charles stood by Lina, but she followed James' mother and joined him. Charlie watchful renewed his question:

"I have answered, I shall go to St. Louis as soon as Henry is ready, and the sooner the better."

The mother's face was calm—the within tumultuous. Lina's younger face was in sympathy with weeping Jeannie and pale Sue. What a sight will that be when eyes shall be permitted to gaze on emotions which the countenance sometimes dimly shadows! One look from Lina had confirmed James' Allie, still loved, now unhoped for, and in his sacrificing self, undesired. He had given his life to his country, and in the deed of gift, reserved no interest in the future. He expected to die, would shun no duty, avoid no danger, but wait. When destiny has been accepted and fate by association become familiar and endurable, if then hope shine, can the emotion be characterized by words? Would Lina have understood him had she seen his true emotion? No, for heart was before understanding, and instinct true to what might be, but was not yet. Between them the atmosphere was loaded with subtle communication, producing uneasiness unexplainable, attraction by which some unknown law of the mind-world binds atoms to its center of gravity. Is the man selfish who desires to draw the loved into his arms and hold tightly within a ceaseless embrace; or, is it

some law of mind-chrystalization by which element-
ary principles are secreted and polarized into a transparent diamond of purest water ?

God sees all hearts. Blessed be this truth! No
one is absolutely unappreciated. He knows, he loves,
he gives, and we can go, cast on him all our care,
trouble, sorrow, and he will sustain and comfort.
Mother and son, Jeannie and Sue, Lina, yes,
Charlie—last because most—Henry and Mary, with
the sober, distant-eyed child, all can go to Him.
Will they ?   Quick as the wing of a bee, sharp as its
sting, heavy as the lid of an eye by poison sting
wounded, Mary took her load, and with the resolu-
tion of a brave soul, tried to cheer by her courage,
and by promptly acquiescing in her husband's sacrifice, said she:

"You may go."

"To-morrow ?"

"Oh! to-morrow! not to-morrow! How can we
let you go so soon ?"

Said James :

"I cannot stay; this place is too unpleasant.
But Henry need not go."

Henry answered :

"I will go with you, and we will go to-morrow."

CHAPTER XIII.

Days pass on rapidly for Leette, whose interest in the Yankee soldier increases, since she must use her greatest caution in acquiring the information she seeks, lest his suspicion be aroused: moreover, he is reticent, answers with reserve, and she is compelled to employ all her acuteness to form the most appropriate and apropos questions; she is bold in forming opinions, outspoken in expressing, for she has discovered a truthful nature which keeps silence rather than tell a falsehood.

Whenever she is baffled on one track, Leette does not abandon the field. That electric life of a woman which the Creator abstracted from the first man, is attracted by the brave, honest prisoner; so that she lingers in his presence, hangs around his couch; and she finds at times the duplicity of her heart vanquished, whereby she is surprised to gain, in answer to a spontaneous gush of emotion from a good impulse, information which could not be extracted by cunning questions. Taking away all she has obtained she connects the fragments, as some old time inquisitor may have laboriously put the tiny flakes of the torn letter, part to its part, until the rejoined document stands boldly forward to testify against the prisoner. Then when time enough has elapsed to dig a grave deep to conceal her motive, she asks a leading question which shall prove her position. In such a moment Leette asked this question :

"How did your brother Henry die ? "

The corporal answers, by saying :—" He was killed while defending our train from a guerilla attack."

Another question follows, "Where ? How long ago ? "

As brief as her question, is his reply, "Near White river."

"In a valley between two hills ! " Leette exclaims rather than asks, while the corporal answers and asks :

"Yes. Do you know of it ? "

Leette continues her thought by asking :

"Was he killed by the road-side ? "

James excited enough to rise on his elbow, looks keenly in her eye, answers her's, and asks his question :

"Yes. How did you happen to know any of these circumstances ? "

Thoughtfully, as if new light had dawned, some conclusion been overwhelmed, she said, speaking as much to herself as to him :

"That was among the first attempts at cotton trading. And you buried him, and you have not heard from your mother since. You have a right to be lonely."

Now to explain this more fully, " I " of this story must unfold another phase of cotton stealing, and a part of the past history of James Manet.

Following the army since the begining of the war were a large class of men of various nationalities, filled with one idea—their own benefit—which was placed above country and above regard for their fellow men. Men who strove in every possible way to entice the soldier to squander his hard-earned pay; charging him a price which yielded unconcionable profits, while the articles of traffic were useless or worse than useless under the circumstances; mere adventurers, waiting for something to turn up. Some, not contemptible Jews or squalid Italians, but influential politicians at home, relatives or personal friends of colonel, general, or commander-in-chief; all waiting for fortune.

This which I now relate turned up for some good *Cincinnati*, perhaps it was St. Louis, it possibly might be Cairo or Philadelphia merchants ; New York and Washington, Boston and Chicago have not been unrepresented. England has been in the market with millions of dollars ready to invest in the cotton business. This turning up for some body, is connected with this story because it excited Col. Solenter and Adjutant Hardone to enter the cotton business. Before I unfold the operation, the politician Sandison's farewell injunction to Charlie must be given, as characteristic, showing as it does, the front door of temptation thrown wide open before he left home :

"Make money. No matter how; but make money. Charlie, I am in earnest, money does everything. Fairly if you can, *but make money.*"

In the onward march of the army a fort was captured. Its walls were constructed of bales of cotton. I do not know the number, I care not, ten thousand, a hundred thousand, no matter, a great many thousand pounds.

One of these war-fortune-hunting gentlemen came to the general commanding :

"General, do you want to make a speculation? Do as I tell you and I will make your fortune. You shall do no dishonorable thing, nor have a stain on your character or reputation."

"What do you mean?"

"If you will sign your name to a document I will prepare: mind! I will not ask you to sign unless you can honorably and conscientiously do so. I will, in case of success, give you a quarter of a million dollars."

"How is that?"

"You know the fort. It is of no account as it lays, useless to the government, useless to any body. The cotton is rotting where it lies. The soldiers are tearing up the bales, and as soon as the army leaves, the rebels will come in and burn it."

"Yes. True."

"Now I am going to submit a proposal to you in

writing;—I and my partners, (distinguished merchants, capitalists, men who subscribe the sinews of
war, in—this time we say *New York State*,)—offer to
pay the government through your Quarter Master
General ten dollars for each and every bale of cotton
delivered us in good order from the walls of the fort,
taking it as it lies. I will make a statement of
the facts in the case, you shall endorse the document
as correct, and recommend the acceptance of our offer
and transmit it as official business to Washington."

" What good will that do you? How will you get
the cotton out ?"

" The number of bales is so great, at least five
thousand—say ten thousand—that the sum of fifty
thousand dollars or one hundred thousand dollars,
paid direct, without any trouble into the treasury, will
seem well worth while and be accepted."

" Well, how will that help you? "

" As soon as the offer is accepted, I will make another. You know the supplies of the army must be
hauled from——rail road depot, and——landing, on
——river and the trains return empty. I will represent
in another document that the teamsters have to lock
their wheels to keep the mules from running away,
and offer to pay five dollars per bale for the transportation of every bale, making twenty-five dollars per
load, to the cars and steamboat. You shall endorse
this application as correct, and recommend the offer
accepted. I will see that the proper influence is
brought to bear at Washington, and in return an order will come from the War Department. All you

will then need do is to hold the army here until the cotton is out."

" I see nothing wrong in your suggestion. I will not promise, but I will do anything I can for you. At present I must think of it."

Perhaps this is not the language used, nor are these the precise words on file at Washington. The facts are not all stated here, and what is stated here may be false. But the one all important fact which turned the head of Charles Hardone, Lieut. and A. A. G. which made Col. afterwards Gen. Solenter, a cotton speculator, that important fact lay in the *report* that the major general received his two hundred and fifty thousand dollars, for the simple fact of writing his name.

Did he do wrong? Wouldn't you have done the same? How many of the people in the United States have the virtue to withstand such a temptation? How many educated minds have power to analyze the moral question involved, and clearly comprehend the moral responsibility?

At 'the time these things were shaping in Tennessee, James Manet and his brother were following the rough roads of South Western Missouri and Arkansas.

They had fought during the three days' battle of Pea Ridge, had seen the skillful maneuver by which the attack was commenced in the rear, when Sigel with his battery and detail of men had covered the retreat of the train on the main body. They had been detailed as guard to their regimental wagons.

The rebels fought like brave men; but they were not a match for the hero of Carthage. Selecting, with his apt eye for artilleric effect, a turn in the road, he unlimbered a section and waited until the enemy were in range, then held them at bay by quick discharges. Another section, with their infantry support, followed the retreating train until a new position of defense was reached, when, in turn unlimbering, they assumed the defensive, and the first section, limbering up, bounded at double-quick to seek their next position to check the out-numbering foe.

And that last day, when the cannon were all massed. The rebels thought victory was secure. Our men were lying on the ground only a few paces in front of the guns. Then Gen. Sigel came riding to the battery, jumped from his horse, examined the ranges, looked through the sights, and rubbing his hands, said: " That will do! fire!" What a burst! Watching its effect, he again rubbed his hands with the commendation, " That is very good. Fire." They did fire. " Cease firing—charge." A new volley ran down the hill into the face of the foe,—a volley of men shooting bayonets. Regardless of the leaden storm which sang death, they pressed to the hostile line of battle, then delivered their reserved fire, amid yells which demons might have uttered, following their charge of lead, as if it was only to forewarn of the engine coming. The enemy did not stop for the cars, and we won the battle of Pea Ridge.

The world is not one garden of Eden. At least

the soldiers who followed the army of the frontier to Helena, will not call those rough desolate mountains about the source of White river paradisical. Black jack oak, hazel underbrush, white and blue ash, inhabited by the crab-sized wood-ticks and the small seed-tick that burrows head, body and all, into your flesh, with a ferocity equalled by the giant who smelled the blood of an Englishman ; and then there was that other little red insect, which is too small to be seen until its bite makes the body pimpled like the measles, itching with irritation, and when mingled with the chafing of weary, sweaty, dusty walking, made the march or the rest almost a purgatory.

That is indeed hard.   This is harder.

The covetous desire of wealth was not confined to the army of the Tennessee.

An A. Q. M., no matter for his name, came in contact with a prisoner, who claimed to be a Union man.   It is not my purpose to explain the means. This Union man told the Q. M. that he had an hundred bales of cotton hid away, and if he would only manage in some way to get for him a box of boots, a box of shoes, a barrel of flour, some sacks of coffee, some sugar, a general variety of army stores, he would tell him where the cotton was hidden.

Now look at the temptation, cotton was worth thirty cents per lb.   The average weight of cotton per bale is 500 lbs., more or less, and the value per bale would be $150, the average exceeding rather than falling short.   One hundred bales at this figure would bring $15,000.

This quartermaster could not withstand the temptation. His own empty wagons could haul in the cotton without suspicion, since seizures of cotton were being made for the government.

How to transfer the stores without suspicion was the next problem. It was solved in this manner. I do not mean to insinuate the author of the suggestion. The required stores were carefully selected and placed in an army wagon. This was put in a marked position in the train, and it was agreed, that the Union man should at the appointed place capture the wagon and carry it off.

This might not be easily done, but a creature of the quartermaster was employed to drive the team, and on the attack he was to start his mules in fright away from the road, and in the confusion his team would not be missed, or if missed, be of too little importance to be followed.

This plan would have been successful, if two honest privates, James and his brother, had not been on guard in the train. When firing commenced they stood at their post. Mary's husband saw the attempt to get out of the train, and drawing a bead on the driver, too many of whom were mere creatures of pay, ordered him to drive on, or he would shoot him.

James had already given one horseman his quietus, and was loading; the position was a run between two hills; a famous spot for killing deer. The rebels had come through the woods skirting the hill over which the wagon road led, and seeing the right wagon, made a rush to head off the mules into the other side of the run, hoping in this way to drive a half dozen teams off on a gallop before the escort could have come up, to secure their own wagon and more. .

The teamster was too hasty, the guard too watchful. On one side Mary's husband, on the other James; the team passed on; Mary's husband went over to James, but before he could reach cover, not until he had fired, he fell shot through the head. The click of hostile caps, the report of hostile rifles were one, and two dead bodies, one hit by the huge minnie ball fell; two more offerings to the curse of slavery passed into the sleep. Offerings to slavery! no! cotton was the direct cause, slavery the remote, and,

Six weeks after, Mary heard from her husband, James sent a half written letter. One letter when he left Springfield, one came after the glorious day at Pea Ridge, and then—nothing—nothing—until her father was too sad to speak or even look, to tell her of no letter. "Nothing mother," answered all enquiries. Waiting seemed forever and ever, and then father came into the house, and the family wept together. Jeanie and Lilly Sue seemed to take Henry's death most to heart. Mary had no more than a deeper eye, a longer look, a sadder quiet, and work over, held her child more fondly, clinging closer to it as time moved him farther away from the present, buried him deeper in the alluvium of memory. This was not their only grief; Lilly Sue was pining, never very strong. The war was eating her

life away. · She was an æolian, every breath exhausted, died away on her strung nerves.

Six weeks after ! Dead six weeks—in heaven six
weeks, and she did not know it.—James wrote. "We
buried him as well as we could. I put his body on
the train, and when we camped at night, one of the
teamsters, who is a friend, took his wagon, (the quartermaster forbade, but that made no difference) and
we went to a barn and tore down the doors, and got
nails and boards enough to make a coffin. It was
only a rough thing, but so much better than most of
our poor boys get, I was satisfied. I washed his
face and combed his hair ; I have cut some off for
Mary, and will send it home with his knapsack when
I have a chance. But I could not make him look
very natural until I tied a handkerchief over his
forehead. I put on him a clean shirt and his best
uniform, and then some of the boys helped roll
him in his blanket, and we lifted him up and laid
him in the coffin. I covered him carefully and nailed
up the box and we took him out under a big tree
where the boys had dug a grave. I felt so bad
thinking of you I did not know what to do. We had
no chaplain for ours had gone home after the battle
of Pea Ridge. I waited until the boys were all gone
and then I knelt and prayed by his grave. I do not
think you, nor I, nor any of us, will ever see it. It
was so lonesome. I thought of you all and dear
Mary. Dear Henry, I wish I had died for him.
Why couldn't I have died ? I have no wife to mourn
for me, no child to leave alone. When I saw him so

still, I wished I was dead too.   He was brave as a
lion, and we all loved him.   I never knew him to
do an unkind act or speak an unkind word—he did
his whole duty and died like a soldier."

CHAPTER XIV.

The last chapter contains these words:

" The one important fact which turned the head of Charles Hardone, Lieutenant and A. A. G., and made Colonel, afterwards Major-General, Solenter, a cotton speculator,—that important fact lay in the *report* that the major-general received his two hundred and fifty thousand dollars for writing his own name."

In looking after the interests of a corporal, who was the victim of a cotton speculation in the department of the Missouri, the history has come upon the political intriguant—a next-door-neighbor—who, in the fortune of war, with more dishonesty, with less ability, and less honor, but political partisanship, has managed to acquire position, fame, and fortune.

Before the " I " turns back to tell how a common citizen of the United States took his first infant-step firmly on the sacred commission-step to preferment ; permit that " I " to offer a humble tribute to the worth of that man, who, with only the privileges and opportunities given to every common school-

child of this now free land, had the great gift of
common sense to recognize and trust the integrity,
the virtue, the holy purity and unsullied honor—
patriotic honor—of the masses, the *oi poloi,*—the
common people—from whom he sprung, and by
whom he was elected, as an *honest man* to be their
President : who, knowing the corruption of the office-
seekers of the capital; the venality of politicians,
influential to Judas-ize their constituents, their birth-
right of constitutional privileges, and their native
land,—paid them their price of thirty pieces of silver
from the nation's purse, and thus made them true to
their constituents and their country. If this history
is ever written; if the brain, the heart of the nation,
can ever become strong to face the rottenness at
home; the war most terrible waged by his soul
among professed friends, who demanded fat places,
fat commissions, and fat contracts,—then shall that
national heart honor more, venerate more, and adore
more the sublime virtue and the spotless honor and
honesty of Abraham Lincoln.

In infinite mercy, in the hour of the nation's extremity, when liberty, freedom and progress trembled
over the brink of slavery, chains and barbarism, was
given to the common people, as a Saviour, an honest
man—the noblest gift of God.

The great redeemed nation and people of the
United States of America may look back on the
blood-stained years of war, now over, with joy and
gratitude to the Almighty; for, as the French revolution, drenched in blood, has been in its results a

blessing to France, as the battles of old Ironsides have been the *magna charta* of England, as the American Revolution gave liberty to the Union, as the death of the Son of God has been productive of the highest blessings to the human race, so this latest, greatest struggle has blessings untold in store for the generations of the future.

The peaceful citizens of the United States are made a nation of warriors; transformed from the enjoyments, arts and ignorance of peace, to the. excitement, science and education of war. A new problem has been solved: The possibility of a nation of independent men volunteering of free will to fight, to suffer, to die for a moral question; and, after the surplus population has been depleted, and voluntary enlistments ceased; the possibility of the remainder submitting to a conscription, assisting the strong hand of military power to take the popular idea of liberty by the neck; consenting to the suspension of the writ of *habeas corpus*; enduring acts of injustice done by arrogance of brief authority, or ignorance of incompetents; and after the peace of the state has been secured, when war has ceased, the most stupendous corrollary of the problem, the possibility of the leaders, generals, colonels, officers of every grade, abdicating peacefully their positions and returning voluntarily to private life: this other, no less important corrollary, the possibility of soldiers returning from war and its demoralization to the uniform tedium of ill-paid daily toil; the successful demonstration to the world that a republic can withstand a revolution. .

I wish I had time to paint with a true pencil the country as it was; not as those jealous of the opinion of the world would have it appear. I am not of the number who shut their eyes when unpleasant scenes are in sight. Man is not perfect, nor wholly evil; even followers of the Meek and Lowly often disgrace the name of Christians. But Jesus is no less a Saviour; for such weak, erring ones he died. By assuming a purity, a holiness, a greatness not ours, we deceive the world, and discourage other people anxious for the same liberty.

I am writing cotton; but before I get at the bales marked " C. S. A," and hidden away in the fastnesses, the thickets, the swamps, the cane-brakes of the South, I must show how simple private citizens did in some instances come up from the common herd. step by step, until they stood above the multitude, dignified by the name, the pomp and circumstance of power,—and became the nation's hand to move its armies, deplete its treasury, postpone it may be the termination of the war; in at least one case, to disgrace the whole land by their lamentable lack of principle.

Charlie Hardone had his hands full. His company dwindled. Political education had taught him to manipulate his muster-roll. Success had been partial, and Solenter, smarting under well-deserved rebuffs, plainly told him his position as lieutenant depended on the full muster-roll of actual men ready to go into camp: told in that cautious reprimand which mingles promise of reward with threats against failure. There were men in abundance, but they would not go with him. Hours of thought strove for a solution. Consultation and plan were frequent with the captain. The offer of orderly, made to James Manet, indicates the plan finally adopted. A company has three commissioned and thirteen non-commissioned officers. A full company must have a complement of one hundred and one men, including one drummer, one fifer, and one wagon-master. Twenty men were already secure, leaving seventy-eight to be obtained. Each officer should be assured • of place, graded by the number of men obtained for the company. Three recruits entitled to position of corporal; five to sergeant,—the sergeant who brings most to be orderly, and rank of first, second, and third sergeants graded in the ratio of recruits, while the lieutenants were each to be responsible for ten new men, or more if possible. Captain Solenter furnished funds for office rent, board, and other expenses—a most important item, as the rooms were not distant from a beer shop.

"Come, boys, have a drink." Out of the office into the saloon, behind the latticed screen, up to the counter. A common shop with a huge square ice-chest, out of which two long brass stop-cocks drew lager or June beer; glasses under the counter; a few old barrels, and a few decanters of different colored spirits; two or three round tables, a number of chairs and a long bench.

The crowd is composed of some recruits, some am- . bitious privates anxious to become officers, a few

11

hangers on and two or three persons from the outskirts, who are half decided to be soldiers. The
arguments of the office with its drum-sticks and fife
are unavailing.

 " Come boys what will you have ?" all are invited, and every one drinks. Bar-keeper asks:
" Going to enlist? answer, " Can't say." " Oh,
yes! now's your time. The best company in the
best regiment in the State. Capt. Solenter is a
brick ; you'll have the finest kind of times." " That's
so," echo several voices, glasses being set down
empty, convey a question as to the application. Bar-
keeper says, " Have another drink boys—I stand
treat to any man who has half a mind to fight for his
country." (Capt. Solenter pays for all this.) " Now
I tell you, if I hadn't this shop on my hands, and a
wife and babies, I'd enlist square off. Whiskey ?
Well that's all right, take a little for your stomach's
sake. There's another thing I have got to say to
you ; perhaps I oughtn't to say it, but it's true for all
that. There never was a better fellow than that
Second Lieutenant of yourn ; he is one of your common kind of men who will take a fellow as he finds
him. You should have seen how careful he handled
Bob Roberts tother day. Capt. Solenter, he's got
the influence, but Charlie knows what he's about,
and is the best fellow in the world." Best fellow in
the world, says every one. And when it comes to
singing he beats Jenny Lind to smash. Hallow!
there he is—talk of the devil—Hurrah! for you,
Charlie ; I was saying you was a tip top singer.

Take something? Boys you mustn't be offended, Charlie lets other folk's opinions alone, if he is rather strict, but he'll get over that by and by. Come now, Charlie, the boy's kinder don't think you can sing, open out on 'em. Take another glass boys."

The young men gather around Charlie; they wait for the song—"Give us the song." He says:

"I don't think the song is of any account. I would not give a cent for men who want to be caught by a song. Volunteers is what we want. Men who love their country. Those men down South have had their way so long they think us mere cowards. Some of them say they can lick ten Northern men. Don't I see them doing it! I'd like to see one man come in here and clean us out." "So would I!" said half a dozen voices, and their eyes flashing, told how powerful and vindictive emotions lay smoulder-ing, while convulsive twitchings of fingers indicated a readiness to fight some one instantaneously.

"They think all there is to be done is to look at us and we'd run. You're all a parcel of poor white trash, mud-sills, or'nary critters. When I think of it, I can't help getting mad. I believe it is right to swear sometimes, and I say, d—n them."

"Bully!" shouts the whisky man, "I'll fight, I'll die for the old Union."

"That is what I call the right spirit," says Charlie. A man is only half a man who will stand and tamely submit to the insults of the South. They have some lessons to learn, and we are the boys to teach them."

" That's so," says the saloon keeper. "For all that, I'd like you to sing that song you gave tother night. Don't be bashful. That, 'Oh ! Susannah, spank Yankee Doodle on your knee.' "

" Oh, sing it, Charlie, sing it Charlie ; that's a fine fellow. There's no one here but us. Sing it old fellow."

Thus importuned, but not without hesitation, he sang,

> " I came to town the other night
>   When all around was still,
> I dreampt I saw old Southern rights
>   A coming down the hill,
> A corn-cob pipe was in her mouth,
>   Old Bourbon in her eye,
> Says she, I'm going to free the South,
>   Oh, Yankee, don't you cry.
>   Oh, Yankee Doodle,
>   Don't you cry for me,
>   I'm going to have all rights myself
>   And spank you on my knee.

> " Ise jumped on board the telegraph,
>   I'll float on every river,
> My cotton's God, all magnified
>   And Yanks are but my nigger.
> De Union's bust, de South's run off,
>   I hardly tink I'll die,
> I'se larf'd so hard, I'se killed myself,
>   Oh, Yankees, don't you cry.
>   Oh, Yankee Doodle,
>   Don't you cry for me,
>   I'm going to have all rights myself
>   And spank you on my knee."

"Bully! Bully! Hurrah, for Charlie! Hip, hip, hurrah! hurrah! hurrah! Tiger, ah! By glory, they shan't spank me; I'm going—come Bill Solomans, you must go with us; all the boys are going; come on."

"Have another glass of beer, boys?"

"That's enough," says Charlie.

"Just as you say," says the bar-keeper.

Come on now, come on—and under the furor, and with the rush, two more recruits were brought to the point and signed the roll and were sworn in.

But all of his men were not bought by a song. Every town for thirty miles was scoured, and money in the shape of expense freely lavished to supply the requisite number.

Meantime James Manet was doing duty in the wilderness of Missouri as eighth corporal. Obedient to orders, which placed him as task-master over drunken men; called him to assist in tying, as punishment, thumbs to high limbs of trees. Think of the mental strain on such a man, when under his charge are thirty-six crazy, drunken, shouting navies, levee-rats and, miners! Did they suffer more, when it became necessary to silence their bellowings by gagging, or was his the pain and torture when the pick-handle was run under the knees, held in the tormenting position of bucking by the fettered wrists?

What were his thoughts at the loosened tongue in strong celtic tone:

"Och, blissed Jasus! Och, howly vargin! Whoop! D—m you for a d—d son of a ——.

Whoop! I'm a fray Amiriken ceetizan. I enlested for the Union. Captin, I'll shoot ye. I'll be G—d d—d to hell, I'll shoot ye. Jist fur a drap o' whishky. Whoop! Hurrah! I'm fray. Ye shan't gag me. I'll die fusht! I wont shet up. Whoop! I'm fray!"

Kind words and soft things will not do for brutes, and one experience of the butt of a musket, in a drunken man's hand, closes the bowels of tender mercies. Besides, the officer of the guard expects every man to do his duty. The officer of the day will curse the officer of the guard. He will heat the swollen expletives in transmitting them to the sergeant of the guard; and the poor corporal of the guard, with enough authority to excite fear without respect from the private, has too little to demand consideration from his superior; and, in the constant and uncontrolled, unbridled play of passion of the distant camp, removed from the restraints of female influence or wholesome public opinion, the poor non-commissioned officer must listen to the unchecked flow of the language of hell, out of lips of fetid breath, and from demonized souls, which in sober moments will call him the best man in the world, and die if need be in his defence.

James was at Rolla, and saw the return of General Lyons' army. The ragged and shoeless First Iowa—men who sprang from cottage and mansion for their country; who walked' all the long, dusty Northern roads until they joined the little army on its march after the running General Price. That company of educated, professional men, who, protesting against the forced marches of one day and the idleness of many succeeding days, received answer from their superior, " A soldier has no right to be a gentleman." Who yet, at the request of that same commander, returned to the battle-field,—for their six months had already expired, and they were forty miles on the road home,—returned by a forced march and joined General Lyon—men to whom he said when he ordered them to charge, and they, without confidence in the nerve of the man in command, asked " Who will lead us ? " " I will lead you, my brave boys." They followed him in the charge. He fell.

Oh, had he lived, Wilson Creek would have been an acknowledged victory, without retreat ; for Lyon had the nerve of a great general, who can see his army melt around him, and of the tattered remnants make a fortress immovable as Gibraltar. In battles with armies, as with prize-fighters, it is the side which can take the most punishment and yet stand up at the end, which comes off victorious. He is a wise general who, by the sacrifice of one-half or two-thirds of his army, defeats his adversary, holds the battle-ground, and saves the million lives of his people. Such was Lyon.

James Manet was within reinforcing distance of Mulligan at Lexington. Curses fell thick and fast because no orders came for them to march. Somewhere something was wrong. He marched with General Fremont to Sedalia. Think of men taking the initial lesson in soldier-life, with their guns slung behind them, long hickory gads in their hands, with which they warmed up the tired—in many instances drunken—stragglers, and by dint of blows forced them to keep up !

Hard as this was, it was mercy. Hovering around were squads of rebels, who, with the guerilla spirit, found the tired sleeper, and left him as Alexander left the sleeping sentinel.

Oh, soldiering was hard to learn. They who think it means simply being sick, or wounded or dying on the field of battle, know nothing.

On that hard march to Springfield, which political jealousy rendered abortive, this incident occurred. A burly corporal gave out. He was tired; a soft man, who gave up at home at imagination, ignorant of himself as a horse of his power. His officers were more exhausted, as on them fell the labor of the march and the duty of keeping the company and the regiment together. Price was running as no one but Price and retreating rebels ever ran; like a long, lean, lank hog, whom you have detected in a field of clover. The officer came to the man, ordered him into the ranks under penalty that he would fix him. Soon after, the corporal fell out and lay down again. The officer waited until the train came up, then he fastened his wrists by a cord and tied him like a.dog to the army wagon, where he made him walk for an hour, then loosed him and sent him to his place in the ranks. Did the corporal shoot his officer in the first battle ? No. A man who enforces obedience

by such means, is not afraid of an enemy. A brave
soldier respects a brave commander. That captain is
dead, but only after rising from the line to the command of a regiment, in whose front he fell, fighting,
with more than one wound.

Have you ever been very thirsty? James Manet
has drunk water in which swine have cooled themselves. But why go on through these horrors? Because by them is tested the will of volunteers, their
submission to an idea, their willingness to suffer, to
die for their country; because hereafter officers almost wholly appear, and while many—the majority
let it be hoped—are noble as the angels of God,
some are exceptions, and as a whole, the most self-
denying patriotism is to be found among the quiet,
uncomplaining men who have for thirteen dollars a
month left happy homes, been nothing but soldiers,
and died alone, squalid, dirty, filthy, without a friend,
nothing but a private.

Charlie's regiment was not called into active service until after the surrrender of Forts Henry and
Donaldson, the evacuation of Columbus, and the capture of Island 10. They arrived as raw recruits at
Pittsburg Landing and awoke to a knowledge of war,
on the early morning, when the pickets were driven
into the camp, and the long roll hardly beat, before
the skirmishers of Beauregard were firing vollies on
the line of battle. There was nothing for them to
do but lay on the ground and fight until that position
became too hot, when they withdrew to form a new
line of battle, from which they were again driven,

not to reform that day, but to renew the fight in detached squads as their nerves or fears permitted.
Charlie was not a coward, neither was Solenter, but
their colonel showed himself a coward, and for
cowardice his place was given to the braver man.
And now remains but one step between Solenter, the
lawyer and politician, and the brigadier generalship.

At this point cotton properly begins. It only remains to say a word of Lina Sandison and leave her
at home.

After James Manet went to war, a fair, unobstructed field remained for Charlie. Events waited
not. New combinations drove old acts, even of evil,
far from thought, almost from memory. Every
day had new excitement so absorbing as to preclude
backward glances, hardly admitting the anticipations
of the future.

The company was full at last. Then through
some turn of fortune's wheel, the colonel of the regiment was transferred. By political and other influence Capt. Solenter succeeded in obtaining the
lieutenant colonelcy over the head of the captain of
Co A. and the major of his own regiment, uniting his
forces with the old lieutenant colonel, who was promoted to a full colonel.

This gave promotion to Charlie, who became first
lieutenant, and through Solenter's influence, adjutant
of the regiment. Solenter, already in conjunction
with others, laid wires for the removal of his colonel
and his own necessary succession to the vacant post.
Thus, before the adjutant had more than a theoreti-

cal, Hardee-Tactic knowledge of his duty, he was in a fair way to be assistant adjutant general.

Of this Charlie was proud.   He was smart, he was successful, praise fell gratefully on his ear, and flattery was to him delicious.   Yet this would have been tame had not success with Lina Sandison also been granted.

Lina Sandison, to do her full justice, had that something which at times receives the name of presentiment, the inward instinct forbidding to do what was soon to be done.   A combination of circumstances hemmed her in, their pressure directed, and acting with perfect freedom, still this indistinct impression came occasionally to haunt, to suggest danger in the future.   A disturbing force had entered her mind. What ?   She did not know.   Often it happens that the heart goes out, nor does the owner know it has gone.   Up to that moment such a thing as heart, love in this sense was unknown, nor is it yet discovered ; a want is the sensation ; something has gone.   Who has it ?   The poor child does not know. Home was happy, morning was lovely, noon was glorious, evening was perfect.   Now what is the matter ?   The heart has missed something.   The heart wants something.   How many thousand thousand hearts have wakened on a morning since the war began, wanting something ! weary, knowing not why !   Ask Lina if she loved James Manet.   She will answer, no.   But when he went to the war, she missed something.   Her thoughts turned to him alone, might have solved the mystery without mis-

ery. But Charlie came with varied attractions,
and his great store of animal magnetism. Some
men, as also some women, have power to attract, to
influence and control others, as a gift. Charlie, so
far as a strong will can, compelled Lina to love him.

Look at his advantages. Young, not bad looking,
genteel, self-possessed, forward, self-confident, making the most of every gift and advantage, and he
had both. Then he was a star in their beau-firma-
ment, and other girls envied her,—tried to catch him.
Besides, he was successful ; he was an officer ; he had
been promoted. And then he was fascinating. Every
advantage was skilfully used ; for Charlie played for
the stake of Lina Sandison as shrewdly, as persist-
ently, as energetically, as for a full company or an
adjutant's position. Politics had taught him to look
far ahead for the main chance. And, when he left
for the war, she was engaged to him,—trying to feed
her hungry heart on his love,—trying to satisfy her
great imagination of her Adam on him,—thinking
how kind, how good, how smart, how elegant, how
beautiful,—making him radiant in the rays of what
she knew she could love, of what she believed him to
be, of what he had made her believe him to be.

CHAPTER XV.

Genius, talent and capacity are governed by no law of primogeniture, nor can be transmitted from father to son as an entailed estate. The Union army was composed of as smart, energetic business men as the world can produce. Men left the pulpit, left the bar, left the dissecting room to fight as common soldiers for their country. Clerks, head-clerks, and book-keepers, left the largest houses of the great cities of America to become privates or non-commissioned officers; individuals who possess in the germ the ability of an Astor, a Gerard, a Baring, a Peabody or a Lawrence. The officers also were capable far-seeing business men. These with half an eye caught distinct views of fortunes possible. The signature of a Provost Marshal, a quartermaster, a general compasses a district, enforces an order which makes a monopoly, whereby any individual can realize a profit of thousands daily.

The first consignment of beer admitted to Vicksburg cleared $20,000 in one month.

Charlie Hardone was no fool. Sandison had given him instructions. Solenter was equally sharp. The commander of a post, he possessed power to make monopolies by special orders. Applications were made almost daily to him by individuals for privileges. These he turned over to his post adjutant Hardone, saying,

"By the writing of my name I give a permit which enables a man to make his fortune. What good does it do me? None. I tell you I shall do it no longer. Whoever wants me to help him, must help me. Now Charlie if you can arrange it to make something yourself and cover me up, all right, go ahead."

Charlie replied, "I will fix it."

Hereupon Charlie worked out his plan which is explained in the following letter:

"*Mr. Sandison:*

DEAR SIR—Enclosed you will find letters of recommendation from Col. Solenter to Bankers in New York, friends of his in whom you can confidently rely. They will do your business for you and recommend you to other parties.

"Immediately on receipt of this, you will, if you know what is best for yourself, let your store go to the devil; realise as much ready money as you can beg, borrow, steal or compass in any other way; go to Solenter's father and get him to endorse for you; then start for New York, where you will buy up all the Tennessee, North and South Carolina and Georgia money you can come at, and then come down here and start a bank.

" I will guarantee $100,000—as *your* share of the profits. There is almost an unlimited field of operations. Cotton can be bought here for ten and fifteen cents in gold, greenbacks will do, but the people prefer Southern money, which you will be able to buy, if you are expert, at fifty per cent. discount in New York.

" You have no time to loose, for other sharp men are on the track. Go at once and let usual business take its own course.

" Solenter will furnish you all the permits and necessary documents for the army lines.

" You had better while you are East go to Washington and see the Secretary of War and the Treasury.

" I also recommend, this is my own responsibility, you to secure the co-operation of your state senator or representative to aid in case of any complication with the authorities. I have no definite plan to suggest. You know more of such things than I. But it seems to me the offer of a share of the profits of the business would be fair. He being on the ground at Washington, would be able to keep us posted and could cover up whenever necessary.

" I think in carrying out the plan, it would be well to get Col. Solenter appointed Brigadier General, and then if he shows himself at all in our next fight, by a judicious manipulation of our home organs, we can bring him so fully before the country as to demand his appointment as Major-General. This will entitle him to the command of a district and then we will have all things our own way.

"I wish only to give you these suggestions. You will need no aid from me. On your arrival here and during our intercourse, it may become advisable to play off on you ; Solenter knows that to perfection. All you do must be done through me, and he must never be involved in any transaction.

"In regard to division of profits. it must be by thirds. And, if necessary, we will each give a portion, which shall be made satisfactory to our agent in Washington.

"The profits on a bale of cotton will rarely be less than one hundred dollars, and, with the facilities we can compass, I have no doubt we can get out ten thousand bales.

"Now I have a thousand things to manage besides this, and of course cannot give my mind to this speculation at all. You can easily understand that you will have to do all the business; be the beginning, middle, end, first, last,—everything connected with it. We know you, have confidence in you, and you must go ahead. You shall be backed up.

"One word is as good as a thousand.

"I am, as ever, yours, etc., etc.,

"CHARLIE."

Cotton goods, once twelve and one-half cents per yard, had gone up as high as twenty-five and thirty cents,—afterwards, higher than half a dollar. Why? Because raw cotton was scarce. What made it scarce? War. What made war ? Slavery. Unpaid labor of black men has clothed our whole people. Has not the low price of cotton goods

reduced the demand for, the value of, all others
regulated by the demand? Who, of all our men,
women, and children, has not sacrificed moral responsibility when cheapening sheeting, shirting, or
prints, over the counter? The whole world has par-
taken of the American sin of slavery. Because the
sub-divisions have been so minute, responsibility has
been assumed unhesitatingly, and the slave-holder
been encouraged in his crime. The demand for
cheap goods encouraged him to rebel,—to establish,
by rebellion, the institution which reduces the cost
of this staple.

In those early days cotton could be bought for ten
dollars per bale,—the consideration being, in some
instances, a pair of boots, or a few gallons of whisky.
or any of the many indispensable necessaries of life.
The cotton supply diminishing, people thought it
must be obtained at any sacrifice. The Treasury
granted permits, subject only to the control of the
general commanding in the field, to whose judgment
the whole trade was confided. The few individuals
first engaged were extraordinarily successful.

Mr. Sandison had anticipated some opening of
this kind; and, on receipt of Charlie's letter, was
ready to embrace its propositions instantly. Excusing himself by the tale of sudden call to Washington, he went East and secured a large amount of
currency at rebellion prices; the bankers and bro-
kers being very willing to dispose of it at any price.
He also secured his agent in Washington. Sandison
was the man, of all others, to accomplish any deli-

12

cate mission. Knowing men, he knew what to leave
unsaid; susceptible of pecuniary influences, he knew
how to exert such influence on others; being an influential party man of long standing, he knew the
character, quantity, and quality of influence he could
rely upon. His peculiar genius and usefulness con-
sisted in knowing exactly how little taken from
different sources of power would unite in accomplishing something unsuspected by any of his many
assistants,—causing them to raise their hands in astonishment, exclaiming, "Is it possible? What a
man that Sandison is!"

This being so, none need be surprised that Sandison left Washington for home with papers, to which
the autographs of the Secretary of the Treasury,
the Secretary of War, and the President himself, were
attached. These documents were the more readily
granted because their intrinsic value was not apparent; because, alone, they amounted to only a
seeming endorsement, which no one deserved more
than he, who, by judiciously preferring his claim, and
withdrawing in favor of those in power at the exact
moment, had put the party under obligations not
easily ignored. The surprise lay not in asking too
much, but asking so little, while the favoring authorities would have been astonished at the effect of these
documents when united each to each, together with
good fellowship, good wine, good cigars, and part of
the profits.

When Sandison arrived at home, for the first time
his wife and family were informed of his intention to

go South. His relations at home were of that independent character that acquiescence was of course.
Self-sacrifice had been taught in his household by
the insatiable hand of party-spirit. In many respects he was a politician in his own family; shrewdly
governing without anger or Solomon's rod. They
loved him. It was hard at any time to let him go.
Whenever he said, "I go," they never thought to
hinder or oppose,—they wept.

Lina has been learning her lessons. You see it in
her face. Childhood has given way to the earnest
woman. Self-forgetfulness has worked into her active life, making her foremost in labor for the soldiers. What no one else will attempt because it is
hard, she passes not by : careless for the light gos-
sip of little minds and diminutive souls : seeking
forgetfulness in doing something for the heroes who
have given life for us. The faint hungry look of
her girlish eye, is more distinct in that of the woman,
who, in her heart of hearts, is getting grey with emotion. There is a fire there, a passion, which restless,
and fitful, goads her to something, makes her wish to
do—and asks from morning until evening, "What
shall I do?"—and when it is all done, it seems so
little !

She is beginning to be the smallest degree disappointed in Charlie. His letters lack what she seeks,
the invisible assurance of entire devotion. Some
words are trivial, some expressions, whose words
are unexceptionable, seem to have no meaning.
She is learning her capacity for suffering. She is be-

ginning to know how much she can love, and desire to be loved by a man whom she can honor in the same degree. She is hungry. Father goes away with only a kiss. Mother does not understand or appreciate her. She turns to Charlie, and is hungry still.

Just before her father goes away, that sad letter from James tells of Henry's death. How awful to die, so suddenly, and send no good-bye to his wife and child!

James writes, " Only the night before he died, as we sat beside the camp-fire, we talked of all at home. Soon after we went on picket. Then, for some reason, Henry seemed sad and lonely, and recalled the sad funeral of Capt. Esmons. He said, since he had seen war and fighting, he was glad our good captain had found a grave among his friends. " You and I, James, God knows where we'll be buried. I wish that at sometime, Mary and my child could come to my grave." And he spoke of mother and Jeanie, Lilly Sue, leaving not out Lina, for she seemed as near as one of us, and then he seemed burdened to know what would become of his wife and child when he was gone,"

Those words!. That remembrance! Hearts are traveling hither, thither, backward, forward, all over our land. This binds us closer to the living, closer to the hillock in the sun-baked clay of Arkansas, and Lina felt ties of relationship, the great, common bond of grief. How much closer after Lilly Sue went away! Sue was very near to Lina, and when the eyes slept, Lina closed them.

Mr. Sandison had no sooner reached his new post, than he sent for George Washington Wirtman to be his cashier. At home he had hired him to carry on his business for five hundred dollars per year and store privileges. He now offered him one thousand dollars and expenses all paid.

Wirtman was a thorough book keeper, having spent his life at the desk. A man of sterling integrity and unbounded confidence in his fellow men; of the number who think every man honest, even after they have cast a shade on themselves. At this juncture, he was the man for Sandison's purpose. His honesty, his unsullied purity, would cover any transactions in the office. He should never know the nature and character of the secret business, and his ignorance would assist in preserving it intact and hidden.

The offer was too good to be refused, especially, as Sandison proposed to break up house keeping, and have Mrs. Wirtman take his residence, reserving only a suite of rooms for his wife and family. Wirtman was in debt for his house, and this seemed to present an opportunity of earning the means of payment and removing the mortgage. He accepted the offer, and was on the point of closing out the store to Sandison's partner, when Lina insisted on taking the store herself, and carry it on. She would hire a clerk to represent her interest. This would realize more than such a sale. Lina was successful, and immediately installed Mary Wirtman as clerk, while she was mother to the fatherless babe at home.

CHAPTER XVI

When La Scheme returned from New Orleans and New York, he came by way of Memphis,—remaining only so long as was absolutely necessary. Whilst absent, individual cotton trade had prospered. Small lots of ten and twenty bales, secreted by planters, had reached the Federal lines. These, in every instance, ran the gauntlet of guerillas, who burned all the private cotton they intercepted. This cotton trade soon attracted the attention of military and naval authorities. A certain proportion of supplies always passed through the lines when the proprietors returned home. It became evident that a large proportion—sometimes the whole—was directly or indirectly applied to the use of the rebel army.

Whenever guerillas were parties, of course the profits accrued to the prosperity of the Confederacy. So, also, if any son, brother, husband, or father was in the Confederate army,—the absent loved one is dearer than self; if not dearer, is only second,—the extra pair of shoes, the warm blanket, the cloth for pants or coat, or the articles themselves, bought and worn through the lines by a rebel, who came in rags, were forwarded to the army. The cases of destitution among real Union men, who, positively in want, unfolded the harrowing recital of their trials, wrongs and persecutions, only aided the contraband trade, and a faithful officer found great difficulty in distinguishing real from bogus Unionism. There was an amount of haggard poverty clinging to all within the state, that the soul of every true man was moved. When not twice, nor thrice, but a hundred times, this was proved a treacherous cloak for a hostile spirit, bowels of mercy were dried, and there was no pity nor compassion. General, Provost Marshal,—every officer, even to the sergeant on picket, became a relentless avenger; a rule invariable, save when there was a bribery of cotton. The Treasury made its regulations for legitimate trade. To the War Department, through the generals in the field, the control of individual cases was entrusted. The navy. by its gun-boats, were concerned in the transportation upon the river, and in the enforcement of the prohibition placed on articles contraband of war.

In a short time these forces arrayed themselves in antagonism. Any person who complied with the letter of the Treasury regulations, was entitled to a permit to engage in the cotton trade. A Jew, a semi-union man, a squelched secessionist, knowing where cotton was hid, came for a permit,—obtained the sanction of one department of government, and then proceeded to get out his cotton. When the War Department forbade, means were used to remove their opposition. In suspicious cases the navy interfered; and here again forces were required which sometimes had arms long enough to touch the Washington center of power; giant connections represent giant capital, and when pecuniary arguments are used, power is measured by depth of pocket.

Instances can be named where pecuniary temptations, too powerful for the moral stamina of all the officers appointed to protect the interests of Government, had been applied; where Treasury, Army and Navy had been bought for a consideration. Each man, excusing his delinquency, salving his conscience with the argument, "I am not bribed; for I only grant a privilege which this cotton speculator values enough to pay for. Government is benefited in no way, and is injured not at all. I might as well make something as have this man acquire fortune by the use of my permit, by the aid of my protection.'

This was all clearly comprehended by Kendal La Scheme,—as well before as after his return from New York. Leette Ledone was to be a key upon his finger-board. to aid him in his plans.—plans which embraced the Confederacy in success, and his own safety and wealth in its failure. His return was direct to Leette. Coming upon Leette and her prisoner unexpectedly, the impression upon his mind was of distrust; fear lest the test imposed had been too great; lest mind and heart had been captured; lest he had lost power; lest his plans should fail by the very means he had chosen.

"Leette!" She started. He had come into the room like a thief. She had waited and watched, yet he had taken her by surprise. "You are getting on well. Have you forgotten your country?"

She took his hand, went into her room, and said:

"Oh, Kendal, I am glad you have come." Leette threw herself into his arms with the abandon of a woman who has a right, who does no wrong. "You can persuade him. I know you can.. If he was only convinced we were right, he would fight no longer. I cannot answer his arguments; but you can. You know so much; you understand the cause of the war so well."

"What have you learned from him? Have you won his love?"

"No. He has been disappointed. I think so. He will not acknowledge it."

"Been disappointed and loves yet. That is the worst kind."

"I taunted him, but he denied. I challenged his motives, called him love-cracked. I do not believe that; he still loves."

"What is her name?"

"He has never told me; but I believe it is Allie Sandison."

"Is it possible! It may be the daughter of my old friend. If so, she is in Memphis. Leette, congratulate me, I am in luck. Who would have thought circumstances could produce such a combination! I forgive your interest in your prisoner. I would like to see more of him, to try him a little.

Then again the two went into the prisoner's room; not at first directing their conversation to the corporal, but talking over him until he involved himself. First, however, Leette acknowledged she had not attempted to deceive him by pretending Unionism. "We agreed to be enemies and immediately became better friends."

La Scheme complimented her on her honesty and humanity, congratulated her on the corporal's improved appearance, wished she could be nurse for the whole army, and carelessly asked:

"Is he an abolitionist?"

"No," answers Leette for him. And her promptness of reply indicates a depth of interest which La Scheme suspected. She continues the prisoner's defence by saying, "He volunteered for the Union when South Carolina fired on the starving garrison in Sumpter. It was a cowardly act I did not approve. I have heard you say the same. He has told me about his first company, how the governor of his state abused him and killed his captain. Had I been in his place, the country should have taken care of itself! I would never have struck a blow! I would have died at home first!"

James interrupts: "My own private feelings are nothing, weighed against the interests of my country. I know my commander would now look from his home in heaven with pain, to see me desert my flag, because he could not die fighting for its honor. I should deem myself unworthy a seat there, if any personal consideration could make me forget myself, could tempt me to become a traitor."

" It is very creditable for you to say so. I would never fight for the Southern Confederacy if so abused."

" You do not know yourself, Leette. I give you credit for greater patriotism."

" Possibly, Kendal," said Leette, pausing for thought, " You are always right." The impulse of personal revenge burst forth in these words, " But I would kill that Solenter the first time I saw him. And that Hardone, too, is a rascal. I know he should feel my vengeance. No man shall ever trifle with me. Oh, let him try ! " and then Leette spoke God's name as woman never should. " He would repent ! "

" Is Solenter a general ? " asked La Scheme.

" Yes," answered Manet.

" Hardone his adjutant general ?"

" Yes."

" Both were politicians before the war broke out, with Sandison ?"

The corporal answered, " Yes."

" They are bad men."

Now this was a mere blind on the part of La Scheme. He was deceiving Leette, for he had already met his old room-mate, and arranged to deliver him a thousand bales of cotton at a certain time, engaging as partner, entitled to one half of the proceeds, bcause he contracted to steal the cotton from the Confederate government, and he also agreed to keep off the guerillas, as far as he could; that is, Gen. Solenter should head an expedition to protect the boats while taking it on, and he would keep them from burning the cotton before they arrived.

La Scheme only pretended to steal from the Confederates.   Gen. Solenter, Sandison, and the Adjutant General did not pretend, they *stole* the cotton from the National Government, from the National Treasury, and are rich at home, enjoying the proceeds after the war is over.   Neither the corporal nor Leette imagined what he meant when he said:

"That is valuable.   Thank you, Leette, I am truly obliged.   You have done well.   Your prisoner is a prize."   Then, as if he had forgotten himself, he used the following language: "You are a Union man.   I have relatives in the North, Union men.   I wish they were dead.   Democrats and old line whigs now all dyed abolitionists."

"Why?" asked Manet.

"I will tell you why.   What right had they to interfere with our local institutions?   What right has any state or individual to question the acts of a sovereign state?   Where can they find; how can they execute; how can they legally perform any act outside of their jurisdiction?   We are free and independent, and for our own benefit joined the North; when we choose, when our interest demands, we are at liberty, and have the power to go whither our sovereign will directs.   You would hinder us, you would try and stop us.   As well, dam the Mississippi or harness a thunder-storm."

"This is a marriage," said Manet.   "Man and wife contract with each other; but they have no

right, mutually, to dissolve the relation; for society
has also its rights, and enforces the law of divorce.
The South has disregarded the rights of the North
and taken the law into her own hands; has appealed
to arms, to the right of revolution; and the question
now is, which is the stronger. We have greater
population, greater wealth, and better still, we have
right on our side. We shall succeed."

"You do not know the spirit of our people. We
never can be conquered. The South conquered the
English in the Revolution. George Washington belongs to us. We have gained every battle of this
war. We are invincible: by birth-right, by creation, God-made to conquer."

"Sir, I cannot see it. Because the slaveholders
of the South have from their cradle lorded a supreme
will over miserable slaves, and more miserable white
trash, they have become impregnated with an idea of
invincibility. You can conquer slaves. You might
be expected to hold on, to weary out the endurance
of your common poor white. But you cannot tire
out a free, educated, thinking man of the North.
You may convince; but you cannot compel, you
cannot master: when you propound the question of
endurance,—throw your money, your life into the
conflict,—he will meet money with money, he will
put life against life, and, as you oppose, he will resist to the bitter end."

"So will we, corporal. We will endure, and you
will fail. When the war touches your pockets, the
d—d mercenary life-blood of your small-souled Yan-

kee counter-jumpers and pedlars will flow in streams
large enough to wash old Abe Lincoln out of his
throne, built of dead men's ivory—sculls and cross-
bones."

" Oh, Kendal!   What is the matter? "

"Nothing."   Nor was he disturbed.   He was only
playing with her—testing her regard for the prisoner
by cruel words.   Would she care for words, without
respect or a finer emotion?   What difference to
him?   None; save as the latent devil desired a monopoly of conquest, demanded faithfulness of the
victim while he took license as he pleased.   " Come,
Leette, I have much to say to you.   We will talk to
the corporal at another time.   I am glad, sir, to see
you so well.   You could not do other than well with
such care.   Your side cannot give you much incon-
venience? "

" Some; but fast healing.   I shall be as good a
man as ever, thanks to Miss Leette."

" There, you are calling me Miss Leette again.
Why do you never forget?   I shall be very angry if
you disobey me."

" I am a prisoner."

" Yes; my prisoner, under parole."

" Almost well enough to go to Richmond."   And
La Scheme left the room, leaving a cruel thought in
the air behind him.

CHAPTER XVII

"Why are you so cruel?" asked Leette, when they were seated at the table, where she entertained La Scheme apart from the household.

"Why are you so kind?"

"Do *you* suspect me?"

"Do you trust yourself?"

"You left me a work to do. You, yourself, said 'Well done.' What would you have more?"

"Have you won his love and trampled it down? Have you not, rather, given him a respect you cannot recall?"

"I like him; and, if I am to have a Yankee husband, I want him."

"You love him. Ah! Leette."

"Don't say that again! Don't you! You know better." Leette's eyes flashed; that lip drew back, —the white teeth shone.

La Scheme was satisfied. It remained for him to direct her passion,—toward himself as long as it suited his purpose, and then—no matter. He said:

" Leette, I will give him one more trial. I will argue with him until you are perfectly satisfied. Before we begin, I will promise to manifest no anger, nor say a violent word. I will do this, though I may be boiling (as if La Scheme could boil) with passion ; and, Leette, I will do this for your sake. Frankly, now, I do not believe the country will be benefited. This corporal is a man too firm in principle to desert ; has too much character to yield to any argument. Still, I will try. After I have failed—for I know I shall fail—you may succeed by offering your love. Not in earnest. That true, abiding affection is mine. I claim it forever. Leette, you know *forever*. If I fail by argument, you will succeed with love. Do you doubt it ? "

" No."

Leette's answer was a conviction. While watching and waiting, association had fulfilled its law. A woman meets an impossibility in striving to nurse, tend, be kind, yet hate. She pitied ; she loved,—not a brother's, neither sister's, nor love such as La Scheme held ; yet, love begot by circumstances and fostered by respect. She, also, with pardonable vanity, believed herself irresistable. Had she not won La Scheme ? Had not others bowed before her ? When had she ever failed in winning, if she desired ; and was a Yankee able to resist charms like hers ? This plantation, her blood, her education, her power, wealth, beauty,—who could resist Leette Ledone ? Would James Manet ? In like circumstances, man may be excused for falling in love. A

deep pit was dug for his. feet, of which he was ignorant. Will he be taken ?

Changing the subject, she asked, " Have you been
successful ? "

" Beyond my hope. I find friends everywhere.
In some places it is necessary for me to assume the
appearance of an original Union man, who has been
driven into rebellion. Generally, I need no false
colors. I find great dissatisfaction with the conduct
of the war by the Administration. I also find the
prime movers making their fortunes out of the war,
and ready to see, or not see, whenever their interests
are involved. I find ambitious men disappointed ;
full of bitterness and gall ; ready for whatever
may come,—even to treason,—if their vengeance
may be obtained. The party out of power will do
anything to be reinstated. Of those who are in
power—who are simon-pure abolition devils—I know
many who would send us amunition by the ton, and
whatever we need, were they sure of concealment
and their profits. The elements of distruction, which
I have counted safe for our success, exist all over the
North. They abound, can be increased, are multi-
plying every day. All that is heeded is organization, combination,—the union and harmony of these
various and conflicting elements in one grand whole.
Then the Administration and Government can be
easily overthrown, without a shot from our side, or
the loss of a man. The subject weighs on me. I
am devising a plan. But, first, I must have money
at my command. Oh, if I only had a thousand mil-

lion dollars! I would buy every sinner of the North, and then they would put the abolitionists in hell. Oh! Leette we must have money! money!! money!!! We must sell our cotton for greenbacks if we cannot get gold; money we must have!"

"Why do you place such importance on money? Our soldiers will do their part. They whip the Yankees every time."

"Yes; but look at the hold they take. Our men, valiant as they are, cannot withstand their numbers. When we retreat from a victorious battle-field, they take possession, and so fortify, that their cowardly gangs can maintain possession against all we can spare to attack. Besides, it is our policy to retreat, to draw them from their base of supplies, and make them starve. We owe to ourselves and humanity not to expose the lives of our men uselessly; and if, by leading Yankees into our land they can be destroyed by sickness, is not the result valuable as a battle? Gen. Bragg is retreating from Champion Hills, Forrest is retreating from Nashville, and this expedition of Gen. Herron's to Fayetteville will end in the same way; while before long you will see that Gen. Blunt will claim a victory at Maysville, won under similar circumstances. I have told you before that we must not expect to be always victorious, that dark days are before us, before our noble generals, before our victorious, our long enduring glorious army. Now I propose, long before it transpires, to take advantage of the revolution in the North to accomplish our independence."

"What do you mean? What revolution?"

"I mean the next election for President of the United States. Every election is in its nature a revolution, in which the issue of an entire change of Administrative policy is involved. Now, if by combining every element of opposition at the North, we can make the Northern people draw back, change their policy, and acknowledge our independence, don't you see we have gained the victory by a bloodless battle? In this battle you have a most important part to play—Money, cotton—cotton, money. Will you do your part?"

"Can you doubt me?"

"No, Leotte. But a single purpose, unwavering, never faltering, is requisite; and I fear lest love, or some other passion, may divert from the noble heroism of absolute devotion to your native land."

With a sudden impulse, the hot-souled woman rose, and went to her open piano, so situated that she looked him full in the eye, her eye expressive of most intense passion, and, running lightly over an accompaniment, sang;

"My heart is a flower, born over the sea;
    It bursteth with perfume—
            Shed only for thee :—
    For thee ;—my love only—
            Shed only for thee.

"My heart is an ocean, pure, boundless, and free :
    It's flooded with rapture—
            When taken by thee :—
    By thee ;—my love only—
            Taken only by thee.

"My heart is a heaven, one angel I see—
I love him for ever,
                That angel is thee :—
My own love ;—mine only—
                MINE!—my heaven is THEE."

CHAPTER XVIII

Flattery is the slime of the Serpent of evil. La Scheme approached Manet with flattery.

"Corporal, I have congratulated you on your nurse. I must award you a palm of victory for winning her admiration. She has even persuaded me to such an opinion of your worth, as to induce me to offer my influence to obtain a parole for you, and she insists that I can obtain for you a commission in our army. She thinks you are an honest man, who follows a conviction of duty, and believes that I can put our cause in such light that you will acknowledge the wrong and no longer fight against us."

Manet was about to speak, when his words were anticipated thus:

"Hear me through. I know this proposition cannot strike you favorably at first. Indeed I told Leette I had small hope of your accepting. She says she knows you better. I, who am acquainted

with the world, know not more than one second to
Leette, who is one in a thousand, and less than ten
in a million. For her sake I now make the offer.
It may be I shall not obtain a commission; but I
can give you wealth beyond your highest expectation.
And I think I can put the rebellion, as you term
our secession, before you in such a light that you
will see it as do Leette and myself, the true harmony of creation—the ordained system for the government of the world."

" How is that?" asked James.

"You are a thinking man. You must have noticed the poor working of our republican institutions.
You know that they are a failure. A republic can
only be maintained by pure men of honesty, integrity and poverty; men above reproach—esteeming
others better than themselves—always ready to suffer, thereby doing patriotic service. This is possible
to a certain point of national existence. The United
States have attained thus far; have come as near
heaven as fallen humanity can attain. Poverty is
the criterion of purity. A wealthy republic is impossible. It will fall by intrinsic corruption, as flesh
drops from a rotten mule. Every republic of the
past has so fallen. All were successful while poverty, integrity, and simplicity reigned. After dominion became extensive, luxury came,—then the
republics of Greece and Rome fell. The time has
come for the fall of the United States of America,
and I only ask you to save yourself in the general
ruin. It can be done in one way: by joining the
aristocratic Southern Confederacy.

"There is a law of wealth which the North has violated. It has thrown to the poor of the world an invitation to get rich; excited the ambition of every miserable wretch in Ireland, England, and Dutchland; made him a discontented citizen; brought him to this land to be a tool of unprincipled demagogues, who, by his aid, overthrow your institutions,—making it necessary for the good of the land to establish the only true system of government—the limited aristocratic monarchy. The North deserves its fate; for it cannot but fail. Every aristocrat in power ought to crush your Northern States, and aid us in striving to return to the only true normal condition of power—the ruler and ruled, the king and subject, the master and slave.

"You have given high wages; the result is, the elevation of ignorance, brutality, and insignificance; the shadow without the substance—dross, brass demanding the place of pure gold. Your servant is clad in silk of the latest pattern,—gorgeously as her mistress. Perhaps, by the accident of complexion, form, and color, surpasses her attractions, and is fit for a decent mistress. Yet this ignorant piece thinks herself the equal of the high-born woman, whose blood is better, purer, and above her own."

"It may be," said James, "she has a mind superior to her station. I have seen humble ones who were infinitely superior to those for whom they labored, in every way save the accidental relation of wealth, which made one work for the other. This is one of the best results of free institutions,—making employer and employed equal. The same rights, the same opportunities are open to both; the servant of to-day may be independently rich to-morrow; neither losing caste, nor degraded in the least. A republican government is one of equality."

"Equality!" contemptuously repeated La Scheme. He hated the word. "There is no equality. Upstart poverty is the most contemptible equality. Codfish aristocracy. Dead, damp mist, calling itself rain. Look at yourself—a common soldier. Who is your commander? An upstart, with half your brains: placed over you by the fortune of political favor. The aristocratic element exists in your army from Major-General to the man with two stripes, captain of a corporal's guard. Look at a man like yourself—the unit of aristocracy. What do you get? Hog-sty quarters in camp; transportation as a cooped chicken, a herded mule, penned cattle, boxed sheep, on railroads and steamboats; living, eating, sleeping (when you get to sleep) in your own filth; or, if on the march, in the mud; while officers are in a cabin state-room, fed at the cabin table.

"I know more of you than you imagine. Your major is a Provost Marshal. Do you know he is partner in that trade-store in Helena? It sells when no one else can; headquarters gets all its liquors and supplies there, free of cost. I went to the silent partner, who does the outside work, and asked him if he had pluck enough to engage in a speculation, which, with some danger, would net him two hundred per cent. profit—perhaps a thousand. He took me

by the hand, saying, ' I am your man.' He is a man
of nerve; he has pluck.

" I told him a lady friend of mine, you, Leette,
had hidden twenty bales of cotton, averaging six
hundred and fifty pounds to the bale, A. 1. Arkansas cotton, worth fifty cents a pound in Helena. I
told him, you and your friends had not a thing to eat
for a year; no salt, no sugar, nothing ; that you
were first quality people, who were wealthy, but the
war was hard on every one, that Leette had not seen
a pair of new shoes since '61 ; that she wanted family
supplies, and would take the whole at fifteen cents
a pound in supplies, or thirty-five cents 'in greenbacks; that the articles of female wearing apparel
she wanted, could only be obtained in Memphis, and
if he would only take the whole off my hands, I
would go to Memphis myself and buy the articles at
Memphis wholesale prices ; paying by an order on
him, while he should charge Leette the retail price
in Helena, payable in cotton at fifteen cents. He
demurred to the price per pound as I expected—
your Yankee cute trader always haggles—I came
down gracefully to ten cents per. pound, he agreeing
to apply for and secure the permits and see the goods
safely delivered outside of the lines. Leette was to
come in, as she did, merely to conform to the regulations, and go through the form. She would not take
the oath, and then we used those other people as a
blind. It was a sure thing of five thousand two hundred dollars, to say nothing of the profits of trade."

Drops make an ocean. A little act of wrong done

carelessly by many individuals, becomes a huge crime, and the several diminutive deeds of corruption done by individual soldiers and officers, may cost a nation its life.

"You are an honest man; you suffered. Your Provost Marshal was bought; your captain was influenced by your Provost Marshal; and your officer of the guard, by the same.influence, was the most insignificant your regiment could afford. It has all come out right; for the gallant little fight you made, has covered the whole transaction beyond suspicion, and I am under obligations to you for it.

"Equality? Those men are your superiors in rank, but they are inferior to you in soul as hell is lower than heaven. There is not place in society for every man to be rich, for every man to be a judge, representative, governor, president; when ten thousand equally ambitious men seek office, the most corrupt will obtain supremacy, because they will use measures to obtain their ends which honorable men cannot. There was once a republic of honest men; our fathers, who lived in times that tried men's souls, only asked a crust and honor. Time has taken those heroes from earth, and left others, uninfluenced by their motives and principles; men born of dirt, with groveling souls, to be rulers of the republic. This the South has endured. We have hoped against hope, and at last we have taken the only remedy, sad and desperate as it is. Revolution! We seek a pure government where only the best men can be rulers, can be leaders. Ariston—aristocracy: the best, wisest, greatest men. Born to be great, born to be good, born to watch over, care for and protect, poor fallen humanity, unable to take care of itself. A noble, high toned aristocracy is the purest and best government the world has ever seen—not that a republic is not a good government. This has been good. The day has past, is gone forever; because a free government requires greater integrity than mankind are capable of maintaining."

"I thought you commenced the war for the sake of slavery; because the abolitionists threatened your peculiar institutions. For this purpose you organized the Knights of the Golden Circle, and planned the rebellion long before they originated."

"Different men have different motives. Different minds explain events as they understand them. I give you my understanding of the relations between North and South.

"I am a Knight of the Golden Circle. I was at Mobile at the time of the formation of that order, and underneath the outside organization, comprehended the subtle intent. It is the simplest thing in the world, and I will explain it to you.

"The civilized world must have cotton, sugar, and tobacco. Artificial wants have been created, must be satisfied, and the South can furnish these agricultural products cheaper than the rest of the world. Cotton, sugar, and tobacco will always bring their value in gold, in every market, therefore they are gold. The land that produces them is the golden land. The Gulf States and Mexico will produce these golden products in the greatest abundance, forming a circle of which Cuba is the center. The Knights of this Golden Circle designed to take this Golden Island of Cuba, and to this end adopted their primary organization. Central America and the Southern Gulf States were also included.

" Underneath all this, was the design to establish a limited monarchial aristocracy. Cotton, sugar, and tobacco are gold. The golden land raises cotton, sugar, and tobacco. The owners of the land must control the labor, white or black, necessary to produce the crops that bring gold. They pay the taxes, therefore, they should make the laws, should rule the land ; they should only vote. Labor without capital is brute cattle-power, and ought to be subject to the rich man.

" Slavery is only a pretext to bring about this grand result. Slavery exists at the North as it does at the South. We have seen it and known it, and it is right. All men have not power to perceive, and blindness is as common North as South, South as North. Party spirit was the entering wedge of distruction. As one by one the old bones of contention passed from public observative politicians inflamed the public mind with new questions. The United States bank, the protection tariff, public improvements, one after another failed to lift ambitious men to public places of emolument. Public men, too lazy to earn their bread by hard blows and wearisome sweat of the brow, magnified this slavery question, which the Knights of the Golden Circle use to excite all the Southern people to that point which culminated in secession, and which ultimately will establish an aristocracy on this continent which shall govern the world."

"What do you mean by saying there is slavery at the North?"

"Look at your country! Gigantic corporations rule cities and villages. You are slaves to them. They dole out wages in their sovereign pleasure. We support our slaves in sickness, and in the decrepitude of old age; corporations shut up shop when they please, and starve their slaves, the poor laborers, without care or responsibility."

"The laborer of the North, sir, is not dependent on his employer; he can at any moment refuse to labor, and then the capitalist must fail; or, if he demands higher wages, must yield to the demand."

"Corporal, I know all about strikes; they are temporary. Length of purse always weighs down starving opposition. Even the educated poor man, lawyer, doctor, or merchant, fall in behind the wealthy, and use their education to mould a public sentiment which will serve the common master—a slave-holder without the duties of ownership, with the rights of a master, the power of pocket, the despotism of necessity, and the lawlessness of a tyrant. Oh, you northern laborers are slaves; mean, contemptible servants of the rich. Do rich men fight your battles? No! they stay at home, fattening on contracts. Poor men have to fight; rich men speculate. They can buy your laborer, soul and body, can find a substitute

any day.   What can the poor man do ?   Leave wife,
children, and home, and fight your battles."

"My father, sir, taught me that desire for property, for wealth, was legitimate—destructive only
when it centered in self.   Capital invested in gigantic enterprises is not necessarily hurtful.   It degen-
erates to luxury and vice when laid up for others—
demoralizes those who receive it unconscious of its
value.   In other lands, where men are not free, capital has been monopolized by a few.   My father taught
me to regard money as water, seeking a natural level.
Some men will be rich ; must I, on that account, be
covetous ?   Nature makes infants, not capitalists ;
nature does not invest millions in entailed estates ;
nature has no lords or nobility ; nature made man as
it made forests.   Why is one tree larger than another ?   Fallen nature introduced a curse—labor.
Labor is not properly remunerated ; and laboring
men have no permission in any other land in the
world to get rich.   Rich men love to get the labor of
the poor for less than its value, as thereby their profits are increased.   I do not see why that should make
a free man destroy the only government in existence
where he has privileges equal to the sovereign, where
he is a sovereign, and where all places of honor and
trust are open for honest competition.   You teach
me that this is the poor man's war.   You identify
yourself with the rich man, and seek to make me aid
your cause by arguments drawn from abuses of your
own side.   You fight for aristocracy ; you fight
against popular government.   We fight for the rule

of the poor man at the ballot-box, for the rule of the majority."

"The rule of the majority!" repeated La Scheme. "Damn the majority!—the most detestable rule on earth. It never expresses the will of either party. Generally a small minority, an organization, society, clan of voters, on the eve of a closely contested election, have power, by deserting and joining, or by mere union with either party, to carry the day. This faction is controlled by an idea, embodied in representative men—and these men have their price. When they are bought they become masters, or are made slaves. The balance of power is the will of the majority—the hardest task-master ever born ; it has ruined this country. We held it until political changes threw the abolitionists into the scale, and forced us to choose between freedom and the damning rule of a contemptible posse of fanatics."

"Sir, this trial of free institutions which you pronounce a failure, I conceive to be a success. The question at issue is the ability of men—common poor trash, to elevate themselves, to govern themselves, to be independent—to be free. The test imposed upon it by your secession, by your rebellion, is the most severe possible. If it stands—if you fail—and I believe you will, then Europe, and all the people of the world, will imitate our example. I think your argument is, that wealth must be concentrated, and must govern, whether in a republic or a monarchy. Permit me to refer again to my dear, dead father. He taught me that a parent's best gift was an education, a trained mind, qualified to fight the world and win victories in the same path he has trod with honor and success.   He taught me that every man of abundant means should lay out his surplus wealth in the channels adapted to benefit his fellow men. This is the royal prerogative of a free man.   The truest patriot, the best Christian, is he who, having well provided for his own, wisely scatters the abundance of his prosperity in assisting his fellow men. You have referred to ancient republics.   Rome perished because her wealthy citizens, without royal prerogative, became aristocrats, and aristocracy is the stepping-stone for unlimited selfishness, identical with unlimited monarchy.   She had no true Christianity, and no true Christian benevolence, no charitable institutions, and no self-sacrifice.''

'' Corporal, you come on religion.   Here you, too, are wrong.   Religion is the child of weakness. Strength is self-reliant.   No man seeks God's aid until he is helpless.

'' Men of keen insight, thousands of years before Christ was born, in their studies for dominion, found that permanent government must rest on power and weakness: power in the king, weakness among the people.   In order to perpetuate their dominion, they made close study of mental weakness, and found superstition, upon which they constructed with all the ability of great thinkers, the present superstructure of religion.   They united church and state ; controlled the sensitive (conscience) weakness of humanity ; condensed the atoms (men and women) of power, by laws of crystalization (military and civil laws), formed Titanic mountains of minerals (kingdoms, empires, and aristocracies.) They learned that the strong point of power lay in controlling the element of feebleness in the subject, and, after careful study, formed systems which we recognize as religion. The Chinese savants have the system of Confucius. The Sanscrit the Budist, and Brahmic belong to southern Asia. Greece and Rome each had their superstition; while the Jews had patriarchs and wise men, who, from association with Arabic and Egyptian sages, and with the wisest men of China and India, sequestered, stole, and simplified principles and theories of law, until they had the greatest number of eternal axioms, and, so far, the system nearest perfection. Then that peculiar genius, Jesus Christ—who stands to morals as Shakespeare to literature, and Blackstone to law—presented his system of morals, which the high education of our civilization prefers to the more incomplete and more unscientific schemes of unskilled thinkers.

"You have imbibed the false notions of progress in religion, and have not attained to freedom. There is a spiritual idea beyond your Bible system, which will some day take its place. But for common, ignorant people, I prefer the Roman Catholic. It has a centralization of power formed by the experience of the most astute, sagacious minds. It never dies; has a single policy; brings forth rulers as a mother babes; suckles them with her ideas, bathes them in her principles, schools them apart from humanity,

14

until they grow up bone of her bone and flesh of her flesh. Whoever comes in power, the church is always the same—permanent, reliable, irresistable."

"Mr. La Scheme, I see clearly that you do not believe in that which is a great consolation to me— the Christian religion as a divine institution, in Jesus Christ as the Son of God. I believe this as firmly as I believe in my personal identity. What the world needs more than all else, is self-sacrifice. I put my principles in practice—I give my life for my country. Heaven sent the great Example, who died a felon's death to give eternal life and salvation to those who deserve no mercy. Since the crucifixion, no one, hating service, has been truly great. Loving sacrifice must characterize our public men. Ambition, in president, secretary, or judge, must be second to right, justice, and country. The senator must sacrifice his self-motors; so the representative, so the soldier, so too, the sailor. Men—all men, public and private—must be willing to do right because it is right; must go forward and do, in the face of frowns, true duty ; perform the acts of statesmen and patriots, tested by a standard of heaven-born purity, by a criterion of honor keen in its distinctions as the eye of an impartial justice."

"That's all fine philosophy. I do not disagree ; but I tell you it is impossible. It is mere theory; practice disowns its possibility. We have tried the experiment and failed. The Confederacy is attempting to save itself, in the wreck, by an early return to that form of government which has withstood the convulsions of ages. I have treated you with the utmost kindness for Loette's sake, and desire now to come distinctly to the point. Will you accept my offer? Throw in your lot with the South, and become one of us?"

"I think your system of government would soon become an unlimited monarchy—a despotism. Your president, Jefferson Davis, is a tyrannical man, and manifests that character which would honor any despot. All he lacks is opportunity. He is the only man for the crisis, which I understand to be a relapse into barbarism."

"Jefferson Davis is not the only man for the crisis. He is only an incarnate embodiment of the secession idea. Every such embodiment is a Jefferson Davis. Any man or woman who has intellect to comprehend the bottom thought, to perceive the underlying principle—the adamantine foundation of the superstructure, to whose erection this war is but an obstacle; and also, when finished, an evidence of success—is a confederate; give him like will, energy, pluck, nerve, and brain, and he is a Jefferson Davis. Our great president is only a representative man. The lobby members would fill his place, were he to die. We permit him to exercise despotic power because we believe in it. The tyranny of a firm will acting in accordance with our principles, even in mistakes, is preferable a thousand times to the vacillating indecision dependent on delegated power. Are you satisfied?"

"Not yet. I thank you for candor. I am under

obligations for your frankness. If I accept your proposition, I must understand all I undertake. It is a question among us whether, by the progress of this war, an end is not put to slavery. In your new empire slavery will be dead."

"Do not take that flattering unction to your soul. As long as a man in the South struggles for Southern independence, the soul of slavery lives. We are seceding because the North threatened our institution of slavery. A principle of government is involved. The few have a right to sell the many, whether black or white. Servitude is necessarily involuntary. England is full of white slaves. France, Germany, and Russia are full of white slaves. Your Northern mechanics are white slaves; your capitalists slaveholders. We believe in the thing; you disbelieve, and act as we do. We see no difference in black and white slavery, and know that capital has a right to own labor. We are honest; you are hypocrites. We call things by true names; you cover vile acts like a whited sepulchre. Slavery cannot die until we are destroyed. With our success it succeeds. When we have conquered the North, we shall be the strongest nation in the world. The North fears us; the whole worlds fears you. We shall teach them the true principle of their own government, and both they and we will control labor and laboring men. We shall have as many slaves as we wish; for poor whites will be slaves. You see now what is before you.

If slavery is right at all, white slavery and black

slavery are identical. Mind has no color, memory
has no color, judgment, reason, have no color. Who
knows but that color to the Almighty eye is so finely
marked, that no two beings are white or black.
White, brunette, brown, copper, yellow, dark, black,
advancing as some minerals, from transparent crystal through white by insensible degrees to opaque and
to black. Infinite purity alone is spotless. Our eye
condemns the black because it sees our own skin
white. God pities our impurity. Men with white
faces have black souls. Purity, chastity, love, do not
shine through the outside covering—[else Leette
would have spat on La Scheme as a Moor, darker
than Othello of Venice]. Villainy, lust, hate, revenge, do not show black beneath Caucassian features. Skin has no influence on the heart. God
made *white* men, with different qualities and quantities of brain, and capacity of brain development—all
endowed with an infinity of future increase. There
are white men whose groveling instincts, and ignorance, put them next neighbors to beasts—white men
whose affections, or absence of affection, develope
consanguinity with the fallen lost, the demon of hell.
Love is love, hate is hate: each has characteristic
manifestations. Size of a fist changes no title of
the quantity and quality of these attributes of the
heart; no more does the color of that fist; neither
does the color of the body. A warm heart may exist in a casing of charcoal, copper, or bronze, or silver. Whiteness of snow cannot warm a marble
heart. Equality of a nigger to a white man! No

white man is the equal of his white brother, side by
side though they stand, unless the mind, head, and
heart are similarly developed.

[In the winter of '63 thousands of hogs were frozen
to death by the intensely cold week after Christmas
and New Years. Were they consigned to the dung-
hill? No! Hams and shoulders were cured from
them for our soldiers, and the remainder tried for
lard. A white man, a rich man, lovely wife, beautiful daughters, to be degraded by the contamination
of a colored clergyman who brought a 2000 dollar
gift to the Sanitary Fair for sick and wounded soldiers, because the equality of the races would thereby be acknowleged! Is a government contractor, a
white man, who cures frozen hogs, or any other shod-
dyite, better than the blackest of the black, when his
"limed soul" hesitates no single moment to make
money on any article, in any way which uselessly sacrifices the life of a gallant soldier? Dust to dust,
ashes to ashes; the soul washed by the blood of Jesus is white. Whatever God may do in regard to
color in heaven, there is a place prepared for souls
dyed by such deeds. Thank God there is a hell!]

James Manet listened with the same quiet expression which misled La Scheme from the first. He answered in as quiet unchanged a tone:

"Before this war commenced I knew nothing of
slavery, cared nothing for abolitionism. I was, I
am, a Union man. I knew of slavery nothing until I volunteered. You are teaching me to hate the
institution so bitterly, that if I continue, I shall be

more rabid than the most radical. You desire to
destroy a free government, to take from American
citizens the privilege of managing their own government, and create an aristocracy. All this for the
sake of slavery. Sir, I hate it because you love it,
because it aids you to fight us—because you used it
as a subterfuge to deceive and mislead your own common people, to cloak your treasonable designs. I
have not been an abolitionist, but I will be from this
time forth, because, by taking your servant, we re-
duce your aristocratic men and women to the simple
laboring citizen, put them on the level of plow, hoe,
churn, and wash-tub. I wish to see every slave taken
from your Confederacy, thereby taking bacon from
your smoke-house, corn from your crib, and starving
your commissariat. When negroes fight, their masters must fight and work too. You know how to
fight, but not to work ; you will fight and starve.
Starvation is just punishment for the crime of treason to free institutions."

"Leette," said La Scheme turning toward her,
" Do you see I was right ? For your sake I leave no
stone unturned. Corporal I have use for such a man
as you. I told you I could make you very rich ; this
promise is not an idle word. I have within my control an immense business in cotton which will make a
thousand men independently rich. If you will consent to be my agent, to act in secret, in conjunction
with me, I will insure your fortune, more money than
you can make by a life-time of labor in the North.
I will even promise more. You shall not come

South, nor join our Confederacy, except your judgment, your free choice, shall move you to do so."

"Mr. La Scheme, it is very easy for you to speak
these words. I am not blind to the importance of
the promises you make. I know how sternly difficult it is to resist temptation. I do resist, I refuse
your tempting offer. Every man worthy to be a
citizen of this free republic, ought to be above bribes,
ought to have a spirit pure. Mine may have had
leaning to wrong, had evil thoughts, spoken wrong
words, but in action I am yet pure. I choose so to
continue. I am satisfied a time will come, is coming,
when free men will be pure men, good men, Christians in holy honor, in honest business, in sacred
home-life. It will come."

"No, sir. Never! never! Man cannot reach
this state you imagine. In all the thousand years
of the past, he has failed. The future is to be as
the past, and the part of wisdom is to care for yourself in the general ruin. If you do not care for
yourself no other one will."

"The difference between us, sir, is radical. You
do not believe in the elevation of human beings as a
race. Your system is founded on the degradation of
fallen humanity. I acknowledge the justness of your
conclusions on your premises. The reasoning is
correct. But I believe in the redemption of the human race. I believe in Jesus as a Savior, I believe
men can repent and reform, can be pure, full of
justice, equity, and truth.

"Mankind, irrespective of color can become Christians, and act on the golden principle—Do as you would have others do. A republic can be composed of Christians, or so large a majority actuated by the principles of Christian morality, as to be what you deny.

"Again, I believe in a Holy Spirit, ruling in the hearts of men. There have been times when I lost faith, when ruin seemed to overwhelm our cause and our country. Out of that darkness it came triumphant. I recognize a power you cannot understand, an over-ruling hand in which I trust. I may die, God lives. You may kill us by thousands; he who holds the hearts of men will not permit you to conquer. He is teaching——"

The world is a school house, men and women scholars. The teacher is experience, dealt with a governing Providence, and progress is marked by revolution.

——"the people of the world a lesson through you and me. When we have well learned, war will cease."

"I shall never learn."

"You may be taught by death. No man ever stopped the lightning. God moves the storm. Where rests the power of your arm to stop a cannon ball? When God moves the world, do you expect it will stay its progress because your will says 'No'? Your argument is the argument of despotism, my faith, that of freedom. My argument may not convince you; but I believe, I feel, I know you will fail. I have faith in human progress, have hope for the human race. God is at work. In our moment of success, you will find failure. When we fail, out of our misfortune will come success. God is for us."

"That is bosh for the man who believes there is no God. Come, Leette, have I not done my part? You shall be more successful."

CHAPTER XIX

"What a good Confederate that Yankee would have made, had he only been born South!" said La Scheme when they were alone.

"He has the best blood in his veins. His ancestors fought in the Revolution," says Leette.

"Oh, Leette, you do like this Yankee!"

"Suppose I do, better than any I ever have seen. How much is that? He is not a coward; speaks his mind, cost what it may; has often spoken to me what made me mad afterwards; for I never once perceived its extent while he was talking."

"Well, well, you have taken a fancy. You may turn him to our side. I cannot. He talks well. Do not fall too much in love with him. I leave him to you; for I go away to-morrow. When I come back I will decide what to do with him."

"You going to-morrow! Where and why? Can you not stay and rest a moment?"

"Rest before I am weary? Rest, when I see the only chance for the Confederacy in my hands? No. This is the golden opportunity. The Board of Trade,

the Treasury officials, and the Army officers are
deeply concerned in cotton stealing. Sandison is
there. I saw him. I know him of old, and I can
do anything I please with him. I [the liar!] needed
to know one fact. This Yankee—how glad I am I
saved his life!—has, thanks to you, revealed it.
Sandison is in cahoot with General Solenter,
through his future son-in-law, the Adjutant General
—this explains my old chum's successful business.
I did not expect this. I can hardly restrain my
joy. They are all politicians, susceptible to a consideration. I shall make them believe me a cotton
thief, speculating for a fortune; and, without their
knowledge, use them to their destruction. The
opening is too good to be neglected."

"Let me go with you. It is lonely when you are
away—so v-e-r-y l-o-n-e-l-y ! I endured your long
delay because of your request to win this Yankee's
love. You are unkind to think that I could forget
for one moment. Send him to Richmond to-morrow,
to-day; but do not leave me; or, if you must go,
take me."

"Perhaps it will be well."

"When shall we send him away?"

"Not yet. I may be able to use him. Let him
remain until our return. How many bales of cotton
have you? How many have you burned?"

"Five hundred after they took Memphis. I have
one hundred and fifty in the cane, and there are a
thousand bales of Confederate States Cotton back
from the slough."

"Are they marked ? "

"Yes. C. S. A. on the heads. I gave them to the government to secure the foreign loan."

"I wish they were safe in New York, and the money in the hands of our Committee. Leette, if you only had all your own well sold, you would be worth a quarter of a million in gold. What folly to burn a pound! What a mistake! Leette, you shall not lose everything. You may go with me. But, Leette, I am a Union man within the Federal lines. Until you have taken the oath — "

"Must I take that oath ? "

That iron-clad oath! Which sounds loudest in the ear of the recording angel—the spoken words of the Union officer, who repeats the comprehensive words to which the indignant, hot-eyed, red-faced chooser of two evils simply nods; or that inward hope, wish, prayer, curse, bursting out of the heart-passion on the wings of a long breath, entering eternity with this definition : "I have sworn. If I keep the oath may I be damned ! "

"A thousand times, Leette. I have, and am none the worse. The Federals know me as a good Union man." These words came from La Scheme's lips with a hiss. "I do not associate with rebels inside of their lines. I should not go near you until you are Union. Never recognize me. If you are introduced, treat me as a stranger or beneath your notice. We must not know each other at first, that we may most aid our success."

"Where shall I stay? When shall I see you?

What shall I do ? "

" Stop with your friend, the Judge."

" They are Union."

" The very place. Their daughters are true. Besides, you must mislead even them. In the delicate business in which we are engaged, one's own friends cannot be relied on,—should be trusted only in extremity. Deceive your own, and your enemy must bé double sharp to see what a friend fails to discover. Act like an enemy, so as to be hated by a friend; you may save life,—may save your country. I cannot tell when I shall meet you; nor what there will be to do. Yes; you may sell your cotton. Not much; begin with five bales,—do not offer more. Can you sell five bales ? "

" I know I can."

" I must go and see our captain, who saw me through the Helena affair. I have business and instructions for him. Be ready to go when I return."

" Yes; and I will say good-bye to my Yankee husband. I must hide him out of the captain's way. I should never see him again if his men took him prisoner a second time."

She went out to see the corporal, and La Scheme, shaking his head, said after her departure, " Leette, Leette, you have too much heart. That good soul of yours has too much love. I must crush it out; must set it on fire with the demoniac which lies in your nature. That Yankee is too true, too pure, and must be removed. The captain will see that done. I have delicate work before me. What can

I do? Wait,—let events decide and interpret them; lead others to the meaning I would have them believe. Oh, what a glorious power!—to see into, read through, the souls of others. I know men; I anticipate their words. If I only had opportunity, I could direct this war, govern this new empire, and succeed,—which is more than I believe Jefferson Davis will do. What a confounded fool he makes of himself sometimes!" With a brain teeming with such thoughts and ideas, La Scheme went out from Leette to seek the headquarters of the guerilla chieftain.

CHAPTER XX.

The guerilla band was a motley mixture. Few made more than pretentions to a uniform. They possessed a marked uniformity in one particular—dirt. Originally, their garments had been white: that is, white as the cotton fibre carded by the coarse hand-cards of the negroes; spun by their coarse fingers into coarse yarn which had been coarsely woven by a coarsely constructed loom, and then cut and sewed by a coarse needle, without bleaching or other finishing process,—white as such unwashed, hasty construction could produce. Some boasted a slightly increased finish, being the addition of a tawny, butternut color, from a decoction of oak, walnut, or other bark. This uniform possessed the essential quality, durability; already outlasting any machine manufacture, and promising shelter from rain, and sunshine, night and storm, for more than one season to come. Night as well as day-dress, blanket as well as over-coat, duster in the thick clouds of a skedaddle, tent in the hasty, improvised bivouac of the canebrake; accustomed to the floor of the log cabin, the plantation mansion, the slave's quarters, or the baked soil—not the stony, sandy New England, not the rich, black alluvium of Connecticut's meadows, not Western prairie, but the red oxide of the corroded Arkansas, or the turbid mud which melting torrents of the big Muddy has laid in layers throughout the lower Mississippi bottoms. In this respect, all the regulars were regularly uniformed.

Another striking uniformity of the Tom, Dick, and Harry of this wild region, is vice. Lazy, ruffianly men, who eat whisky, drink whisky, live on whisky when they can get it, on its substitute, corn, when they can not. Scum of both armies, with all a soldier's faults, with none of his virtues. Thieves, who would plunder, though at the risk of life. Brave devils, who had the blood of murders coagulating on their souls, boasting in the exploit, and calloused to remorse, exulting in their wolf-hyena-life; carrion birds, not all buzzard, since they had degenerated from the eagle; possessing all the ferocity of the one, while they digested all meat of friend or foe, with the horrible appetite of the other. This is the genuine guerilla.

Another part of this band, gave it dignity and character. These were planters. Every citizen was enrolled with the proper authority, and assigned to the commanding officer, who had power to order them into active service. They called themselves home guards. Plantations, slaves, and families could not be left absolutely manless. Some must oversee the labor which produced the subsistence for the army in

15

the field and the people at home. Yet, all must be organized for self-defence and personal protection. The captain, major, or colonel, generally knew his section, gleaned the poor, and desperate with whom he engaged in the active duties of conscripting, and waged the common guerilla warfare; while he favored the rich, granting them exemptions, and never called them save on important occasions, when numbers were essential, or their presence was necessary to inspirit or to check the regular band, which went into danger, took the heavy blows, and were of no particular account if they were killed.

On this occasion, notice of an expedition from above, had been received and transmitted by Southern sympathizers. The captain had ordered every man in his company to meet at this place, armed.

Rapidity of communication among a united people, even in remote and sparsely populated districts, is marvelous. In this section of the South it was conducted by women. The news was obtained from headquarters by the means of secret emissaries—proslavery men who visited the saloons and offices, and learned from clerks, with most unexplainable facility, every movement; men, so well posted, that they could guess all they could not buy with the official seal and stamp affixed. A plate of butter, a load of wood, a harmless female, conveyed the word outside the lines. Southern women ride on horse-back. Once on horseback, by short cuts—devious paths in swamps and canebrakes; tracks on the levee, when direct; by dry beds of streams; by the public road, if near and safe—girls, young boys, old men, carried the report fast as animals could go; so that, it was often said, no boat could leave ·Cairo, Illinois, without her name, character, cargo, destination, and number of troops, proceeding faster than steam, informing all the bands by telegraph.

Leette was a carrier. Her *Janie* stood waiting in the stall, sure-footed, fleet; dark night or broad noon made no change in her swift passage through deer and bear tracks to the station, whence another took the news, good or bad, direct to rebel headquarters.

The guerilla band were gathering when La Scheme reached the captain's rendezvous. Before he arrived, loud tones of a revelling song reached his ears. First came the chorus:

> " Drink, men drink,
> O drink your fill to-day;
> For life is bonny, and love is sweet,
> And fighting is our play."

When the cotton speculator rode up, and was recognized, a guerilla, sitting astride of a barrel of old Bourbon whisky, raised up a tin pot and roared out the following stanza:

> " Oh wine was made for boys and women,—
> Old Bourbon is the drink for men;
> When balls and bullets come a whizzing,
> Give us old Bourbon then."

He repeated the last line and then took a big swallow and passed the pannikin, which the other

guerillas took, imitating his swallow, and then joined
in the roaring chorus :

> " Drink, men, drink,
>   Oh drink your fill to-day ;
>   For life is bonny, and love is sweet,
>   And fighting is our play."

" Empty it out, boys, and pass it round." It
came back to the king of the revels, who drew a
spigot, from whence spirted the precious liquor.
"Never mind the canteen. Second verse." Then,
raising his tin goblet, sang :

> " Oh peace was made for girls and women,—
>   War, stern old war, was made for men ;
>   When on the battle-field we're charging,
>   Give us old Bourbon then."

Just then a black servant came out of the log
shanty with a broken pitcher to be filled from the
common stock. The non-commissioned officer, who
had the same in charge, put the full dish to the negro's mouth, spilling the liquor down his throat and
over his big thick lips, while the band yelled out :

> " Drink, men, drink,
>   Oh drink your fill to-day ;
>   For life is bonny, and love is sweet,
>   And fighting is our play."

The men passed the can again. There was a certain method about the whole of this revel ; a sort of
restraint, mixed with a peculiar license, which was

unwilling to get drunk, though quite ready to be anything but sober. Short drinks and quick turns seemed in order. This hindered the darky, who was awaited impatiently, and called from the shanty.

" Coming, sar," he answered.

Yet the men were in no particular hurry, and the slave had to await their half-drunken convenience. The captain—master—came to the door, angry at detention : saw the new arrival, and instantly called La Scheme. As they went into the house the song broke out again :

> "Old Bourbon whisky's made in heaven;
> Old Bourbon is the drink for men.
> Drink Bourbon whisky while we're living;
> Dead—drink old Bourbon then."

" Glad to see you, La Scheme. You are the man we want. We are to have a stirring time. Our men are getting ready."

" What ? I do not understand. Where did you get the whisky ? "

" That came through the lines on a drift-pile. Some of our friends on one of the Memphis packets. It was well done. We got it several days ago. I give it to the boys to put them in good heart. There is an expedition going down the river. I imagine they have got wind of the cotton I am watching. Don't I wish they may get it ! "

" How can you prevent it, if they have more men, —especially when you have no artillery ? "

" I will send it to heaven with a fire-brand, and

leave them ashes. Trust me to outwit a Yankee. Sit down and take a drink; there is plenty of time."

Outside the guerillas were singing:

"Drink, men, drink,
   Oh drink your fill to-day;
   For life is bonny, and love is sweet,
   And fighting is our play."

Who would think that La Scheme, the Confederate, was at the bottom of this expedition? That he had improved his time at Memphis in such a remarkable manner. Least of all, how could the guerilla imagine any plot hidden in the mind of a Confederate like La Scheme? And if, as was true to a certain extent, this cotton was sold to benefit the South, why did not the speculator, like a man, tell the guerilla captain, and obtain his safe-guard? Could La Scheme doubt for a moment which the captain would prefer to do—destroy two hundred and fifty thousand dollars, or make one hundred and twenty-five thousand dollars,—ashes or green-backs? In truth, La Scheme's original plan involved a disclosure to the captain; but his suspicion of an affection between Leette and the corporal had changed the design to that which is soon to be developed. La Scheme possessed a happy faculty of turning every accident to the best account. The whisky and the preparation of the guerillas were moves in his hands. He had a defined plan, or rather a skeleton, of what was to be done at the mercy of circumstances; and his disposition was so well subdued

that, like the master of the chess-board, the check
of an antagonist was only a false move which exposed and mated his own king. Consequently, La
Scheme·was simply their old friend—shaking old
friends with the hand-grasp of warm friendship—
greeting new acquaintances with that cordiality
which intoxicated them with the pleasure of genial
good-fellowship. They drank all round, and enjoyed
the men's chorus heartily, saying "Bully for the
Bourbon," as the loud strain, repeated, entered their
ears :

> ' Old Bourbon whisky's made in heaven,—
>   Old Bourbon is the drink for men.
>   Drink Bourbon whisky while we're living ;
>   Dead—drink old Bourbon then."

As if the word "dead" had suggested an idea, he
asked the captain :

"When do you expect them ?"

"Any moment. I must send out a scout now.
These men have drank about enough."

Rising from his seat he went out, and gave orders
to a subordinate, which were obeyed by a general
mounting and departure of the band—but not before
the precious whisky was brought inside.

"We do not often get an article as good as that.
One of our side got it particularly for me. It will
not last long ; while it stays let us enjoy it."

The capacity of a corn-fed soldier of the South to
contain whisky, is astonishing, which makes them re-
semble that object of their special hate, a Dutchman

—on the principle of the arithmetical rule of three,
viz :—as lager beer to a Dutchman so is whisky to a
Johnnie. These soldiers were gentlemen—gentlemen who had not seen whisky for ten months, and
they drank with the freedom of soldiers, and the capacity of an empty two-gallon jug. La Scheme enjoyed their thirst, for he was too wise to imitate their
example. He, however, absorbed their attention by
his account of Memphis and the army there, and the
state of feeling existing at the North. When their
cups were empty, he warily suggested some hope of
success, or some promise of aid, which filled them
with joy, and called for more fluid to wet it down.
Keeping up their good fellow-feeling, he put them in
that frame of mind which cares for nothing, and
would rather fight than eat. About this time the
lieutenant dismounted and entered the shanty, saying :

" They are here."

" How many ?"

" One gun-boat and three transports."

" Send for the lower squad ; bring in all the de-
tachments. Are your men all right ?"

" Yes. Shall I fire the cotton now, and fire on
them afterwards ? we can concentrate then."

La Scheme spoke : " You had better concentrate
now. Ledonc's Point is the best place ; and in case
of a retreat you can have the cover of the levee and
the quarters. You had better not burn any cotton
until you see it is in danger. They may not land
here at all."

He knew that orders had been issued to gun-boats to shell, and troops to land and destroy, any plantation which harbored guerillas. What motive had he for the destruction of Leette's home? Was it Corporal Manet? Certainly he could be otherwise put out of the way.

"That is the best place," said the Captain, "but I fear lest the Yankees will land and burn the buildings."

"I think not," said La Scheme; "They will not do that unless we fire on them; and even then we would meet them by a good volley, and prevent their landing. But you know best; you must take the responsibility. I would not have Miss Leette's old home destroyed for the world."

"Mount!" commands the captain; "we have no time to lose."

The Mississippi river, in its course to the sea, runs from a direct line with the waywardness of a headstrong girl. The meanderings of its channel are similar to the three wonders—too wonderful for the wise man, Solomon. Often a steamboat, bound up or down, heads toward every point of the compass between sunrise and high noon. Many, many times, between Cairo and New Orleans, the eye can see over a narrow peninsula to the river below,—a short mile, or, at most, not more than five; yet the stream runs twenty miles around the almost-island to make that little distance. Such was Ledone's Point. Leette's plantation was on the neck,—gazing at both rivers, yet nearer the south than north. La

Scheme, riding with the captain, contrived to lead him to occupy the north side, from which the attack could easily be renewed on the southern side, there being ample time for riding across, and other preparation, while the boats were getting round.

Arriving at the place, the guerillas dismounted and tied their horses in the woods, out of sight of the river; then went to the levee and lay down in a position to command the approach. In the distance, coming down, were dark clouds of coal-smoke from Uncle Sam's big chimneys—taxes upon future generations ascending thick and fast into the air; one dollar a moment, this expedition, to be paid by children's children as the price of union, liberty, and a free government.

The gun-boat was not molested, but passed beyond the point; so the first transport. Each transport held a regiment of volunteers, who were packed away in every possible place. On shore, the trees heard no rustle save the breathing of their own leaves; no voice but the twittering of home birds, who saw no cause for disquiet or wonder in the watching, waiting forms, so near the color of the soil as to seem mounds — newly closed graves. Nearer and more near came the boat. Two companies, detailed to repel attack, were in line of battle on the roof. At ease; the nation's soldiers rested on their guns, for they were tired. No one had fired on them all day; nor the previous night, when they lay at the bank with their pickets out. The soldiers not on duty were seeking the little comfort possible ; guns were laid along the deck. A few were watching. The channel came close to the bank ; the boat drew near. On the other side, the Mississippi spread its mighty current over a great bar. The smooth, shining surface spoke of no danger ; but the pilot knew, if once he left the channel, the boat would be as hard and fast aground as Noah's ark before the flood, or, when the waters falling, it ran aground on the summit of Ararrat. What matter if the rest of the world was an ocean ? The boat could not swim : so on it came in the current ; nearer and more near, until the distance seemed so short that a biscuit could be tossed on shore. Still the guerilla would not give the order, " Fire."

He loved Leette, and could not bring his heart to endanger her old home; to bring the house where she was born to ruin. He hesitated ; while thus poising, that man who hated Leette because she saved the life of James Manet caught the eye of La Scheme. The eye that tells without speaking, caught a look toward him, then at the house. With a scowl of rage and hate, the guerilla raised himself, aimed at the pilot-house, and fired. Instantly, a volley followed ; guerillas loading and firing without command, bullets singing the leaden zip, zip, zip, among the Federal soldier's ears ; a volley taking them by surprise, which they feebly returned. The next boat was treated to the same ; but they were prepared, their pilot ran as far from the bullet-bank as was possible, so disturbing the guerillas' calculation of distance on the water, that the balls fell short and harmless. When this was discovered, the gang left the upper point, ran to their horses to be ready for a new attack below, when the boats came round.

One man lay stiff, and stark, and cold. The guerilla who fired without orders. His captain strode to his side. "God d—n your soul to hell, go home!" The poor worthless soul rode on a pistol-bullet out of the sun, out of the woods; away from the American bottom, with its river—Father of waters—its mighty bosom, sandy, snaggy; its quaint forests; its cane-brake; its rebellion; rode faster than railroad; as the lightning, to try the realities of the beyond. How far was La Scheme guilty? He did not encourage him, he did not command : such encouragement, such command, would have met disobedience; he only looked "Don't fire, that house belongs to Leette Ledone," and the guerilla fired, and went to hell.

The boats came round. Now the guerrillas had the down side. Boom, boom, boom, burst from the gun-boat; shell followed shell. The transports landed, their troops debarked, formed in line of battle, and charged double-quick upon the foe, — uselessly; those horrible shells! those infernal gun-boats! Horses and riders beat a quick retreat; and when the infantry were running eager to avenge the assasination of their comrades, the cut-throats of civilized warfare, were beyond their reach, frightened by a shell.

They found the butternut, and rolled his carcass

into the river—food for cat-fish. Long before this, La Scheme sought the plantation, at the door calling, "Leette! Leette! Quick —quick for your life!"

She met him, cool and collected, her eye flashing fire.

"What?"

"The gun-boats—the gun-boats!"

"I do not care, Kendal."

"They have been fired into. Don't you hear? They will shell your house. Didn't I tell you? Where is your horse? They will burn your house and take you prisoner. Let the corporal go. Save yourself."

"He is safe, and so am I,— Sam, get my horse,— Uncle, take care of the house, or run off, as you please.—I am going to stay and see it out."

"Leette! and ruin all my plans? Oh, Leette!"

She yielded again, and went with him—not a moment too soon. The gun-boat had the range, and a shell burst near the quarters. Old Aunty was coming out, and a fragment disemboweled the innocent burden-bearer—wronged from infancy, wronged in maturity, killed while being righted—free by the Proclamation, killed by a fragment of the Proclaimer's law-enforcer—free by the law of God; gone to heaven where the dead white guerilla could not go.

When the troops came all was as it had been abandoned, save that a shell had already fired the mansion. They completed the work and left but chimneys.

CHAPTER XXI

India has its jungle, Mexico and California their chaparral. Some vegetation never attempts to grow straight, shuns right lines as nature abhors a vacuum. Such is the mesquite. The laurel, too, emulates perfection in crookedness. A generic term exists in every language, which gives utterance to the idea obtained by contact with dense, luxuriant, tangled vegetation. There is such a thing as impenetrability without crooks or curves. In the South this is called cane-brake.

Suppose a field, a farm, or a county, covered with newspapers—the New York Tribune, Times, and Herald; add the London Star, Times, and News. Let every letter—capital, italic, little, big, cypher, or figure—grow straight into a bamboo cane, one, five, ten, or thirteen feet high. That is a slight comparison with the canes growing in a wild Southern forest. A small cane-brake is of little account as an obstacle; very valuable to the grazier, whose cattle winter on the green fodder—growing fat, while

Northern relations are shivering over dried grass or meadow hay. A small cane-brake is of no more account than a few cypress trees. The mourning cypress, the base of whose trunk is a swollen bulb ; a gigantic lily on top of the ground, whose flower-stock has no leaves, whose flower has no garment ; its net-work of veins and fibres standing stiff and stark in the air, like an inverted umbrella without silk covering. The tree which stands to other trees, as the ancient mariner to other men—

—— "Lean, and lank, and long,
As is the ribbed sea sand."

But when a cypress swamp and its concomitants is populated by a cane-brake and its entanglements, there is no likeness save to itself. It remains unique, alone,—a cane-brake in a cypress swamp. It is a jungle, yet not a jungle ; a chaparral, yet not a chaparral ; it is a canebrake in a cypress swamp, which, to be appreciated, must not only be seen, but where one must be lost and feel the sensation of trying to get out.

In three minutes Leette's horse passed the cleared land and entered the cane-brake. Not the dense mass described, any more than a forest of oaks means the California live oak, girding thirty or fifty feet. Little scrubby cane—pipe-stems, with macaroni limbs and vermicelli branches ; the poniard-leaf, long or short, always narrow, always brittle, and suggesting stabbing. Then came a slough—a low bottom, where were scattering cypresses ; then higher land, where was a cane-brake. Leette had darted before and left her companion.

La Scheme followed. To his animal the distance was a ten-minute task. On entering the wood he lost her. His first suspicion, James Manet. La Scheme believed in will-power. He conceived himself the master of any woman, of Leette. Abandoning the excitement of passing events, he drew in those tenaculæ of mind which perceive; the antennæ of the soul which, snail horns, abstract sensation from the atmosphere; concentrated his vital electricity on Leette, and willed her return.

An half-hour passed, during which he gave his animal freedom from the rein, and permitted him to choose his own way. Exerting one intense current of thought, sending the command to the flying woman, "Come back." Lapse of time did not discourage, only gave proof of that power which drove her on. He believed an actual contest pending—a battle going on between the invisible antagonisms of will. He knew he would conquer. When assurance came, as it did to his mind—self-deceived perhaps,—when he experienced a relief of tension, he said to himself, "She is coming," and then gave attention to the place whither his horse had borne him.

It was a Robin Hood's nest in the forest. He paused under an enormous cottonwood, permitting his horse to graze while he looked around him. The mind, freed from bolts and bars, took in nature, and he relieved himself by talking aloud:

"This *populus monilifera* is magnificent. Ages

on ages must have passed since it was a feathery
seed, borne on the wind. Perhaps, left by the flood
of old Mississippi, when Cæsar was a boy and Mark
Anthony a baby. There is the *quercus alba* and
prinos. I wish you were staunch and copper-
fastened; loaded with ordnance for Vicksburg.
God! what a hard time there is before them, ignorant how these Yankees can fight. *Ulmus alatus,*
winged-elm; no great value; but I love you because
you are of the South. There is the liquid-amber
styracifua and the *myessa multiflora*—sweet and sour
gum; and you, Mr. Hackberry, *celtis mississippien-
sis,*—cord-wood: Oh, wouldn't the Federals be glad
to have you to make steam! You are a nettle-tree.
Had you been known to the Romans and Greeks,
they would have planted you in hell for switches for
young devils. The furies would have no need of
snakes, crowned by your thorns. What a wood-yard
Leette might make of *fraxinus americana, pubescens,
viridis,*—ash—red, white, and green; no matter
whether dry or just cut. She is the one; burnt her
whole wood-yard to keep it from the dyed wretches."
As if a moment of relenting came over him, he
paused: "Good girl. Loves me. Nothing but a
woman. I must sacrifice her. Too smart; would
be a tyrant when I relaxed the rein. I will use
her well, and put her out of the way. This is the
flood of fortune's tide, and I must make my fortune.
Men are dying by thousands. What matters the
life of one woman!"

The tall trees stood thickly, twining branch among

16

branches, shutting out the clouds, the sun, and sky.
Their tops, a firmament, supported by living pillars,
whose base was a distinct creation, or rather a chaos,
the wildest of the untamed thickets of the American
bottom. An impenetrable wilderness of leaves above,
a similar wilderness below, trunks between, like telegraph poles, save in size. The cane was impregnable; nature's abattis, straight, contorted, interlaced,
interwoven, twisted and twined, over, under, betwixt,
around, between, by climbing woodbine, thorny vine,
morning glory, wild grape, and gorgeous with the
trumpet creeper. Up to his head, above his horse,
sitting in his saddle, he could not reach the height of
the tangled mass of living leaves and flowers. The
peculiar cane-brake of the South; and this was the
haunt of guerillas, accessible by one narrow path
leading through.

Another half-hour, Leette came. He did not say,
I knew you would come; she did not tell him what
feeling prompted her to seek him here. Both felt a
need: he to command, she, the want and willingness
to obey. Neither asked Why? Strong minds anxious to know, prefer to wait rather than question,
when thereby they fear to manifest weakness.

Leette spoke first:

"I went back to watch them. They have burnt
every thing. Broken down my arbor, killed my
hogs, my tame cows, taken my mules, my poultry,
my fodder, my corn; what they have not taken they
have burned; what they have not burned they have
destroyed. They found the thousand bales of Con-

federate cotton, and almost took me. Oh! if I could
have burned it," patting the neck of her racer,
" poor Janie, good Janie. Janie saved me." The
mare curved her lithe, beautiful neck, proud of the
caress of her mistress. La Scheme continued silent,
waiting. Leette's mannner repressed emotion, which
burst out, " I wish I was a devil. I'd torment the
dyed brutes ! They fired at me ; ordered me to halt,
and fired at me. The fiends ! I'd be willing to die
to send them all to hell. God Almighty ! how I hate
them ! "

This was La Scheme's opportunity. Her mind
was ready. For such a state of soul he had been
waiting. " Leette," said he, " Are you woman
enough to consecrate your life to vengeance ? Dare
you swear to live only to punish and revenge until the
South shall be free ? "

She answered, " I dare."

" If I will find you opportunities, will you give me
your solemn word and oath, to be true, to be secret,
to be faithful even to death ? Never to flinch, never
to waver, to endure torture without confession, to
suffer without a word, to look danger and death
face to face for the sake of vengeance ? Can you ?
will you ? "

Again she answered " Yes,"

" Leette, I have been seeking a woman of great
character, energy, and will. You are such a one.
Shall I prove my confidence by initiating you into a
secret band, of which you are now to know no more
than that I am a member, a chief, and have the
power."

She answered, " Yes."

He continued: " Every step has its test and its oath. When your courage fails you cease to progress, and no future mystery will be revealed ; while the knowledge gained amounts to no more than an opportunity to join an organization of which you know one member. Have you will to proceed ? "

She answered, " I have."

" Dismount, and I will test your courage."

He never followed the same primary initiation twice. The persons he used were bound to him by test oaths other than those of common and universal existence over the South. He was able, by his powerful memory, to hold every individual sworn to him by chains of iron; that infinity of memory which carries a consciousness of ten thousand acts of numberless persons — as mother earth remembers its myriad fields of ripening grain, forgetting no stalk, no beard, no grain of barley, oats, or wheat.

Standing on the ground, he took her arm, unbuttoned her sleeve, rolled it deliberately to her shoulder, clasped it above the elbow with a firm thumb and forefinger until the small purple veins stood clearly under the white skin; then he let it loose. She held steadily where he left the arm extended in the air. He then took from his pocket a small flask, unscrewed its tumbler-top, gave it her to hold, and renewed his grasp. When crimson blood again revealed its channel, he drew from a secret hiding place a dagger; with its point pierced the tissue, opened the vein, from which warm life spirted in a continuous flow. Whilst jetting its bright crimson on the ground, he fastened his eyes keenly on her face, watching for a quiver of a muscle, or a change of color. Satisfied, he took the little goblet and caught a measure of blood; then, removing his hand, suffered the wound to exhaust itself in slow drops. Leette's countenance seemed to ask, "Well, what now?" He spoke, saying:

"You are not afraid of blood. It is well. Follow me in the words I speak. When your courage falters, stop. With you, always, rests the command ' Proceed!' I admit no weak, hesitating follower."

"Thou Beginner of all things,—Elemental source of life,—Disposer of all secondary causes,—Life of the sun,—Substance of the earth,—Spirit of the air,—Pervader of water,—recognizing Thy presence in this blood, and hailing Thee, by the name common to mortal tongues, I invoke Thy recording ear, oh, God!"

Leette repeated every word. As his thumb and forefinger had been on her arm, his glance pressed on her eye to catch the shock of each new idea. Speaking as to an echo; waiting until both call and echo had printed on the air,—the photograph, which travels into the limitless space; where sound waits in patience the day when every idle word that man has spoken shall come in witnessing judgment; summoned by the great, prosecuting Attorney of heaven's tribunal, to confront the prisoner at the bar, thus: "Here am I. Remember! Thou didst speak me." Gazing, waiting; his scrutiny was satisfactory, and he proceeded

"You are a true daughter of the South; love its mountains, glens, hills, valleys, plains, and majestic rivers, above all the rest of the world. You love its institutions: particularly the ancient, patriarchal institution of slavery; given by God to Abraham, confirmed by Moses, and sealed in Solomon. You believe slavery the true foundation of civil, social, and moral existence—designed to equalize the relationship of daily life, and, passing beyond the grave, to reach ultimate perfection in the eternal future; that the throne of God is established on the principle of servitude; God, himself, the alone Emperor of created and uncreated worlds—obedient to the eternal principle of master and slave. Do you so believe?"

Leette replied, "I do." He continued:

"You also believe color a test of capacity; that nobility of endowment is found alone in the white race, who are by nature rulers of the world, and that a select few of the white race are designed to bear dominion and rule—to whom belong the land power, wealth, and slaves of the world. This you also believe?"

Leette again answered, "I do." He continued:

"You believe the many—people of every nation, clime, and color—ought to be the slaves of the ruling class; without right to knowledge, education, wealth, or power; to be ruled without right to vote, or govern themselves; and you are one of the ruling class. This you believe?"

She answered, "Yes."

"Then declare: All who oppose, by thought, word, or action, my right, and the right of my class, are my enemies."

Leette answered, "I declare them my enemies." He added:

"Swear to follow and trample them under your feet."

Leette replied, "I swear."

"Now repeat this oath after me. 'I will recognize and obey the orders of my superiors. I will offer to the glory of my country, and the success of these principles, my life. None of the so-called treasures of the heart—neither of home, love, honor, modesty, chastity, or purity—shall for an instant check me; but be offered willingly, if thereby advantage may be gained for the cause of the South; and thereby be established in the Western world the time-honored·institutions of the past."

Then La Scheme, taking a small book from his pocket, opened at a blank leaf. Handing it to Leette, he took the measure containing her blood. Into this he dipped a gold pen, and, giving it, said:

"Write the words, 'I swear,' and sign your name. In thus doing you sign your own death-warrant. The space left blank will remain until you shall have revealed a secret, or violated an oath, or turned traitoress. Then shall be written the sentence of a secret tribunal,—which shall be executed, even to opening your heart, and writing from that inkstand the word 'Fulfilled.' Do you hesitate?"

"This is my answer." She wrote rapidly, in a clear, running hand, "I swear,—

"LEETTE LEDONC."

Making, also, that little scroll which is now put on legal documents in place of a seal. Saying, when it was done, "You have said no word against our enemies the Yankees."

"Girl!" said La Scheme, "Why are you not a woman! Our enemy is a principle, and those influenced by it. I am a Yankee. You, and all members of this league, see in this war now raging more than a simple struggle for the Union. We have enemies in the South. We have valuable friends in the North; men who will, when we have gained the victory, bring every state to become a member of the Golden Circle. But hold! Before I make any developments — give either signs or pass-words, or reveal any secrets—you must take the anathema. Repeat it with me."

"I will obey, though obedience cost all that I hold dear : that which is dearer than life, eternal salvation. To that end may I be anathema maranatha, if I refuse, and I call on the curses to curse me.

"Cursed be my body; cursed be my mind; cursed be my soul; let all that has power to pain, blight, scorch, and sere, unite and curse my morning, noon, and night—make my morning misery, my noon agony, my night torture,—make my sleep torment, my dreams hell; give me a broken back, withered and limping limbs, an aching tooth, a smarting eye, a parched throat, and a sore ear; fever in the blood and madness in the brain; take from me the love of my friends; give me to the dogs of my enemies; hide the star of hope; make me a contempt, an astonishment, a hissing, a desolation—downtrodden, spit on, fed with swine, bedded with beasts. May eternity curse my soul with the heat of damnation, make my love hate, my bliss blackness, my memory blistering, my reason distraction; my strength weakness; powerful to suffer; dying, yet never dead; living, yet never alive. Torture me with the fire never quenched; gnashing of teeth, wailing and weeping; revenge never accomplished; fury impotent; frenzy insatiable. Give me a useless hope of forgiveness, and a tempting view of heaven lost forever. Thus let me be anathema maranatha, if I do not obey. Amen."

"You have sworn. Your motives are high and pure. There remains another oath:

"My country's friend is my friend, her enemy my enemy. I will not bear ill-will, hatred, nor revenge in my heart; neither will I lift my hand against my most bitter personal foe, while he is the friend of the Southern Confederacy; her friends, though my enemies, though they may have wronged me in my nearest and dearest feelings, though worthy of death for their deeds, shall still be mine. I will forgive them, I will protect them, I will feed, care for. and bless them, I will watch over them by night, I will guard them by day. And if in this I fail, may the curse of curses accompany me in overwhelming agony, and I be damned, damned and thrice damned."

Then he raised his dagger, holding the little drop of fast blackening blood in the other hand.

"I swear, if unauthorized, you reveal this inter-view, or word of mine to any soul on earth, you shall meet punishment. Hands you know not shall strike the blow, ears you dream not in existence shall hear your tongue, penalties you are not yet permitted to know shall be enforced, in witness whereof——"

He held his dagger in imprecation toward heaven, raised the tiny goblet, and drank her blood!

"——You have freely given allegiance. You have no choice, you must obey. Once having laid hand to the plow, never look back. When you tremble, let another bolder go forward, going die in the furrow."

Leette replied, "Do you think your oath startles me? No!!! My word of honor is better than all the oaths you can invent. Oh! I hate them so! I wish I had that live one here! I tell you I would tear his heart out with my teeth in less time than you would kill him! I love you because you hate them."

"And I have made you swear, because I know you so well. You would do as every Southern woman would: let the enemy know you are an enemy, and put him on his guard. That is the act of a fool. You must conceal hate. I have chosen you, because I know that you can conceal that hate, and deceive them; can lure them on, until they are beyond hope, and then, push them over, laughing while they dis-cover who did it. You have to learn, and I know you are capable, the intense satisfaction produced by consciousness of doing, of saving your country, when none but yourself know your effectual work. In-deed, you must conceal your agency. You must seem to be inconsistent to every principle, while you are sublimely consistent to the idea of your labor. This is the reestablishing of aristocratic monarchial government in America. The democratic idea is a fallacy. Every man who so believes is our friend. We must use him, even if he is armed to fight us. The North has more aristocrats than the South. Of these, many wage the bitterest war : but the best is, that our fastest friends are those democrats who pride themselves on their democracy, our fastest friends would be our worst foes if they knew. You must understand all this before you can be of the greatest possible use. When our enemies play into our hands, we win a double victory."

" I can do all you desire without an oath."

" Leette, tried in doubt, danger, and death, you are true, else I would never trust you. Your heart and soul is with the Confederacy, or I had never loved [bah ! of what material was his love ?] and honored you with this confidence. Believe me, I understand and appreciate all your great qualities, honor and esteem and worship them. Yet, it often becomes necessary for a man engaged in great enterprises, to do many things inconsistent with his professions and his principles ; acts which render him subject to the charge of—worse than ingratitude, worse than meanness, worse than criminality. To guard against any possible danger of the impulses of your mind, when you should for any reason get angry with me, I have laid on your soul the binding power of an oath. You have willingly entered its sacred limit, hedged

yourself for time and eternity within its eternal wall
of obligation, and are no longer bound merely by
what you now regard a pleasant duty, but by the necessity of almighty responsibility, and implicit self-
imposed obedience, unquestioning, unhesitating, even
when disagreable and hateful. More than this, you
are now a member of an organization. This imposes
new duties and new responsibilities, which reach
beyond our individual selves, over-top our loves, our
hates, and compel us to lose our own likes and dis-
likes in the general good. There are elements of
destruction sufficient to destroy the whole North; but
they are useless because unorganized. The essential
element of success is secresy. Now that you are
bound to secresy, not only by consciousness of an
oath, but by the bond of secret organization you
have that whereon to think. I am inclined, yes I
will give you more, I will test your honesty, honor,
and faithfulness, by telling you I never shall marry
you. What I have told you of marrying a Yankee,
I shall exact for the benefit of the country. I do
not attempt to conceal or deceive, I do not fear you
nor your anger. More eyes than mine watch, and
will compel you to fulfil. But I know you better
than you know yourself. From this time forth you
must be like myself, dedicated to your country.
Think, when I sought you first, I won your love as a
woman, in order that I might consecrate your soul
to the cause of patriotism. You gave me your heart
expecting to be married. I test that heart by a
higher and more powerful ordeal than common

woman can endure. Will you bo faithful when your lover immolates you and his own love on the altar? Think!"

CHAPTER XXII

"Shall I introduce you, Miss Ledonc?"

"No. I am a stranger,—a rebel. I want to be left alone."

Leette has come, in obedience, to Memphis. She is here in the loyal, squelched secessionist family, where La Scheme has consigned a fiery, passionate brain, maddened by the word "think." What has she not thought! Every thought has been a boiling bubble in her mind-cauldron, bursting to scald—falling into the fused thought-mass, to bubble, burst, and scald again.

Who am I? Leette Ledonc. Where am I? In the South. I was happy; l was rich; I had a home; I had a country; I had a character; I had a lover. What am I? God Almighty! and oaths which the unwilling ear had stopped out—but the obedient recording sound waves answering nature's law had left their earotype—came in awful succession, pattering intense footsteps on the roof of her tongue, which education, as a lady, ordered to halt, and forbade to vibrate and echo in the ears of others. Still, they

were palpable to the stern recording angel, as each
fused type of passion knocked and pounded on the
door barred by propriety.

She had lost faith—faith in herself, and faith in
the man to whom she had given the disposable self,
God gives to every woman. Divided and thrown
away—her soul—that she had left—was so uneasy,
so lost, so alone, as to be of value — less than
nothing; at sea with nothing at the helm, without a
rudder; without a God, save as innate necessity for
religion gave meaning to the oath, "G—d d—m."

The lady of the house called another lady by a
gesture which Leette had never seen but once before.
The signal, repeated, told Leette she was not alone
in a secret. Repeating the same, and adding still
another, the young lady came direct and sat beside
her, saying:

"I am very glad to see you. When did you ar-
rive?"

"An hour ago. Do you live here?"

"No. I am here" [a sign which Leette again
recognized] "to spend the evening. I had orders to
be present."

"What is the token!"

"Obedience without question."

"Do you ask or seek explanation?"

"The heart, consecrated to a great work, never
questions—only 'What shall I do?'"

"What is the work to-night?"

"I know not. It matters not. When it comes it
will be done."

" The penalty ? "

" Death."

Leette had more food for thought. There was something which she did not understand. Soon after, drawn from her thought by a movement,— they were in a recess where the lady of the house had left her,—whither this member of the secret band had gone, she asked :

" Who is that officer ? "

" General Solenter. He has recently returned from an expedition down the river."

" He burnt my plantation, gin, and quarters. It was his gang that stole my cotton. Vengeance ! "
The other lady placed her arm around her.

" Your name is Leette Ledonc. I am to meet you here."

" Who told you ? '

" Kendal La Scheme."

" You know him ? "

" I am to be his wife."

" Wife ! "

" I am ordered to tell you that none are worthy to govern a kingdom who cannot govern themselves. The vengeance of fury is impotent. Be calm and obey."

Leette was silent. Comprehension of the genius of the man who had become her master flashed, and she, too proud to obey a woman, remained silent until another figure passing made her ask :

" Who is that ? "

" The Adjutant General Hardone."

" Charles Hardone."

" What do you know of him ? "

" Is that woman his wife ? " ˉ

" No. His intended, Miss Sandison, daughter of the banker. She came here to nurse that old man yonder, Mr. Wirtman, the cashier. Everyone respects him. Miss Sandison devotes her time to hospitals and cares for the wounded. One of these immaculate Yankees. Her lover is very faithful."

" I will tempt and win him from her. Come with me."

Will—what is it ? Purposeless;—with a purpose. Time past, absolutely lost. Time future, pregnant with the results of earnest, persistent labor; a point, a line divides purposeless from purpose. What is will ?

Leette went to her chamber. There at her disposal were garments adapted to adorn and enhance her natural beauty. Leette selected from these, those adapted to her style of beauty, with unerring judgment. A slave performed menial offices, and she consulted her companion on disputed questions of toilet and taste. Engaged in the Eleusinian mysteries, she loosed her tongue from the stiff formalities of indifference, made a virtue of necessity, and took the leaguer of secret oaths into the sisterhood of a common confidence, the sympathy of common rebellion, telling her the story of her wrong, and her will to be revenged. Leette did not tell how La Scheme had trampled on her love, never ! no, never ! Leette had not asked the meaning of the firm set of her lip, the

17

gritting of her teeth, when this other, by the word
wife told of La Scheme's perfidy. It meant revenge—without answer or even question, when,
where or how—revenge on some one, on something,
revenge in its first burst, in its full fury, was directed
on the burner of her house, on the invader of her
state, on the successful Yankee. As for La Scheme,
there was a suspension of feeling; a question whether he was false. Let him if he dare. She was his
master, he might. think otherwise; that will which he
had conquered was able to master him or any one.
Knowledge of his present plans, the will to thwart
them, made him her slave. In an instant, Leette
Ledone had become the woman Kendal La Scheme
had discovered, the Hazael who had evil concealed in
her nature to qualify her to be a devil, Jezebel.

When Leette, adorned with the best and latest
of the fashions—the first time since the war commenced,—saw herself in the drawing-room mirror,
she was strangely startled. Never before had that
Leette been seen in a looking-glass. The inner woman asked, "Who am I?" Thought, "Ah! I
remember. Good-bye, Leette. Good-bye forever."

The lady rose, astonished. Some Southern women
would not resume the fashions because their rebel
sisters were reduced to single skirts and dresses.
Fashion belonged to the North. The South disdained
the Northern fashion. Leette in pride had rejected,
but now resumed, these garments, which transformed
her into a regal beauty.

Leette went to her entertainer, by proud manner

freezing any word which surprise or courtesy might
have prompted; took, as of right, the chief seat.
With a gesture of command seated the lady who had
been with her at her side; then entered with skill
and easy self-possession into conversation. First,
saying to the lady:

"Bring the General here. Do not let him know
I wish to see him. You may say my plantation has
been destroyed by Federal soldiers, and I am a
Union woman."

The lady of the house found General Solenter in
conversation with Alina Sandison, Mr. Wirtman, and
his adjutant. Addressing him, she said:

"General, you have never seen one of our Southern belles. A young lady, whose plantation you
burned on your last raid down the river, has come
through the lines and sought refuge with me. I
have persuaded her to come down this evening, and I
would like to introduce you, if you have no objections."

"She must be a rebel. Has she taken the oath
of allegiance? If she is as beautiful as you describe, she may be more dangerous than a regiment."

"Oh, yes; she is a good Unionist. She has been
under the cloud of circumstances, as have we all.
She was born South. Her home was here until you
burned it, and now she has to seek safety elsewhere.
I think she has the proper protection papers. If
she has not, I ask you, as a gentleman, to assist
her."

Taking his arm, she drew the general away. On

his part, turning to his friends, he invited them to
come.   Mr. Wirtman declined; but the adjutant
general, putting Lina's hand in his arm, followed.
A general without his adjutant general is a house
without a wife.   Passing through the drawing-room
door, the splendid beauty of Leette Ledone came as
does sunlight on the eye when emerging from some
subterranean cavern.

"Is not she magnificent!   That is beauty.   Lina,
I have heard of Southern beauty.   I have seen it.
You do no know my contempt for all the females I
have seen South.   They fell below my imagination.
So much is written of Southern beauty, I had con-
ceived a grand ideal—a perfect woman.   I was so
disappointed.   This equals my grandest expectation.
Isn't she perfect?   What an eye!"

"She seems to me too queenly, Charlie.   I have a
choking sensation as I look at her.   See that mouth!
It is unrelenting.   She could kill her enemy.   I hope
she will never hate me."

"I wonder who she can be.   What a grand presence she has!   Solenter is fairly broken up.   Bully!
Wont I have the joke on him!   Let us go and find
out who she is."

Leette had no intention of knowing Charles Hardone at present.   Taking the general's arm, she led
him in her promenade away from the place where the
two were standing, and so averted the threatened introduction.   Before she met the general, she had
requested her lady friend to perform on the piano
until she should stop her promenade.   That lady

asked to be excused: "Play for Federals—for miserable Yankees? No! Her harp was on the willows." In reply, Leette said, "None are worthy to govern a kingdom who cannot command themselves. The vengeance of fury is impotent. Be calm and obey."

When Leette took the general's arm, this young lady, turning to the mistress, said, "Ask me to play, and take no denial." The hostess proposed music; invited others, who successively refused, and then asked this one. She entered upon that line of excuses every lady-performer has by heart, until a quick, imperious glance from Leette recalled her to obedience, when she arose and sitting at the instrument, ran a prelude upon the keys—such as an accomplished woman who has had no servile labor to stiffen her delicate fingers, who has had harp-strings and mother-of-pearl keys from infancy, can instinctively perform—a combination of memory-thoughts without words; now wailing, now triumphant; soft on occasion, then increasing to victory. Forgetting herself in her music, she fought the battle of the Confederacy on the keys before her—skirmishing the attack, charging on the double-quick, thundering the repulse, mourning the dead; weaving in snatches of old lessons and old songs—the "Marseillaise of Freedom"; "The Mocking Bird of the South," and "The Bonnie Blue Flag, that bears a single Star."

Lina Sandison, repelled [instinct] by Leette, had no anxiety for acquaintance. The promenade removed the event. This music drew the attention of Charlie, who was an enthusiast. Together the two, pledged to be one, stood listening; drawn near the piano, to lose no single note of the varied harmony so lavishly shed in obedience to command.

This was Leette's time. Advancing in her walk until she stood behind the performer with the general; heedless of the music; near enough to be heard by Charlie and Lina; she said to the general:

"I was not to blame for the act of the guerillas."

"They killed five of my men, and wounded twenty. I am not responsible for the results that followed. Had I known you were a good Union lady, I should have spared your mansion and quarters. The orders are very strict, and must be obeyed. There is no other way of preventing this outrage. Open warfare is legitimate; but to ambuscade a transport, and kill as do those assassins, is not justified by any laws of civilized warfare."

"You do not know who you may injure in this indiscriminate destruction. I do not care so much for myself in this instance as for one of your own Union soldiers who had been taken in a skirmish by the guerillas and left at my house. I took care of him myself. The best Yankee I ever saw, gentle, patient and brave—a hero. I learned to love him. He told me his history. How he loved his mother! I think his father was dead, and she had married again."

Leette saw her arrow had struck. Lina Sandison's attention had been gained. Leette put her hand on the player's shoulder, and she ceased, turning partly from the instrument. Leette fixed her eye on the General, directing her conversation to him, not losing a movement of either Charles Hardone or his intended: "Poor fellow! He had been wounded in his right arm, had been ridden down and ribs were broken; his shoulder was injured, I think dislocated, a sabre cut had lain open his temple, and his head was otherwise bruised. The most dreadful sight you ever saw. I nursed him until he was nearly well; his wound had closed up and he became the good looking man he was. I think his brother had been shot somewhere in Arkansas. I had to coax him back to life, for he did not care to live. Poor fellow," she used the word as if it agreed with her feeling, and drew a deep sigh, "he had been disappointed in love. A noble man; none but a Northern woman would or could have trampled on such affection."

Lina without introduction, interested, by premonition, asked, "What was his name?"

Leette, turning full upon her, answered, "James Manet."

"What became of him?" asked Hardone.

"The shell from the gun boat which set my house on fire, burst near his bed, threw a beam on his body, and he was burnt to death."

"Horrible!"

"Perhaps you knew him?" This to Lina. To the General, "Are these acquaintances of yours?"

"Excuse me Miss Ledone, permit me,—this is Miss Sandison."

"Her first name?"

" Alina," answered Charlie.

" That cannot be, the one was called Allie."

" Your friend seems moved," said Leette coldly. To the performer, " Did you ever play ' The Battle of Prague ? ' " She answered,

" So long ago I have forgotten. Miss Ledone, Adjutant Hardone is a performer, and a beautiful singer. Persuade him to sing something for us."

"General," said Leette, with a bewitching smile, the Adjutant is under your orders. Will you issue one for the benefit of the company ?"

" Perhaps, Miss Ledone, a request from one lovely as yourself—one who has sheltered and nursed a friend of Lieut. Hardone, for Manet was an intimate friend before the war—may be more powerful than a command."

" A friend of yours !" offering her hand to the Adjutant. " Then you must be a friend of mine. James Manet was as fine a Yankee as I ever met. You must have loved him. I loved him. Will you sing for me Adjutant ?"

Allie Sandison did not wait to hear what reply her betrothed would make. She knew certainly that James was dead. His foster-father was in the next room. To him she would break this news.

" Why does Miss Sandison leave us ?" asked Leette.

" James Manet's father is in that room," answered the General. " When Miss Sandison came among us, it was at the request of Manet's mother, Mr. Wirtman being very sick. Miss Sandison had a charge for this same Manet."

"Ah," interrupted Leette, "I may have touched a tender cord. Was Manet a Corporal?"

"Adjutant, what was Manet?"

"A Corporal, when he enlisted. Oh, it is the same, I have no doubt. Lina feels badly. His sister Lilly and she were great friends, before Lilly died. I think Lilly gave her some charge for him. Lina would have saved his life if he had been in the hospital; she is a glorious nurse. She saved old Wirtman's life. I am sorry for Mrs. Wirtman. James was her idol. Such is war. Poor fellow! he had hard luck."

Miss Ledone prompts the pianist, "Adjt. Hardone is not only a singer, he is a composer. He has songs of all kinds."

"Really, Miss Ledone, you must excuse me, I have a very bad cold. I could not do justice to my voice to-night."

"Now Adjutant, said Leette, coquetishly, "you would not refuse *me*. I am not accustomed to denial, and perhaps I will promise to grant your request when you are very much in earnest."

"On such conditions I cannot refuse. But what shall I sing?"

"Love! love! We have the reality of war. Sing of love; an old song, one you made before there was any war, when we were all brothers. Did you make songs then?"

Leette looked into his face with an earnest, innocent question, as if the deep woman was not scheming to measure his soul, to fathom the amount of pain this death of an old friend, who had relinquished his opportunity to gain a woman's love, abandoned it in his favor when the right was certainly disputable, the pain this death gave him.

"I did sometimes think I was a poet then, but since I have been ashamed of my early efforts, and have almost forgotten them."

"How can you say so. You are too proud. You cannot forget. Do now, General, (flattering) sing us one of those old love songs."

Thus urged, Hardone seated himself and sang the same song, the same air, that James Manet heard when he relinquished claim to Allie Sandison's love. Allie Sandison, now a true woman, heard those words, that chorus—

> Love's sweet tone, love alone,
> Proving that though time roll by,
> Love can never die,

and the evening before the war came back into her mind as a picture. The sofa, the piano—her piano, Charlie singing, his abrupt invitation, her answer, the good-night, and that No so clear that James' voice seemed in her ear. Then the good-bye in the church yard. Henry dead, James, both dead. Lilly Sue gone, and James Manet loved her, and went to the war because he loved her; killed, too, when a prisoner, by a shell from one of our own gun-boats. She remembered her dream.

"Beautiful, beautiful," exclaimed Leette. "You are a poet. You must sing often to me."

At this moment, Kendal La Scheme came to the general and shook hands cordially with him.

"Who is that man?" asked Leette.

"One of our cotton speculators."

"Is that so?"

"Yes. Very successful. He has made a million of dollars."

"Will you introduce me? I have cotton to sell."

"You, cotton to sell! How much? I can help you."

"Is it possible! How fortunate! You know I have lost everything save a few bales of cotton, which are hidden away to keep the Confederates from burning them. If you will be so kind as to show me what I am to do, you will put me under the greatest obligations which I shall be most happy to repay."

General Solenter speaking to Leette says:

"Miss Ledone, permit me to make you acquainted with Mr. La Scheme." She bowed most distantly, then moved away with Charles Hardone.

"One of these aristocrats who think the ground too good for their feet," said La Scheme.

"Or perhaps you are too good a Union man," suggested the general.

"I do not know. She may have some cotton somewhere. Then she will talk to me if I show the greenbacks. Money buys them all, General. She wouldn't be bad to take, eh, General?"

CHAPTER XXIII.

A woman, really fallen, is nearer the devil than a fallen man. Leette hated herself because she loved La Scheme. Hated him because he had deceived her. Yet loved him because he hated the Yankees. Admired him for his manly physique; was fascinated by his animal magnetism. Yea, verily, wept for vexation in her thought-moments, because she had to love. She acknowledged to herself that he might trample, discard, neglect; yet would, could not but love him. This galled her pride, and tears brought no relief. She took vengeance on her own weakness by revenge on others. How a proud heart is cauterized by seeing itself read, understood, and applauded by the one of all others it would deceive! Yet, even in this comes consolation.

La Scheme avoided Leette's presence in person; making care for her comfort keep an unseen presence in constant memory. The lady of the League took her home.

" How long have you known Mr. La Scheme ? " Leette asked when they were in their apartments.

"Since Memphis was taken. Not until very recently has he formed the League. Very few are permitted to enter, lest all should not be true. You, chosen to danger, are appointed to command; we to obey. Visitors will come to see you; each of whom will leave a parcel, which must be passed safely through the lines. Ignorance tells no tales. Most of those who come here will know you only by the sympathy of rebellion. You must do the rest. Kendal has great confidence in those he cuts away and sends abroad to pilot their own course. I know you are a pilot since last night."

"I am a pilot—captain and men to spare. La Scheme is right."

The mansion of Leette's friends had been erected by cultivated taste, regardless of expense; had been furnished after its master and mistress returned from travel in foreign parts, where they came in contact with every appliance of elegant life and luxurious ease. Its pictures were painted by masters of olden time; were paid for with the wages of men and women, and by the sale of their children. Its carpets were soft as down; its library adorned with elegant editions of standard works. Music and art were not neglected. The owner of thousands of human beings and large plantations, in Tennessee, Mississippi, and Arkansas, had all that heart could wish. Why not? The garden was beautiful as Eden. Prolific in shrubbery; box-wood borders; roses, whose fragrance and name was legion; climbing, twining woodbines; grapes; honey-suckles;

hedges of evergreen; magnolias and peach-trees; annuals and perennials; and the fairy, spidery crape-myrtle; evergreens trimmed into polygons and diamonds. All this without sacrificing the green lawn. A conservatory, a small fountain, wide walks, narrow paths, a summer-house, an arbor, bee-hives,— all of these, and more, were arranged with skill by lavish expense of labor and exquisite taste. A flower of the Spice Islands transplanted.

What a home those wealthy Southerners had! Nature opened a full lap and besought them to adorn life with beauty. God gave them the richest, most glorious part of the Union. They cursed it first with slavery, then with rebellion. Satan and his angels fell from heaven.

Such a home La Scheme gave Leette Ledonc, as a base of operations. Master and mistress were her slaves. The gentleman she called Uncle was an absent rebel. The lady she called Aunt, the young ladies she called Cousins, were too bitter secesh to open shutters or doors to the invader. Leette threw everything open. They would not complain of soldiers, whose taste for beauty picked flowers and evergeens (with the license of children on May-day) in a rebel's garden. A few regiments of lovers of nature would pick all the flowers in Paradise. If that Paradise was in rebellion, would trample the borders, break down the plants, ruin the walks, and make the Garden of Eden a desert. Leette would not complain, would do better—obtain a guard which should protect the premises and her contraband or war. A bold woman, Leette, to beard the lion in his den. Many an old man has lost his spectacles over his nose.

To this end Leette prepared an entertainment of the rarest viands, exhausting the sutler's stock of delicacies and the wines of the wholesale dealer. It would not cost more than one bale of cotton. Everything was skillfully prepared by servants, who were personally attached to those who loaned them to accomplish the mission entrusted to her care.

General Solenter and staff were special guests, treated with distinguished consideration. No one obnoxious to the federals was permitted to be present. No one whose hatred to the Yankees was beyond control, who could not hide and conceal contempt and scorn, so deep it could not slip from the eye or curl on the lip, was invited. A sort of living torture, where the victim is self-immolated.

In the beautiful, glorious sunset, she led them to easy seats on the colonnaded portico, whence they could look over the broad river, glistening with gold, to the opposite bank; before them the treasure of art, and still more distant the wild realm of trees, rolling their forest of green, in long waves, toward the setting sun. A slave brought a box of fragrant cigars, and the gentlemen were left to enjoy their ease.

On her return, the General, feeling that glow of enjoyment, compounded of good feeding, good drinking, good smoking, coolness after a tropical day, fell into the trap set so deftly.

"This is magnificent! Such scenery! Such luxuriance! Such beauty! I could live here forever.
No wonder your people love their homes. I should
fight for them if in your places.

Leette quietly pointed to the fence, which had
been torn off for fuel, and through which, as if by her
orders, certainly for her benefit, two soldier boys
made entrance to the garden, pulled some flowers,
and quietly looked at the General on the piazza.

Volunteer officers, who owe their position to ability,
to patriotic devotion to the cause of their country, who have won their spurs in fair fight, are res-
pected. These men were not afraid. When they
enlisted in his company, he had promised them a
sergeantcy for obtaining five men. This they had
done, and he violated his word. To be sure, he was
now general, but they knew him before he was even a
captain; and as their eyes caught sight of him in
magnificent ease, they cursed from the select vocabu-
lary of a soldier's oaths; ending each brimstony commendation with words like villain, rascal, and devil.

He heard no sound, but seeing their eyes, and
knowing their cause for hate, comprehended the sig-
nification of their low ejaculations. It angered
him, and Leette's look of silent comment on his power-
lessness [military despotism cannot bind the soul]
touched him to the quick. Gen. Solenter turned ab-
ruptly to his adjutant:

"Order a detail to do guard-duty on these premises to-morrow morning and continue the same until
further orders. You understand?"

Hardone looked at him with surprise; then at Leette: then at the soldiers, before he answered, "I do."

"Attend to it, then." To Leette he said, "If my men give you trouble let me know of it immediately. I will teach them to respect private property."

Leette could not keep joy from her eyes, though no action expressed emotion. In that cellar was concealed a hundred pounds of rifle powder, in her trunk a box of opium, in her wardrobe and drawers of the other ladies in the house, quinine, percussion caps, and other small but valuable articles. Each new day increased their store from the secret agents who were found and organized by Kendal La Scheme. No underground railroad was ever more successful, or transportation more safe.

He had formed a band of complotters on the basis of Alexander the Great. A mule loaded with—not gold, but cotton, entered. and was stabled in the patriotic city of New York. Secretly, by marks known to the initiated, articles of necessity had been concealed in barrels and boxes, shipped to various localities, from whence, by re-shipment, they found their way to Memphis. This was a commissariat from which the South was to obtain supplies, and the rebel army indispensable medicines, percussion caps, boots and shoes, and even clothing.

Every day, males on the outer line of brotherhood, passed into the hands of females, sworn only by their deadly hatred of the Yankees, over the counter, small parcels which were deftly hidden in their morning

18

purchases. Leette Ledone was placed here to super-
intend their passage through the lines.

By her first move, she obtained a guard. Of
course, no bulky articles could pass either way; but
at this time, as always, medicine was in great demand
both for the country and the army. At this time,
aided by the winter, holding Grant in check at Me-
ridian,—all along the course of the Yazoo from Old
river near Vicksburg, past the batteries at Haine's
Bluffs to Yazoo City and thence to Gen. Pemberton's
head-quarters, medicine was more necessary to the
comfort and life of the army than powder or boots
and shoes.

Leette's second move was a pleasant one to her.—
She had determined to wound and vex the Yankee
girl, to make her jealous, if no more ; if possible, to
destroy mutual confidence, break her heart. To that
end the smiles of a coquette were lavished : La
Scheme's lessons in will power, the animal electricity,
which every strong will can exert, coupled with tempting female display, was thrown around the Adjutant
General who was fool enough to believe himself the
fascinator, who had no more principle than to go
willingly into the meshes of the human spider.

"Enter not into the path of the wicked, and go not
in the way of evil. Avoid it, pass not by it, turn
from it and pass away. The lips of a strange woman
drop as a honeycomb and her mouth is smoother than
oil. But her end is bitter as wormwood, sharp as a
two-edged sword."

The soldier who can forget himself, his honor, his

country, and speculate in cotton, finds it easy to violate the plighted troth of his youth and tread upon
the heart he has taught to trust in him. Charlie Hardone never dreamed where his steps would lead when
he, (crafty Leette) boasting of his horse, was led to
challenge her to try speed with the fleet racer Janie.

She accomplished another result. She brought La
Scheme back. This was their conversation :—

" Have you forgotten ? "

" What have I to forget?"

" Yourself and your country. The sale of cotton,
whereby you provide sinews of war. You have taken
up a low-lived Yankee hireling." ·

" What right have you to be jealous? You, who
have a wife in every place."

" Then you listen to every idle rumor."

" Call you idle rumor the true words of one sworn
to communicate your own commands? Ordered to
speak this word to madden me."

" You deceived! Leette Ledone! You! I thought
you knew me better. Woman, why cannot you raise
your thoughts higher ! Are you, too, caught by the
chaff which blinds common birds ? "

" Kendal La Scheme, do not imagine you have
power longer to deceive me. I am free. One bond
remains between us, and one only—I obey while you
remain faithful to our country. All other links that
held me are broken. Master in the art of deception,
thou art deceived."

" Then, at length, we know each other. I have
not worked in vain, since, by breaking your woman-

thought of love, I have made an army for my country."

"Beware of my vengeance. When you marry other than myself, as you have sworn, I will enter your house and destroy your peace. Her you falsely call wife shall wish herself in hell rather than have crossed the path of Leette Ledonc."

"I laugh at your threats. I fear not. The day will never come. Do not you who follow the beck and nod of this false abolitionist perceive no cause of fear? Already you are marked."

"Ha! ha! How much quinine have you given me? Where is it now? When my friends are mis-led, well may I fear no detection from an enemy. I rode him a race. I led him beyond the lines. They did not challenge me. Oh, no! The Adjutant General needed no pass. His company was beyond suspicion. I took out more at one time than you got out in a week; won the race with Janie, who came back much lighter than she went."

"But you were thrown?"

"You are well informed. I thrown? Janie throw me! What penetration! Yes, I was thrown, and when thrown was rescued by a woman, who has sent the contraband of war to a man who loves and would die for me."

"Not James Manet; he is dead."

"Ah! you believed that. Master, mind you are not the equal of Leette. He is not dead. I am glad you are jealous of him. He is alive, if he loves me. Such love is priceless. I never would have given

Allie Sandison to Lieut. Hardone. She has a heart.
I'll trample on it. You ordered me to marry a Yankee, and kill him. I may obey. You promised to
be mine when he was dead. Dare to violate your
word! Contraband to a corporal in the federal
army! You are blind! You command me to speculate in cotton,—you, an old speculator, who have
made a million dollars. Oh! Kendal La Scheme,
you never will deceive Leette again. I am speculating. I have ordered ten bales of cotton, delivered,
and I already have the price in my possession."

Then La Scheme took Leette down. "Leette you
are a jewel—a priceless jewel. Your name shall
have a place in history, when we are free from war
and possess our independence. You are better than
I ever expected, than I ever imagined. I have only
one fault to find. You did not make it absolutely
necessary for the boat which gets your cotton to
carry supplies to the plantation."

"Did you know it?"

"Of course I knew. The money came from Sandison's bank. The General is a party to the transaction, and asked my advice before engaging. I
approved and urged, because you have been stripped
of all your property. Well done. I was only trying you. The test is eminently satisfactory. Go on
as now. A rich reward awaits, whether you crave
the destruction of your enemies, the success of your
friends, or your own aggrandizement. There are two
things, now, of prime importance, and you have better opportunities than I. To your consummate tact

they are entrusted.   I cannot be more than assistant,
until the moment for assistant to be chief.   The first
is to get from the Adjutant the news of this expedition to Vicksburg.   The second, to sell those thous-
and bales of Confederate States cotton.   Are we
friends, Leette?"

La Scheme offered his hand.   She took the hand,
and called herself a fool when he had gone.

CHAPTER XXIV

Two minds conflict. The strength of two independent creations, endowed with infinity, eternity, and personality, meet in antagonism on equal ground, with like determination and energy. Death only can end their strife, if neither will yield. Will they fight after death? Endless war is hell. There is no peace, saith my God, to the wicked. Can the souls of men and women, who hate the people of the North, ever dwell in unity again? La Scheme—a politician, a mere self man—can accommodate himself to any change. Can a woman—who, from the almost impossibility of being a soldier, is unable to inhale the actual, real, absolute experience of a campaign; made up of thought-lightnings, will-electricities, eternity-anxieties, huge foreshadowings of impending destruction; of watch in battle, in thunder and rain; without fire, shivering; in camp, starving; in the smoke near burnished steel—can a woman, with the soul of a man, make up her mind to yield and accept peace from the hand against whom she has rebelled?

Leette Ledonc had come to no such pass. Hate was furious when within the mind. But new emotions expelled those equally strong, and she was a mirror when with Alice Sandison, whose society she courted. Why? This was the reason. From her a casual remark opened a shutter in the Adjutant General's office. Another from Lina's father put her face against the window. Charlie Hardonc threw it open. General Solenter by an inadvertent admission, invited her in, and the combination of all these varied nothings were clear as her eye behind the Adjutant General's shoulder reading the official order from the Commander-in-chief.

Leette was a mirror in which Allie Sandison saw a friend, because for the moment, pure thoughts and good intentions were reflected. Allie Sandison, positive in her character as Leette Ledonc in hers. Allie the woman, no longer Lina the girl. Character developed, mind mature, will, strong with the immobility of educated principles.

I remember standing nearly two-thirds of a whole forenoon on the paved levee in front of Memphis, Tennessee, while a captain who had oversight of all the steamboats, as a deputy Provost Marshal, most earnestly deplored the demoralizing influence of the war on soldier's wives, on young females who came into the lines searching for wounded brothers and friends. Official duty put him on guard where he must watch closely every man and woman who came into or went out of our army lines, a scrutiny which

palliate l no hypocritic sanctity and excused no pitiful
evasion; where he saw so painful sights as made him
declare that purity was exceptional. Traveling wives
of soldier and officer, nurses in hospital too came
within his observation condemned; and he asked
with the earnestness of a grey haired man:—"What
is the country coming to?"

Allie Sandison, in the midst of such corruption,
was no negative. The Almighty God of virtue made
her spotless; every one seeing, felt her purity.
Many, females in particular, often deplore their
small opportunity of usefulness. Why were they not
men? Why did not Providence make them saviours
of their country? Allie Sandison,—unconscious of
doing anything, Allie Sandison,—living a pure woman, where men were distrusting themselves, distrusting God, distrusting all men, all women, losing
faith in all their former conceptions of possible virtue
and holiness—where man's own birth was branded in
common oaths as doomed offspring of contempt—
Allie Sandison, a living refutation of that idea born
in the border thought-land of perdition—Allie Sandison, any woman, every woman, who so lives as to
impress cotemporaneous minds with the truth of
angelhood and purity; white-robed in words, white-
robed in thought, white-robed in action,—has fulfilled one great mission of life. That woman who, in
this war, has come in contact with the army, and
maintained a spotless Christian character, may thank
God for the opportunity of vindicating the honor of
womanhood.

This was the Allic Sandison, who, thinking no evil, also sought the society of Leette Ledone. To the pure, all things are pure. The angel fallen can assume the semblance of light. Addison says hypocrisy is the homage vice pays to virtue. Leette Ledone thought neither of the Bible nor of Addison. While Allic sought to win a mistaken love, to show her Southern sister's .professed Union heart tinctured with bitterness, that a true Union woman had no hate, no ill-will, no animosity, Leette, conscious how poorly she concealed her mind, professed to love the kind spirit, and sought to hide every part of herself which had an evil countersign. There were mutual attractions as well as repulsions. As a hoyden girl calls her gentle mate to the seat on the extreme end of the board, whose center is balanced on a fence between, so Leette played with Allie, designing when she was well up in the air to let her fall.

James Manet was a link between. No true woman can ever hear of a man's generous love unmoved. When she cannot love back, she respects—gives that love next to love, pity. Thinking him dead, she, regardless of consequences, chose language which his heart would have thrilled to hear ; which made Leette jealous and revengeful. Her big heart, longing for love, unsatisfied; avenging her wrongs on one engaged to another. 'What did the rebel care for Charlie Hardone, that she strove to win him from his allegiance ? Why did she begrudge the affection she knew James Manet gave without reserve, without hoping for return ? It was useless to her who loved and hated La Scheme. But while with Allie, her face was unsullied by a frown, or tossing on the leaves of emotion to indicate a tempest breaking on the strong branches of the trees of passion; her black eye was a perfect foil, telling no tales. Her cheek had ever a smile; her lip, bound by the will to please, found no trouble to obey the impulse of good nature. Besides, respect paid involuntary tribute to innocence, good intentions and love, so far as to call forth an aspiration. Oh! I wish you were a rebel! But being a Yankee, no matter how great the attraction, she must hate.

Leette was a mirror, where Sandison saw a mere scheming, worldly-wise woman, who was smart even to surprise him by her sharpness; who had no conscience in a bargain; who asked, demanded as a right, what would have sent a man to the guardhouse and military prison for suggesting.

Leette was not a mirror to Charlie Hardone, in that a mirror reflects. She gave him pictures; but not those his imagination would have seen; since he had broadly put his foot on the slope of destruction and walked backwards. He was between two angels—above was his affianced, calling him upwards; behind was Leette, calling him down. His face turned over his shoulder — backwards, where enough was exposed to tempt him to turn his back on truth, purity, and love. In fact, Allie loved him too well.

Around the head-quarters of many Western generals [the East I know nothing of. It claims virtue.

I tell what I have seen, and I have seen no great
pretensions to immaculate purity among people of
the West] are numbers of fast men, whose interests
lead them to fawn upon those in power; who lie on
the ground to be trod on; who laugh and truckle;
do any mean act to gain their ends. These men
pander to vice; are ever ready with a cigar, a treat
—whether a single drink, a plate of oysters, a champagne supper, or a gallon of whisky. They tell
barn-yard stories, sing fancy songs, and are " Hale
fellows well met," without a shame.

Allie loved Charlie with eyes wide open to see the
gulf which threatened to overwhelm her future. A
Christian, knowing he had taken a Christian's vows,
she did her duty and plead earnestly. With an appetite for vice, the apple he had before him was too
tempting. Charlie Hardone entered her presence
degraded, and was a whited sepulchre.

General Solenter was a Hardone, with more style.
A leg of butchered sheep is no more, whether simply
boiled in a common pot or prepared *mouton a la
Francais*. Necessity compels common men to keep
others at a distance; else, contempt would sink them
deep as their desert. The less absolute merit—the
more style, the more pretension. Leette Ledone was
a mirror to his weakness, and with him assumed hau-
teur—put on more style than the Empress Eugenie,
the pride of Napoleon and pet of France.

These reflections of her mind-mirror were varied
by the appearance of others—La Scheme, guerillas,
rebels. Each moment had full possession; exclusive

—so that Leette had as many personalities as came for reflection. Behind which her own proper identity lay hidden; a reality at midnight, when curtains vainly barred out mosquitoes; but thought, too busy with its own pain, was unconscious of any live being save Leette Ledonc.

CHAPTER XXV.

One thousand bales of cotton at the time I am now fixing as the date of this transaction, would sell in Memphis for upwards of three hundred thousand dollars.

Three hundred thousand dollars!—is worth a risk. There was no risk in this case. One hundred thousand dollars paid to Leette would put the cotton on the bank ready for shipment; with not merely a pledge from guerillas not to burn, but a detachment to protect it. More of this hereafter.

I was in Chicago four years after the first nomination of Abraham Lincoln, when that party which was stigmatized as Copperhead met in the mammoth amphitheatre to nominate a candidate who should combine all the elements of antagonism in existence at the North to crush out the policy of emancipation, of Unionism embodied in Abraham Lincoln. What element united those antagonisms, fused them in harmony over the watchword *peace ?* The old Simonpure pro-slavery democrat who voted for Brecken-

ridge ; his deadly enemy the banking-protection-pub-
lic-improvement-fossil-old-line-Whig ; and that anomaly the radical black stripe abolition Fremontist ; individuals blaming Fremont as they also blamed Lincoln
for what was not done ; under valuing what had been
done ; uniting with that very large class of luke-warm
patriots ; men of strong party prejudices unable to
reconcile support of the Union, since support of the
Union contains death to slavery, with their life-long
support to that institution. Timber, out of which
circumstances wielded by traitors, can mould treason.
God knows, it is his law, though men ignore its truth,
that seed sown will germinate. Dragon's teeth sown
will grow into fighting men ; and his Providence has
thwarted the energetic plans which would have nipped
off the parent stock, only to spread deeper and wider
at the root, and multiply indefinitely the evil to be
more securely developed in coming time. Slavery is
the evil. Slavery is the curse of free government.—
Black slavery is the positive, white slavery the com-
parative and caste the superlative degree of wrong.
While the lower is tolerated small progress can be
made in ameliorating the condition of our own kith
and kin, in elevating the only absolute and imperishable ground of distinction between man and man,
namely, truth, virtue, holiness, and knowledge. Had
the rebellion been squelched,—slavery remaining, the
result would have been valueless.

Had the grand principles of anti-slavery been
choked down the unwilling minds of men, the steady
progress of conviction would not have been. Such

thoughts as influenced Gen. Fremont in his proclamation were impossible, at the time. The time was,
and Gen. Fremont was the man, to enunciate the
principle. Abraham Lincoln was the man in the
right place, to say, as he did say : " Wait, the principle is correct. Hold, practical emancipation is not
yet possible. You have advanced a new idea—a correct idea. I will not trouble, only suspend its execu-
tion, until public opinion has come up, embraced its
truth, and men are not only practically convinced,
but are its earnest advocates." The mill of events
grinds slowly. Those minds which grasp the future
are too apt to be impatient—to get angry with the
plodding mass, who cannot see, cannot comprehend,
the true logic of events. These stubborn, blind men
have not received mental illumination; but daylight
is approaching, when all shall see. The expense is
awful. Life, limb, happiness—all that man or woman holds dear ; new conscriptions, new outlays of
public money, new taxes, new duties—because the
opposition, in self-will, refuse to recognize the progress of human events. Do not become impatient.
The responsibility is not yours. In the creation of
the earth from chaos, cycles of years seemed uselessly wasted while fire cooled into solid rock, while
vegetation and animal life went to decay—forming
solid masses of carbon, sufficient to supply a purer
atmosphere, a more delicate vegetation, a more ex-
alted animal life, until time shall end. The moral
universe may be in a similar transition period ; and
the convulsions of human struggle, epochs in the pro-

gress of soul life, onward and upward. They who comprehend—who desire to urge onward the movement—should not grow impatient. since the Creator, whose work they are, in whose plan they act, governs the progress—wisely choosing his instruments —justly perfecting his designs. Have faith. Trust God, who doeth all things well. When God has done with a man, he drops from public observation. Do not resist God.

All these contradictory elements, which were meeting in harmony, burying the hatchet and affilliating in political brotherhood, were unable to defeat the destiny of the age: for slavery is barbarism and State · sovereignty conflicting with National Union is destruction. Their rallying cry, Peace! Peace! at any price, even to dismemberment of the Union and abrogation of the Constitution by the seceeding States. Let them go if they wish, Peace! Peace! This cry was made more loud by the proceeds of cotton, smuggled through the lines; cotton which some of our own officers in the field assisted to pass the lines. They were paid for the permits to get it out. Their honest (?) devotion to their country threw every obstacle in the way of open, free trade, and their public record is beyond impeachment, yet they themselves took bribes, opened side doors by which the enemy went out and in loaded with money to outflank, to battle in their rear against their fathers and mothers, sisters and children; by which they bought that political element, always for sale, and attempted to ruin the country. Thank God they failed!

19

The poor soldier must fight, shed his blood—die. His family must meet the treasonable laugh, the contemptuous pity of the copperheads; because the national officer was so covetous, so vile, so degraded, as to traffic in cotton.

Many a quiet looker-on in that misguided, ambiguous conglomeration of political pudding-stone, [there were diamonds, there was fine gold. How can a diamond shine without its glorious setting? How can gold be known when mixed with mud?] knew that Southern cotton, transmuted into English gold or Northern greenbacks, paid the passage of members of secret organizations to the scene of political conflict; armed them with pistols, and furnished them with powder and ball.

This is a long way from Leette Ledonc. Nor does any woman appear in this chapter, dedicated to none but Union men—supporters of the Administration and Federal 'officers. Again I disavow any intention of stigmatizing any particular man; nor the army or navy as men, or as a class of men. I point out no individual. If the pen draws true portraits, it shall not have, like the earliest attempts at art, the words, "this is a cow," to distinguish the features of brigadier from colonel, or major of the gold leaf from him of the two silver stars. The act and its consequences are wrong. Whoever has been guilty deserves condemnation. Let conscience stand accuser. Let truth, set home by conscience, be judge. Let a calm, unprejudiced public try every officer who comes home from the cotton regions enriched by the war beyond the just savings of his army pay. If there is guilt, let the penalty rest only on the criminal. There is but one way to reach the wrong-doer, and that, the just contempt of an indignant country. When men are known to be guilty, if the public sustain and honor them they partake of the guilt.

"One thousand bales of cotton. We must have them." Charles Hardone was seated with General Solenter in the private apartments, where none came uninvited. .

The general was sitting in an easy-chair, his hands thrown behind his head and his feet resting on the table. He was smoking a real Havana from a box just opened, and only a few moments before sent in by a cotton speculator, who wanted a permit endorsed with the general's name. The side-board held a bottle and glasses standing on a waiter. The adjutant general interrupted his remark by pouring some liquor into a glass, approving the flavor thus :

"That is tip-top. Smooth as oil. Some of La Scheme's ?"

"No," answered the general. "His cannot come up to that. This came from an old reb, and has been in the country for twenty-five years. La Scheme told me of it. In fact, tried to get it himself, but failed. You can't guess how I did get it."

"Of course not, since you say so. If La Scheme failed, no one need try. That man is cute as the devil. What he abandons no one need attempt. I wonder if there is more where it came from. A raid that way wouldn't be a bad thing."

"That would not go. Do you remember the dinner at which we were the guests of Miss Ledonc?"

"You don't! D—m it! I do remember. I'd have got tight there if Lina hadn't been on hand with her Bible quotations."

"Ah, old boy! look out or you will be in love with this rebel."

"I am already about the same as you are. You better keep straight or I will write your wife—" At this point a knock at the door interrupted them.— "That is Sandison come to work out this trade."

"How are ye, Sandison," says the General not rising but extending the hand unoccupied by his cigar, apologizing with the words, "*the nearest the heart.* Have a drink? Charlie, ring for another glass."

"Not for me, thank you," replied Sandison.

"Oh, try this. You never tasted better,—sample it—genuine article captured from a rebel — thirty years old."

"She is not thirty years old; not more than twenty."

"Who?" asks Sandison.

"Miss Ledonc."

"If she is not thirty she ought to be. She has the oldest head on her shoulders I ever saw for one so young. Do you know what she wants now?"

"No, what is it?"

"One hundred thousand dollars down, and five thousand dollars worth of supplies delivered."

"What are they?' asks the General.

"Salt, flour, beef and pork, whiskey, and a general assortment of plantation goods. She had a list of articles, as long as the moral law, from a cotton card to a paper of pins. Can we work it through? It is worth the trial; but a hundred thousand dollars does not turn up every day. What say General?"

"This is a new dodge. Greenbacks have always done the biz before."

"Not always. There have been small lots of supplies which have been worked out without your knowledge,—Hardone knows; we would not trouble you with them. This is too big and I dare not venture without your approval and consent before hand. You see, at least it is plain to me, although she does not say so, that the guerillas must be bought off or they will come in and burn the cotton while on the bank. In fact she hinted as much."

"This is a big thing. If we fail it does up a cool hundred thousand. I have tried every way but she will take no risks, the money must be paid down.— Then we must charter a steamboat. Here is trouble again. We have to take in the Quartermaster."

"Oh, the General can manage that well enough. A special order will do it."

"Yes. But how to get the supplies on board. The supplies must go, and they must be permitted by the Treasury Agent. It would never do to pay for the cotton and then slip up for five thousand dollars worth of supplies."

"It is a hard case, Sandison," says General Solenter. "Suppose you get the supplies on board, the navy will interfere; Admiral Porter's order is very strict, and these navy fellows are jealous as can be. They know how to obey and would be more than glad of a chance to pick us up. I am afraid it cannot be done."

"It looks scaly enough," said Charlie. "Besides, the new Treasury Agent is so sharp he will seize the cotton before we know what is up."

"That is true," says Sandison. If it was anything less than a cool two hundred thousand I would not touch it, By G—d, I cant make up my mind to give it up."

"Neither can I," says Charlie.

"Nor I," says the General. "Take another cigar. We must work it out some way. If we can't, no one can."

"That's so," says Charlie.

"It is a tremendous risk for me," says the General. I have at stake more than you. While you in failure loose only money, I loose money and chance my reputation. They may order an investigation."

"Buy off the judges or the witnesses. We will stand our share as part off the expense account. We can control the *reports* of any such investigation ; and if necessary, a judicious outlay, will mould public opinion at home by the leading articles in our party organs."

"Can you do that, Sandison ?"

"Oh, yes ; I have done that many a time. Your reputation does not trouble me. We can fix that. I am bothered only on the question of supplies. The

Provost Guard is on the levee, and the Treasury detectives are always on the watch. I do not know
what is best."

" It is best to get the cotton, of course."

" Ha! ha! ha! That is the mischief, Charlie."

For a moment look at the situation. One thousand
bales of Confederate States cotton, which once within
the Federal lines, by the laws of war, belongs to the
government, are offered for sale for $100,000 in green-
backs, and $5000 in supplies.

Cotton can be legally bought for greenbacks, but
not C. S. A. cotton.

The Navy forbid steamboats to land, save under
their guns, on penalty of forfeiture of boat, cargo,
and the imprisonment of officers and crew.

The Treasury confiscate all cotton which is brought
within the lines contrary to the rules and regulations
of its department.

The General in command also has his orders re-
stricting trade in the staple, violation of which involve
like forfeiture and penalty.

This opens the field to the quartermaster. Oh,
had all men been honest — had all generals, all
treasury agents, all quartermasters, and their aids,
clerks, and assistants, let alone the accursed thing;
preserved carefully all the cotton which came within
the lines, and forwarded it to market; had all collec-
tors of customs, United States marshals, agents of
the War Department, carefully husbanded the proceeds from such sales—an amount would have been
realized which would go far to decrease the great

debt, and thereby diminish the taxation so heavily weighing down the whole land!

The temptation was too great. Young men, old men, generals, colonels, captains, lieutenants, chaplains, nurses, have yielded—have sinned the sin of Achan. Some have, by the enormity of their transactions, dipped their souls in the blood of as pure and noble soldiers as ever died for their country. God forgive them.

Whoever would condemn too harshly, let him remember the Forgiver who taught, "Judge not, that ye be not judged," and left the prayer, "*Lead us not into temptation.*" Let him ask himself what he would have done if two hundred thousand dollars had come within his grasp—two hundred thousand dollars in less than a month. Two hundred thousand dollars! two hundred thousand dollars! Who would not do wrong for two hundred thousand dollars?

For a time each smoked in silence; each thought. At length, heaving a long breath, General Solenter said:

"Sandison, you must make the best bargain you can. I do not care how you fix it; only do not involve me. Keep your own council. You will get the thing through straight. Have you employed La Scheme?"

"No. He has played off on me in this matter. I know not why."

"Then you must pay him well. He will come in; and you know he is always successful."

"General, I will try. It is a hard matter."

"Go on. Don't come to me until it is absolutely necessary. Then, I will do all that any man can."

"General," says Sandison, "the only question is how to do it. We can buy every man who stands in our way; but that would not pay. Nothing would be left. There is a way of getting privileges from the Treasury Agent, and making one hand wash the other, on the principle of one good turn deserves another. Do you understand? It is all right?"

The General nodded.

"Then that permit business can be easily arranged, and we can get the goods on board by your endorsement. Your order will carry the guard. Nothing is left but to get through the navy."

"Blast the navy!" says Charlie, "We will risk that. Once get the cotton on board and safe here, I defy all the navies in the world to get it away from us."

"I would rather be on the safe side. I know a man in charge of a gun-boat,—an old friend, who would do anything for me. I think I can work through him. It may cost us a pair of silver-mounted pistols and a basket of champagne. It can be brought out somehow. I shall charter the first boat I find."

"Go ahead; the sooner the better. That woman is a sharp piece, and, as near as I can make out, has already taken ten or twenty thousand dollars earnest money from other parties. First come, first served. She told me herself."

"Did Miss Ledone let you know that?"

" Yes," replied Charlie.

" You must be thick with her."

" Charlie uttered the Englishman's interjection, coloring while he added, " Do you think I would let her get the start of me ? Two hundred thousand dollars are not to be picked up every day."

" La Scheme told me the same. He said he had advanced on this lot. We must work off his claim. He said it was a speculation, and was willing to bet on it. If he lost he would win on another. He told me he would look out for Miss Ledone, as she was keen as a briar, but did her the justice of being up to her word. Shall I close with her ?"

" Yes," answered the General, " and under the circumstances I will send one of the Quartermaster's boats. As soon as the cotton comes in I will order it seized, and put a guard over it. The rest will be easy."

CHAPTER XXVI

The following letter, written about this time, explains itself :

"*My Dear Mrs. Wirtman:*

"I wish I could lay my head on your bosom and cry. Do not show this letter to mother. Poor mother ! I would not make her any more unhappy. I enclose one for her. I am sad and so lonely.

"Mr. Wirtman is nearly well, and attends to business, but his heart is not here. Since he heard of James' death, all energy seems gone. We have learned no new facts. Leette—is it not strange for me to call her that name—is a strange woman. I wish you could see and know her personally. I fear, yet am fascinated. She seems to be good. I cannot tell what I think, for always, after a visit, I feel relieved as of impending evil. She insists that I call her Leette. James did. For his sake I do not turn away, as I would gladly do. No return can be too great for kindness, such, as she says, she gave to him who is sleeping. Oh ! what a death ! And she says

I am the cause. Do you blame me? He died for
his country. Didn't he? Leette says it was cotton.
I wish father would go home. I hate the sight of
the bales laying on the levee, for every time I see
them they seem covered with blood—his blood. Do
you forgive me? Can you forgive me?

"Why do I write you thus? I ought not, perhaps,
but I cannot help speaking. You always seemed so
dear. God forgive me, if I am wrong. I write you
because I am so lonely. I knew Charlie drank, but
I did not think him unfaithful. I will not think
that now, although Leette says, "All men are rascals.
The war has made them all villains. There is not
an honorable man in the North or the South. The
good men are all dead." She is so bitter! Poor
girl! some one has injured her, and she is revengeful. I cannot believe all are wholly bad. She tells
me dreadful histories. Oh! this cruel war!

    *   *   *   *   *   *   *

"I take my pen again. I have been reading my
Bible,—that one Lilly Sue gave on her death-bed.
You remember. It belonged to James. I have been
praying. I am strong again. The Saviour is a sure
refuge for those that trust in him. I have committed
my soul to his care. 'In the valley of the shadow
of death I will fear no evil, for thou art with me.'

"I cannot comprehend the situation of affairs
here. Father is very busy. I hardly see him, day
or night. I should be very lonesome, but find enough
to do. And if you could only go with me to the
Overton Hospital, and look into the eyes of our poor

sick and wounded men, when I read to or write for them, you would feel that I am not quite useless. There are blessings everywhere, when we look for them. 'Little deeds of kindness. Little words of love.' I know what that means now. When I make one of those sick soldiers smile I feel happy. I worked all one afternoon to get some socks right for a poor hollow-eyed man; and wasn't I paid when he said, ' That's just like my mother '!

"Charlie does not like me so much in the hospitals; but he has so much work, he does not find time to spend with me. You know I cannot be idle. Before long the army will go to Vicksburg, and then I plan to return home. Father will accompany the expedition, and will not leave me alone here; though I would gladly stay and take care of the wounded. I hope Mr. Wirtman will go home, too. The bank is not making much money. Father says your husband is too honest. There, I am coming back on to the sad things again. Isn't it awful when you are beginning to be afraid of losing faith in your father? I do not think it is right to make money as men do here; and I feel so badly to think how my dear father works to get it. Have I a right to close my eyes?—am I wrong in seeing anything in him which is contrary to my standard of right? I do love him. I wish he would come home.

"My dear, dear friend, what can I, what should I do? Pray for me. I need strength to do my whole duty. When I get home I shall never want to go away again. I wish Charlie and I were only happy

together, and no more war; I would be willing to
work hard all my days. I want to talk to you. I
am not satisfied with this writing. I am tempted to
burn what I have written. Love, love, love. Good-
bye.''

While this was going, another letter had been
written by Mrs. Wirtman, in reply to that informing
her of her son's death. With much that was irrele-
vant, there was this which follows—telling her secret
thoughts; also, suggestive of what may have been
the nature of the correspondence between these persons during the kind watch which Lina Sandison was
keeping over—saving the life of George Washington
Wirtman.

" I cannot believe he is dead. I, his mother, who
first felt his heart beat, who have loved him from infancy, fed him on my breast, watched, tended, prayed
over him during childhood and boyhood, sent him forth
to battle for his country. Life of my life, heart of
my heart, I have not yet lost him ! My heart is yet
whole, and the news which you sent is not, cannot be
true. James is yet alive else I should know it. I am
confident he still lives. When he dies I shall have
warning ; my heart is still whole, I shall see him
again. Call me foolish, Allie, it was his name, and I
shall call you by none other. I am a foolish, loving
mother. I will not give him up. That woman was
mistaken, or worse. I fear her on your account.—
Beware, dear daughter ! Do not trust her too far !
And Charlie, forgive me, Allie, if I give you pain, I
fear lest he may not be worthy. Do not place your

affections so entirely, on anything earthly, that their precious treasure shall be wasted. God preserve and keep you, darling, and return you safe and quickly home.

" Tell my husband to come home. Let money perish rather than be gained at the price of honor. I would rather live poor and die in want, than feel one single moment, that abundance was procured at the expense of truth, justice and country.

" Dear child it is time for you to come home. I thank you, I bless you for all you have been to mine and to me. Your mission is ended,—but—I am selfish ; I do not think of your father, of Charlie. Stay while you can be of service to them, and then come home,—come home and bring my husband with you."

CHAPTER XXVII.

In what the pilots of the Mississippi call a *blind field*, a lone widow occupied a log shanty. The cultivation of the South clears from the trackless woods only the smaller trees; while the large monsters, of pre-Adamic proportions are lazily girdled, to slowly decay. Cotton and corn were planted among these trees, tomb-stones of past vegetation, whose shadow, rising with the sun, shed all day long a regret on the green, tasselly stalk, the delicate silk of the corn, and on the flowering, flaky cotton. The very soil was a grave-yard of immortal seeds. Every year a campaign, through which the stolid, thick-lipped, thick-skulled salamander slave waged war with the weeds. Weeds, whose tiny mustard-seed produced a young forest for the birds of the air to occupy as playing, singing, and feeding ground. When any field was once abandoned, neglected, not more than two seasons, the posterity of dead forests jealously reassumed possession, and young cottonwood trees sprang in cane-brake profusion from the soil. What a tangle is a blind field! Weeds, cockle-burrs, briars, morning-glory vines, ticks, nettle trees too young yet to be a bush, stubborn hickory saplings, ash shoots striving to become trees; all, every, each, whatever of bush, shrub, vine, nettle, wild, untamed, spontaneous nature riots in producing—all of this, with nothing to hinder, grows in a blind field.

The log shanty had been abandoned, five or six years before the war, by its owner, who was a poor wood-cutter. The widow, who now occupied it, had a cotton history. One of the witnesses against the civilized world—that civilized world which, ignoring its own damning responsibility, holds up its hands in holy horror at the cruel war its own cupidity has engendered.

Calico, prints, muslin, sheeting, shirting, were only a shilling (York), a rial (Spanish), a sixpence (English), a levy, a bit, a fib, or any other name which means twelve and one-half cents, per yard, previous to the gigantic moral maelstrom which has put the price of cotton from seven, eight, and nine cents, per pound, up to fifty, seventy-five cents, and one dollar. All because of slavery—unpaid labor of the African slave. Who, by its incessant and unlimited demand, impregnated the Southern mind with the immortality of King Cotton? The old world. England first of all. What did it do for England? Put free white labor on a par with the forced labor of the black slave. Cotton which can be produced for a sixpence must be manufactured for a sixpence. Cheap clothing makes cheap labor, cheap food; so that every

20

laboring man in the world, whether manufacturer or agriculturist, was degraded to equality with the poor slave of the South. The great land-holder, the great corporation capitalist, alone reaped the benefit. The white man, the laborer was degraded ; his family starved.

The husband of this woman was a poor, Southern, laboring man, without land, without slaves, with no more than the God of nature gave a black man— hands, feet, and stomach. The slave-holder despised him, because he was poor. The slave despised him, because he had to work. A poor white at the South was worse off than a nigger ; because the latter was invested with the dignity of his owner's wealth. So when the war broke out, the poor white was driven to save his own life from a bayonet. The army swallowed him, while his wife and family were drowned in the heartless neglect of an aristocracy which hated poor white trash.

This woman had more energy than her husband. She cultivated a field of corn with her own hands ; she even made a bale of cotton—that is, she raised, planted, hoed and picked with her own hands, two bales, of which she gave the overseer one, for gining and baling the other. All this, because God made her human. She could not disobey the command, as does many a proud dame, *Be fruitful and multiply.* Her heart could bear its own stabs, whether inflicted by the heartlessness of husband or the cold, cold world ; but not the cries of a daughter bare-footed at twelve years old, a boy gaunt at seven, or the heavy tuggings at her breast-heart of the infant hungry, hungry, hungry.

When the lines were opened, she took her cow and mule, yoked them together to her wooden-wheeled cart, loaded on her bale of cotton—how is more than I can tell you : not a surplus nail or bolt kept the wedged frame of unhewn sticks together—and wended her creaking way, bare-footed, to the Mississippi, carrying her babe in her arms, while the other two children rode the bale of cotton, or clung to her tattered dress, beside her.

Before she reached the river, a kind man met and warned her of guerillas burning cotton, and urged her to return. Said she :

"I am a pore, lone woman. I want some flour and doings, and some traps for the children. My husband's in the army, dead long ago for all I know. He can't write, and I can't read if he cud. No one 'll hurt them 'uns, shore."

But the guerillas found her, burnt her cotton and her cart ; took her cow and her mule, and left her alone with her children, far from her home, and obliged to take up quarters in a deserted log house in a blind field.

This field was a part of the plantation of Leette Ledonc. Because her uncle opposed, this woman received her permission to remain ; the same motive fed the family with rations of corn meal, and gave permission to take all the corn they could eat from the standing crop.

When La Scheme left her house to go to the ren-

dezvous of the guerillas, Leette without comprehend-
ing, save as the storm impending oppresses the atmosphere, took an impulse to put James Manet out
of the way lest he might be injured without her consent.   There was a tincture of the coquette in this
impulse, as La Scheme seemed to be jealous of her.
She felt so secure of him that a little wholesome sport
would be only pastime.   She immediately went to
James, and said :—

   " There is danger abroad of which I know nothing.
I am your friend.   I would preserve and protect as
far as is in my power.   Will you trust me ? Will you
wait until I come and tell you danger is removed ?"

   Leette was sincere.   Trust begets trust.   James'
nature forbade her to conceal.   The Leette of La
Scheme was not the Leette of James Manet.   The
game was on her side, but underneath the game was
a true fear, a true resolve, " I will save you."   James
consented, and she put him in the log house in the
blind field, binding him to keep within until she
should give him permission to depart.

   James had already gained strength.   His recovery
was rapid.   Time was on his hands, and only one
small book to occupy that time, to relieve a captive's
intense wish to get away.   A book which teaches, "Do
with thy might what thy hands find to do."   What
could he do ?

   Teach that little girl her letters ; tell how that little Testament was given before the war, when every
volunteer was armed with God's promise of mercy ;
before the blue uniform had been issued or the volun-

teers had ever handled a bayonet. By-and-by he devised a plan to shingle the roof from the inside, sending the mother and children to a roof half washed into the river, for old shingles. Old shingles attract no attention, make no noise. Afterwards he studied how to fill the cracks from within so as to add comfort without suspicion; and one day when they were all gone, he found a loose board under the corner where he made his bed. Looking for opportunities to escape, when bound by a wall of parole so thick and high that, while honor was at stake, he would not go out of the open door into the blind field to gather even a stick of wood or a beautiful snow-white flower. What an eternity the sound of the distant cannon of our friends holds on a prisoner! They did not come. Was it wrong to lift the board and plan for escape when the chains of honor might be lifted? It was only a chance. A prisoner must take chances. James took the chances, and little by little dug a hole unnoticed by either mother or children, and connected his hole with the outside of the house.

About this time, a slave who had escaped his pursuers, came for refuge. The widow refused no one.— Out of the same pot from which they all eat their hulled corn, without spoons or forks, he was fed. He received the lion's share of the hoe cake made of meal pounded between two stones,—not the cake, the corn from which it is made, for Leette's granary of meal was burnt long ago. Leette who was safe and would come back by-and-by. James almost prayed to be taken prisoner again that he might chance his escape. The negro had escaped.

" The Hounds ! How did you get away ?"

" Yah ! golly ! Me knows, hounds neber catch me !"

" How is that ?"

" Dis yer way,—cober up de smell."

" Can you do that ?"

" Yah ! yah ! golly ! Done dat ar plenty, when I steal de sweet potatoe and de hog."

" How was it ?"

" Burn de cow horn and rub him ober de feet and de legs. No smell dar den."

James went bare foot to save his shoes, and burned a cow horn which he kept smoking in them. It was unpleasant to sleep over such a perfume, but it was a chance for safety, and he permitted no chance to escape.

He was much alone, for he had aroused the hopes and desires of this mother to get to a free land where children could go to free schools and obtain a free education. She had no means of her own, nor any expectations, until he suggested her gathering all the loose cotton at Leette's plantation, and separating the scorched, saving only that uninjured ; and while she was thus employed, each child, even the baby playing in cotton, he was patching and making sacks out of the refuse rags which she gleaned from the negro quarters. The sacks were all there ; the hole was there ; the burnt smell was there ; and a slight chance of escape was there ; but where was Leette ?

CHAPTER XXVIII

There can hardly be found a place in human experience more galling than the dependence of a strong mind and will on irresponsible military power, when that military power is in the hands of ignorance, self-conceit, and arrogance; or even if the center of power—itself pure, noble, and honorable —is surrounded, battalion deep, with assistant clerks and mercenary hirelings. To be snubbed by a lieutenant, when you know your cause is just—when he is angry because you have told him his error; when you have called for justice, and he has denied because he has the power; when there is no redress, since your application for justice must necessarily go through his hands in the regular red-tape progression of military official business—to be thus snubbed is hard, to the very superlative of eating your own heart up; which thousands have done— some in silence, and others in the guard-house, for the indiscretion of thinking out loud.

The life of such a man as La Scheme was a living

Prometheus, with the difference of mind consuming itself; a carniverous cannibal eating his own heart, which grew as much in the night as he consumed during the day. He was self-immolated; chained by his own will to the rock of exposure. He was like a certain Frenchman, arrested by Ben. Butler, at Fortress Monroe, for some offence which deserved immediate penalty, which was inflicted without delay —a fine of five hundred dollars and hard labor on' the works of Fortress Monroe for six months. "But," says the Frenchman. "Silence! ' says the angle-eyed general. "Certainly, monsieur general," says the Frenchman; adding, as he told the story, "I could bite his nose off."

Thus Kendal La Scheme, day after day, applied at the various offices which controlled the cotton permit business; working for himself, for others, by others, through others; observing the men with whom he had to deal—studying their weaknesses, their companions, and their peculiarities; laying them under obligations to him if possible, and making himself useful every way, without suspicion. Leette was only one of the irons he had in the fire. She was one so near as to burn. Little as he cared for women, she made him jealous; afraid lest she might run away with his own bridle, and never account for proceeds.

"You love Charlie Hardone, Leette. You forget your oath, and your duty."

"What do you care whom I love? I used to love you. I hate you now. I know what a fool I made

of myself. You are a villain, La Scheme! a deep-
dyed rascal!"

"No matter about the rascal. The tongue that
uses the word is familiar with the idea guilty or not
guilty. The Adjutant General is spooney on you,
and you play with him. Why don't you seek higher
game?"

"You are jealous, Kendal La Scheme. A man
of conquest, like you, ought not to begrudge a pitiful
Yankee Lieutenant, to his future wife, particularly
as she is instructed to marry a Yankee, and kill
him."

"You cannot marry this one, since he is engaged."

"Which means that I, Leette Ledone, your affianced wife, am to marry another, whom you shall
choose, when you please to appoint the day. No, sir.
This arrangement is in my own hands. You are
under contract. I am released from obligation.
When you dare to marry, then watch for my vengeance. When I marry the man I chose, dare to
interpose and I will murder you as coolly as you
drank my blood. Kendal La Scheme, you have made
no saint of me. Beware how you arouse your own
creation!"

"That is right, Leette. You talk as I would have
you. Now you look as if you could tread on any
Yankee soul, could bite and champ their hearts, but
I fear you will never accomplish it. Even this Adjutant loves his Northern girl too well, to more than
flirt with you; and she is a good angel, who despises
in her heart, pities, the poor Southern fire-eater—

forced by circumstances to be Union. She hates the business you are engaged in, and has tried to persuade her father to have nothing to do with your thousand bales. If she can only get her lover engaged in her plan, down goes your hundred thousand dollars, down goes the confederacy. Shall she do it, and you alone responsible ? No ! This thing must be, despite opposition. Can be, must be done while the iron is hot. Are you going to be outwitted by a Yankee girl ?"

" Has she gone against me ? I was sparing that fellow on her account. Well, I will trust to no one in future."

" No one ?"

" There may be one. Ah! you mean yourself, La Scheme. Trust you! Yes. I know how far I can trust you—when it is for your interests."

" And the interest of the Southern Confederacy."

" Just that ; no more. We understand each other. You are true as long as the cause is safe. I know no other cause, and am ready to die for it."

" Right, Leette ! Go to-night with this pass through the lines. Tell the Captain to press all the teams, and have the cotton on to the bank at Laconia, for a boat will come for it in two days. Tell him this is a government transaction, and I have the permits from both sides, and that I will have supplies for him and the army. Every one of his men must work with a will, for high parties are interested and the boat must not be detained. Now remember and obey."

Leette did not go first to the guerilla captain. Where? To the blind field to James Manet. Impulsive and wayward, not all bad, a good angel struggling, striving for possession, Leette had resolved to offer her love to James, and if he would accept, to try and be good. How much she intended by such a proffer is impossible to set forth. She acted on an impulse. She wanted love. One love to love above the world. Ten thousand other loves might come to her mirror, flit before it; behind all there must be another, pure, imperishable, all her own exclusive possession, to which, weary, she might return and rest,—be at peace. All of the imaginary lover which was necessary to fill the void, she centered on James Manet, since La Scheme had ceased to be any longer her thought-Mecca.

"I am very glad to see you," said James, thinking only of liberty.

"Are you, really?" was her blushing reply.

"Certainly. Can you doubt it? Why have you been away so long? I have watched, and waited, and watched, and yet you did not come, and now I am quite well. Oh, how glad I am. But you are weary and worn. You look tired. Are you sick? I shall be very sorry to have you ill, and your home is destroyed. Did you find no friends? Have you been in trouble?"

All this was spoken while warm hands were retained in meeting. True sympathy on the part of James; since it came spontaneously, without a repulsive feature. They were alone. Yielding to an impulse, she threw her arms around his neck, burst into tears, and said :

"Love me, love me."

"Leette!" exclaimed James, astonished at this strange action. She answered :

"I am so lonely and miserable."

"Poor Leette, what can I do to make you happy?"

"Love me."

"I do love you."

Simple words, which mean much or little as they contain meaning. They did not carry to her heart the solace she craved; but they were soothing, and she needed comfort after a sleepless night, in which her horse wondered at the maniac impetuosity which forgot love to Janie in the cruel whip. Recovering herself, she said :

"I have heard of your mother. Your father-in law, Wirtman, is in Memphis."

"Is my mother well?"

"Yes. But your sister is dead."

"Lilly?"

"Yes."

"Who told you?"

"Allie Sandison. Charlie Hardone is there, Adjutant to General Solenter. I hate them,—I knew I should hate them."

Lilly Sue dead! When? She did not know. Allie Sandison in Memphis, not married, but soon to be, else why there? Leette noticed the change of his face, was maddened by the electricity of repulsion, as she had been gladdened by its attraction.

"She is going to be married to him in a week before the army leaves for Vicksburg." Impetuously to him—"You love her yet,—I know you do."

"No ; only as I have always loved her. Allie is a dear good girl and I wish her to be very happy. I loved my sister Lilly more than any one of the others, and she loved me. I feared lest she should pine away when brother Henry was killed. She thought me dead and did not wish to live. I shall never see her again."

"Dear James, let me console you. Love me—permit me to love you. I know what it is to be alone."

"You shall be my sister."

"No more than sister ?"

"Leette !"

"Do not Leette me ! I am alone, I want something,—some one. I am nearly crazy. I want some one to love me who is worth loving. I know it is un-lady-like to ask you. I hate what is lady like. I am only Leette Ledone. I want love, love, love ! Wont you love me ?" She seized him and looked steadily into his eyes. There were tears there.

"Poor Leette !"

"Yes, I am poor Leette. Make me rich Leette. Give me an honest man's love. I have money. What is money without love ? Oh ! for a home ! James, give me love and home."

"And country, Leette ?"

Their relative sexes seemed a mistake, up to that question. Mild, gentle, kind as a woman ; raging, furious, vindictive as a man, her will seemed already triumphant; but that word country was adamant, and there his will was firm as her own.

"My country, not yours," said she. "You were a dead man; I gave you life. You belong to me. My country is your country. Love me; be mine; come to my home. I am rich. We can be happy. James, you will love me. If you don't love me, I shall hate you—hate everybody."

"Leette! Leette!"

"No more Leettes to me. Say you do love me; you will love me, or I shall believe there is no love on earth. Every man is a villain,—a rascal,—a devil. I shall hate the race, and live for vengeance. You do not answer me; you dare not refuse. If you do, I will wreak my vengeance, not on you alone, but on those you love. I can do it. I can reach far into the North, to their very door. Forgive me, James, I am going crazy for love. You do love me, —you will love me. Speak, James, I am hungry for love!"

"Leette, I owe my life to you. Always shall I love and respect—always cherish deep, grateful affection in return. I thank you. May God bless you. An evil spell over your mind blinds every perception of truth. God has not abandoned earth. Goodness, virtue and holiness still live, and there is forgiveness for all. Mercy came from heaven for lost men. While I have been wounded, lessons of duty have become fixed in my heart, and hate and revenge have yielded to the teachings of Him who reviled not again. Leette, I wish you were a Christian."

"Love and respect, Jesus and religion ! I want no love and respect. There is no Christ or religion ! I want nothing but love, and you will not love me. Oh ! it is because I am a Southerner. I hate you. I am a true daughter of the South. You are a Yankee. You shall go to Richmond. You shall starve at Belle Isle. You shall know better than to despise the love of a Southern lady."

"Leette," said James, "I shall not change. Goodbye. When you need, if the time ever comes, for me to return your kindness, I shall gladly prove my love. If I ever take one of your men prisoner, I shall care for him as you have done for me. I would gladly love you, if I could, but my heart is dead since I entered upon this war. I do not expect to see it through, and how could I pledge my hand to a foe of my country. I love you and can forgive. The end has not come yet, and when it does come, it will find me faithful to the Union, the whole country. I am your prisoner. I gave you my parole of honor. I now withdraw it, and shall escape the first possible opportunity. All the love man can give in gratitude is yours ; but I never could marry an enemy of my country."

"Neither could I. Do you think I was in earnest? No. I was trying you. I promised La Scheme I would. I knew I should make a failure. You may escape if you can ; the guerillas and bloodhounds are on your track. We are enemies now,—we always have been. You mean, low lived Yankee, begone !— Get out of my sight !"

James without a hat and without shoes, walked
slowly into the blind field toward the woods, toward
the slough.

Leette frantic, mounted her horse to ride to the
headquarters of the guerilla Captain. Her love despised. How La Scheme would laugh! He should
never know. She would never tell. La Scheme was all
now. Had he been true she would love,—yes, she
would die for him. When one thing fails, exclusive
attention to another may bring happiness? No. Business, cotton, money to injure the enemy, she was
still unhappy. Leette was right. She was nearly
crazy.

James returned to the house after she had gone and
took his shoes; without them he could not throw the
hounds off the scent should they follow him. He took
them in his hand and went out barefoot again.

CHAPTER XXIX.

Leette found the Captain with his men, was invited to partake of their hospitalities, and gave them the latest news. That which pertained to the supplies was particularly agreeable, and all necessary arrangements for cotton readily concurred in. Incidentally, Leette said :

" Captain, you remember that Yank I took under my protection. I saw him to-day down in old Jim's shanty. A woman has harbored him. He insulted me. I think it is high time for him to go to Richmond."

" Or to hell ! dog him ; and I will soon send him there."

" Oh, do not hurt the man. He will do for exchange."

" Of course I wont hurt him. Lieutenant, tell Bill Wolgo to come here."

On his appearance, the captain said :

21

" Bill, there is a Yank down in the old blind field."

" The devil there is ! " was the classic reply.

" Can you bring him in ? "

" Can a duck swim ? "

" Oh don't be too sure, Bill," said Leette. " This fellow is one of the cute ones—one of those Yankee pedlar chaps, who make you uns believe the moon is made of green cheese. You can't catch him. Besides, he has the start. I saw him go into the brush."

"When I get on his track all hell couldn't save him. I have trailed a deer and bear all day and taken his scent the next morning."

" There you are at the dogs again. You must not let them bite him."

" Oh, no. I will call them off before they eat his clothes up. Who would have thought when I trained my pups they'd had such prime game. That's all Captain ?"

" He won't be taken alive."

" Then I'll have him dead.

" Not if you stay here. Take half a dozen boys along."

" All right, Captain."

" A new uniform with boots complete," said Leette, " if you bring him in alive."

" I will do it."

Bill Wolgo was a lynx-eyed man. A non-commissioned officer, without education, save as a rifle and axe had taught lessons of wood-craft. His heart was big, not symmetrical; shrivelled as to nobleness, honor and rectitude, save as honor exists among thieves. This commission was in his line, particularly acceptable.

Without delay he put his gang in motion toward the blind field. Arriving there he made search but found nothing,—the bird had flown. Enraged at this escape, Bill taxed the widow with concealing the Yank. This was denied, for since morning she had not seen James Manet. Bill had not taken his dogs, after the promise of the uniform and new boots, both of which were needed, particularly the latter, as his shoes, stolen from a dead soldier, were falling to pieces, and he had no stockings; or rather, those he wore had no bottoms, constant use without washing having rotted the feet. The loss of reward was enough to arouse his passion, add to the fuel a burning taunt of failure; then, picture the fury with which he reappeared before the shanty and commanded the widow to produce the Yankee son of a dog she had concealed.

All this time, Bill's partners were driving through the woods, beating the bush for a trail, and examining every sign. There was one barefoot track leading broad and fair to the slough. It went into the mud, then turned after floundering knee deep, came out and walked by a path into the cane-brake, then it followed the path and was lost; but the path led to the river.

While they were arguing the probabilities, whether he had gone into the woods; whether he had swum the slough; whether he had broken trail by climbing and using the grape-vine; or, may be had a skiff, in which .he had escaped down the river ; or, perhaps, had attempted to swim the current and been drowned : while they were thus arguing, one man had been sent for, the dogs. Meanwhile, Bill cursed the widow, overhauled her house and played general havoc.

The dogs came, and were set on the trail which they followed, until they too, were at fault. Bill was now beside himself. His mind was an ocean,— an ocean has but one element, water,—his element was passion. His ocean was full of waves; all the intensity of his nature raging; every yelp of his fierce dogs infuriated him ; every obstacle maddened ; thinking himself on the trail, he pushed forward to be baffled, to be thwarted. He cursed his dogs, cursed his men, cursed his horse ; damned himself, damned his name, damned his eyes, damned his soul, damned his mother, damned Leette, damned his captain, damned God, damned heaven, damned hell, but with all his damning, did not find the Yankee corporal.

In this state of passion he returned to the shanty and again called out the widow. Terrified before, she—no word of comparison can express the horror of fear which this human candidate for hellish immortality inspired. An emotion which all a mother's love led her to combat for the sake of her children, who strove to hide in her tattered gown. The girl and boy were quiet, frightened into silence ; but the babe would not be still. What with the baying of hounds, the swearing of mad men, and the screams of the child, there was a bedlam which rendered Bill Wolgo more furious.

"Shet up, dog you! If you dont shet up, I'll blow yer brains out."

"Hush! hush!" said the mother. But no amount of soothing could stop the outcry.

"Make him, or I'll kill yuh both, dog you!"

The mother pressed her child closely to her bosom, more and more closely, although nourishment was not necessary to check that scream. It became quiet, and she told the simple truth.

"He's dun gone. Don't know whar. May de Lord neber have mercy ef I know whar he's gone. I can't tell ye, because I don't know. I beg you 'uns to let we 'uns alone. I don't want nuffin' to do wid you 'uns."

Profanity, again I allude to the common language of the common people of the South; so far as my observation of the war has gone, it was one tissue of oaths. Leave their conversation to the simple word separated from the intensifying adjective, and it was tame as mere slang devoid of ideas can be. With those warm expletives, every thought was a hot shot, discharged from a red hot cannon, and singed wherever it fell. I cannot pretend to transcribe the conversation of Bill Wolgo. It was too devilish. It nearly frightened the poor, lone widow out of her senses. Curses and threats, that suspicion of being favorable to the North, equivalent to death, or that worse than death—persecution. No where to go— no home—no husband—no friends—no money, and three children.

At this moment, when Bill made a motion in his

anger to cut her face and breast with his whip, the mother turned to protect her child, and uttered a scream of anguish. She had smothered her own offspring.

The child had opened its mouth wide, in one of those inhalations which an angry or terrified infant is in the habit of giving, when silence follows a scream, to be followed by one louder as soon as a new breath is taken. Then the mother had pressed its open mouth against her bosom, and had checked its subsequent convulsive efforts to escape by pressing it more tightly, until the impulse of affection had proved destruction.

"Oh! my God! Oh! my God! He's dead! He's dead!"

"Dog rot the brat, I am glad of it. Shet up your yaup, or I'll merder you 'uns. I orter skelp ye for harboring a Yank."

"Bill, Bill, they've got the scent."

"Where?"

"Here," another voice shouted, "In this drift pile."

"Set it on fire. Smoke him out. Make it too hot for him."

In a few minutes the pile of drift and old logs, part of a tumble down stable, now overgrown with cockle burr and briars, and so tangled as hardly to admit even a dog, was on fire. It was so large and thick as to render it immovable, without great exertion; and if the Yank was there, he could either come out or burn to death. The dogs were howling, as only a hound can, when he is near his game. To render certainty more certain, one came out with an army shoe.

Leette Ledone had too great interest here to keep long away. Passionate, her love had its regret. She loved La Scheme more than judgment approved, so as to yield when the opposite hate was removed. And her regard for the Yank was sufficient to draw her to see the end. She came to learn that her vengeance had been accomplished; the shoe had been her gift, she remembered it. In its accomplishment, she had been the instrument of death to an innocent babe.

It is never right to do wrong. When once evil has been done, its consequences are beyond control. It may stop harmless. It may set others in motion. All subsequent ruin and devastation can never be atoned for by the plea of innocent intention. "How great a matter a little fire kindleth."

Leette, with a woman's impulse, took the widow under her protection. The dogs refused to follow any new trail, which satisfied the hunters that their victim was consumed in the flames, since he had not come out. Some said they smelt burnt meat. They had done their duty—obeyed their orders. Nothing remained. Bill called off his dogs and retired. Leette could do no more than promise a coffin for the dead, on the morrow. It would have been charity to have kept watch with the bereaved, but this was impossible. That dead child would have had company.

There would have been a spectre arising from the flames. She was not beyond human feelings, and James Manet had a mother.

CHAPTER XXX.

Dear Mother :

"I am alive, safe, and with my regiment again at Helena. Thank God. A beautiful Southern lady, Miss Leette Ledone, saved my life, when wounded by the guerillas, who took me prisoner on picket. I have run many hair-breath escapes—the last of which is not least. As this is freshest in my mind, I will tell you all about it.

"I was getting on nicely with my wounded arm, and my ribs were healing rapidly, when Leette came and told me danger was threatening my life. She promised to take care of and save me, but I must agree to obey her implicitly. I consented; for I have had experience with these guerillas. She then led me to a lonely log hut, where a poor widow woman was doing her best to keep three little children from starvation, and took my word of honor to stay in the house until she came back; for, if seen, I should be killed. While here many things occurred. Leette's plantation was burned by our men, and I would have tried to escape but for my word.

I was thinking all the time of you, and how I should escape. I felt that something was wrong at home— I almost knew it; and, when Leette told me Lilly was dead, you cannot think how sadly I felt. She is in heaven, darling sister, where I hope to meet her before this war is over; for, though I have been so wonderfully spared through these past dangers, I cannot expect to survive those which are yet to come. Mother, I shall never be taken prisoner alive again. I had rather die. Soldiers must die for their country; and I cannot but think, if more of us were willing to die fighting, we should end the war sooner, and thus save more lives for our dear native land. It is worth it all, dear mother; and I want you to be very happy in thinking how glad I shall be to have shed my blood for the benefit of millions yet unborn. Do not sorrow for me, for we shall meet in a better land.

"And now while I think of it, I wish you would thank Allie Sandison on my account for her kindness to father in caring for him when he was sick. You cannot know, dear mother, how much is her due, for you never had any experience with the terrible diseases of this climate. God bless her. She is soon to be married, Leette tells me. I am glad, for she deserves to be happy. I hope Charlie may be spared through the war, and they enjoy the great blessings of peace, when God shall permit it to come again.— Charlie is very smart and is Adjutant General.

"But I am forgetting how anxious you must be to know how I made my escape. Well, while I was a prisoner in the log house, I was thinking of getting away, for I had never given my parole not to escape, only to Leette. I knew this was my best and only chance for 'God's country.' Oh, this is not wicked! If you knew how pure, how good, how holy the North is in comparison with this slavery cursed land, you would appreciate our feelings when we think of home as 'God's country.' 'God's country' was far nearer the Mississippi river than it is Richmond, and I was right. So I dug under the shanty and made a tunnel to an old barn which had tumbled down and become full of weeds, briars, and drift wood. I got it fixed to my mind and ready, all but one thing. And God sent that to me,—the way to escape the bloodhounds. They set them on my track and had nearly caught me, for I lost one shoe which the dogs found and so discovered the place where I got into the old barn. I had stopped up the hole to prevent them from getting in. Here again God was on my side. Thank our pastor for that little Testament. I have it next my heart, and when I am shot it shall be still with me. How it has comforted me! I have faith in God. Bless Him for his preserving care of your son.

"Those guerillas were in such a hurry they set fire to the barn, thinking to smoke me out. They did not know I was safe under the house in my tunnel. I had profited by the negro's secret and so scented, you would hardly call burnt cow horn a pleasant perfume, but it saved my life. I had my shoes and bed clothes, not much but burnt cotton, and the boards where I slept I also rubbed with it, and the logs of the house. I heard the hounds run over my head, smelling and sneezing, but they did not detect me.— You may believe I prayed then. Oh, mother, God does hear prayer, and he will deliver our beloved country safely out of this terrible calamity he has permitted to come upon it.

" Dear mother, one of the saddest things happened there that night. That widow had a little baby boy, which she smothered to prevent it screaming before the dreadful guerillas. That night after they had all gone and left her alone, Leette went away last. The next morning she brought a small cracker box for a coffin, with some white cotton clothes for a shroud, and then think she set the guerillas on me ! 'and she actually dug the grave and assisted at the funeral. What a woman ! She did not think I was alive. She did not know I had been minister. Your son James a minister ! But I was, I preached comfort all that long night to the poor mother. I had the words in my heart, for I have learned many chapters. I have not been idle, and I prayed over the little body with her, so that she felt resigned. I told her the babe had gone to heaven. It did seem to me as if Lilly was with me, and I told the poor woman she was : and I told her I knew the child was an angel, and had one friend among the angels. The bereaved mother believed me. She said, ' It made her feel easier to think that he was not among strangers.'

" This woman has several bags of cotton, which I wish she could sell, as she wants to get North, where white men are free and poor white children can get a common school education.

"This is a great way off from my escape, but I have so much to tell you I do not know how to write. I shall have to try and do it, by-and-by. I must, and in a very few words. After the guerillas thought I was burnt to death, they did not come near the house. Not long after I succeeded in calling the attention of a gun-boat, passing up the river, and I was taken on board, and here I am.

"There is soon to be another move to Vicksburg, and we are to go. I am glad to be able to fight again. You may think it strange, but I wish you would write Leette and thank her for her kindness to your son. She saved my life. Leette is a great rebel, and has had some bitter disappointments, which have made her lose faith in all men. I cannot hate, and yet I cannot love her. She hates the Yankees. I want her to know my mother can forgive. I am sure she would love you. God bless you, dear mother, and write very, very soon to your

Affectionate son,

JAMES."

CHAPTER XXXI

Leette returned to Memphis after her thousand bale business was arranged; but not until she had visited the rebel army. Like one of those possessed, the spirit would not permit her to be at rest. As soon as her mission to the guerilla was accomplished time hung heavily; therefore, away went her fleet racer to the camp where her friends held General Grant in check. Here she soon tired of the sights of sickness and suffering—contrasting the garments, the rations, the hospitals, and all their want, starvation of supplies, etc., with the abundance which existed in the Federal camps at Memphis. Quinine—ten dollars for a single dose was freely offered by men in the raging fever.

In the South medicine is given in quantities to astonish the profession at the North. What, there, would be enough to kill a patient, hardly produces any effect upon the poisonous diseases of this climate.

The impulsive Leette—craving excitement; carrying in her soul a raging adversary, which kept her ever active; striving to run away from herself—took up the will to smuggle through the lines sufficient quinine for the army. The comparison of a mirror continues to represent her mind. Before that mirror, spurring her weary animal, faster, faster, was the great word, "Quinine." There was painted the army sick, without quinine; well, with quinine. It buzzed in her ears and rang in her brain. In Memphis she saw only one sight—a room where quinine enough to supply the whole army was hidden. "Get it out, Leette," seemed to be sounding like a thunder-call. How? I do not know. Not by walking her horse, fifty miles from Memphis. So she struck poor weary, patient Janie, willing but worn; with every blow saying, "Quinine, Janie. Get it out. Get up, Janie. Quinine! We must get it out. Quinine, Janie."

Such driving will exhaust any animal. It was too much for Janie. Another horse supplied the place, and, broken down, the favorite followed, a day behind, to enter the stable for the last time.

But, at Memphis, a new picture came upon the stage, driving quinine from the mind as effectually as if it had never been. This was Charlie and Allie.

Before she left, there was a report that these were to be married. Going into society on her return, Leette saw them together; saw that Allie had recovered her influence over Charlie, and that she had lost ground. She remembered her first impression, and the wish for revenge. She remembered the charge to win a Yankee's love, then trample it down.

She saw herself thwarted by a man who had loved
this very Allie Sandison ; that James Manet, who
refused Southern love, Southern home ; and the same
woman was robbing her again. What would La
Scheme say ? As if to enforce the thought, she
turned her eye from them to meet his—speaking to
her the very words of taunt. And, as if that was
not enough, the happy pair came to her—Allie saying :

"Miss Ledone, we have heard from James Manet.
He is in Helena with his regiment. Can you tell how
he escaped ? Aren't you glad ?"

"Have you heard the news ?" asked Charlie. "We
are going down to Vicksburg next week to clean that
out and open the Mississippi to New Orleans."

Leette had need to think,—to work, lest her plans
should be frustrated. Undoubtedly they would be
married, immediately. No, never. Her heel must
crush that out. A peculiarity in great demons lays
in sacrificing the malignity of gloating over their tri-
umphs before the face of the wronged, not taunting
them with, "There I told you,—I did it,—You suffer now,—How glad I am." The devil enjoys the
ruin,—the wreck, and chuckles to himself over the
misery wrought. A plan was devised in a moment.

"Allie, you can judge of my surprise when I
reached home, to hear that James was alive. I had
forgotten that I told him to hide from the guerillas,
those wretches who fired on the boats and drew the
shells of the gun-boat on my plantation. I heard
they were coming, and now remember distinctly tell-

ing him to hide. I sent him to a deserted wood-chopper's hut. But in the alarm and confusion of the battle and conflagration, he passed out of my mind, until some one said he was dead, killed and burnt as I told you, and I believed it. You may be sure I am glad to hear of his safety."

Just here La Scheme's presence became a consciousness. To catch his eye, to know that he understood, to read his thought of gratification in a defeat similar to his own, prompted a change of story.

"Allie, would you believe me? He waited there for me. He told me,—no, I will not tell you before Mr. Hardone. That is a secret. But you need not be jealous, Adjutant. James is a fine man, and I can't tell you what he told me. His love is worth having, I know. He thought you were married and there was no more hope for him, so he gave—there I am telling James' secret. He is a dear fellow. I do not wonder you love him, Allie."

"How did he escape?" asked La Scheme. "You had his parole." Those keen, sharp eyes were fixed to read her secret. Knowing he mistrusted, she would not permit him to have the satisfaction of even looking those hateful words, "I thought so."

"Not parole of honor. You know he never would give that. His parole of love, and I gave it back to him to redeem after the war, or when he got a discharge."

"That does not explain his escape," La Scheme persisted.

"I do not know how he escaped."

22

"Mr. La Scheme," said Charlie, "How can you be so ungallant as to ask a lady such a question ?— She desires to conceal her instrumentality. This is a mixed company. It might not be safe. Not every one would have courage to aid a Union soldier to escape."

Leette, on her part, turned an angry, haughty look of contempt on La Scheme, saying,—

"When I saw him last, he was going barefoot into the woods. Towards evening, I heard the dogs barking in that direction. I could not stay, but rode down. When I got there they had a brush pile on fire. If I must tell you the whole truth, a soldier's wife had just lost a babe, and I did not think of any thing else but comforting the poor mother who had taken care of him when I was gone. Are you satisfied ?"

La Scheme understood the question, but did not answer. Allie and Charlie saw a woman's true kind heart doing good. But over Allie's heart was the same disagreeable sensation which made her feel suspicious, of which she was ashamed,—angry at herself because she could not like one who had been so kind.

The position in which Leette was placed was far from desirable ; add to it a most intense anxiety to know of the success of the cotton trip, and it will be easy to understand her eagerness to leave this unpleasant neighborhood; so when La Scheme offered his arm for a promenade, she readily accepted. Yet this position was not entirely satisfactory, for La Scheme demanded an explanation, and he would ob-

tain the truth, her denial to the contrary notwith-
standing. Oh! how she hated *his* penetration. Consequently, she began conversation by asking,

" Were you successful in the cotton ?"

" Yes, but the boat and every one on board was
arrested as soon as she came here. Every detective,
every provost guard, every treasury agent, large or
small, was after the cotton."

" You were not arrested ?"

' No ; I was too sharp for them. I had everything
arranged, going on the boat myself."

" Did you get the money ?"

" To be sure. They would not trust me, nor
would I them. So it was agreed to deposit the
amount in the safe of the boat, in the charge of the
clerk, subject to my order when the thousand bales
came on board. I let it remain until we reached
Memphis ; but after we had the cotton all shipped
and were backed out, took Sandison to the office,
passed papers, and took his acknowledgment before
the clerk that it was my money. Then, as soon as
we landed, before the guard had time to get on board,
I drew the deposit and went ashore. It was well,
for I should have been kept a prisoner ; but they
were not sharp enough."

" Will they take you now?"

" Not the slightest danger. I have put the money
where they cannot get it and that is all they are
after. But how about this Yankee?"

" Hush! that animal is watching. I never liked
her. She suspects, La Scheme. La Scheme, you

must manage to separate the turtle doves. I must speak to each alone."

" Leette, you cannot deceive me ; you failed, as I knew you would."

" Failed? I would not have succeeded for worlds. Miserable fanatic! he was too low for my contempt! I am angry with you, since your wish made me waste such attention on the dirty dog. I wish he was dead. When I saw our poor men dying for want of medicine—when I thought what abundance there was in the Yankee lines—I could not contain any longer. And then, after I saw his sleek, fat face, so changed from the pale, wounded prisoner, whose life you saved, saw—and seeing, knew—the detested Yankee wretch owed it all to me: I,—I set the blood-hounds on him. That is all I know about it. There is something more important, and you must help me. Quinine; I must supply our army with quinine. The quinine is in the city, and I must and will get it out."

" More important than quinine is the news you have heard to-night. Where is Janie. You must carry this information to headquarters immediately."

"Janie was brought in yesterday foundered. I shall never ride her again."

" You must go immediately. The Adjutant has a good horse. Try and get both a pass through the lines and his horse. The more difficult his consent, the more persistent his opposition, the higher must you bid. Promises cost nothing."

" But the quinine; I will not go through the lines without the quinine."

" That is an after matter. Now you must get the
pass. Orders against any person, whatever, leaving
the city are most stringently enforced; several I
have got beyond the inner pickets, have been arrested by the cavalry. You have a most difficult
task. Begin by separating the two fools. You can
lead her. She hates me. Your only chance for a
pass is through the Adjutant General. I will lay
the track you shall persuade him."

La Scheme led Leette again near the Adjutant,
and his intended saying, as they met in their promenade, "Now is your time." Instantly Leette, meeting Charlie, said:

" You will not be jealous if I give Miss Sandison a
particular message from the Corporal?"

" Certainly," said La Scheme; "Miss Sandison
is too honorable to be under any suspicion of lack of
affection to her intended, though," turning toward
Hardone, "that Corporal is worth a woman's smile.
Do not fear, Miss Ledone has received token of his
love."

Manner is everything. The insinuations of actions
and looks were inimitable forerunners to slander.
Leette said :

" Dear Allie, you cannot know how much pain it
gives me to be compelled to confess what I now must
do. But you were a friend of James' mother, and
you loved him. It is very sad to injure the good
name of any person in the world. No temptation,
however great, could make me do so. I would lose
my soul first. But what would you think if I should

tell you that—Oh! I cannot: How can I so debase your good opinion of me! How can I tell you this wrong act of one whom you so loved—whose friends are so respectable. Oh! Allie, pity me."

The hypocritical actor put her hand on Allie's shoulder, and shook hysterically while several deep sobs choked down tears; she was too proud to weep. Allie was horror-struck at the awful something; a midnight thunder cloud, full of blackness,—electricity,—thunder,—hail-stones,—rain, which had, without warning, taken tempestuous possession of a clear, summer sky.

" Oh, Allie! I was alone. I did not expect it of him. I did love him so. When I found he was alive I was so glad. I went to him, and he—oh, forgive me. I was —"

Again she put her head on the hand which had not been removed from Allie's shoulder. They had gone from the others, and were by themselves in an alcove. That hand which held Allie by all the will-power the earthly demon could summon. The same will which, with all its strength, strove to crush the heart before her.

And Allie—was cold as stone. The meaning did not dawn clearly upon her. Those who have travelled on the great Mississippi have often observed on foggy mornings, after the sun had risen and the snow-mist been scattered, the beautiful gossamer veils, which become more attenuated and spidery every second the sun looks at them,—have sometimes sailed behind them, whereon they were under their shadow. The meaning Leette intended Allie should infer was indistinct, yet palpable as the shadow of a gossamer fog on the Mississippi. She was silent, waiting. The positive and negative of animal electricity were in repulsion, and unable to explain. Allie could not overcome her aversion to speak.

Then Leette, realizing her failure, took the next desperate step in falsehood. Almost groaning, she said :

" Oh, Allie ! would you love me less if I was to tell you I was a mother without being his wife ? "

Seizing the hand which lay on her shoulder and throwing it violently from her, with a whole sea of scorn-waves in her eyes and face, Allie repeated, " A mother, without being his wife ! It is false ! " When she threw Leette's arm away, so violently it turned her around. An expression of hate passed over the averted face which would have made Allie fear. But when Leette turned again, the consummate actress had resumed her role, and appeared unchanged. Leette instantly seized her hand and put it to her lips.

" Forgive me, Allie, it is true. Oh ! I am so wretched. Won't you pity me ? Do not cast me away ! I am alone, an orphan. My home is burnt, my friends lost ! I am alone, alone ! No one cares for me. It is no use for me to love ; where I love I .always find misery. Allie, do not look at me so. Oh !"

Putting her hand on her breast as to relieve a sudden pain, Leette gave a half suppressed shriek. Allie drew her to a chair and seated her there. La Scheme who had been a careful watcher at a distance, was approaching, having left Charlie in the smoking room. Leette placed her hands on her face, for the effort of acting had been wearisome, and while it was thus covered, she permitted it to assume the natural expression of molten passion. She was mentally a vulture, and hungry, ravenous to consume Allie's heart.

Allie answered, " Whatever there may be I freely forgive. So far as I know there is nothing. Whatever *you* may have done, I believe him incapable of a dishonorable act,—not the act of which you charge him. It is impossible. He has too good a mother, he loves her. Rather than believe him guilty—"

Allie paused a moment; strong emotions were struggling. At this moment La Scheme was near enough to hear her words, for Leette to hear his approach. She turned a face on fire with hate and rage toward him; but at his mute look of warning, it changed, and when Allie resumed,

" I would believe you a false, perjured woman."— Then unable to check the strong impulse of instinct, added, " and you are."

Leette sprang before her turning away.

" Stay! leave me not thus. I tell you the truth.— You are too good, too unsuspecting. You do not know what this war has made men. How it has debased them ! Oh! if I had never known ! I was once unsuspecting. God forgive me ! What I am now he has made me. It is the holy truth ; I declare it on my sacred honor.

Still Allie was unconvinced. Her ears heard these frantic declarations, but her heart was unconscious. A deaf and blind person in a room where the stove habitually smokes, may be uneasy at a breath more pungent than common, but on that account does not imagine the house on fire. Leette had been disagreeable from first acquaintance, and Allie, though uneasy, was not convinced. Between the word of a woman she disliked, and the memory of a man she honored, she clung to the latter, she replied by only one word,—

"The dogs?"

"I saved him; I took him from them; he owed his life to me, and he trifled with my honor."

"It is false! James Manet is incapable of ingratitude. I do not believe you. Let me go."

Allie left her without a look. Leette gazing on her departure like a caged tigress hungry for blood, was recalled to herself and another school of deception by La Scheme's cutting comment,—

"Failed again!"

"I have not failed."

"You lied."

"I did not lie. I deceived a Yankee. I do right. In such a cause lies by the millions are blessings. I have planted a thorn in her heart which will stab her to death. It will go to her home and stab his mother. I wish it would drag her grey hair in sorrow to the grave. If it could only disgrace that old white headed father-in-law, and blight the prospects of his sister, I should glory in it

"Leette, you are a jewel, I knew it, I always knew it. You have done for Sandison's daughter. Try your hand on this Adjutant General. I have failed, I cannot get even the prospect of a pass for you. I told him of another thousand bales of cotton. He replied that General Sherman was an old fool and had closed the trade entirely until after Vicksburg was taken. It is impossible for you to get through on that plea.— Not that he personally was unwilling, but the orders were too strict and he dare not disobey. Your pass must come from the General commanding himself.— The Adjutant General is the only man under heaven who can do anything for you, and he tells me he cannot. It is useless to ask."

Allie Sandison, leaving the alcove, found Mr. Wirtman, her only friend, in the mixed company who occupied the parlors. She joined him, thinking Charlie, as was often the case, might have been called away on business, and he was not always kind enough to excuse himself. Mr. Wirtman, too much of a gentleman to neglect any person—to Allie more of a parent than her own father—cheerfully took her under protection, and, when a message came for him to come home, "A soldier wants to see you immediately," he said, "You, too, Allie. Perhaps it is James."

Thus, when La Scheme sought the adjutant general, and brought him back, he found no one save Leette, who having accidentally overheard the message to Mr. Wirtman, and the name James, had a key to open her new operations ; though she did not use it, as she first intended to excite his jealousy, for Charlie said, anticipating her words :

" I know what you would say. La Scheme has told me. It is useless. I cannot give you a pass on any consideration whatever."

" She shook her head with language which beauty makes more eloquent than words. He smiled, but replied :

" I mean it all. You cannot tempt me. I know of the cotton : but that is blocked for the present. Besides, we ran such risks on the last, and the Government is watching us so closely, that the General will do no more business in that way. We shall never buy on our own account again." •

" How is that ? " asked La Scheme.

" We shall demand our share in cash before we sign a permit. Not a pound can come in or go out until its owner has paid us for his privileges. We hold the cards, then, without risk of detection or fear of loss. So you see I have no need of any cotton now. You will have to wait, Miss Leette, until General Sherman goes away before you can get out the cotton."

" General," said Leette, " are you really in earnest? I liked you so well. Why! I thought we were partners! I must have dreamed."

" I feel highly flattered," was Hardone's retort, " to be a partner in your dreams. Was it a pleasant one ?"

They were interrupted by a voice saying, " You are joking, Miss Ledone."

"Mr. La Scheme !" said she haughtily, " Would you throw discredit on my word ?"

" By no means. Excuse me. I beg your pardon. I will intrude no longer."

He left them alone.

" I did dream we were partners, General. Why aren't you General in place of that fellow? You are so much smarter than he. I wish you were. I should be afraid of you.

" Why ?"

" I dare not tell. You would be too vain. But it is no use for me to wish. When are you going to be married ? Oh ! do you think she loves you ?"

" Of course, why not ?"

" Why ? I—I ought not to say a word; but I am an impulsive Southern woman, and if I like a person I cannot hold back like those cold females who inhabit the North. I have talked with her, and she has no passion, no fire, no enthusiasm. She is all hospital, and she does not care. I won't say it ; it will hurt you. No ; you are a man. Yes ; I know you are. You love her, and she does not love you. I know whom she does love,—that Corporal ! Do not shake your head, nor turn away. I am not jealous. I would be if you loved me. Oh ! how I would—"

Charlie turned toward her, eyes wide open, and saw her hands on her heart, while she withdrew an expression of loving possibility from her face, assuming the bashful consciousness of being surprised.

" If you do not believe me, go to Mr. Wirtman's and see for yourself."

Charlie knew Allie had cause against him. None
are more sensitive than the guilty. He had not
reached the point of guilt where sensitiveness becomes shameless. Before he had quite gone, Leette
put her soft hand on his arm and detained him.

"You are going away so soon! Perhaps you will
die. I may never see you again."

He put his hand on his forehead, murmuring to
himself, "Is it possible! She does love me."
Leette's face was covered by her handkerchief.
Kindly putting his hand on her shoulder, he said:

·" Miss Leette. Leette! I am astonished."

"1 cannot help it. I never could be calm as
Northern women. And you are going to war, and
may be killed. Whereon she drew into his arm
and put her head on his shoulder.

" But, dear Leette!—"

" Oh! am I dear to you? Just a little. I felt it
in my heart. I knew you did not hate me."

" Hate! No. Oh, no!"

" Then give me one good-bye." She raised her
lips, which on his part were met, while she drew on
a beautiful smile, and looked lovingly from eyes she
had reddened by rubbing, said, "You will think
of me, Charlie?"

" Of course I will."

" And will you do me one great favor before I go?"

" Certainly, if it will make you happy. What can
I do?"

" Come and see me when you return."

" I will do that certainly. And now I must go."

"So soon?"

"Yes. Good-bye. What, another? I am rich." She held his hand—following him a little, detaining him a little. Then said:

"Oh, Charlie!" [he stopped and looked at her,] "Janie is dead."

"Not your racer, Janie?"

"Yes. I want to bury her, but cannot get out of the city lines. O dear! I loved her. She saved my life."

"Is that all! I will give you a pass to do that. That is easily done. Come into the library."

In a few moments Leette came to La Scheme, her eyes flashing with the fire of victory. "I have it! I have it! It is mine! Hurrah for Leette Ledone!" She held up the slip of paper and waved it in the air. He took it from her, and read:

"Miss Leette Ledone has permission to take the dead body of her horse Janie through the lines, bury it and return.

"By order of Major General Solenter.

CHAS. HARDONE, Capt. & A. A. G.

"Quinine! Quinine!! Hurrah!" and without noise she gave vent to expressions of jubilant joy.

"Janie is not dead, Leette. And if she were, you could take out no quinine with her."

"I shall kill her and fill her with quinine. She served the Confederacy in life, she shall serve it in death, and be buried with its life in her keeping.— Oh, I did cheat him. I made believe love, and took him in. Soft fool! devil!" Here she trampled with her foot, and wiped off her lips, and threw back her hand, as though she tore off the kisses he had placed there and trampled on them. "But it was worth it all. Quinine, quinine, who would not cheat a Yankee, even at the expense of a kiss, for the life of our army ?"

CHAPTER XXXII.

No wounded soldier, without strong motives, refuses a leave of absence. James Manet, just escaped from the rebels, the blood hounds, the fire, was none too well, especially as a new campaign was at hand.— Whatever other inducements, and they were many, he had, to visit Memphis, see his relative and hear from home, he had this also, to aid the poor widow, who had been goo   nd true in his extremity. He knew of the difficulties connected with cotton, merely by report, until his return to Helena, where he was foolish enough to imagine that the story of the widow's destitution, her guiltlessness of wrong in the war, the starving condition of her children, and her kindness to himself under such circumstances, would be sufficient to obtain speedy relief from the authorities, especially when corroborated by himself. Little, how very little, did he know of the vampire appetite existing among those in command, for *blood money.*

The rules and regulations of the departments were

justly, honorably, wisely strict. Against the prudent foresight of General Grant and General Sherman not one word can be spoken. I remember distinctly when listening to a bargain which involved several million dollars, which brought fifty thousand dollars worth of goods, salt, flour, whisky, boots and shoes, plantation supplies, on board a steamboat for a cotton trip up a celebrated river. That those men who had permits and papers from the most unexceptional authority, united in declaring that in all their intercourse with military authorities, whatever they may have paid other officials, these Generals were above suspicion. Honest men do exist. Noble, glorious examples are found among our Generals. That which deserves condemnation is the exceptional instance like General Solenter, whose turpitude was so well known among the clerks and subaltern officers of his department, that they felt secure in all minor acts of black mail which they practiced upon every individual who was base enough, or weak enough, or too much pressed by business to incur the delay brought about by them ; when under the plea of red tape, they hindered, blocked, opposed the usual course of business, that they might be paid for doing their duty.

To make this phase of the cotton business stand out in its clearest light, I copy the trials of a man in a large Southern city where an honest General succeeded a renowned cotton speculator, whose name ought to descend to posterity blackened by the pity of every just lover of country. Pity for the weakness which was not satisfied with the honor and respect of a land

23

full of friends.   Sad regret that such a man, who had
enjoyed the confidence of his native State, who had
filled offices of the highest trust in the gift of his constituents, of his party ; whose name had been before
his admiring countrymen as candidate for the highest
office in the gift of a free, honest, honorable people,
should have fallen before a pecuniary temptation.—
Alas ! what treasure of gold, of rubies and precious
stones can compare with virtue lost, with honor sullied, with reputation tarnished forever !   There is
one man whose name is justly despised, the traitor of
the first Revolution, Benedict Arnold.   When the history of this war shall be justly written, the General
Solenters of the army who have uselessly sacrificed valuable life on the shrine of the god Cotton, will mark
a new era of contempt, and be held up to the detestation of all the good, pure and patriotic of mankind.

Before this memorandum is transcribed, I will relate an incident which I will only vouch for as current
in private conversation in New Orleans.

A Texan broad brimmed hat, a long wide cape, rebel
grey overcoat, with a large bulky planter's form within, applied to a certain Provost Marshal General for
a pass to go out of the lines and purchase cotton.—
This was refused as contrary to orders.   The appli-
cant persisted, finally proposing to pay for the pass
in gold : and the Provost Marshal accepted the offer,
wrote the pass ; whereon Texas produced a bag of
gold telling fifteen hundred dollars in coin on the table, which was paid.   When the pass was folded and
put away, Texas unfastening his outside coat, threw

it open and displayed the stars and buttons of a Major General in the United States Army. The Provost Marshal saw his position and burst in tears. Well might he weep, for the Major General wrote an order from the President of the United States arresting the unworthy officer, and put him in custody of his own guard.

This was done in the Department of a commanding General who was beyond the shadow of suspicion, a General who has made himself hosts of enemies by his determined hostility to every phase of the cotton trade. The prohibition ought to have been perfect, final, complete. The possibility of exception opened the door of temptation, thereby put a premium on every chance of the trade. Less damage perhaps would have resulted had the door been thrown wide open, and every one permitted to get out all the cotton his individual enterprise could reach.

Again, the lack of judgment exhibited by some of these officials was wonderful. Whenever any steamboat brought cotton within the army lines, cotton was seized, in accordance with the regulations, which was perfectly proper; but not this alone, the boat which brought it was also seized, and if not confiscated put to an aggregate expense, causing thousands of dollars of loss to the owners. Even this might have been endured by loyal men, had there been any certainty the cotton so seized would be sold and its proceeds turned over to the Government. But in many instances, if not in every instance, commanding officers or quartermasters found ways to put the proceeds into their own pockets, until steamboats passed by hundreds and thousands of bales, laying exposed on the river bank and afterwards burnt by guerillas, which might have assisted to defray the expenses of the war and diminish the taxes which oppress and burden the land. Had the plan been adopted of paying the steamboat's salvage, or even freight, those millions of pounds would have been saved, as they might have been with slight exertion. To the truth of which statement I call steamboat men, who have followed the river during the war, to witness.

Often the General commanding was entirely ignorant of the misdeeds of his inferiors. Then, he was not responsible. But there were Generals, like Solenter, who received the price of blood, let them, when known, bear their curse, unmitigated obloquy, the detestation of every honest man and woman in the land.

To return to the process of obtaining a permit to get cotton. On the twenty-first of a certain December a man obtained permits from the Purchasing Agent of the United States, in accordance with the orders issued by the President, to purchase two hundred bales of cotton. An honest man, who was determined not to pay a bribe. This is his record:

" Hurried to Colonel S——'s office. Waited most of the day before I could obtain an audience. Handed in my permits, and received instructions to call *to-morrow.*

" Dec. 22d.—Called. Was told I must name ves-

sel and crew, and give bond with security. Not
time to-day. *Call to-morrow.*

" Dec. 23d.—Filed bond and named vessel. Was
told all right. *Call to-morrow.*

" Dec. 24th.—Office closed until the 25th.

" Dec. 25th.—Permits not ready. Had to be recorded in adjoining office. *Come to-morrow.*

" Dec. 26th.—Went and spent all day. Succeeded
in getting permits signed. Went to Gen. C——'s
headquarters ; was told I could have my papers *to-
morrow.*

" Dec. 27th.—Papers not sent in. *Come to-morrow.*

" Dec. 28th—Forenoon.—*Call in the afternoon.*
Afternoon got permits and hurried to Admiral P——'s
office ; was not detained five or ten minutes.   Then
went to Provost Marshal's office to get passes to go
through the lines to the point where the cotton is.—
Too late to do business that day. *Come to-morrow.*

" Dec. 29th.—Spent the day to get Col. R——-'s
signature.   Pass sent to Gen. II—— by Orderly ;
not be signed *until to-morrow.*

" Dec. 30th.—Was told permits and passes had
been lost ; persevered and hunted them up ; found
them too late to be signed by Gen. II——.   *Come
to-morrow.*

" Dec. 31st.—New order issued ; pass to issue from
Col. S—— and be endorsed by Gen. II——.   Went
to Col. S——'s office ; waited all day and failed to
gain audience.

" Jan. 1st.—Got a hearing too late for the General's signature. *Come to-morrow.*

"Jan. 2nd.—Col. S—— had failed to send pass up to head-quarters. *Come to-morrow.*

"Jan. 3rd.—Waited nearly all day, and got my pass."

If this was the process in later time, when the President's order encouraged honest men to engage in the cotton trade—when military detectives were watching officials, fearing they should be detected—what must have been the delay and detention when Generals like Solenter saw tens, hundreds and thousands of dollars waiting only to be taken, ready to drop in showers, so-ever their permits were granted?

James Manet found cotton a hard road to travel; because he was unwilling to do wrong. As this is the story, we turn back to the place where we left Mr. Wirtman going to his rooms to meet a soldier who might be his wife's son; for, already, he had sent a letter, soliciting for him leave of absence for a few days, and obtained the endorsement of General Solenter.

The rooms of Mr. Wirtman were in a sequestered dwelling, which had been assigned Mr. Sandison, near headquarters. On their arrival they found James in the parlors, engaged in close conversation with Mr. Sandison.

Allie Sandison did not willingly accompany Mr. Wirtman. Doubt hung over every step. Should she believe Leette? Which of all her representations should be believed? That James went to war because he was disappointed in his love toward her? That, thus disappointed, he had forgotten

patriotism so far as to be a traitor; thus, by implication, throwing a heavy responsibility on herself?
That he had not only been treacherous, but base?
And if this was false, if James was all his mother
believed; if he loved truly, and she more than half
wished—that is, a something which grew warm in her
heart was not sorry if it might be so; while another
self, with all of cultivated affection, regarded every
such emotion as treason to him who held her promise;
who, holding that sacred pledge, was, day by day,
putting affection to a test which dwarfed and more
than checked its growth; the care of a gardener,
nourishing a rare and costly plant in a conservatory,
forgetting his daily attention—leaving the doors and
windows open for the chills of evening, the damps
and even frosts of neglect,—like this of to-night,
leaving her alone: forcing such a meeting as was to
come upon her unwilling. And then that other
something, the other somebody, the true Allie Sandison springing away from the Lina Sandison of
girlhood, uneducated by war, with an instinct like an
orange-tree blooming in its own dear native soil,
drawing bashful from fear lest Allie Sandison should
be recognized.

James Manet met them unconscious of else save
joy to meet them alive, unchanged, save as the mind
and heart grow strong and old, as thousands of our
volunteers have become, from puny minded boys,
brave reliant men by the teachings of a short campaign. No calumny could look in his calm, fearlessly
honest eye, and believe him untrue; unconsciously,

Allie Sandison became all Allie leaning on his words, drinking them without asking for a reason, while he simply, briefly told the saliant points of his experience, dwelling most upon what concerned others.

At length Sandison drew the attention of all to the topic which had been interrupted when they came.

"And so La Scheme is a traitor as well as rebel. I am sorry for it. He was my friend, room mate and classmate in College. I thought well of him, and even now I can hardly believe what you tell, though it must be true. Why! I have been engaged with him, and never have seen a dishonest act yet."

" His plans are too deep, Mr. Sandison. His foresight is remarkable,.more wonderful his knowledge of human nature, most extraordinary the facility with which he adapts himself to every one he meets. I have seen him win slaves for the study, play with them for amusement, when no one was by ; I unnoticed, wounded, silent and a prisoner. He was a politician before the war ; while we soldiers are fighting with powder and balls, he is doing more fearful destruction with the very weapons which opened the conflict terminating in bloodshed. He trusts in politics. I have heard him condemn Jeff. Davis for neglecting the politics of the North ; now he has opened the cotton trade on his own plan, and, as he says, transferred the seat of war to the North. I know he counts on your aid and assistance. In his opinion every Northern politician has his price ; excuse me for thus saying, but I do believe he thinks he can buy you. "

" Yes, James, you are in this, if not right, not far

from right. I know La Scheme. I read him. He
never deceived me. I have made use of him when he
was using me. Politicians use each other, the wise
man, the sharp man uses his adversary against his
will if possible. Now, he has helped me in the cotton
business, I have aided him; both have made money.
If he attempts to use his profits to the injury of the
nation, I believe I am smart enough to checkmate him
there."

"Oh, that cotton!" exclaimed James. "I wish
there was no cotton and there had never been any."

"Not that, not that. We must have gold to
prosecute the war,—gold to sustain the finances of
the country. While I am getting out cotton, I am
doing the nation more service than any individual
volunteer, since thereby I move the army in the field,
the people at home, and the nations abroad, who
watch the variations in the market value of our gold."

"Oh, Mr. Sandison, more than either gold or
cotton is common honesty demanded among those
who manage the finances of the war. If cotton is
to come out at all, let every one have an equal opportunity. Bring its price down; but do not permit the authorized agents of the Government to mon-
opolize it themselves, at the expense of the whole
country. The widow who fed me cannot get her few
bags of cotton away, because the authorities will
give no permission; while some persons obtain permits every day. Oh! I wish we had an Andrew
Jackson or a Napoleon at the head of affairs : some
one who would shoot two or three rascally Quarter-

masters,—hang an incompetent, speculating two-and-a-half or five per cent. Surgeon General,—or gibbet a Brigadier or Major General, who sacrifices the men entrusted to his care."

"Have a care, James, what you wish. Abraham Lincoln has not power."

" Why has he not power ?"

"He will not be sustained."

"True, he will not be sustained by politicians, political papers, and political expediency men."

"Why do you not include the whole country? Every intelligent man at the North is a politician."

" No, not a politician, but a voter. I will wish that the people, the whole people,—the whole army, —were moral enough—had back-bone enough, to compel officers to do right."

" There are honest men in the community, James," said Mr. Wirtman. "You must have had a sad experience thus to impugn your whole country."

" I have had a sad experience, father. I never knew what human nature was before I came into the war. Certainly it was never so developed at home. I acknowledge there are good men in the community. We need a San Francisco Vigilance Committee to unite honest men in common defence; and, as avengers, elect an honest jury to bring to justice the high and titled rascals who rob the country, and go unpunished through the elevation of their position or the magnitude of their villainy. La Scheme is a rebel, yet he goes through the lines unmolested, protected he says, by influences which hold back the hand of the President. Senators are his partners. Oh, don't they have pay enough? Better pay them fifty thousand dollars per year if money alone can raise them above such baseness. I wish the land was full of honest men."

"You speak strongly."

"Why should I not? Brother Henry was killed for the sake of La Scheme's cotton. Our picket was attacked for the sake of La Scheme's cotton; some of our men were shot and two murdered before my eyes, on the same account; five others went to prison, two of whom starved to death; then Leette's plantation was burned and old Mammy killed, by an expedition after cotton; my own wounds and imprisonment all came from it; and it does seem to me as if no new operation was undertaken until the last base was exhausted of that detestable cause of the war."

"Well, James," said Mr. Sandison, "I have been in the business, but I never engaged in cotton to benefit myself at the expense of my country. As long as it was legitimate I had no hesitation; but the moment it aids and comforts the enemy, I wash my hands of it. There is one transaction in which I shall engage, or rather which I will take off your hands, the widow's, give yourself no further concern. I will see it safely brought into the lines and sold for her benefit. Now a politician is not necessarily dishonest and a traitor; when they forget and become such, they deserve punishment and contempt; but in this struggle where brain meets brain, honest men must use the weapons best adapted to the conflict. If they throw shells, I reply with one of larger calibre and more destructiveness if I can. I know La Scheme. He is a party man, my enemy. Soon his scene of action will be transferred to our elections at home.— There I will meet and expect to defeat him as you will meet and conquer his powder and shot in fair fight. I believe I put a just estimate on his honor, on the permanence of his principles, and I would trust him so far, and only so far, as our interests were identical."

Thus ended the conversation of the evening.

CHAPTER XXXIII.

At the table the next morning, James was asked, "What do you think of Miss Ledone?"

The question came from Mr. Wirtman. Allie listened eagerly. This was the answer:

"She is a deceitful, dangerous woman, I know not how to describe. I have occasion to remember her kindness most thankfully. At one time, no sacrifice could have been asked for her sake, which I would not have granted. She can be an angel—can change to a demon. If she is simply a creature of impulse, I can pardon and forgive; but if, as I fear, she is a persistent wrong-doer, wearing a mask intended only to aid her designs, Leette is unworthy a place among honorable people. I think she cannot be trusted, if for no other reason, because she is intimate with La Scheme, and—but she saved my life; I will not even injure by telling what I think."

"Intimate with La Scheme! What do you mean? Neither have attractions for the other: they are rather at sword's points, which is more a cause of wonder, as both claim to be Union."

"I told you what I thought of La Scheme's Unionism. I have seen both away from Memphis. Soldiers know what value to put on professions made within the lines. Go with us on a march, and you would trust every Southerner so far only as his interest is dependent on your own safety."

"Then Leette is a rebel, James."

"Not a doubt of it. I know she is, unless she has been converted. very lately, and Leette is not easily changed. One of the last things between us touched this very point. My parole was indirectly given to her; when I withdrew it distinctly, she gave me up to the guerillas, and I made my escape, though they attempted to burn me to death."

"Burn you to death! Then you did not give her your love. I knew it was false!"

"My love, did Leette say so? What could be her object?"

"Can she be a woman! Impossible! No woman would try to make a man's reputation villainous at the expense of her own!"

"Allie, what does this mean? I do not understand."

Allie, laboring under strongly excited feelings, did not reply, and James continued:

"Can she be mad? Her last interview was more of madness than sanity. She offered me her love, but at the sacrifice of my country; then, when refused, she threatened me with vengeance."

Allie exclaimed:

"Is it possible! Can this be her vengeance?

What for ?   It must be so.   I understand her contradictory action ; she was the lover—she is the rejected—she is the villain.   This is her revenge.   Her
object must be to injure you and wound your mother
through me.   What a vindictive schemer !   Can this
be all ?   She may not love, and this may be the plot
of an angry rebel.   I doubt if she has any heart at
all.   I never could overcome my dislike, and I am
glad of it.   What a miserable she is !"

An interruption came at this moment, from Adjt.
Hardone, late to breakfast, and in ill-humor from a
headache, occasioned by too much Bourbon ; one of
the instances of which the army commissariat has a
few, where officers never in their lives drank so much
whisky, because bought at government rates, wholesale price, and guzzled by the gallon.   He remembered his conversation with Leette, and seeing James
he addressed Allie angrily, asking :

" Why did you not wait for me last night ?"

She answered, " Why should I wait when you left
me without explanation ?   Can I follow wherever
you go ; or, can I even stay when without protection, I am subject to unnecessary insult ?"

" Insult !" repeated Charlie, " no one dare insult
my intended,"—laying stress on the my, to inform
James of their relationship.   The same word enforced by a threatening glance, then, as both word
and glance were lost on James, he continued : " You
had no wish to wait for me, while greater attractions
were in store.   I was not surprised to find that you
left me for such company, after what Miss Ledone
told me."

"Miss Ledone!" said Allie. "Ah! you will oblige me, Charlie, by never quoting her authority
again. Your present anger is excusable. She has
been slandering me to you, as she slandered James to
me. She insulted me, leaving me no choice but to
come away with Mr. Wirtman. I am glad I came,
since she is now unmasked."

Again the last word was the text.

"Unmasked! What is there to unmask? Leette
is a good Union woman."

James laughed. "Leette is the best rebel I ever
saw,—tried to make me desert, and even persuaded
her lover, La Scheme, to offer me a commission in
the rebel army."

"No no! no!" exclaimed every one simultaneous-
ly. Allie added, "The wretch!"

"Certainly she did. She never pretended to be anything but a rebel, and was true to her principles. As
a rebel and belligerent, I respect her for doing all in
her power for her cause. I never believed it possible
for her to be else than a rebel. A Union woman in
Union lines indicates a capacity for deceit I had not
believed possible."

"You have not fallen in love with her? She told
me so," said Mr. Wirtman.

"I did love her for her kindness. I do love her
for saving my life. I shall never cease to regard myself as owing courtesy and good will, but nothing
more. She put the dogs and guerillas on me; even
if she did not really love me, I never could marry
the enemy of my country."

Then Charlie received an impression. Leette told truth that James loved Allie, loved her beyond his own just right ; else, why had not the superb beauty dazzled James' fancy and thrilled his imagination ? Charlie did not know Leette as a poorly clad rebel, with nothing but form, face, and hands to recommend her to notice and love. The trappings of wealth remained in Memphis and their fascination. The halo of large plantations and cotton bales, was ●cality to the poor Union prisoner who saw them burning, knew them confiscated ; who saw how helpless each Southern lord and lady became when her slaves were gone; who saw those slaves going whenever, wherever the God-sent Yankee army opened a passage through the Red sea of slavery to the Canaan of freedom.

Allie Sandison, too, received an impression. James was honest, true, and unchanged, and, as contrasted with Charlie, so much better, that she honored the corporal more than the Adjutant General.

General Solenter, very much at home, came in, to see his friends, pass away the time, hear and tell the news. Observe the peculiarity of this meeting of Major General, Adjutant General, Banker, Banker's daughter, Cashier and Corporal. Before the war their caste ranged, Chairman of county political committee, village lawyer, two clerks, an old man without particular employment, and a girl. The lawyer was nobody, neither the clerks, nor old Mr. Wirtman ;— Mr. Sandison, the politician, was everything, and the girl his daughter. When the war is over, the great vortex of equality will swallow up and forget the tem-

24

porary distinction, save as bravery, honor, ability and
nobleness of character have convinced the common
people of eminent qualities worthy of lasting remembrance. Even now, the General and the corporal
met and shook hands in the present,—with the past
buried,—as cordially, as equally as if both were not
decorated with either two bars or two stars. After
the first greetings, the General said,—

" The commander of the outside pickets has reported a curious case of smuggling through the lines. Early this morning a female, with the dead body of a
horse on a dray, passed the guard, going to bury it
outside. Their papers were right, and no more was
thought of it, except the length of time they were
gone. New orders have been issued making unusual
watchfulness necessary on the part of the guard, and
when the female did not return, suspicions were excited, and the drayman arrested. He pointed out the
place where the body was left, but it was not there.—
Immediately a detail proceeded to scour the country;
and what do you think they found?"

" What could they find?"

" Yes, Miss Sandison, what could they find? You
cannot guess."

" Was the woman a spy?"

"More than that, a smuggler; for at length the
horse was found. Its entrails had been removed and
the vaccuum filled with *quinine.*"

" Is it possible! How could you tell?"

" By the broken bottles. That one speculation
must have been worth twenty thousand dollars at

least, and be of incalculable value to the rebel army."

"Who could have done it ? It seems too much for a woman to attempt."

" I know of one woman capable of doing this, for she has done it before."

" You mean Leette, James."

" Yes. Leette Ledone possesses the spirit capable of such an action, and the nerve to carry it through successfully. But she did not do it alone. She had some man to help, I feel sure I know him ; the same who planned the surprise of our picket at Helena, La Scheme : a man who deserves his name, whose great skill consists in concealing his own instrumentality. Leette is a spy, and La Scheme is her director. She has taken her quinine and gone to inform the rebels of the progress and starting of the expedition for Vicksburg."

" We shall see before long," said the General. "A detachment has been sent after her."

" No cavalry can overtake Leette when mounted on her Kentucky racer, Janie."

"Janie is dead." Charlie Hardone exposed himself. Guilty of violating orders, the turn given to the conversation surprised him into a confession which unraveled the whole mystery.

" Janie is not dead," said James. " I saw Leette myself, from a crack in the log shanty, seated on Janie, who looked as handsome and showed as keen an eye as ever."

" Miss Ledone told me herself."

" And asked you for a pass to bury the mare ? and you gave it ?" asked the General.

"That was what she was doing when trying to injure James whom she had sought to murder. I think you have cause for anger. She was too smart for you. I would be ashamed, Charles Hardone, to be deceived by a rebel woman."

"Adjutant," said the General, "you have made a great mistake. The very thing of all others to be avoided has been accomplished by you," and then he swore and cursed the Adjutant General; and the Adjutant opened his mouth and replied, exposing to Allie an acquaintance with such words which she had never imagined. This did not continue. It was a burst, a thunder clap, after which the storm held up; General Solenter going away, Charlie following, James already gone, Wirtman and Sandison leaving also, and Allie was alone.

CHAPTER XXXIV.

When the Adjt. General left the house (evil favors its own) he met La Scheme, and told him what had happened—charged him with being in communication with the enemy, and accused him of conspiracy. La Scheme, on his part, listened quietly, assuming the manner of innocence—restraining words : only deploring the sad transaction, and pronouncing the whole a mistake which could easily be explained. He declared Leette had not gone away, but was still in the city, and should be forthcoming.

Immediately he took measures to find and bring Leette back, for she had remained to receive important documents, which he was to transmit before she went below. Moreover, by the same fortune, which has been alluded to, Leette was unwilling to leave Memphis while hate was unrevenged on Allie, Charlie, and James.

It may seem strange and inconsistant for Leette to remain outside the picket lines, hoping to receive dispatches, when no person could pass without the signature of the General commanding. This, however, was very easy, as has been already alluded to; and, in this particular instance, a large, sensible dog had been trained to pass between two houses whenever sent. He conveyed the command to come back in disguise, in place of the expected papers which she was to forward to the enemy.

When La Scheme met Leette, and told her the situation, he said:

"Leette, you must marry the Adjutant General." She exclaimed: " I will die first."

He replied: " You deceived me, Leette ; attempted to act alone, and failed. The consequences may be fatal, and certainly will be, unless you rely implicitly on me. I am unlike other men, as you are unlike other women. I have thrown myself heart and soul in this war, because the war exists ; if we were at peace, I should fight just as hard for my politics to conquer. Most persons long for a home, for rest ; a place where they can be at ease amid the pleasures of love and family. I want none of them. The times do not admit of peace. Children do not appreciate the kindest care, the greatest love. I find every father a miniature King Lear, taught to know—

> " How sharper than a serpent's tooth it is
>   To have a thankless child—"

My existence finds its intense happiness in the conflicts of political life. I study the human mind and make it my slave. I form plans based on the universal principles of human nature ; then lead the men at my disposal to do my will. Leette, do my bidding and all is well. Let me, as a friend who knows you and loves you—this is no idle word, Leette—impress upon your mind the danger of your present position ; charged with being a spy, in danger of death—which you do not fear, or of long and solitary imprisonment, which is unpleasant, but worst to be checkmated.

"Leette, you are superior to common womankind. I frankly acknowledge how far you have exceeded my expectations—expectations originally large. I knew, but did not dream, of the capacity within. To develope all that wondrous power, to teach you how great you were, it became necessary to trample on the heart—the love which woman, mere womankind regard their destiny. The spirit world knows no distinction of sex. I did love you, I do love you, and you know it ; you have felt its strength. No unkind act can drive me from promoting your wellbeing.

"Now let me ask—I do not require any answer, answer yourself frankly, and remember no feeble specimen of womanhood is being interrogated—has not your heart a capacity to love more than one man ? Have you not a power, a capacity, to give from the immensity of your nature a love, differing in kind, in quality, differing in degree ; a passion, large and complete, to different objects, different men ? Is not that love, in every distinct manifestation, greater by a two fold power than your sex commonly call a first, only true love ?

"To-day you love me, Leette, and I love you.—

Closely examine that affection, appreciate it, then let it exist. Mine will continue, whatever disposition you choose to make of the gift.

"Do not wax angry with me, if I tell you a truth which you wish had no existence. Leette, you love that Corporal. I do not blame, I honor you, since your noble soul appreciated qualities which no true woman knowing, could fail to love. This is a law of mind. Your great mind, Leette, obeyed. The affection felt toward me, cherished toward him, are not identical; both can, both do, exist. In such a heart as yours, Leette, as mine; there is room for many others. I assure you, that upon examination, you will find another affection—a certain love for this Adjutant General. But more of this hereafter. I am not blind. I can tell you of another; perhaps, if I had time, if I knew your whole history, could point dozens—your own memory can recall the experience. But one more is enough for our present purpose. Leette, you love our efficient assistant, the guerilla chief—playmate of your girlhood. He is content and satisfied with the share you concede to him; for your heart is large enough for us all, can give in a day more than a Yankee wife in a lifetime. Why then be jealous of other hearts equally large with your own?

"Now let me explain to you our present position. My life, yours, hang upon the same thread: the stroke which kills me, destroys the work in which I am engaged, to which you are bound. This present crisis, improved, will make us successful; neglected, will cost us all we have already done, and probably destroy us together. There remains one course alone, by which our mutual safety is secured and our cause, the cause of our country, is saved; by which all the proceeds of the cotton already sold, the sums which will come from that hereafter obtained by my organization, shall be judiciously used to foment trouble in the ranks of the people at the North.— That only course is for you to marry the Adjutant General.

" This seems impossible. I can accomplish it all : and Leette, by the power you have given, by the solemn oath you freely have taken, I command you to obey. Whatever of power these may have upon your mind, weigh carefully before you refuse. But Leette, I do not only command, I as a man to a woman, soul to soul, for the sake of yourself, for the sake of one whom you have loved, I entreat you to do right; more than this, above this, higher than this, by your love of country, standing where I see more and beyond your farthest gaze, I assure you there is only one safe path to tread, and that is this which I now point out."

Leette at first treated La Scheme with small civility. She was a prisoner, his captive, held in iron chains by her oath, a bondage she hated, but could not escape; voluntarily assumed it would last forever. She gradually became interested, did not interrupt; for when his eye, his voice poured forth its impetuous torrent, it carried her mind along, as the breaking up of Spring puts barns, houses, and farm yards upon the foaming tide hastening towards the sea. Thus had it been when he wooed, and he was again a lover, a magnetizer, exercising his old power, returning like a flood, until she yielded. La Scheme took consent as his without the tongue signature. Her eye and heart had responded. They left the place of meeting together to return to the mansion which had been her home. Innocence fears no scrutiny. That house was under military surveillance; to go there would be full proof of the falseness of the charge against her. While thus going, Leette was recognized by Allie Sandison, also passing through the street, in company of the Adjutant General and the corporal.

If Miss Ledone ever could dress so shabbily, I should call that woman with Mr. La Scheme Leette."

"It is Leette," said James, "I have seen her so clad often."

"Arrest her at once and take her to head-quarters," said Charlie.

"I am not a Provost Guard."

"That need make no difference. It will excite less attention and be better for her. I will prove to General Solenter I am innocent of any intentional violation of orders. He was too hard on me this morning. You will show your consideration, and certainly you are under some obligation to her."

Immediately, James obeyed, followed Leette and her companion, while Hardone hastened to his office to anticipate their arrival, and inform the General of what he had done.

La Scheme heard fast steps approaching; then the

word " Halt ! " Turning, he looked the Corporal in the face, who said to him,—

" Sir, I am ordered to arrest your companion and accompany her to headquarters. I wish to spare her feelings in every possible way. Be so kind as to face about and precede me. In this way no one need be aware of her arrest."

Leette moved to resist. La Scheme in a low tone spoke the words, " I told you ; trust me and obey." They did as ordered. No one on the crowded street thought the Union soldier in blue, on duty. Acquaintances met La Scheme, the cotton speculator, in company of a woman, nodded and were recognized; taking no notice, not thinking his companion a spy, not imagining the tremendous pendulum of anxiety beating in his or her heart. Anxiety hangs over an abyss waiting to drop off. Some believe themselves falling though they have their arms wound round a certain probability of success ; others, believe they will succeed, when their finger nails are dug into the outermost bark of the straw failure. This was La Scheme ; never hurried, never excited, equal to every emergency, powerful in self-reliance. Though both were surprised, were ignorant of the absolute charge brought against Leette, were most eager to obtain some clew of the extent of the conflict to be met in the future, neither spoke a word nor asked a question. On the part of the corporal no word was uttered except the direction " File right," " File left," as they turned different street corners. At the entrance to headquarters, when challenged by the guard, the corporal

went forward and said to the soldier on duty, " Prisoners by special order.   Call the orderly," whereon
they were passed into the gate, meeting the orderly in
the hall.   A moment's conversation between them,
then a soldier off duty was called to stand guard over
the prisoners, for so James represented both until he
reported to the Adjutant General in person.

　Headquarters were situated in one of the largest,
finest private mansions in the city ; a noble sample of
luxury, adorned by a lofty colonade in front, reached
by a flight of marble steps ; steps, which in peaceful
times had cooled the bare feet of the African ; from
which the little lords and ladies,—masters of the sunny South,—had looked with satisfied scorn upon passing poor trash plodding on foot, and with satisfied
pride upon the prancing horses of aristocrats like
themselves enjoying the air, which their magnolias,
jessamines and crape myrtle, their marble platform,
their mosaic paved hall made cool and delicious.—
Those large parlors and reception rooms were now occupied by war desks and war papers.   The velvet
carpets had been removed, to be out of the way of
muddy army boots and sharp steel spurs.   Still,
there were remnants of splendor on the walls ;
pictures which had made bright eyes grow brighter,
none the less appreciated by the earnest art loving
soldier of the Union ; mirrors, that the young officers
on detached service consulted ; where the bearer of
despatches discovered the effects of his haste, causing
him to make his stay in the saloon as short as possible.

　Every one was busy.   Officers coming and going.

Reports received,—orders sent. The head work, the heart pulse of a great army was beating here, almost noiselessly. Each private or officer had work to do which must be, which was done ; and the two persons waiting the General's convenience in the hall, excited no remark, drew no peculiar attention ; hundreds, thousands had so waited before ; some to return to liberty, some to be sent to prison, some to death ; some lost, some recovered property ; to the hard working men who represented the nation, all was in the line of business, of duty ; performed in accordance with the laws of war, after a decision arrived at upon the facts before the Court ; each act driving some other out of sight into forgetfulness. And some things were done, as was this, now before the General Commanding.

The Corporal came from the General's office, saying, " You will come in." Following, they passed an orderly with a sword, entered a large parlor where were desks, officers and persons in waiting, and continuing, reached a boudoir, where General Solenter sat alone.

" This is a bad business, Miss Ledonc."

Her disguise was no more than the primitive style of dress in which Leette was first introduced at Helena. The General saw her shape more as nature designed, though fashion did not imprison feet in steel, like the dungeon keep of an old castle, whose naked top was barred to the noon day sun and the twinkling sharp-eyed stars. Leette asked,—

" What is the charge against me ?"

" A spy, and furnishing rebels with contraband of war."

" 'Tis false! Where is my accuser? I demand the proof."

" One accuser stands by your side. The Adjutant General is another. You have taken quinine outside of the lines, and were taking news to the enemy."

" My presence here refutes the last charge. The other is false as hell. I am a Union woman. What could I do to aid them? I defy my enemies to the proof."

Said La Scheme, " The Adjutant General informed me of these charges. I knew them false, and immediately sought Leette. This corporal had won something of love which her kindness in saving his life, ought to have made respect, if nothing more. She, like a true woman, could not endure his presence in the society of a preferred rival, and weak as woman is, had put on sackcloth, hiding away from the possibility of meeting him. I found her, and was bringing her to meet you, to explain these appearances, when his mean soul must needs add insult to ingratitude, and drag her, thus shabbily clad, into your presence. I know but little of Miss Leette. Your knowledge goes as far as mine. Does it not entitle her to respect and consideration as a woman?"

" It certainly does."

" Then, why keep her under arrest? Let her go upon her parole. I will be responsible for her appearance when and where you order."

" No. The charge is too serious, at this time, too. She must remain in custody."

"General," said Leette, "I do not wish to be relieved of guard so long as I am under suspicion.—Watch me. Let my accuser be my guard. I am innocent, I fear no investigation. James knows me and I dare trust in him though he has proved unkind. Oh, James, how could you!"

"This is all foolishness, General. The woman is not competent to watch her own interests. She ought to consult her friends. She should change her dress and appear more like a sane person. I almost fear she is love cracked. General, she needs female care; I will be surety for her."

"No. La Scheme, you may consider yourself under arrest, with the privilege of the city, to report here every morning at nine o'clock. She must remain in charge. I will yield this ; corporal, you shall take her to her friends, and remain as a guard near until she shall be prepared to be restrained her liberty.—You will then accompany her to the dwelling occupied by Mr. Sandison, and remain in charge until relieved, giving her the liberty of the parlors and the portico, not letting her out of your sight, nor holding any intercourse with any one, except in your presence. There is a small ventilated room, back from the parlor which was made for just such prisoners. I will send you written orders."

CHAPTER XXXV.

The parlors of the Sandison dwelling were lighted, and company was gathering, on the evening of that day. Leette never was more elegantly attired, nor ever looked so handsome. She attracted attention, and was treated so courteously by her guard that no uninformed spectator would suspect her to be a prisoner under arrest. When asked for music, she unhesitatingly complied, requesting the Corporal, as a favor, to turn her pages, and gracefully accepted his arm who invited her to play.

With this part of our characters we have not now to do; but with the Adjutant General, who took La Scheme by the arm and led him out upon the portico.

" I have orders to write the Judge Advocate, commanding him to examine Corporal Manet under oath, preliminary to drawing up charges against you and Miss Ledonc, for trial before a commission."

" What are the charges against me ?"

" Being in communication with the enemy and aid-

ing them with contraband of war. All that saved
you was the engagement of the witness as guard."

"And," said La Scheme. "The fact that I had been
engaged with the General himself in cotton speculating, which I should be most certain to reveal, and
which my partners at the North would so publish as
to ruin his character. No, no, the General has not
considered all the bearings of such a charge against
me. You need only suggest this to him, and tell
him I can explain whatever he desires to understand,
and he will perceive it is for his interest to let me
alone. I have friends in Washington who can easily
procure my release, even if a commission should find
me guilty. And you, who know something of such
things, ought to be wise enough to perceive I stand
in no danger. I know too much. Why, Adjutant,
so far as you yourself are concerned, you would
never permit me to go to trial. Now I want you to
understand me—I do not threaten, I know better—
but I can make more money in cotton than any other
live man, and he is in the business and it will not
pay for him to confine me. I should certainly remember it. It would not pay to have my ill-will inside the other lines. This is all talk : your own
good sense tells you what a foolish, inconsiderate
folly haste would be in this matter, and before the
evening is over you will be glad nothing has been
done."

He paused a moment, then continued :

"I thank you for giving me this notice. I expected as much, and am happy not to be disappointed.
25

I have been interested in you from the first. To tell
the truth, I had rather see you make money than
any person I am concerned with, even the General.
Good-will calls for a return in kind. I ask only
the opportunity to make you one of the wealthiest
men on the continent. Another person might doubt
my ability: this very charge indicates the ground of
my confidence. I am in favor the other side of the
lines, by which advantage I am enabled to deliver
any amount of cotton at any safe point. The idea
of delivering contraband! My dear sir, our last
engagement was undertaken with that express understanding. It is too late for you now to profess
horror at the event, particularly when a mere Corporal attempts to expose. Face it down. Your
word, the General's, is double, treble, will overwhelm that of any private; especially when, as in
this case, the goods were immediately divided among
individuals and never benefitted the army. The
people at the North have confidence in you—are
predisposed to believe you are honest, as you are.
I hold it right to use these side opportunities to
make money. There is no reason in the world why
you should not make your share, while irresponsible
foreigners, and men too cowardly to fight, are making fortunes every day. I think I have said enough
on this point.

"That Corporal could not understand how and
why I should, in the legitimate course of business,
seem to aid and abet the rebels. I did, but it was
when in your employ, doing your business and de-

livering your goods. You know the whole transaction, and have the money in your pocket. Now judge, ask the General to decide, if or not, I am guilty."

There being no reply he resumed:

"I am inclined to think the Corporal has some secret cause against you. I know he is a smart, sharp fellow ; and learning from the accident of his imprisonment that you were making money, sees that he can reach you through me."

Charlie gave a start. His jealousy was aroused. They had turned and were looking through the open window. La Scheme continued :

"See him now, pretending to guard Leette while he is really paying attention to Miss Sandison. It may be you do not read human nature as I do ; but no great penetration is needed to determine an understanding exists between them, and perhaps more.— He has a long head. He won't touch you, oh no! but he will involve Leette and me, knowing I am your agent; that, in order to defend myself, I shall have to call upon you, to prove the authority under which I acted, and then he hopes to see you brought down. Did you ever give him cause to hate you ?"

Charlie answered slowly, "Y-e-s, but Solenter was most to blame. I never gave him credit for such scheming. It looks likely. I do not believe Allie is party concerned."

"No, I do not think she is. She is not smart enough. How did it happen you ever fancied her ? Such a talented man as you are could have your pick, among the richest, and most splendid girls of the country."

"She was the pick."

"You thought so then: you were too much in a hurry. She is nothing but an unsophisticated country girl, and will never change—no more calculated for you, and the society in which you will move, than a maid servant for mistress of your establishment. You are rich already; before the war is over will be worth a million, then your little Western village will be too small, and you will live in New York. I know what I am saying, I know where the cotton is, and you, I, and the General can get it. Now, Adjutant, why don't you try and get Leette? She thinks well of you: somehow you make an impression. You sing and play, and all that—fight, too. Leette is worth winning."

"Indeed she is!" said Charlie. "One of the most affectionate creatures I ever knew. If I was not engaged, I should be tempted. Isn't she splendid! She is a gem!"   .

This burst from Charlie was produced by the graceful reception given to Gen. Solenter, who then came into the room. La Scheme immediately said:

"Now is your time; you know what to say. In these matters the General will do what must be done, and you know, you nor he, can afford to compromise my safety. Say to him also from me, that Miss Ledonc is innocent; and were she not, we cannot afford to have an investigation at the present time. You understand me?"

"Yes. I think I can arrange it, though that confounded pass I gave last night has made him cross as two sticks; not that he cares, but General Sherman may chance to light upon him, and he would rather see the devil."

"All the more reason for not stirring at this time. Would it help him any to be known as cotton speculating? and it will be known. Hush it up; let it die; certainly no damage has yet been done—make a farce of the examination. Always keep such things in the dark. Tell the General to see Leette himself, and he will be satisfied of her innocence."

"I will see what can be done."

Thus saying, the Adjutant General went on his mission to his commanding officer.

While the interview between them was progressing La Scheme held aloof from the gay groups in the parlors. These were large rooms, lighted by gas chandeliers, with great bay-windows: the former owner having sought to realize the splendor of nobility. Curtains of heavy damask hung over the recesses, mirrors of French plate glass reached from floor to ceiling, and oil paintings decorated the walls. There were portraits of master and mistress. Ah! had they been here, would they have gazed unmoved on the lace and shining decorations of the officers of the nation? Would those selections of their taste and wealth have occasioned happiness; the means, as they now were, of adding to the pleasures of Yankee soldiers—the aiders and abettors of flirtation with conquerors of the South? More than one of these thoughts were present, interfering not, rather heightening, the zest of enjoyment.

From one of the alcoves the Adjutant General came from his interview with his commander, saying to La Scheme when they met :

"I believe it is all right ; he will see Leette himself and give her an opportunity for explanation, and if satisfactory, that will be the end. He admitted the force of your suggestions, and said he should not have moved in the matter had it not been for outside pressure. Let us go in. Didn't I tell you ?"

Leette, the rebel, is walking with the General, who has destroyed her home, whom she hates most cordially ; and though he holds her destiny in his hands, she does not change a feature. From infancy, society has educated her to deceive. She has been more true to herself since the war broke down restraint and permitted nature to think and act out loud, than when peace imposed the white lies of graceful society upon her. She returns easily to the mask which art puts upon the soul.

" General, what return can I make for your gentlemanly conduct this day ? You do not know how I appreciate your consideration. I am tempted to believe that you do not share in the motives of my accuser, or else, do not believe the truth of the accusation. Is it true that James is the only witness against me ? What does he say?"

" Miss Ledonc, I do not know. As yet the charges are not put in writing. I have ordered the examination to take place to-morrow ; as soon as the Judge

Advocate has framed the specifications you shall have a copy. To tell the truth, I am very sorry this has ever happened, for I had entertained a different opinion of you ; indeed, it seems impossible now."

" It is impossible, General. It is not true. The charges are false. General, if I can convince you, cannot these proceedings cease ? Must I still be a prisoner, and be subjected to the indignity of a trial before that dreadful commission ?"

" I fear you must. The matter has gone too far. It is too public."

" Why who knows it but us ? Few even of my friends know of my arrest. It will die of itself."

" You mistake, Miss Ledone. It will reach home and influence the public there."

" I understand. That Corporal, that woman's tongue, you fear. I can remove that, because he can prove nothing against me. Will you confront us ?"

" Certainly." Turning from their promenade they met the corporal, who was following at a respectful distance, doing his duty when his prisoner was in charge of the General himself. At a motion, he advanced, and the General addressed him,—

" Corporal, state when, how and where you became acquainted with Miss Ledone ; also the evidence you possess of her character as a rebel and a spy." He answered,—

" I first saw her on the street in Helena in company of Mr. La Scheme ; next, when she attempted to run the picket guard : and afterwards, when she saved my life from the guerillas, which was given to her in consideration of her services as a spy and smuggler of contraband of war."

'It is false!" exclaimed Leette, "and if I were a man I would crush your perjured tongue down your lying throat. You are meanly and cowardly false to lie against the character of a woman who saved your life! You are a liar and you know it!"

"Mr. La Scheme told the guerillas this was true in the speech he made when dividing the articles among them. They left me and went with him, saying, 'Let her have him. Let her have the dyed Yankee. Bully for Miss Leette!' and those of our boys who were present can prove it."

The exclamation of Leette, loud and fiery, drew the Adjutant General and La Scheme to hear the conversation. Upon hearing his name, La Scheme said,—

"Since my name has been mentioned, it becomes me to explain my appearance among the guerillas, and my connection with this affair. I do not blame Leette for anger under such circumstances; certainly, if I could have imagined how ungrateful the corporal has proved, I would have spoken no word in his behalf. I see my old friend Sandison. I am glad to welcome you under such circumstances, for we knew each other as college mates, and he can confirm the facts I now relate.

"When we were in college a boy used to black our boots and sweep our rooms, a small matter of a penny a day, which we settled by gifts of old clothes, boots, &c. He was a reasonably smart enterprising lad, and we were pleased with him ; were we not, Sandison?"

"Yes, and his name was James Manet, now before us. Go on."

"I recognized him among the prisoners, as a guerilla was about to save the trouble of toting his carcass to the other side ; and with difficulty saved his life, by asking Leette as a woman, to do what was beyond my power, as a man. Even then, the men were not satisfied, for he had shot several, (much to his credit, which made me the more anxious to save him,) but I myself was sailing under false colors, and had a narrow and delicate path to walk to save my own life and accomplish the cotton mission I was on. You know gentlemen, and I need not explain, how that demands peculiar finesse ; and I must say, under the circumstances, I had no great regard for truth. I thought the end justified the means. Besides, our friend here, could hardly be said to be in a condition to gain very clear ideas, as he had been ridden down ; which blow had broken three ribs, while a stone upon which he had fallen had stunned him, leaving that scar on his forehead. Besides, he had a pistol wound in the arm. Such a pitiable object you never set eyes on. Had I not a good memory I would have passed him by, but I never forget a face I have once seen.— Under these circumstances, gentlemen, it is more than hard for Miss Ledone, who is innocent as a babe, to receive such a return for her kindness, since all he is to day, he owes to her care."

"Very true," said the General. "There is, however, one thing unexplained. Where did the articles which you distributed to the guerillas come from ?"

"That was a matter of special permit from the General in command of the Post, to Miss Leette, for the slaves on her plantation. It was all right. Corporal, were not the papers properly signed ?"

"Yes, the signatures were correct, but the ambiguity and quantity were suspicious, and therefore I stopped them."

"You understand how such things are, General. I was getting in the cotton : Leette saw difficulty was inevitable and foolishly attempted to come to me. The Corporal fired and drew the attention of the guerillas, who were after my cotton to burn. They went in for a fight. I got the cotton in safe, and then went to look after Leette and arrived in time to save the corporal's life. They used to say one good turn deserves another. I should be very sorry if such an act of hospitality should endanger the life or even safety of Miss Ledone,"

"I do not believe one word of it," said Allie Sandison. "The cotton was guerilla cotton. You must have been with the guerillas, and Leette must have been a spy. Why did you tell the gang, Leette was going to Yazoo city ? Why did Leette tell me, James insulted her ; why did she set the guerillas and bloodhounds on his track, and try to burn him to death ?"

"I did not try to burn him to death."

"You did, you know you did. You offered him your love. You tried to seduce him from his allegiance to his country, to make him a rebel, a traitor like yourself. And when you failed, like a fiend, for no

true woman would set blood hounds upon the track
of the bare feet of one whom she loved; would come
and look coolly on when the house was burning, where
every blast seemed full of his scorched flesh and burnt
bones. Yes, like a fiend! you called off the dogs when
your work was done. You thought it was done. You
with a woman's heart to leave that poor widow alone
with that murdered babe! Yes, murdered babe! and
you murdered it. When Bill Wolgo, hounded on by
you, stood cursing that lone, unprotected woman,
threatening her infant's life, unconsciously stifled its
feeble breath, the act was yours."

"It is false! Girl, you lie!"

"It is true," said James Manet, "I saw you myself."

"Where were you?"

"Under the floor!"

"The dogs did not find you!"

"Leette!" warned La Scheme. He was too late.

"I know it. I had found the slave's secret. I
threw them from the track and outwitted the hounds."

"This has gone far enough," interrupted General
Solenter. "I see clearly there will have to be an investigation. So far as you are concerned, Mr. La
Scheme, the explanation is satisfactory. Adjutant,
leave Mr. La Scheme's name out of the order. I am
sorry for you, Miss Ledone, but the examination must
be held. Corporal, I leave her in your custody for
the night, or until relieved. See every want attended to so far as possible."

"Stay, General. Do not leave before you hear

my answer to this monstrous accusation. While I was astounded by it, I could not but admire the effrontery with which this young maiden espoused the cause of her discarded lover, and the readiness with which she substantiated the tale he has privately tattled in her ears. He is an honorable man and she is an honorable woman; they are witnesses, and I am accused; but, thank God, I am not guilty. Can such a preposterous story be credited a single moment?— No sane man or woman can believe it. Nor would these unless they had been guilty, and desired to create an impression of innocence, by accusing others more pure than themselves of crime."

"Miss Ledone," said Allie Sandison, "do you believe in the God whose name you so easily take on your lips? You do not answer. How many times have you told me there was no God? Before this war commenced, civilized women never wore jewelry made of dead men's bones; never sent requests to lovers to bring them from the battle field, trophies which savages love, and cannibals gloat over. Your slavery has cursed your souls. A woman who can heat an iron, and drop burning sealing wax all on fire, to blister the bare back of her half sister, because the passionate blood of the same father resents the ignominy of being a slave, is capable of setting blood hounds on one she has loved, for not reciprocating her passion. Into the face of such an one, I hurl all insinuations with contempt and scorn. What I am I can answer to God. What you are, God only knows. May he have mercy on you!"

There is this peculiarity of a black eye; if the facial lines are thoroughly under control, it tells no tales; it burns like the sun, but writes neither innonocent or guilty upon the jury-mind watching the prisoner countenance for evidence. Leette's face was a foil, with only one expressive member, the thin upper lip which clung to her smooth teeth as if two double purchase blocks were straining on either side to part it over the jaw. The lips opened with a smile of scorn, as she answered,—

"I am not yet on trial before His bar, if He has any. I would expect no justice there, were He a female abolitionist, fickle to love and unlove in a single breath. My God is unchangeable."

Here La Scheme interposed. "A woman's quarrel. General, this is too small business for us. Will you give me a moment while they fight it out between themselves. When women dispute on love and religion, the contest bids fair to be interminable."

This remark broke the circle. Allie left the room with her father. Leette said to her guard, "After so much discord I would like harmony. May I play on the piano?"

It was not yet late, and callers were still coming; the large rooms admitted various groupings, none had presumed to intrude upon the General, so that an occasional loud word merely attracted attention or excited curiosity which had not been gratified. Leette was so highly excited that a vent was indispensable; her knowledge of chords, her memory of past lessons and favorite subjects, enabled her to vent upon the

instrument, the passions of her soul; a wayward,
weird medley, which none but a skilled reader of musical passion could interpret.

CHAPTER XXXVI.

When General Solenter had retired from hearing he looked at La Scheme, and simply said, " Well?"

" What do you think of Leette, General?" was the reply to that question.

" It will go hard with her."

" You do not believe her guilty ?"

" Appearances are not in her favor."

" Would you approve the sentence, if a commission should find against her?"

" I'd hang her high as Haman."

" General, Leette must not die. You need not save her: simply do not interfere : that will be enough. I will give five thousand dollars just to let the matter rest, and when an opening comes to let her slip out. We have had dealings, we have secrets, and it is best for us to be friends : we cannot afford to be enemies. Leette has many strong friends who have cotton, and by her influence we can make many a cool thousand. I will induce her to procure another steamboat load for half the other cost."

"You know her very well now. I thought so : no matter, I want no more boat loads of cotton: the risk is too great ; that form of business is closed: the danger of detection destroys the value of the proceeds—the anxiety absorbs all else, and interferes with regular business. That is final."

"I understand your position and your feelings.— You do not object to the profits, but the risk. I agree to take all risks. You shall have no share in any transaction whatever : before anything is undertaken, I will pay you in solid cash, or its equivalent, for the privileges you give, and chance the rest ; or, if you prefer, you shall have one half gold and one third of the net profits of every venture. You see, that in failure, you retain the amount advanced.— You can lose nothing, for you invest nothing. Is not that fair ? I furnish all the capital, run all the risks : you simply grant privileges and prevent opposition."

"Yes, that removes the difficulty. But why do you press so for Miss Ledone ? You have not fallen in love ?"

"No. I thank you for the opportunity for explanation. I made her acquaintance in that Helena cotton speculation. The officers are in there, as they are here. You know all about it—"

"Yes, yes. Go on."

"I found her a smart one, more than equal to me, and for a time kept away from her. Then your expedition down the river burnt her plantation, and brought her here ; that caused our transaction for

the thousand bales, which opened my eyes. I have
studied her; I have found how I can use her to advantage. She has done me a good turn, and I never
desert my friends. You, General, see what she is.
I know I can make her pay. I want to make my fortune on cotton. Leette knows where it·is. We make
her a cat's paw to pull our chestnuts out of the fire.
She does not know my motives. I do not often find
a woman to be trusted. She has not failed.thus far,
and, if I can bind her by that woman's failing—
gratitude, I am safe for a million or two as my
share.

" Now, as to the charge of being a spy. There
can be no other. The idea of her killing a favorite
horse, and taking out its bowels. Bah! the idea is
its own refutation. No woman could do such a thing.
(She did not; he himself had done that work.) I do
not deny the possibility; when you think a moment
you see its improbability. So you see the only
charge is that of being a spy; and I assure you, for
I have studied her, that she is a Union woman as far
as it is possible for a Southern born female to be
Union. She has passed between the lines on cotton
business; and every one so passing can be called a
spy, unless they are deaf, dumb and blind. A woman will talk—will tell what she sees and hears   I
pledge my word of honor, Leette has done no more.

" Now, as for this Corporal. I deceived him my-
self, when I first saw him, so that he really believed
I was secesh. If I had been, why did I save his life ?
I had but to keep silence, and he would have been

2ö

murdered. General, you understand politics well enough to know how to lead a crowd : one man must have sweet, another sour—all things to all men ; and in doing this cotton, I am, of necessity, compelled to seem a rebel, when I am not. If they knew where I was, and what I am in the federal lines, the very next time my neck was in the rebel camp, I should have no moment to ask for mercy.

"This Corporal has seen some things he cannot explain : has heard Leette and me speak words of a treasonable character. Can you not explain them all ? How does one of your spies act in the confederacy ? Would not Miss Ledone be a fool to talk Union before guerillas, who would take her life in an instant? Would you not, in a rebel camp, be the best rebel of them all ? General, it is hard to suffer for one's good deeds. Because a wounded prisoner, out of his head, could not perceive what I was doing—that I was as good a Union man as himself—I am endangered. You know better, and as soon us you consider, relieve me from suspicion. The same, in a different degree, is true of Leette. I tell you, Manet has a private spleen to vent against her, and is not to be trusted."

" I think you are right," said the General. " But the matter has gone too far for me to interfere. I do not know but your suggestion is a good one, talk to the Adjutant General."

" If you let it rest in his and my hands, we can manage to keep you from any possibility of suspicion. Only let it pass until this expedition goes down ; the coast will be clear and all shall go well. The Adj't. is a clever fellow, and sharp : if anything goes wrong can be made responsible. He has already done a thing or two, and can do more : in case of necessity he can resign. He is safe for an independent fortune. Now, General, I think we understand each other. I would consider myself under obligation to speak to Miss Ledone alone."

"Yes, you shall have the opportunity. Come, and I will order the Corporal not to interrupt. You are a good friend and pleader. I hope I may have such, if I ever fall in trouble."

"True to death, General. We will make common cause, and I will defy the world to tarnish your reputation while I am in your debt for any favor. I almost wish it might come, to enable me to prove my ability and sincerity."

"God forbid!" said the General, leading to the piano, where Leette was still playing.

La Scheme took Leette aside to the window, near the piano. She looked a question ; he answered :

"I have failed entirely. The only point gained is to delay the charges and specifications. The General says it will go hard with you, and if found guilty you will be hung as high as Haman."

"If it were not for one thing," said Leette, "I would not fear. You remember what you told me of will. I have never doubted my will, nor have ever failed to conquer, except that woman and my prisoner. He has a power over me ; I never intended you should discover. Whence it sprung, how or when, I know not. He is either ignorant or careless to manifest it ; and she,—there was a repelling influence which never relaxed, which I could not overcome—foiling my every attempt to win her confidence. These two have me in their power. I feel helpless : powerful to fight, yet restrained from striking a blow. I could not be more angry. if the confederacy was overthrown."

"There is only one way of escape, Leette—"

"The way, said she interrupting, "which will make them happy, by bringing them together.— Never ! They shall be miserable while I live and I will torment them afterwards."

"Foolish girl ! How short-sighted you are ! How jealousy and hate blind a woman ! Listen to me, and I will prove this to be your best revenge.

"Which hates the Corporal more, you, or the Adjutant ? You, who confess him master. Don't shrug your pretty shoulders or wrinkle your sweet face. Whoever possesses a will you attempt but cannot conquer, is your master, though you may not be his slave. Which hates him more ? The Adjutant, who knows his intended loves a man whom he had injured. Loves ! yes, and always has and will, and would were she the wife, and faithful, too, of the General. You mistake when you imagine you would make her happy, by moving him out of the way. First, the Corporal would not fly to fill the vacuum : he has gone in for the war, and the will you cannot approach is the desire to die for his cause. He is happy in thinking one he loves possesses the true affection of a rising officer. I see how his eye glances, every thought is right, and he would suffer more in the pain this blow would inflict on Allie Sandison than joy in the hope it would open to him. Second, the woman herself would be wounded in the tenderest quick of heart life. Her honest love rejected, by the choice of another, she does despise—you know how thoroughly; judge by the guage of your hate. She will return home discarded. Drop into her reception home the invidious rumor, rejected because the temptations of army life proved too great and she had fallen; then, think you, the loss would be pleasant? No! twice no! for she does love her intended; a love she will miss, as you miss mine. That makes you start. You see my theory is correct. A woman with any size of heart, can love a dozen.

"Now, the Adjutant hates him. I will arrange; yes, I, my will is not conquered. I know I shall succeed, if you will take my road, and not set yourself in defiance of my labors for your life. The Corporal shall be sent to the front, before she knows the news. She shall bear her burden alone, and in the chance of war he shall die. A will like his, lives in battle because the life is charmed. He has already been shot; the next will end his days, and the one he loves be twice a mourner."

"I have heard you," answered Leette. "I grant your position as slave, which you shall recognize by unfolding truthfully to me what new plan you have devised—into whose combinations I may come—where I must play so important a part as to be indispensible. If you fail in the least, I will die here; since I know when I am no longer of use, you care not how soon I die."

"Leette, if you make conditions, I also will make them. First, tell me, and I will answer as frankly, will you do my bidding to save your life and be free?"

She answered, "I will."

"This then is the order: Go to New York as the wife of a federal officer; open one of the most fashionable establishments in the city; draw the society of influential people. Under this curtain the work for Northern disunion shall progress. Your house will be a center of movement, of news, of all else necesary to our plans. You shall be mistress of a kingdom, in which the thought of a Yankee husband will be forgotten, save as it becomes necessary to further our designs. I am sure you cannot wish or ask for anything better. Do you?"

"No."

"Then I will go and find the Adjutant. You see it is late, midnight, and yet you cannot escape; for that sentinel is on duty, out of earshot, but he does not trust you nor me. He obeys, the most dangerous man in the world."

When they came out from behind the curtain, before La Scheme left, the corporal advanced, uttered the military word, "Halt!" La Scheme remained curious to see what next.

"Miss Ledone," said the corporal, "you have a pistol in your bosom. I will take it if you please.—

Do not deny, nor refuse to deliver it," said he, after hesitation on her part. " I saw you put your hand to it when Miss Sandison was speaking to you ; when you took my arm I felt it, and you touched it as you came out, to see if it was there."

Leette took the small patent four shooter and gave it without a word, an opportunity La Scheme thought too good to escape, and he said,—

" Master !"

Leette's eyes flashed upon him, but he had turned carelessly and left the room. Soon after, servants entered, closed windows, dropped shutters, turned off the gas, save in one burner which led on the front centre marble table, a Turkish hookah with a shade ; then, they, at his direction, locked the doors of the back parlor, and he prepared for his vigil.

Leette was no longer at liberty. Respect for her feelings, for the orders of the General no longer required a loose rein, duty had been done where every person was an aid ; now, darkness brought responsibility, and duty put on its stern face and led the prisoner, with the respect which adheres to a daughter of man's first mother, to the room which became a cell, the moment the command was given, "Do not leave this room, under any pretext, to-night."

At that hour after midnight, when deep sleep falls on men, the corporal, weary with his responsible duty and unrelieved, sat him down on a chair to rest after his slow pacing backwards and forwards before the large folding doors of the inner parlor. His back was toward the door of the apartment where Leette was a prisoner ; remaining in this position a time, he fell into that half dream sleep, which often overtakes the watcher fatigued by previous exertion.

When Leette entered her jail, she left the door ajar, had noisily unrobed to convey the impression of retiring, while she retained garments sufficient for a full dress ; then threw herself heavily on the sofa bed ; whence she, looking from her darkness, into his dim light, watched every step of her guard. The thought of her soul was,

"I wish I could kill him. He is the only witness against me whom I fear, 'my master!' and La Scheme taunted me. Then I would be master, I would be revenged on Allic, on them all. He has my revolver, I dare not shoot if I had. I can stab him. That is safe. He did not suspect that." Then she felt for a pearl handled poniard and found it there. She watched and waited, but the regular light footstep, the regular passing from before the single stream of light falling on her eyes, told him watchful, and she dare not try his hand, well armed, awake. The steadiness of the motion of the corporal became at last wearisome, and losing her excitement in its continual lullaby, she dropped asleep. When the sentinel sat down, the change aroused her with a start, which also jarred the sofa. For a moment, everything was impalpable, then her situation came back upon her ; and to eyes awakened from sleep, the dim light of the large rooms was clear day. She saw the corporal as she prayed,— if intense desires can take form of prayer,—he might be asleep. She lay perfectly still to let him sleep, then came and pushed wide open the door. It moved noiselessly, yet she unsatisfied, only looked at the corporal, took at the glance his whole position, and went and lay down again, fastening her lynx-eyes upon his motionless form to detect any sign of watchfulness, and so far as will has power to put antagonists in sleep, to magnetize him by spidery webs more strong than wire net works or iron bars. Becoming satisfied he really was asleep, she left her couch and came silently, until she stood within reach behind his back. At this moment she stretched her hand to its full distance, calculating the range of the heart, which was unprotected, even by an arm. Then the peculiarity of her position, the possibility of detection and its consequences, gave pause. She drew her dagger near her head, lifted her other hand in the position of listening; that concentration of being in the ear, which makes a pin fall louder than a sledge upon an anvil, and the jar of a door like a clap of thunder ;— there was no pin fall, no jar, no creak of boards. Again she drew up her arm to strike; again hesitated, in this instance looked straight before her,—then dropped her hand and went into her chamber.

She had seen in the tall mirror reflected, her own murderous face, her own uplifted arm, her own un-clad form : none of these had paralyzed her soul, un-nerved her will. She had also seen the reflection of the Corporal's clear eye fastened on her own ; and seen him not only awake, but *holding her own revolver pointing at her head!* a hand more firm, a will more fixed, a finger more prompt than her own. Her master !

His sleep had been the strange wakefulness of exhaustion, where mind awake, the body sleeps. He had sat his chair before the glass which reflected her door, well knowing egress was impossible without that faithful reporter painting her passage. When she came armed, he had covered her form with the revolver by the reflection, until it rested where she discovered him waiting to shoot, the instant the assasin's will became action.

Leette came from her room as soon as she had put on her dress, handing her poniard to the Corporal.

"You have spared my life twice. I will not thank you. I wanted revenge. You are my master, for never before have I held such respect for you. Since looking at your eye in that glass, I feel no fear. I will look into the future as steadily. I can die once ; no more : I can look death in the face until it comes a thousand times. James Manet, you have taught me to wait death fearlessly; in life and death you can count on Leette."

Sternly he replied, "I am ordered to hold no communication with a prisoner. Your place is in that room. Go!"

CHAPTER XXXVII.

The lateness of the hour interposed no obstacle to the will of La Scheme: a will that courted obstacles, grappled, turned, twisted them over; or, that impossible, examined them front, flank, and rear, never hesitating, never yielding, but surmounting and leaving them behind as trophies of his triumphant progress; for if unconquered, they were baffled, so baffled as to indicate the skill which propelled his plans in spite of their opposition. Thus it was he could direct Leette, whose will of impulse could not be mastered in particular instances; causing him great anxiety, compelling the formation of new combinations, when she stubbornly adhered to her own independent choice. The will of the corporal was different in the respect that he obeyed duty, adhering to his own view of personal obligation; an unconquerable obstacle, which had it but calculated and schemed to accomplish any object with far seeing resolve, would have been irresistible. The one was quiescent, the other

active ; the corporal was true and full of principle :
La Scheme plausible, and careless of any law of God
or man, in performance or violation, success consecra-
ting and ennobling every act of right or wrong.

The Adjutant was alone in his quarters, preparing
for rest. La Scheme waited for no introduction, but
dove into the middle of his subject. In other cases
he might have wandered around, waiting for his victim to catch and suggest the idea ; here there was no
need : he knew his man, believed him ready to become
a tool, and needing only the firm strong hand to push
him on. The men who planned the rebellion, and in
general, men who can plot, devise, and invent, are
cool, calculating and treacherous; themselves never
enter the house of danger, but stand without on the
threshold : blind and brave tools are selected and
pushed into the fire. Themselves are great Generals,
who stand in unscorched command to win laurels in
victory, or secure safety and immunity in defeat.

"General, Leette must be saved. There is but
one way. You must marry her, send her beyond the
lines, and when the business opens up again, your wife
will be beyond suspicion."

"Me marry her ! That is impossible. I am engaged. "

"Break your engagement. Such things have been
done. How many times have you done it ? I tell
you, General, your reputation, your character, your
fortune is in my power. I can make or break you.
I know what use you have made of the General's name
without his knowledge, and if you should arrest me

or permit me to be arrested, and if you do not devise
with me ways and means of saving Leette, I will de-
nounce you to the General, have you tried before a
military commission, where you well know you would
be found guilty. I would spend more money than
you could,—and you would be condemned. I could
condemn the General. To save himself, he would let
you slide. You are not blind; you, with half an eye
can see how he makes you a scape goat. He will
never turn a hand to save your property when his own
house is in danger of fire."

"Let us go to the General and talk it over with him."

"I have just come from the General. I know all
he can or will do; it amounts to anything you dare
do. You see the responsibility. He will do whatever you say must be done. The less he knows the
more irreproachable will be his reputation ; when
that is protected we are safe. We must consider every plan, and adopt the most feasible, then go to him.
Leette must be saved. We have no moment to lose.
That examination must be prevented, and the corporal sent back to his regiment. What will you do ?"

" I do not know how I can marry her."

" Do not get‑angry at my frankness. I think
enough of you to talk English. Listen, whatever
may be your conclusion, I have been over the ground ;
if you can find a better way of escape, tell me. At
present, hear, accept what I suggest at its value, re-
jecting at pleasure. I desire to save Leette ; this is
my only excuse. She is rich ; owns two plantations
in Mississippi and one in Arkansas, all in her own

right; she has made money in cotton; I need not tell you how much. You also know she can make more; she knows the ropes and has the inside track. Ten thousand bales will not begin to cover your share, and cotton will rise to over a dollar before the war is done: and in case the war is over, her husband will be a millionaire. In the Confederacy she is all right;— and as a Yankee's wife, her husband's and her own Unionism will save her property from confiscation. So much for that: now for her rival.

"I am somewhat of a judge of women, and I tell you, General, Miss Sandison does not love you, and you know it. She may think so, I believe she tries to; perhaps she does, after a fashion. But you are a man of the world, not to be tied down to any one pretty girl. She perceives this quality and tries to persuade herself to love as before, but cannot; you know it, and the reason. It would not hurt her badly to be deserted; she would have a crying spell, of course, and would be better afterwards. No consideration for her feelings should restrain or hinder a moment. It will be better for her to take the present pang, than to waken up by and by and find you do not love her; a thing sure to happen when she takes the position your right demands, and she is not qualified to occupy. As for her father, you are under no obligations; you have made his fortune; he is in your debt. The State you came from makes no difference, for you can go East and make a new home where money will cover a multitude of sins.

"Now for Leette. A woman who loves, loves forever, through good and ill. Leette is this to you, has a passion that questions nothing, knows no barrier, but loves and will die for its object. Miss Sandison thus does not love you, because she does love this Corporal. She is attracted to and by him : is repeled from and by you. Why ? You know better than I. Men marry for money ; fools for love. Money does all things, and none know it better than you. But when you can get not only money, but love and ambition, a man ambitious and talented like you is more than fortunate. You love action. In place of sitting down in an unknown country village, living and dying in grub-worm-bloated content, you may have a wife ambitious as yourself, and make an impression on the country to last forever, writing your name on the page of the world's history. Your money, her money, your position will make you a Representative, a Senator, a Governor ; any office in the gift of the American people can be obtained by a judicious manipulation of the party wires. What do they care where the dollars come from ? Whether from an ice contract, a Surgeon General's percentage, a Quarter master's stealings, or a General Commanding's private pickings ?

"You know what you·receive when you get Miss Sandison. I know one indispensable,you do not, cannot receive,—love. What does Leette bring ? She is handsome, accomplished, well educated, has traveled, is a lady, perfectly at home in society, and she loves you. Miss Sandison is not more than this ;— whatever woman possesses to attract a man, that has Leette; and now, if under circumstances like these, you give up a lady who is attractive as Miss Sandison undoubtedly is, else, how could she have won you? What will be the affection of one who owes you life itself; who will love with natural fervor enhanced by an imperishable debt of gratitude? Is it not worth a risk? Is it not worth a sacrifice?—can that be called sacrifice which is given up to attain such a prize?"

"Well, La Scheme, what can I do?"

"I will tell you. Leette must go out of the lines for the present. She ought to form the acquaintance of monied men, who can buy our cotton, who can own steamboats, and do our business, inside of the lines, and manage all necessary transactions up North. Sandison has had this in his hands, and received his third. We can do the work for less money, or rather I want to stand in Sandison's shoes. You and the General will take your share, and whatever else comes, after the expenses are paid, shall be divided between Leette and me. I think the only safe course for her to pursue, is to go North. While she is there, she can find a home, and get everything ready against your return. Now, how to accomplish this:

"You have some blank sheets of paper, with the signature of General Solenter under the word *approved*. Fill out a pass, or rather an order, for Mrs. Leette Hardone to go North out of the lines and send her by the first boat. Then, one of those same so filled, will send the Corporal back to his regiment

in Helena. I will go with Leette, and see her safe
cared for in New York, finish some business I have
there, and be back before you take Vicksburg."

" I have only one objection. Allie—"

" There !" interrupted La Scheme. " you have
adopted the Corporal's name. You were accustomed
to call her Lina."

With a grimace and shrug, which betokened annoyance, Charlie continued: " Miss Sandison has
decided to go up on the first boat, and it would be
unpleasant, you know."

" Oh ! that is easily arranged. I will get a minister, and have the performance over in two hours.
I heard a whistle as I came in, and before long the
Clerk will report for orders. You can take one of
those same sheets approved in blank, put on what
dispatches are ready, and send her whooping."

" That is an idea, by gracious ! I'll do it. I hear
them knocking. You go and get Leette ready. I
will be there in less than an hour. I will tell them
I will come on board with despatches myself."

La Scheme was prepared for every emergency ;
knew where to go for a priest who could obey. First
he went to Leette.

" Corporal," said he, " call Miss Leette, I come
from the General with verbal orders."

Manet replied : " Mr. La Scheme, I cannot admit
you without direct written orders—"

" What is the matter, Kendal ?" asked Leette,
coming lawlessly from her cell, in full dress."

" The General has consented to send you North,
27

on tne petition of the Adjutant General, who vouches for your character, and proves it by marrying you. A steamboat has arrived; in an hour you are to be ready ; at that time the Adjutant General will be here, and a minister. Be ready."

" I am ready," was her answer.

" What does this mean ?" asked Mr. Sandison, who came down soon after, having been awakened by the noise. " Has a boat arrived from below ?"

" Yes, sir ; and La Scheme has been here with an order to Miss Ledone to be ready to go North."

" Well, I am glad of it. Lina was going by the first boat to get away from that woman. Now I will go to sleep again, and wait for the next boat. I will not punish her, by sending them together." So saying the political cotton speculator went up stairs again to his sleep.

From this moment onward there was no hitch nor interruption. The minister came, the Adjutant General, and La Scheme. Leette had a great heart bound when she saw how providently thoughtful he had been for her, in bringing along her trunk. It stood by the door, guarded by a big negro, who, by his faithfulness to a master denying him freedom, was proving a capacity to honor and enjoy the same should it ever become his own. The ceremony was brief, the Corporal being witness, then was handed him the following order :—

" HEADQUARTERS, &c., &c., &c.

" You will permit Mrs. Charles Hardone to pass

from your custody, to take the first boat for the North.

"By order of A. S. Solenter,
"Brig. Gen. Commanding.
"Chas. Hardone,
"Approved, Lieut. & A. A. G.
"A. S. Solenter,
"Brig. Gen. Com. Post."

On another sheet was the following, the headings and signatures being the same :—

"On receipt of the within you will proceed by first boat to Helena, and rejoin your regiment, to take part in the expedition against Vicksburg.
"Chas. Hardone,
"Approved, Lieut. & A. A. G.
"A. S. Solenter,
"Brig. Gen. Com. Post."

Feeling that his duty would not be done until he had seen his prisoner safe upon the boat, he followed them down to the gang plank. Leette had watched him, and there she called to him, took him so aside as to be unheard, and said:

"I hate you, James, but you are honorable, and I shall save your life again, or my name is not Leette."

Before she could finish, La Scheme had interfered, by saying to the Adjutant:

"This Corporal seems bound to meddle in all your affairs."

The Adjutant stepped up to him, and said:

"Corporal, the boat just below is fired up for Helena.   Go on board, or you will lose your chance."

Within the next half hour, both boats were steaming for the opposite parts of the compass; one for God's country and life—the other for rebeldom, war and death.

.

CHAPTER XXXVIII.

In the city of New York, on a street conveniently near the center of business, there is a building whose narrow front conveys to the observer no idea whatever of greater capacity than its neighbors. It has an English basement, entered from the pavement, under a flight of stone steps, where large dining halls and well-appointed cooking apparatus are located. The house proper begins on the second story. A hall, containing a wide stairway, and a long, narrow room, absorb all the street front. The building is deceptive, expanding in the rear to double and triple its external promise, opening, to the great surprise of the stranger, upon a range of lofty and elegant parlors, flanked by suits of anterooms adapted to the reception of aristocratic guests. These parlors are located at the head of the hall stairway, apparently on the second story, really in the third, and most effectually removed from any observation of the street. This dwelling, secured by La Scheme, was occupied by Madame Leette Hardone, wife of a Union A. A. General, and therefore above suspicion, whose fashionable elegance, wealth, beauty, and expensive entertainments rendered her dwelling a favorite resort.

Here were accustomed to assemble the underground leaders in that Northern conspiracy, which only failed to succeed, by how little, eternity alone can tell. No uninitiated person, entering the gay and festive company, which never failed to gather every night, would or could have imagined treason, criminal as that of Jeff. Davis, stratagem more subtle, masked beneath the bright fascination of this pleasurable gathering; although the tone of sentiment was not patriotic and the songs were tainted with rebellion. The laugh and song were loudest, the wine flowed fastest, and mirth was most jubilant, when the bulletin announced national defeat.

Madame Leette Hardone *boarded* here, occupying a suit of rooms on the main floor, directly in the rear of the library, which belonged to La Scheme. This library was a peculiar institution; like the reading room in an Exchange, in its assortment of newspapers from every part of the country and Europe. It had its music, and its art; pictures to take the eye, a piano for the ear—where some performer constantly afforded a pleasing distraction should any two individuals become too earnestly engaged in conversation. Books filled the shelves; those best adapted to please a general reader, standard works of the best historians and novelists, with a fair sprinkling of that durable binding which tells of skill in law. A door, which closed itself, led out of this room into another. A door with a spring

latch—a door which never opened without showing a
magnificent, canopied, mahogany, French bedstead,
suggesting privacy and forbidding any uninvited visitors. Behind this door was a desk ; at this desk La
Scheme wrote, consulted and managed the varied
details of his business, connected with the next election. By the side of this desk another door, locked
and forbidden : it communicated with Madame Hardone's sleeping room. This door was opened on occasion, when such secrecy was thought necessary as
to forbid the knowledge of communication even from
the trusted inmates of the house.

La Scheme did not take residence in New York
city. Business—the organization of secret societies
—led him to every state and city of the Union ; nor
was he so unskillful as to declare himself or his object, he only sought to know whom he could trust,
knowing he could trust but few. At times he would
visit a city to listen to the strong denunciations of
Union men ; a most certain way to inform who were
proper tools. subsequent organization was confided
to other hands. The genius of La Scheme was wonderful : it grappled treasonable souls, used their own
treason, drew from them the earliest suggestion of
resistance to the national Government, and thence-
forward seemed but their tool. Nor was he in the
North alone. His brain was one vast system, which
could, like the blind chess player, remember every
move played against himself by dozens of chess antagonists, on different boards, in different rooms,
and resume at any moment the game where broken

off. In returning to Memphis, he visited Albany, Buffalo, Clifton, (Canada,) Detroit, Chicago, St. Louis, and Cairo ; on his return, bringing reports from the whole South and money from every agent he had engaged in his great scheme, his path led another route, via Indianapolis and Cincinnati, Philadelphia, Baltimore and Washington. He resembled those house-wives whose habits are so well formed, that, in passing through a room once, the whole is set in order : in going up stairs for their work. they do not have to go again for thimble or spool,—their work-basket always provided, for they never forget that spool of No. 100 Coats' thread they intended to get when they went down town.

Without naming the particular day, save to say the month of October or November, in the year 1863, La Scheme, wth his pass key, opened Leette's door, for a private interview. She said to him :

" Ah ! it is you ! is it ! What do you want now ?"

" You must go South immediately."

" You forget, my dear sir, that you are not my husband, and you very well know the General has resigned and expects to find his wife in New York, as soon as he can reach home. Home ! I hate that word. I have no home while the Yankees invade my native State. It may be he will make this home."

" Your happiness need not be disturbed, for he must go with you, and your home may be South. I wish you joy in your wedded bliss."

Leette uttered a profane word, with which this

page shall not be sullied, and said :

"I will not go. I hate him. I will never be his wife. The mean wretch! I shall tell him plain truths, when he comes to me."

"Do not go too far! Do not overshoot! You may hit adamant, and be killed by the rebound of your own ball. You borrow trouble before trouble comes."

"La Scheme, what are you doing? I am disgusted with this miserable life among cowardly friends: I hate these black abolitionists, but I hate more these mercenary males and females, neither one thing or the other, whom you have drawn around me here in New York ; and I am one eternal lie from daylight till dark, from dark until dawn. I will endure no longer. I have decided to go to England, where I can be free. At Paris I can live a gay, untrammeled life, associated with counts and kings, nor see a single mean Yankee to drive me mad. I remain here simply on account of my oath. Oh! if Janie were alive! If I could only do something! I would love to risk my life on a raid for quinine! You keep me here, shut up, tied,—a mere doll baby. I am sick, tired of this life. I want action : to live where I can breathe freely—in England or France. I do not accomplish anything. I would rather die!"

"Have I not told you, Leette, that you were doing an invaluable work here—to-day deceiving the Yanks and making friends for the South ; that I could not get on without you; that you exert an influence for our cause in New York of greater value than two-thirds of all the cavalry raids since the war

began? Where is your patience? No matter.—
There is work, active work, now, for yôu. Will
you do it?"

" No, I will do nothing. I have worked in the
dark long enough. You are perfectly unreliable. I
have no confidence whatever in your faith, nor your
word. You promised to be here a week ago. The
time before this, you exceeded your covenanted return so much that I lost courage, and the opportunity of making ten thousand dollars. Even now,
to-day, I am loosing by your delay."

" Why do you not use Longcheat?"

"Use Longcheat! Use a thief!"

" Then," said La Scheme, " I am necessary to
you."

" Yes, until I can make a tool of some other one.
Let me think: perhaps I may endure my—bah!—
Well, Charlie may be useful after all."

" He will be useful. You nor I can afford to give
him up. He is your husband, and you are his wife–"

" Blessed privilege!" broke in 'Leette. " I do
value it. I wish—yes, how I do wish, a stray bullet
might hunt his heart before he leaves New Orleans!
I would wear colors for joy."

" Madame Hardone, I am displeased with you."

" What if you are! It is not so near a first time
as to terrify me. What do you want? You never
come here unless there is something—some little,
contemptible thing—for me to do. Oh! if I was a
man!"

" You could not have saved Vicksburg, nor rescued Port Hudson. You would only be a single man. Suppose you were Beauregard or Johnston, would you chafe less at the causeless enmity and opposition they·meet from our own side, their best friends? No, Leette; here at the North you are doing more for the South than any General at home in the Confederacy. Only follow my direction, and you shall be more serviceable than the President himself. Be patient, and wait, as does our brave and noble Lee. Hold on, and soon you, with them, shall win the victory. But, let me tell you, if we fail, you and I, and our friends here, that the Confederacy is done for, our States are conquered, the slaves are free, and we are slaves."

"I do not believe you. What am I doing? What can I do? I did more when I was in the lines.— There was some excitement there."

"Leette, to what end is this opposition? Why are you perverse?"

"Is ignorance perverseness? When have I ever refused any reasonable requirement? Tell me what are your commands."

"I want twenty millions of dollars. With this sum I can carry the next election; put in Washington a peace President, who will give us time and a peaceable separation."

"You cannot do it, Kendal. It is impossible!"

"I can. I have learned and know it, not only possible, but feasible, probable and certain. While you have been here, ill at ease from my absence, I have tested the whole North, and know the price of every leading politician. I do not now include our own friends, the true, unwavering Democrats of the North. The politicians, who encouraged us in the first act of secession, are our friends and can be relied on. There are others, more than a few, who are unaproachable. I do not care for them. A sufficient number of professed radical Republicans can be bought out right. A larger number will slowly yield when we have started the current. I know they are already joining us, and the current will be overwhelming. I have the names of those who are reputed to be strong friends of the administration, who can be made bitter foes ; and there are some of the most distinguished and influential Republicans, who are not yet prepared to accept the logic of the abolition idea. These men will readily go on the other side whenever they can do so with consistency. Some of them have made advances already. Money, money, oh, for money !"

" This may all seem plain to you. It is midnight to me. You told me this same thing when we came North, and now all you have done is to spend the Confederate money, and speculate in gold and stocks with our own. We have increased our wealth, but this discourages me. I see money in profusion dispensed by the Government among all its creatures, and the people not only do not object, but encourage this expenditure. They were never more prosperous, and make more money and spend more than they ever could had there been no war. Politicians, upon whom you so much rely, seem to me the best satisfied with this state of affairs, and would rather continue the war than put it to an end. You must make me comprehend not only your plan, but satisfy my judgment of its feasibility."

" Willingly. Leette, before I begin, permit me to kindly remonstrate against your perverse opposition to me, this mixture of love and hate. Can you not perceive how impossible it is for me to remain in New York? But no, you do not, cannot understand until I speak more minutely of my past work, and what I have still before me.

" First, the money in circulation, of which the people have so much, which they spend so freely, is a mere paper promise to pay, and can be repudiated at any moment. A reason, a very good reason for its extensive circulation, is the lack of confidence in its permanence, which impels those who hold, to rid themselves of it as soon as possible. With greenbacks they pay their debts contracted in coin ; and they buy lands whose value is permanent like coin ; or they invest in stocks of railroads and mines, which, though they fluctuate, have a coin value. Your eyes are blind not to perceive in this external prosperity, real destruction. 'All able financiers are posted. This is the reason I advised you to speculate in gold. You have been successful. The ten thousand you refer to is a mere bagatelle. You have lost nothing. Invest to-morrow, and you will make more money. Hold all the gold you now have for six months, and you will triple your investment. This influx of paper, this inflation of the market, only precedes dissolution, and is, to my mind, the most valuable indication of our success. Still, I know you will not be satisfied with this alone. Listen then to my report.

" I went to Albany, and found things prepared, as I had been promised they should. I did not act myself, but had posted thoroughly a smart young lawyer, whom I paid a thousand dollars to do the talking. He did the business well and was successful.—Before you, who know my design, no concealment is required, and a few brief words will suffice to state his argument.

" The Emancipation proclamation makes the negro and white man equal. The slave, no more a slave, and entitled to trial by jury can *talk back*. What white man, that is a white man, will ever stand a nigger's lip ! If you call a nigger a man, he is entitled to the rights of a man : personal security and personal property, equal rights to education, to self-possession, and family possession ; to personal wealth, and the right to govern his family and his property ; from which proceeds the right to vote upon all questions which involve his pecuniary, personal or family influence, all of which united, make him a free American citizen.

" Leette, the Black Republican could not stand that. He was too much of an aristocrat to endure the idea of a nigger equal, a nigger voter, a nigger senator, a nigger governor, a nigger president, and he fell into the trap I set for him. He is all right now. He belongs to the select few who were born to rule the world. Already he has done his share of governing, and by means of the various strings at his command,

makes white men his slaves. The mudsills of the
North look up to him, bow down before his throne
and worship, and were he only South, had he been
born South, he would be as great an autocrat as could
be desired. He is just like ourselves.

" I have been at Buffalo. I have been in Ohio.
The men with whom I have consulted are sure of success. So too am I, for we are built on eternal principle, and there is no logical principle diffused through
the masses of the North upon which the Republican
party bases its actions. Very few even of the leading
thinkers have adopted any theory which is based on
eternal truth, like ours, in which God is the Master,
and Creation the slave, in which star governs star of
lower magnitude, and Cherubim, Seraph, Arch-angel
and angel govern those who are below them. The
principle of slavery is the God-given principle of the
universe, and we must succeed because failure is im-.
possible. They fight for the Union,—so do we. Our
united aristocratic Confederacy.

" In this united Confederacy, these men, possessors
of great influence, will join us, but we must pay them
for the influence by which they command franchises and
accumulate their wealth. At present, these franchises, their wealth is at the disposition of the Black
Republican idea, and it becomes necessary for us to
mould the opinion of the country, so as to direct their
power into the new channel. We must pay them a
price which will make it an object for them to change
and bias the country by their independent and pon-
derous influence. We must have money. Twenty

millions will do the work. Twenty millions will not
only supply our friends with the sinews of war, but
buy all the influence we need. There are cheap men
whose influence can easily be obtained ; five or six
millions well spent in Washington will not only keep
in our hands the key of every department, but employ
and protect in the Cabinet itself, a politician who will
obey our every direction."

" Kendal, what a man you are !"

" Why then distrust me, Leette ?"

" Because I am a woman and need love."

" Love ! weakness ! no love now. I want no love
to interfere in my plans. My ambition is too high.
Why was I not in the place of Jeff. Davis? The d—d
fool ! If I had the reins I would conquer without
another battle. Even if the Confederacy should fail
under his direction, I should not lose hope; for out
of the wreck could elements of success be gathered
which will restore the principle of sovereignty, the
principle of slavery and create the new empire. Leette
can you not rise above humanity, above the mere woman, and be a God ?" .

" I can, Kendal, I can. · Tell me what to do."

" There are a million bales of cotton up the Red
River. General Solenter is in town. Your husband
will soon be here. Plan a Red River expedition."

He paused. She was silent. Then he asked,—

" Do you understand me ?"

She answered him thoughtfully, " Yes."

" Will you undertake it ?"

With the same deliberation as before she answered,
" Yes."

He took her hand, drew her to him and put a kiss on her forehead, saying,

"Success. When shall I introduce General Solenter?"

Abstractedly as if her mind had gone from her body, pondering that which was before her, she answered,—

"Bring him to-night. I am ready."

Then she put her arms about La Scheme, as a mother might grasp her boy going into battle, put him away without a tear, but a sigh which was between a sigh and a groan.

CHAPTER XXXIX

La Scheme left Leette to form her plans. By simply saying the word Red River, the subject presented itself before a strong, active mind; and he could safely wait while it was revolving itself. The fact of confidence, such confidence would stimulate Leette to profound thought, and even to originate a plan better than his own. La Scheme had learned this most difficult lesson for a strong mind : to permit other strong minds which he must use, to follow their own, not his preconceived path in reaching the goal, —the victory being his object, regardless of anything else. But he did not design to leave Leette uncontrolled. He knew her impulses were not absolutely reliable, and left her to follow them so long, and only so long, as pleased his purpose. La Scheme sought his spy.

The lady who told Leette Ledone, when she came to Memphis, that she was to be the wife of La Scheme, is also a member of this household ; faithful

by her oath, faithful by her love, faithful by her
jealousy. The matchless La Scheme convinced her
of his devotion, by his manner and his kind treatment, and proved his disregard for Leette by giving
her the name of Madame Hardone. It was necessary,
however, to satisfy Leette, and between a natural
wickedness, which delighted in making two females
uncomfortable, and absorption in work, he aroused
the passion of jealousy, which watched Leette, morning, noon, and night.

As soon as his interview with one was over, La
Scheme sought the other ; unless the object could be
better attained by absence. To-day he went directly
to her private room, took his accustomed chair,—one
presented by himself because convenient for two,—
and called her to his usual place when with him. He
used a word with which Leette had been familiar.

"Darling, I am tired. I wish to rest a few moments, and have come to you. I do wish war was
over so we could have a home."

"Has anything gone wrong, Kendal?"

"No. On the contrary, everything prospers too
well, so that I anticipate some drawback. This
makes me doubly anxious for the fate of this evening."

"Why is this evening so important?"

"Leette !"

"What of Leette ?"

"I expect the Federal General, Solenter, and—
You know what Leette is ; she may forget her obligations and make mischief."

" Why do you trust her? I do not need watching ; you confide in me."

" It is too late now. Besides she has had dealings with the General. I do not believe she will so far forget herself as to drag up by-gones. At any rate I shall be with them part of the time. Will you keep particular watch for me to-night, and let me know instantly should anything occur ?"

"You cannot doubt it, Kendal !"

"No, oh no! I only asked because I appreciate how much you are doing. I see how weary you often look, and I would not think of increasing your many cares, were I not well assured of your love of our cause."

" Sometimes, dear Kendal, I do become discouraged and disheartened, but never when you are kind If you were always as now, I should never have a dark day."

" Woman, woman! nothing but a woman after all. I ought not to expect so much from your sex. I thought *you* could comprehend my task and the constant mask I must make of my countenance.— Believe me, my heart is unchanged! No matter what my actions may seem to say, heed them not ! When my words are cruel, forget them. You know me; like myself, you are in an enemy's country. I never doubt you. Give me the same trust. Confide in my honor and truth."

" I will."

" I knew you would, darling."

There is no need to follow this interview, for this

book has failed utterly, if the politician La Scheme
has not a clearly delineated character. Nor will any
time be occupied in a description of Leette's draw-
ing-rooms and parlors, the company, the music, the
dance or the supper. General Solenter was there ;
and with him, and the Red River expedition, as connected with cotton, we have only to do.

When the grand entertainment was over, and the
hour for guests to begin to think of home was at
hand, Leette invited the General to a private *tete-
a-tete.*

Again, as once before, the General commenced his
conversation by saying: " This is magnificent !"—
Well might he say so ! The floor was carpeted with
softest Wilton. The center table was of rose wood ;
and now its marble top was set with a delicate col-
lation, arranged in silver—fruit, cakes and wine.
There was only one window. This extended across
an end of the room, which was heavily draped with
velvet damask, at this time looped on one side, so as
to discover a large bay-window, filled with tropical
plants, whose fragrance filled the room. The most
conspicuous among them were two trees, an Orange
and Lemon, adorned with buds and fruit, also a
White Cape Jessamine and an Oleander, so covered
with blossoms as to transport the mind to the sunny
South. Between the drooping folds, which rested
against the snow-white curtains of delicate open
work, hung a silver cage, in which a Southern mocking bird sang its tempest of melody. It is not often
that birds sing out of season, but the room had a

strange, soft beauty to-night, which affected even bird nature; for the jets of the gas chandelier had been curtained by alabaster shades, lending an atmosphere of enchantment, which drew a soft, deep, canary song from the bird's throat, swelling into triumph, until it mingled with the distant band, as Leette opened the door, and it died away, when General Solenter sat down and gazed at the luxurious exhibition of Leette's taste.

Leette had invited him to sit down in one of those modern inventions, which refuse to admit a third to separate two intimate friends: invented at the suggestion of that song which sings, " Thou art so near, and yet so far." She took the other seat, and doing so pointed to an Armenian hookah with its long, snaky stem and amber mouth piece, waiting for use, and said,

" Imagine me your Circassian attendant and permit me to fill the bowl with genuine Turkish tobacco and light it for you. I love the smell of fragrant smoke, and this is doubly pleasant since it passes through ice cool rose-water."

She did not wait for a reply, but proceeded to perform the office. While doing it, La Scheme knocked. Leette expected him, and without leaving the pipe said, " Come in." When charged and lighted, she turned, and with admirable deceit, said,

" I did not anticipate this honor. Please be seated."

He took an easy chair. She brought him a box of cigars This chair had been placed opposite the General, and Leette said,

" Mr. La Scheme, you have my chair. But if Gen-

eral Solenter will permit me, 1 will take the unoccupied seat by his side, and we will all be accomodated.
I shall have to depend on you, Mr. La Scheme, to do
the honors."

"Certainly," said both gentlemen. One making
room for Leette: the other pushing the table between
the couple, and himself drawing up opposite. There
was a moment's pause and the General spoke,

" I have always felt there was some excuse due you
for that affair at Memphis. The truth was, I was
under obligations to Sandison for some favors, and he
also was concerned in our cotton business. But then,
you must acknowledge, the circumstances were very
much against you. However, it has all come out
right. All is well that ends well."

" Yes. Bygones let them remain bygones. You
and I, General, buried those memories long ago, as I
have reason to know; and Leette, by her escape and
long residence at the North, has wiped out every
stain on her character. has she not?"

" To be sure. The mere fact that she was the wife
of our Adjutant was sufficient. By the way, that was
a smart dodge of yours. I do not know which to
attribute it to. Miss Leette deserved her escape, and
I am glad she was so successful. I notice you continue to use the Adjutant's name, though he denies
having ever done anything but permit you to use it.
However, he is now free. for his intended is dead, and
he can now have the opportunity of marrying you in
earnest."

" Dead! Allie dead. I thought so." Leette seemed to the General to be grieved; on the contrary, she was glad. Hatred toward a rival, rejoiced in this result, and now she could think of the Corporal as suffering. His rejection of her love had wounded her pride more than the injuries of La Scheme. This, then was complete and one war was at an end. Solenter continued:

"Yes. I am sure of it. The last I heard she was dying. She had not been expected to live for some time. That corporal was mixed up in it. You know that the Adjutant denied the fact of his marriage to Leette here, and we did not any of us believe it, except, you know, as—a mere—a mere— You understand, a form. But Manet said something which did the business."

"I am glad of it," said La Scheme. " You now see, Leette, that I was right. All I ever told you has transpired."

"I am glad, now I am vindicated. General, you can no longer doubt me. Oh, if I could only have shown you at that time, it would not have cost me so much suffering. Only to think, that those who wished, who plotted to injure me, should have been instruments to work their own destruction!"

"Let it go," said La Scheme. " The past is buried. General, take some of this wine. You will find it equal to any we had at Vicksburg. Those were rough days in the trenches."

The General filled his glass and emptied it at a draught, and La Scheme immediately filled it again. He took and drank again. Already, the General had been drinking freely at the public tables, and it was when his manner gave signs of weakness, that Leette took him to her room for this private reception.

"Yes, I prefer this to being under fire. Those," pointing at Leette's eyes, "may be a dangerous battery. I cannot see it." He did not see a whole Red River expedition, a defeat, with a wagon train left on the field, and hundreds of soldiers slain, and also thousands wounded and murdered by the exposure which drained their life, drop by drop, in the hospital. He only saw in those eyes, in that dress, a display of passion, which the figures in alabaster typified. He was sufficiently beyond restraint to put his hand on her shoulder, where she permitted it to remain. "I can see," and he closed his eyes, "that two-story house in front of Logan's division, where we planted our battery at last; and remember my first look at those works, when to show a head was a signal for a hundred rifles to crack, and those rebels were no fools at shooting either. How slowly we worked on! The boys were pure grit, and ran their parallels, cut down their scarps, and slowly worked up to those works. I wish Pemberton had only held off one day. Would'nt we have gone in? I guess not!"

Now this was not pleasant for either Leette or La Scheme; yet neither flinched, in either face, eye, or shoulder. But La Scheme turned the conversation thus: "That was a glorious victory, and you did not make any money out of it. Oh, no! I saw some pass, and if what I hear is true, that was nothing.— How was it, General?"

"You are an ignorant fellow, La Scheme! What made you leave? I had another grand offer, which would have been successful if you had a hand in it. I told Charlie you never failed. but he thought he could work without you; and so when the boats were up the Yazoo, and commenced—just as I expected. they were fired into and the cotton burned. We only lost ten thousand each. I shall make it up yet. I am going to see what can be done about Red River. How many bales are there up there?"

La Scheme winked at Leette, answering, "I do not know,—more than a million. Leette has been talking to me about Red River. I will give you permission to talk to her. It will be safer. That reminds me that I have some business letters which must be attended to before I retire. So, good night and success." Thus saying, he left them together alone.

CHAPTER XL.

James Manet went with the great expedition, was one among the thirty thousand good men, who made the rank and file of Sherman's army,—elbowed his way on the crowded steamboat—stretched his limbs on the rough deck—*cooked* his rations and *boiled* his coffee when he could, or *gnawed* his hard-tack and ate his meat raw, when he could not—debarked up the Yazoo, at Steele's bayou, and advanced on the enemy's pickets—was defeated with the expedition, and took a sad heart back, until the victory at Arkansas Post restored the morale of the army. Afterwards, he built him a roof of cypress shingles in the side of the mud levee, at Young's Point, and plastered the cracks with his shelter tent, waiting until Old Perseverance crossed the big river, and led his troops in the rear of Vicksburg. Nothing but a private, who never disobeyed an order, always ate his full rations, and never looked over his rifle at random : a private, who made it a principle to empty his cartridge box, every time he went out, into the trenches ; and that he went into the trenches his full number of times may be inferred from the number of rounds issued to his company—namely, thirty-three thousand, which were expended during the siege.—one among two hundred thousand free men at Vicksburg.

After the national troops had taken possession, had leveled their approaches, had dismounted all the rebel works, using them for the outer picket line, —when they were employed on the inner line of fortifications, which our engineers rendered impregnable; while the main army had moved, or was moving, to other fields of battle, Mrs. Wirtman wrote to her son:

" Where is Chas. Hardone? Why does he not write Allie ? She has received but one letter since he left Memphis. Mr. Sandison has had a falling out with him on some account, of which he explains nothing. He has abandoned the cotton trade, returned home, and resumed politics, and is very busy forming lodges of the Union League for the approaching election, and hardly stays a day at home, following the track of that La Scheme and that most detestable woman —Leette.

" We do not know, and cannot guess, what the trouble may be. Mr. Wirtman thinks it arises from the cotton of that widow who lived in the blind field. I suppose you know it was confiscated and sold, in spite of all Mr. Wirtman could do.

" We say very little about Charlie, for Allie is not yet strong. My other letters, if you received them, (and he had not) have told you how sick she was after her return. Allie is not yet well. That

climate produces awful fevers—almost as awful in
their effects as their experience. I would not live in
it for anything in the world, and wish you could come
home right away. I think one reason for Allie's
slow recovery is her anxiety about Charlie. She
says very little of him, but I think she must have
heard the miserable story which was circulated, and
of which I wish to ask, if you know or can explain it
in any way ? It came from some of Charlie's friends,
amounting to a statement that he had broken the
engagement, because she had been improperly intimate with some of the officers. Was this the reason
why Mr. Sandison had trouble with him ? Do you
know the reason ? I wish you would write if you
know.

" James, why don't you write to Allie ? She would
be glad to hear from you. And, my son, I must
chide you for not being more hopeful. You do
wrong to think you will die before the close of the
war. I cannot feel so. I know I shall see my dear
boy safe at home again. I believe, too, he will be
very happy in the love of all his friends."

To this James replied :

" *My Dear Mother :—*

" Is it possible that Charles Hardone has been so
base as to deceive Allie up to this time ? Has he
.been so deficient in moral courage as not to tell her
he was married to Leette on the night we left Memphis ? He receives Allie's letters, for he tells me the
news from them when I see him, (not very often.)—
What a coward he is ! Then you do not know he

has resigned his commission, and is acting independently as a cotton speculator ? He is with General Solenter as before. I think the whole move was simply to make money, though Charlie pretends the War Department has failed to recognize his services, and charges Mr. Sandison with having used his political influence to hinder the Governor from forwarding his new commission. Charlie says, 'General Solenter only received his Major General's commission by accident ; that Sandison was opposed, but withdrew his opposition, on the condition that I (Charlie) was to be passed by. And so I am made the scape-goat for all offences.'

" Only a short time ago, our Division, General Solenter in command, was ordered to attack a party of guerillas on the Big Black River. I believed it then nothing but a cotton raid, and so it proved, to my satisfaction at least. We took along a train of empty wagons ; they came back loaded with cotton. Charlie and La Scheme were volunteer aid-de-camps, and I am told were overseeing the whole business. I was not there, but at the front skirmishing with the men who were guarding it. This was C. S. A. cotton, and the boys were paid for tearing out the marks on the heads, and sewing in new heads. La Scheme bought the cotton, and the best of the joke was, that he had not paid the Treasury Agent, who confiscated it. Would you believe me, mother, if I told you he bought it out for fifty thousand dollars ? So every one says.

" The talk now through Vicksburg is of cotton, cotton, nothing but cotton. Almost every one who has an opportunity engages in the trade in some way, and the most astonishing sums are said to be made in the business. I know this must be true, for my duty places me often on the outside picket guard, where every pass must be examined, and all articles must be strictly searched. The orders are very strict, and we enforce them most strictly. But some days, thousands of dollars worth of goods pass through the lines, every one of which are properly permitted, and we cannot possibly find a pretext for seizing and confiscating them. Why do some favorites obtain permits when no one else can?

" Are you interested in these things? Do you believe them? Allie will be; she can: for she has seen the cotton trade, and knows what tremendous temptations it contains. I never dreamed human nature was so depraved. Every one seems to have been bitten by the golden serpent, to imagine that they have only to engage and they will succeed, make a fortune in a month. That has destroyed poor Charlie.

" Here I am reminded to tell you how I know he is married. I was present. I have the order yet which Gen. Solenter sent me to discharge his wife from custody. Leette had behaved badly that night, and I followed her to see her safe off on the boat. On the gang plank she beckoned me, and whispered in my ear, " I shall save your life again, or my name is not Leette." Before the words were hardly out of her mouth, Charlie ordered me on board a transport bound for Helena, and afterwards came and wrote an order for instant departure, so I had no opportunity to say good-bye to Allie or father.

" I will send home my orders, for you to preserve in case they should be needed. I would have sent them before, but never had any confidence in mails which were forwarded through our Adjutant General's office ; but now a regular post-office is established here, I have no fear of the mails.

" I cannot hope as you do, mother, that I shall see the end of the war. I feel a presentiment of defeat and death. I cannot survive defeat. If 1 die, you can tell Allie that I loved her, for now she is free I do not think it will be wrong, but not without. You understand, mother, *not without.*

" Good-bye, dear mother. Love to Jeanie, Allie, to father and all.

"From your affectionate son,
JAMES."

CHAPTER XLI.

Perhaps no greater proof of the ability of La Scheme can be given, than his power to keep in one dwelling several females whom he had taught to love him. This would have been impossible without the great underlying principle of self-sacrifice, to which he appealed as a last resort. With this principle, with his secret oaths and his acute perception of the treatment each different woman-nature demanded, he was able to harmonize and produce an apparent impossibility. Besides this, he possessed a remarkable power of systematizing all business ; and he gave each person a particular sphere, a particular suite of rooms, a particular circle in which to operate ; so that all were occupied in minding their own business, were waited on in their own apartments, and only met in the common parlors when policy or impulse prompted them. The war against the Union was a common bond of sympathy ; their mutual oaths a common bond of union, and in those oaths there was an obligation to deceive their enemy, which united them

29

most strongly by one common obligation of deceit. They had their antagonisms,—had their jealousy,—their hatred; but stronger than anger, than hate, than jealousy, was the oath to treat an enemy as a friend, when that enemy was a friend of the Southern Confederacy.

The lady of the house was Madame Hardone. Her sphere demanded more intellect,—the nearest approach to a man. Leette was the man-woman of the establishment—one who dared say what no other female in the house would speak,—one who dared do what none other would attempt,—one who feared the opposite sex by neither day or night, and would jostle her path through a crowd of men as fearlessly, more fearlessly, than a man, because she was a fearless woman—such an one as brave men respect.

The lady of the parlors was the pianist of Memphis: more choice in her manners, more delicate in her allusions, more equable in her temper, more guarded in her language,—impressing her guests with respect for a lady. Upon her fell the reponsibility of doing what impulsive Leette left undone—a sort of binder up of broken heads, soother of wounded feelings. She pervaded the parlors with a quiet watchfulness, which prevented intrusion or observation of what might else have seemed suspicious. Of all others, she was one to be a spy, embodying the idea of vigilence; and La Scheme knew whom he had chosen when he asked her to stand guard on the evening General Solenter was to be won over to a Red River expedition.

Her observation was not confined to the parlors
It included the whole house, which had been so ar·
ranged that every outside door communicated with
an ante-room, by means of speaking tubes, through
which every arrival was communicated to her, the
moment the ring or knock was answered at the door.
This ante-room was the first reception room, and
opened with large folding doors, (run upon wheels
into the partitions,) upon the great parlors where
each guest was lost among the fashionable pyramids
of lace, velvet, silk, from which, as Venus from the
sea, beauty, adorned with sparkling gems, arose to
swell, dazzle and charm the vision of those so favored as to find entrance here.

The whole of the long evening had passed safely
and quickly " as a marriage bell." The exit of the
principle personages had been accomplished without
observation, and the guests were taking their departure, when the watchful sentinel at the door spoke a
name in her ear which made her start—it was Charles
Hardone, Adjutant General. The master of the
house had come. What should she do ? How could she
prevent a scandalous scene in the presence of the
guests? If La Scheme were only here ! But he
was there also. What should she do ?

The Adjutant General, dusty from his long ride
in the cars, was shown, by her direction, into the
library. Then a servant was summoned to show him
a-room, and, in want of something better, her own
was put at his service. On his part, this whole affair was a mystification, which he could not under-

stand. Why did not Leette receive him? From her letters, she seemed a loving, waiting wife, [he had not been taught how young an animal he was— his eyes would soon be open,] but here was a party, at which she should certainly be mistress; where she ought to be doing the honors, and yet she had not come to meet him, only sent a servant and her compliments. "Well," he thought. "perhaps she is unable to leave her guests; I will go down."

When he entered the room, a lady he recognized as a Memphis acquaintance, received him, and introduced him immediately to a lady with whom she left him and returned to other duties. Charlie, looking everywhere, saw no Leette: as soon as politeness permitted, asking for his wife, learned that General Solenter had been there, and that was all. This lady had been instructed to be ignorant, and refer the Adjutant to the other, who kept busy to avoid him. But Charlie began to grow wrathy: he had not been in the army and captured Vicksburg to be flanked in his own house. He went to this lady and demanded an explanation, which now she found impossible to avert. She informed him Madame Hardone had retired, and counseled him to wait until morning. But with an oath he demanded her room, and went there. She, anticipating trouble, by the front stairs, sought the library and the private room, where she hoped to find La Scheme.

Charlie was lighted by a servant, who guided him by the private way. Charlie did not wait for ceremony, but opened, went in, and closed the door. The

room was only dimly lighted, and he was unable at
first to distinguish objects.

Just at this moment the gas, without hands, burned brightly! La Scheme had been warned and turned it on; then General Solenter caught sight of the
man whom he recognized with these words, "The Adjutant, by G—d!" Leette started, and both confronted him, when Hardone exclaimed,

"Solenter! what do you in my wife's apartments?
Draw and defend yourself!"

Before he could reply, Leette had drawn from her
pocket the same pistol she had surrendered to the
Corporal, returned at her request by the Adjutant's
order, stepped before the General, and pointing it at
her husband, said:

"General Solenter is my guest, partaker of your
hospitality. I shall not permit him to be insulted in
my house, even by the man who has a right to call me
wife. General, will you step into the library and tell
Mr. La Scheme not to return. I have something to
say to this man alone."

The General was only too glad to go away. Leette,
gazing directly at Hardone over the bright barrel of
her four shooter, as long as it was pointed at him,
dropped her hand to her side, when his Henry's Re-
peater was turned upon her, curling her lip in contempt as she said:

"A braver man than you dare to be, taught me
not to be afraid of death. Oh, now, put down your
six-shooter; it wouldn't sound well to have it said
you shot your wife." Then, when he returned the

weapon to his belt, she put her's too out of sight.
She pointed him towards the chair in which La Scheme
had been sitting, herself standing by her seat, with a
look which seemed to inquire, " Well, General, what
have you to say ?"

Hardone commenced, " This is a pretty welcome
to give a man in his own house !"   She interrupted,

" General, no curtain lectures.   Perhaps you are
ignorant with whom .you have to deal.   My little
friend I showed you a moment ago ought to have convinced you of the value of anything in that line.   But
you do not know me.   I must teach you never to
trifle with Leette Ledone.   Oh, you thought you was
doing a fine thing when you disowned your marriage
to me among the boys in the army.   Do not deny or
shake your head.   I have the authority of a better
man than you, General Solenter.   Oh, now, do not
get wrathy.   He is not dead yet.   Monsieur Innocence, who married a wife for the sake of her cotton,
her slaves, her plantations,   jilting and killing a woman you did love, you to assume to put on airs!—
with me ! No ! No ! ! Try that on some one else."

" What did you marry me for ?"

" To save my life.   And I can be grateful for a
favor.   Do you think the way to win my love is to
distrust, disgrace and dishonor me, because you find
a gentleman alone in my boudoir ? I who have rode
alone through the Southern Army ! You have made
a fool of yourself, and insulted your wife by a base
suspicion, which does credit to a knowledge of human
nature, learned among females with whom I do not
associate."

" I beg your pardon. Perhaps I was too hasty."

" You need not beg. That is no winning game with me. I would have you know I put a value on you of dollars and cents, just such as you put on me."

" But La Scheme said you loved me. "

" Bah! You are not such a fool! Come, Charlie, dont make me think you were soft enough to believe that !"

" But the quinine !"

" Oh, yes, you sold yourself cheap that time,—for two kisses. It was contraband of war, and you knew and were paid for it as you have been often since. Do not try any patriotic dodges on me. They will not win. I know you, dollars and cents. You shall have your full share."

" That is all very well. But you are my wife, and having sold myself as you suggest, I too, have a share in the transaction, and as purchaser, have rights in Madame Leette Hardone which I shall assert and maintain."

" Don't be too sure of it ! Don't be too sure of it ! Your experience has been limited. I advise you to make as few experiments as possible at my expense. You are matched by no Northern dough-faced girl, but a Southern fire-eater, who will never forgive an injury or fail to revenge an affront. Now let us understand each other. It is to my advantage to appear your wife; you shall lose nothing by seeming my husband. Oh, I do not care particularly as long as there is no absolute antagonism between us, what you may do, where you may stay,—in a word, I concede what I know you will take, full license without a question. But I demand similar rights and privileges, no espionage, no jealousy, perfect freedom for myself, as full as if I were again Leette Ledone and not Madame Hardone."

"I shall not give it."

"I shall take it without the gift; and I advise you never to interfere, for I shall always carry my little friend, and give you fair warning. Leette Ledone never fired at a man without killing him."

"That is cool."

"Why should I be hot? This explanation must come, sooner or later. It is not for your interest to become angry with me. More than one marriage has been for convenience; and as for love, you believe in it no more than I do. Let us talk business. I have invested your funds and made twenty thousand dollars for you. I have been able to pay the expenses of this establishment on a single speculation. Sit down like a reasonable being and let us make a bargain. How much will you take to let me alone?"

The Adjutant sat down. But their conversation was interrupted, as will be explained in the next chapter.

CHAPTER XLII.

When General Solenter came into La Scheme's room, the door of the library was open, and the piano sending out its loud tones. Paying no attention to music, he came to La Scheme, saying—

"The mischief is to pay now."

"What is it?" asked La Scheme, as if ignorant of anything unusual.

"The Adjutant General came in and imagined I was intruding on his rights. Why didn't you tell me?"

"Why should I tell you? I saw your own order, in your hand writing, endorsing the marriage. It is too late to plead ignorance."

"Well, what shall I do? I cannot afford to break with Charlie. He knows too many of my secrets."

"Did Madame Hardone speak to you of the Red River expedition?"

"Yes."

"Then I can put you right with him. We will anticipate his action. I will go and explain the cir-

cumstances, by taking him in as partner and planning
the details of the expedition. What do you say?"

"Go on. Get me out of the affair if you can. I
know your ability, and consent to follow your lead.
Whatever you say I will assent to. Can we manage
Leette?"

"No. Leette is beyond management. There is
only one way to lead a woman. . Make her think she
drives the team. We will try. Come,—now is the
best time to do what must be done."

Entering the room, they found the happy pair
vis-a-vis. La Scheme instantly went to Charlie,
saying—

"I am glad to see you, Adjutant General. You
could not have arrived more opportunely. The General on the one part, and your wife, representing
the Confederacy, on the other, have just agreed to
work out an expedition up the Red River, which
shall make every officer engaged independently rich.
In a word, the Confederacy will sell out the whole
country, and you have come in time to share the
work and reap the profits. I am glad to see you,
sir, very glad to see you. General, sit down."

This was said pointing the General to the seat by
Madame Hardone. Leette moved and the General
took the seat.

"The General tells me you seemed excited. I do
not wonder : it was a mere accident, for I had just
left them to make a little memorandum of agreement
which I will read to you. By the way, I think this
matter ought to be settled at once, both to satisfy you

and set the General in a true light, as well as remove
any wrong impressions which may rest in your mind
concerning your wife. Excuse me, General, won't
you ask the lady who is playing on the piano, in the
library, to step in."

The General went out, as requested. La Scheme
had two objects; one to defend Leette, the other to
secure an additional witness to the agreement. Besides this he wished to afford Leette a clue to his intentions, that she might not mar the success of his
plot.

"Madame Hardone, the General told me you did
not wish our immediate return,—desiring a private
interview with your husband. He also tells me that
you had settled the terms, as far as they can now be,
in accordance with the suggestions we have received
from the South. But I decided that it was more
important for me to see the Adjutant General and
enlist him in this business, and if that could once
be done, for you and him to go immediately South.
He can complete all the arrangements in the Federal
lines without suspicion; while she will take all correspondence, and act with the confederates, on the
other side."

The General here entered with the lady on his
arm, and La Scheme, turning to her, said :

" Lucille, how long had I and the General been
gone when the Adjutant came ?"

" But a moment."

" Did you know of the proposed Red River expedition, and that there were arrangements to be made
to-night ?"

"Yes. I suppose you desired not to be interrupted, and therefore interposed all the delay I could. I beg the pardon of the Adjutant, for I was not aware that he was to be a party concerned."

"Now, General Hardone, you see what we have been doing, and can explain all which seems dark to you."

"Mr. La Scheme," said Leette, "you need make no explanations. There is no necessity for explanations. I am offended that you imagine them necessary: Gentlemen, my husband and myself are on no such terms as to require your good offices. Be pleased to attend to business."

"Certainly," said La Scheme. "You know, Adjutant, there are a million bales of cotton up the Red River and its tributaries. These can all be gotten out by stationing a force at Shrevesport. Now, a proposition has come to me, agreeing to sell all this cotton, on satisfactory terms, to be decided here after. And, if the Government is so disposed, all the fortified places, and their heavy ordnance and ammunition, will be delivered, with little or no loss of life, in consideration of a definite sum,—absolutely nothing compared with the expenditure the Government will be obliged to make if they fight it out.— The sum suggested is one and one half millions of dollars in greenbacks. All Confederate States Cotton to be paid for at the rate of fifteen cents per pound, one half payable in greenbacks, balance in supplies, while the people are to have the privilege of making their own contracts as they best can.

"These are. the terms in general, and General Solenter has taken upon himself the labor of suggesting and starting the expedition. Is it not so, General?"

"Well—I—think," the General spoke with hesitation. La Scheme immediately appealed to Leette, saying,—

"This was the substance of your conversation with the General, I believe?"

"Yes. You remember, General, what you said of the cotton up there,—how the officers were very anxious to move the army up the Red River; and you remember that you told me it would be the most popular expedition, among the officers, that could be undertaken?"

"Now, Madame Hardone speaks, I do remember. But I think it will be hard to get the necessary orders from Washington. I do not know how the subject can be broached there without suspicion."

"There is money enough to be made in Red River cotton to buy a dozen Washingtons if they were twice full of speculators. There will be no difficulty after it once is started and the right men are within the ring. You know who they are. That Senator and Representative of yours can help do the business in the Departments. Shall I read the agreement?"

"No," said Hardone. "The less we hear of agreements the better. This, like all our cotton transactions, must be strictly confidential. Agreements would sound well printed and published! I shall put my name to no paper."

"The Adjutant speaks solid sense, as he always does. I should have been in many a tight place if he had not kept me off from paper."

"General, there must be something to prove to the authorities that the agreement will be kept."

"They must trust to our honor from the word 'go.' There can be nothing else."

"How shall we divide the labor?" asked Leette.

La Scheme answered, "The General must do the work in Washington. He knows the ropes. The Adjutant must lay the track in Mississippi."

"And what will you do?" asked General Solenter.

"Make myself generally useful."

"Where do you put me?" asked Leette.

"With your husband, on the Mississippi. That reminds me of the necessity for haste. Some one ought to go down and communicate progress immediately, to start to-morrow morning."

"I will go," said Leette.

"Without plan, project or details?" asked General Solenter.

"You must not attempt to form any plan, or anticipate any details. Your first idea should be to suggest the expedition, and get the right man, an unscrupulous politician, appointed to lead it. Details will follow naturally."

"General, you are the man to take charge."

"Not me, Adjutant. That would not do."

"Well you would be if I had the appointing power."

"Gentlemen, the hour is early, and time presses. You will only have a few hours to sleep before Change.

This thing, if undertaken, must be made to succeed. What say you, shall we try?"

"I say Yes," replied Hardone. "My voice is Yes," said his wife. "I am afraid to say Yes, though I would like a hand in," said General Solenter.

Then La Scheme taking up the subject, said, "The expedition is decided. Each of us is supreme in our own place, and we all work to one end,—the expedition. Lucille, will you prepare me a room? General, I will not see you leave us to-night. We will need to talk this over before we separate, especially if the Adjutant and his wife go down to New Orleans to-morrow. It is late now and he is tired. We will leave him."

This was the signal for departure. Lucille left first, Solenter followed. Would he remain alone with that amiable couple? Not he. La Scheme followed and closed the door. When once in the library, La Scheme addressed the General.

"You have made a narrow escape. It was all I could do while you was gone to calm the Adjutant. You were uneasy under his eyes all the evening, and I was compelled to make up many things to protect you. I prevaricated most egregiously when I professed to have received any proposition, but I know the sale can be brought about. There is only one thing now to be done. You must put a bold face on the whole matter and commence work. Assistance will come of itself, as soon as the officials know there is any money in it. Of one thing you must be very careful, not to permit Hardone to get the better of you. If ever a man wanted to kill another, he was one this evening. I have laid his suspicions. The only way to keep them down is to get him off to Vicksburg and New Orleans, while you work at Washington.— When you join your command, the music will be in your hands."

La Scheme showed him a room, and left him,—joining Lucille, he said:

"Lucille, nothing in the world could be better. We shall have a Red River expedition. Our cotton will be sold. I will get our twenty millions, control the next Presidential election, choose a peace President, and our country shall be free. Then, hurrah for Lady Lucille, and the noble lord Kendal La Scheme, Duke of Mississippi!"

CHAPTER XLIII.

No one knows the author of the Red River expedition. It has no father. It ought not to have any honorable origin. In lieu of any other, Cotton Stealing offers the explanation of the preceding chapter, which may or may not be eminently satisfactory.

Every one engaged in that expedition remembers how easily Fort De Russy was taken, and Alexandria captured. They will remember the universal stampede of government and every other team after cotton, so that even the gunboat boys were on special service, until very shortly piles of cotton bales lay on the banks of Red River, and the army and navy seemed a giant thief stealing cotton. They will remember how as the expedition proceeded towards Shreveport, a holocaust of burning cotton preceded, and how at last when that long train of cavalry went in advance of the main army—the wagon train loaded with stores, the quarter master's train, the ammunition train, the paymaster's train, were all thrown in advance of the infantry ; and they will remember how when we were

30

attacked, and our troops were defeated, that train, those stores, those supplies, those quartermaster and paymaster chests, were captured. Every one engaged in this expedition will remember this, and they will now look back upon it as some dream of romance, which Congressional Investigating Committees, and army court martials have proved a mere figment of the brain for which no one is responsible.

But there is one poor private who has a realizing sense of the expedition, and a positive belief as to the originators, the policy, object, and cause of the failure of the expedition.

Corporal Manet was in the fighting corps of the old war-dog, A. J. Smith, and when the routed corps, which had been only brought into action by brigades and divisions, been whipped in detail, ran to the rear in unavoidable confusion, he was in the front with other good and true men prepared to receive the rebel charge.

The rebels came on. They were perfectly acquainted with the number, position and quality of the forces comprising the expedition. They knew how many had been captured, how many had been routed, but they did not know old Grizzly and his Western cubs, who sharpened their claws and ground their teeth at Vicksburg. Perhaps they had been informed of the incorruptible ones and expected to have some hard work to do ; at any rate they formed more than one line of battle and rushed to the charge.

They were repulsed. Every one knows how gloriously they were repulsed. The army found space to breathe and was saved. All honor to Major General A. J. Smith and the heroes of Vicksburg!

In that first charge the line in which James Manet was stationed, was forced back some rods. Before his comrades retired he had been wounded. His leg was broken. They tried to bring him off, but failed, leaving him with seven others wounded. Said James, "Boys, fall back; don't mind us. We shall die anyway. We will kill a few more before we go." .

There was no time for compliments. The line maintained its front only a few rods in their rear. Charge after charge was made by the rebels, but it never reached the spot where they were fighting. Over their devoted heads the bullets, the balls, the shells of both friends and foes were flying. Each man with the will of one who sells his life dearly, loaded his gun, waited for a shot, and fired on purpose to kill. Before the day was gone, they had been complimented by the particular attention of a battery and a regiment of sharpshooters. One by one those brave souls said " Good-bye, Corporal." Now the words came faint from the lips of a farmer boy, who took a bullet from behind, when too eager he exposed his head, and was shot in an artery, which bled him to death. They could not ease his twisted form ; they could not move themselves. They did not weep. They fired finer. " That was for Billy." Thug, came an Enfield bullet. " Charlie's gone. It's my turn next, but I must take one more with me." The air was soft and still as summer morning, while the battle waged on either hand. One short moment seemed an hour to those, who, waiting for a shot, fired at the smoke; or rather, each moment was an hour in coming, each hour a fraction of a second when gone to join eternity. Another charge came, and Long-legged Sam fired his last. He was killed by the premature explosion of one of our own shells. The Corporal fought on until every round was expended, and then took cartridges from his comrade's boxes. At last, a shot, which had its mission, struck his arm above the elbow, and his work was done. Not dead, but bleeding to death.

At evening, some of the boys came to find the wounded, examined each, pronounced them dead, and as the order for retreat had been given, left their bodies to be buried by the rebels.

A battle field at night is awful! Gettysburg, with its three days conflict, Seven Pines, with its woods on fire, or Shiloh, or Lone Mountain; every battle of the Rebellion had its hour of midnight, when no star shone, but exhaustion lay in stony coldness all over the ground like a hoar-frost dew in early autumn.

In the haste of battle, men had not moved from where they dropped, dead-ripe fruit upon the ground. The wounded were still, because the cold had chilled what little blood was left. There were no shadows, because shadows suggest light. Darkness brooded above the tree tops, sombre in daylight. Darkness, below the matted mass of limbs and leaves, did not brood, it penetrated like a November fog on the coast of Maine. Darkness was visible-black moistened and mixed with air, and penetrated the locks of the dead; penetrated the garments of the dead and made them dank, more dank than the soulless clay they covered. In that horror of darkness, there were little streams of light, where our dear boys were dying. It was no earthly sun, nor earthly moon, nor star, but as the pulse froze and the heart sank in that darkness, the light of another world dawned, and they lived to live forever.

On that field there was one artificial light making horror visible. A company of faces black as the night they peered into, guided by a woman's white voice in their search among the dead. There was a man, too, who said :

" Leette, it is useless. He is not alive; wait until to-morrow."

" I will not wait. I said I would save him, and I will. "

" Why would you save him? What is he to you ?— Why have you such interest in this Yankee?"

" It matters nothing to you. I want my own way and will. You need not remain. Go, fill your appointment with General Solenter. Tell Monsieur Hardone I am looking for his rival on the battle field. I come back when I get ready. Go."

" I want you, Leette. Something may yet be done. For if we can, we must redeem this terrible defeat."

" Defeat ! La Scheme, Defeat ! This is a glorious victory. We shall take the whole army prisoners, and capture and destroy those gunboats."

" Leette, you are blind, blind, blind. What is a victory on the Red River? What if the whole army was taken prisoners ? This would only prolong the war. While Grant and Sherman,—while the Army of the Potomac and Tennessee are unconquered, this victory amounts to worse than nothing. All these lives are sacrificed,—uselessly, uselessly. Our men have no brains. Good God! why can't they see!"

"La Scheme, the Federals violated their pledges. They took the cotton without paying for it, and as soon as they began to steal, Gen. Kirby Smith ordered the people to burn, and they did burn. So would I. They are a glorious race. I never was more proud than when I saw the smoke of our million bales. Then I went in for revenge. Oh, it was glorious! I only wish for a perfect rout on their part."

"' Blind, blind, blind. Suppose they had stolen a few thousand bales; ten thousand, twenty thousand, what of it? Now, we have burnt a million. They are gone, ashes. My twenty millions are lost. We have gained a victory, but at what an expense? A million bales of cotton and five thousand lives. We have lost our chance at Chicago, lost our President, lost our Peace, lost our Confederacy. And that NAVY was to blame. The army came up to its word, and filled its pledges. Oh, Leette, what difference did it make, whether we bribed the Navy by letting them steal, or paid the Admiral? We could not buy him, and so our short-sighted General set the cotton on fire because they took it for Prize-money. We could have afforded to have given the Navy ten millions of prize-money. Perhaps we can redeem the defeat yet. I tell you, we are defeated by those gun boats without a shell."

"You can do nothing, La Scheme. If our Generals were willing, our soldiers are not. They will take the whole expedition prisoners and the gunboats too. Go, if you want to. I have not had my revenge on the Corporal yet. I shall find him, and find him alive. Go."

Victor Hugo, in his "Miserables," in accounting for the defeat of Napoleon at Waterloo, asks:

"Was it possible that Napoleon should win this battle? We answer, no. Why? Because of Wellington? Because of Blutcher? No. Because of God."

There was every reason in the world why the Red River expedition should have been a success—every reason to expect it triumphant; but its success would have been the indirect means of replenishing the treasury of the Confederacy, and establishing its credit at home and abroad; as a consequence prolong the war, and, it might be, establish the Confederacy and Slavery. The expedition failed because of God.

So thinks Cotton Stealing. Perhaps Cotton Stealing is wrong. Let whoever thinks it wrong answer this question. Would people who did not hesitate to burn three crops of cotton—a million bales—with their own hands, rather than permit it to fall into the hands of federals, have held back one half or two thirds of its purchase money when sold? or, would they have willingly paid all to their government to secure their freedom?

La Scheme knew what they would do, knew what results he could accomplish with the money, and in the strength of that knowledge regarded the confederate victory of Red River the worst defeat his cause had ever sustained. Was it or was it not?

Leette did not think. She was following an impulse. That phenomenon so unexplainable, which occurs in some lives; perhaps sometimes in every life, where an unseen power drives on in an unusual direction, apparently objectless, to accomplish great good : as when a captain at sea alters his course, in obedience to an influence he cannot resist, and rescues the forlorn survivors of the burned steamer from a watery grave. Leette was seeking James Manet. She knew where his brigade and division fought: knew where the fight was thickest he would be, and when the foregoing conversation passed was standing near him. He heard her words and kept silence. James Manet was willing to die, since his death had rendered such plans abortive. James Manet would rather die on the field of battle than be subject to her vengeance.

The same power which was driving her on, directed her steps, and Leette found the Corporal, still alive, sensible, but very low. She ordered her assistants, two slaves, to place him on the stretcher, and took him out of the woods. As soon as she got to a surgeon, her influence brought him to her case, and on a hasty examination he decided the leg ought to be taken off, as also the arm. Nevertheless, the operations would be useless, because fatal, and the prisoner might as well die without unnecessary pain.

" Doctor, will he die if they remain ?"

"Yes."

" Then cut them off. He will not die."

" How do you know?"

" I feel it."

" I would not stake my life on your feelings."

" No one asked it. This man belongs to me. He can do the Confederacy no more injury. He saved my life once, and I promised to save his. The responsibility is mine. Cut, and you will do no more harm than kill, only finish what two bullets failed to do."

This was all that was said. Other cases demanded his attention, and the surgeon gave the signal for the operation. In an instant, James was placed on the platform, which answered for a table. Leette took a knife and cut his bloody garment from the wounded limbs, and then the surgeon, with a quick movement of the knife, commenced the operations. There was no chloric ether, or other anæsthetic, to economize strength and preserve life, but there was a strong constitution unmarred by hereditary taint, unpoisoned by excess or imprudent exposure. The Corporal endured the operations without a groan, and was taken by his bearers to Leette's quarters. Here, under her care, he slowly improved, until, as time passed, he was able to be moved. Then she carefully took him near the lines, and left him in the care of persons she could trust, saying these farewell words :

" Get well as soon as you can, and go home. You have one arm, one leg. Your mother will be glad to see you. Then she said good-bye,—turned to go out,

—came back, and said to him, " Oh ! I forgot to tell you Allie Sandison is dead !" This was her revenge.

CHAPTER XLIV.

Allie Sandison was not dead. Allie's mother was dead. Leette's perverse heart would torment, because she loved to see her victim writhe. He would not writhe to please her; then she did her best to keep the Corporal alive, because if he died he would join Allie sooner. Her heaven had no separations. The tale was to him the same as true. Leette had been bearer of tidings of the death of his sister Lilly. After having saved his life a second time, and in despite of her words indicated an affection which, though wayward, must be deep and lasting; to believe she would or could trifle with his feelings was impossible : consequently when he wrote home from the hospital, it was merely to tell how he was, where he was, and how he got there, the chances and changes of the past, and the hopes and expectation of the future.

"Mother, you and father Wirtman have work enough to do, mouths enough to feed, without the

care of your poor, useless, wounded, crippled boy.
The country will take care of me in the hospital
until I get able to travel on my crutch, and then I
will pay you a visit. It will be a long time before I
can leave this hospital for one nearer God's country,
although I know I should get well faster and be better where the weather is cooler. Perhaps if Allie
was alive she would be my nurse, for she used to
love wounded soldiers. It is all for the best. I only
wish the war was done. I have but one sorrow in
my maimed condition; it is, that I was disabled in a
cotton raid. I have one joy, that it was a failure.
The size does not compensate me for my loss, and I
cannot think of the poor boys whose bones are bleaching on the battle-field, except as murdered by our own
Generals. May God have mercy on their souls. I
do not know where the guilt rests. Leette says they
will never be convicted, that even parties in Washington were partners in the transaction. In one of
her clear moments, Leette told me; every part was
perfectly understood, and the amount of profits, the
lay of the great whale cotton to the sailors, boat
steerers, captain, mate and crew, who stayed by
the ship in Washington—do you understand me?—
was agreed upon. One thing is sure, we poor privates did not come in for any share, except bullets
and death! And Admiral Porter threw the shell
which burst the bubble and opened the pretended
fight into an actual battle, resulting in our sad defeat; he and his gun-boat men took the cotton as a
lawful prize of war, and as soon as Kirby Smith and

Gen. Taylor found it was not going according to contract they ordered the people to burn, and they did
burn millions.

"Mother, I thank my Heavenly Father every day
for such a mother as you,—for the religious education you have given me. I believe I see God's hand
in this defeat, and I am reconciled to my loss. If,
as Leette tells me, this great expedition was set on
foot by rebel sympathizers, in order to bring out the
million bales of cotton which fill the Red River country; they reaping the rich harvest of gold; the advance in price which the war has brought about, and
with which rebel emissaries designed to purchase the
unscrupulous politicians of the North—to hire them
to attempt the destruction of our free institutions,
I shall never regret the failure. But was Hazael
any the less to blame for saying, 'Is thy servant a
dog?' or was Jezebel any less a harlot because
she was unsuccessful? Oh! I wish if they were
guilty, there were some on our side who would throw
the men like General Solenter out of the window,
that the dogs might lick their blood in the streets.
I never expect they will be punished. The very
gold their infamy has procured will buy judges, who
will conceal the sin. I wish the people would brand
every cotton officer, high or low. It could easily
be done. for honest wages are known to every one.
That general or soldier who comes home rich over-
much, came not honestly by his gold. But I am
tired of this cursed thirst for gold. I hope I shall
soon be able to move to God's country. Then I will

pay you a visit. When I am so far recovered as to be able to leave the hospital for good, I shall try to find something to do. But I am useless enough with only one leg and one arm. If I was only learned, if I believed the people of the United States would listen and be convinced by me, I would travel all over the Union and hold up my stump, telling them cotton did it, and ask them to judge every cotton officer and make him ashamed of his covetousness. I cannot fight, 1 cannot die for my country on account of cotton."

Allie Sandison has learned her lesson. She has lost her mother. Death teaches! She has lost her intended. Love teaches! She has lost her father. Though yet alive, she has lost him, in that she has lost the ideal of a father's love,—found the reality in what a political, cotton-speculating schemer can give. She has seen the world; tasted and found it hollow. One thing she has found in all this experience,—to distinguish the true from the false; and she loves Mrs. Wirtman with a child's affection, Mr. Wirtman so much, as to wish her father no politician, but an honest man like him. Her lesson has been a hard task,—has cost sleepless nights, weary, restless days, —fever in the heart, throbbing in the brain, and tears, often unshed, scalding when at length they would flow. She has learned to regard the loss of Charles Hardone's love as a mercy, but a mercy which cost a long sigh—not because it is gone, but because he was not what she loved; because so much

of her youngest trust was wasted on him. Gradually has she been weaned from that sorrow, for she
is thinking of another.

Back in childhood she remembered stolen glances
at school, when James sat on the other side ; little
kind acts of school children, when she loved to play
a little with him. Then, as she grew older, the
bashful reserve. lest other boys and girls should tease.
Love was the thought—love was the feeling, which
ignorant, she knew not. She knows now.

She remembers the New Year's party : her special
invitation : clear as noon day come back tones retained in her ear, tones of love, and with the recollection,
the memory of longing, waiting to catch them in
Charlie's voice : a sad disappointment : stronger
words had failed to reach her heart, and she knew now
it was James' love for her which had filled the voice,
her love for him had heard the tone, and that love
which demanded like expression only to be disappointed.

She remembered the Wide Awake celebration : how
James led her from the crowd, how in the press, he
put his guardian arm and held her closely to keep her
safe. That memory was a pillow, she, old as experience made her, coveted to rest in, for it was love,
and she did not then know it.

She remembered the fatal evening of Charlie's ·
song, when one sensitive word decided James' course;
and she knew now, was certain now, that a timid love
refusing to recognize its own existence, dare not, in
Charlie's presence, speak boldly out and say, " I love

you." When that fatal letter, telling of Charlie's perfidy, came from Memphis, Allie was tried as never before. She was prostrated by the mental struggle which was combined with physical weakness produced by the poison malaria of the hot summer in Memphis, and the poison atmosphere of its sweltering hospitals. She went low, deep into the dark valley, from which returning health brought a new woman, to bow humbly under the chastening rod which took to Heaven her mother.

Hence-forward, her home was with Mrs. Wirtman. Mary was her sister, and Henry's child her pet. One day came news from Red River, a defeat. James' brigade had stood their ground and beat back the victorious enemy. No letter from James. Then, waiting with a heart-ache for many a day, followed by the report, "Died from his wounds on the field.'

When the word came of her son's death, Mrs. Wirtman mourned with that worse than death-grief, the I-am-afraid-he-is-dead, balancing quickly against the I-will-not-believe-he-is-dead. Then Allie Sandison was nearer and dearer than any other one, because he loved her. The mother brought out the son's letter, and Allie read the words in his own hand writing, "You may tell her I loved her." The women love each other better the more they loved him. They were both in mourning garments, and believed their hearts would wear weeds until they should also go where the weary rest.

At length the wounded prisoner reached the National lines, was once more an inmate of a national hospital, and wrote to his mother. Words cannot tell the joy in the house and in the heart. The morning after, Allie said,

"Mother, he is lame and has only one arm. He is in a Hospital. Would it be wrong for me to go and take care of him?"

"No, child. Go, and God bless you."

"Go, Allie," said Mr. Wirtman. "You saved my life, perhaps, you will save James'. His heart is down. Tell him he is no burden. Bring him home. If he had no legs and no arms, we would make an altar for his mutilated form, and worship him as a sacrifice for his country. Bring him home the moment he can come."

Come into this hospital-tent. Look on those wounded men. See that poor maimed man bolstered up with a stump resting on a rubber, and a leg upon another, over which two small bits of ice are dripping. His wan face is patient, waiting, and he is thinking of home, of mother. A lady enters with the nurse. She is not fashionably clad, wears the quiet, noiseless dress of the hospital, a new nurse. She looks quickly from bed to bed and hastens to him. He extends his well hand with one word, "Allie!"

31

Richmond is taken. Lee has surrendered. Johnston's army has also laid down its arms. There is no armed opposition east nor west of the Mississippi, for Texas is occupied by the national troops. The war is over. Cotton is falling, and the Western gunboat flotilla is to be sold under the hammer. This story ends where it really began, on the borders of the lake whose wintry face looked upon the days before the war. Abraham Lincoln, the honest man, is again President, and the country is safe.

Upon the high bluff before alluded to, stands a cottage,—in that it is not two stories high,—but more like a Southern planter's home on the sugar coast, in its pillared portico, its large rooms, and the comfort which strikes the stranger, who passes along the smooth green lawn, where every evening the lovers of nature stroll to gaze upon the lake, illuminated by the summer rays of the setting sun. There is a garden of shrubbery, where roses, flowering almonds, sweet seringa and snow balls riot in profusion ; and there are locust trees, maples and elms shading the side walk, while a few steps beyond, at the edge of the bluff, is a thriving grove of young cedars. At the foot of the bluff are sand hills, sprinkled with bushes, and several small ponds, which are now almost covered with lily pads, soon to be kissed by the water-angel of purity—the Water Lily.

The day is closing in beauty, and on the porch sits a soldier just home from the wars. He has not yet learned to do without his crutch, though he hopes soon to do without a cane ; and you will notice, as he rises with his company, that the lady by his side steps up and puts his wounded arm and empty sleeve over her shoulder. This is Allie's home, and this is her husband, the Corporal.

The Western man has been invited here, at the close of the war, to be told of the falsity of his predictions, and also to meet some strangers, who have, in passing through the country, called to see the bride and groom. The company has not only Mr. and Mrs. Wirtman, but Mr. Sandison also ; and that tall, keen looking man is Kendal La Scheme, while the lady talking to Mrs. Wirtman is Leette Hardone. In the door, watching the lake, is Mary Wirtman, looking as she did the first time we saw her ; but the babe of that day is a laughing, frolicking girl, who makes herself perfectly at home among the strangers, and shies away with childhood's bashful sport from Kendal La Scheme, who is using his arts to win her confidence.

" Where is Charlie ?" James Manet asks · this question, which more than one would have asked, had not various reasons restrained. Leette turns to La Scheme. repeating :

"Kendal, where is Charlie, my husband? You know."

"I beg your pardon, Mrs. Manet, I should have told you before. I really forgot. The Adjutant General requested me, if I saw or should meet any of his friends on my business tour, to give them his best respects, and apologize for his inability to call himself. When we left New York, business was very pressing, and before this time he has gone down the river to attend to the necessary arrangements connected with his wife's large estates. There are other important matters which he has in hand, connected with the reorganization of the State. Indeed, it was impossible for him to come. I hope you will excuse him."

"There, James! I knew he would do it well. I told Hardone he should not come. You know La Scheme of old. He has not changed."

"Really, Madame Hardone, I did not expect that from you, but perhaps you are better known in this circle than I."

"Now, I suppose, I shall be compelled to tell you the whole truth. I was jealous of him, and to quiet me, he told me a lie. He said you, Mrs. Manet, was dead, making me give the Corporal very unpleasant tidings, which almost cost his life. Now, James, don't say a word! You know how badly you felt, and really Mrs. Wirtman I do believe he would have died had not Mistress Allie gone so quickly to his relief. I was afraid to have General Hardone come here, for I knew how badly it would make him feel to see what a fool he was in his boy-love,—no offence intended, Mrs. Manet. I assure you I approve of your good, final good judgment I mean, for how a woman could have chosen to set one side such a noble,—but—ah! the Corporal is here, and I will not praise before his face."

Hereupon the Western man, to introduce a new topic of conversation, asked La Scheme,

"What business leads you through this part of the country at this time?"

Sandison answers for him.

"He is looking up the odds and ends of his secret organizations, K. G. C's., O. A. K's., and what not, preparing for a new campaign. Come, La Scheme, acknowledge the corn. We beat you fairly at the last election."

"You would not have beaten us if—"

Before he could finish his sentence James interrupted by saying,

"If God had not been against you."

La Scheme shrugged his shoulders, lifted his eyebrows, and continued,

"—if it had not been for the Union League. That checkmated our plans, and the fact of time. We did not fairly get at the work: if we had only commenced early, or had a little more money you would have seen another result. But there are as good fish, &c. Our day will come."

The Western man again spoke:—

"Then, you do not consider the war ended."

This time Leette replied, "Ended! It will never

end. The foundation principles are eternal! The North is successful, because she has more resources, and more men. The Confederacy was exhausted and gave in for the moment, her spirit is unconquerable."

" Then, Leette, what you told me when I was first wounded and a prisoner continues true, that you fight for the principle of aristocracy against a democracy, the few against the many."

" Yes, James, and we shall succeed. I would have been discouraged had I never been North. Had this defeat come upon me when I was on the plantation, I should have died. Now, I can rise higher than such low forebodings. You have the elements of our success and your failure in your midst; and in time, our politicians will reorganize their battalions and fight the battle again. Then, there will be no such word as fail. We are enemies still. This is only a truce, and the next time we come into battle,—beware !"

" Leette! Madame Hardone!" said La Scheme, " How inconsiderate you are !"

" Kendal La Scheme, I will be natural now. I will throw off this eternal mask. I know one brave foe, and I honor him enough to stand boldly before him. We are quits on the past. I throw him my gage for the future. If the world was full of such men there would be everlasting peace."

" Leette," said James, "I accept the trial. You will fail, because God has ordained your failure. Free institutions and a free people will rule not only in this land, but in the world. I grant you that an ignorant, unenlightened, unchristian people are subjects of an aristocratic government; but knowledge, education, and christian principles are capable of self-government. And the time is coming when the world shall be educated, for God has promised that all men shall know Him from the least to the greatest, and the world shall be full of His knowledge and His glory. What that means absolutely, I cannot tell; but it does mean that white men and black men shall be honest men, pure men, good men, doing as they would others shall do to them: that there shall be universal equality, a universal ballot, equal rights of personal liberty, personal security, and personal property: that free men shall bind themselves to no party, nor to any set of party principles, but the truth; so that the only question before the world shall be, What is truth?— Now, I do not expect this in one day, nor will the great result be obtained without contest, defeat and victory. You throw yourself on the one side, and will in the end fail; because your cause is the cause of despotism, ignorance, and evil. I put myself on the other, and shall succeed, because mine is the cause of education, of progress, of liberty, of universal, human brotherhood, and it is the cause of God!"